SACRED BAND

SACRED BAND CHRONICLES • BOOK I

JOSEPH D. CARRIKER JR.

NISABA PRESS

Nisaba Press is the fiction imprint of Green Ronin Publishing, publishing novels, anthologies, and short fiction tied to the rich and varied worlds of Green Ronin's tabletop roleplaying properties.

Printed in the United States of America

Green Ronin Publishing
3815 S. Othello St. Suite 100, #311
Seattle WA 98118
Email: custserv@greenronin.com
Web Site: www.greenronin.com

10 9 8 7 6 5 4 3 2 1

GRR7102 • ISBN: 978-1-949160-56-7

Printed in the U.S.A.

NISABA PRESS EDITORIAL DIRECTOR: Jaym Gates
EDITING: Madeline Schrader
GRAPHIC DESIGN: Hal Mangold
COVER ART: Mel Uran
PROOFREADER: Samantha Chapman
EXECUTIVE PRODUCER: Chris Pramas
TEAM RONIN: Joseph Carriker, Crystal Frasier, Jaym Gates, Kara Hamilton, Troy Hewitt, Steve Kenson, Nicole Lindroos, Hal Mangold, Chris Pramas, Evan Sass, Malcolm Sheppard, Will Sobel, Owen K.C. Stephens, and Dylan Templar

To all my real-life heroes.

*To my mother **Dotty**, a hero who braved a terrifying world to raise three kids all on her own, demonstrating to us what courage and conviction looked like.*

*To my brother **Chad**, for braving the world we grew up in, and doing the best he knew how.*

*To my sister **Tiffany**, for her own superheroic transformation from my baby sister into an amazing woman and mother.*

*To my partners **A.J.** and **Chillos**, for their heroic love, care, and undying support as I wrote this and every other one of my books.*

This is for each of you.

THE WORLD OF THE CHANGED

This is not a world of superheroes.

In the mid-1970s, the Surge happened. No one knows exactly what caused it or even what it was. Recording and sensory equipment across the globe went haywire for exactly 108 minutes on April 24, 1974. When the Surge passed, it left in its wake transformed individuals invested with tremendous powers. They are called the Originals.

Since then, the ripples of that original energetic Shift have criss-crossed again and again, resulting in Echo Events — localized spikes in strange energetic phenomena, resulting in devastation, injury, loss of life…and the gaining of powers. Those who not only survive these para-natural disasters but also gain powers from them are called **Echoes.**

The powers of science and industry have found occasional, often accidental ways of repeating these spikes. Most of the time, those subjected to the experiments die horribly. But sometimes, they emerge with abilities, as the **Empowered.**

This is a world of people with powers who are carefully monitored and shepherded but also protected by a government agency: the **Department of Transformed Persons Affairs,** or the **DTPA.** The tasks that superheroes used to undertake are now jobs for the Changed in elite military or law enforcement units, philanthropic aid organizations (like the Golden Cross), and emergency response teams at state and federal levels.

Government and corporate sponsors pay top dollar to Changed with the talents to aid them in their efforts. It is a federal crime in the United States to engage in super-powered vigilantism, and has been since the Denisov Measure of 1993. Most other nations followed suit shortly thereafter, removing the impetus from its citizenry to engage in such acts.

Those countries that did not follow suit often mandate roles for the Changed. Sometimes this is obligatory civic service. Other times the Changed work in contexts of war, disaster relief, or advancing national interests in various forms. Changed with particular skills can find themselves in extralegal roles, often against their will, at the mercy of the government that controls them.

These days, becoming one of the Changed means living a life of discretion and avoiding using one's abilities, selling out to a corporate sponsor, or being the pawn of a government.

SACRED BAND

CHAPTER ONE

Odessa, Ukraine
April 17, 2013

"When the weather matches what you feel, my little Kosma, important things are happening," his grandmother once told him. On a day like this, he couldn't help but remember the old woman's warnings.

Outside, Odessa was dismal and rainy, its sky reflecting what everyone inside the Warwick Bar was feeling. Normally, the nightlife spot in the heart of Odessa's city center was more upbeat. Oh, the music still played, but no one was paying much attention to it. In fact, the volume was lower than normal, especially for a weekend night. Too many people were staying home.

It was hard to blame them. The *Verkhovna Rada*, the Ukraine's parliamentary body, had that week presented the draft of a law that would make it illegal to talk about homosexuality in public and in the media. This was just the latest in what felt like an avalanche of contemptuous legislation doing its best to make the Warwick Bar's patrons invisible, if not flat-out illegal.

"It's just the first step," the bartender Taras said to an older man seated miserably at the bar, nursing his drink. With barely half his attention, he handed a pair of drinks to a familiar young man with curly dark hair, high cheekbones and a tight t-shirt that showed off his pecs. The young man, a regular by the name of Oleksander, promptly slid him the money for the drinks.

Normally the jacked, shaven-headed bartender would have flirted a little with the young man, but not tonight. He barely noticed Oleksander was there, taking his money and doling out change before returning to his conversation. "They make everyone stop talking about you first. Make it shameful to discuss your gay sons, or your gay brother. Make it illegal to teach about homosexuals in schools or write articles about us. That way, once no one is allowed to even know if you exist or not, there's no one to notice when you start disappearing. It's already happening!"

Snatching up the drinks, Oleksander fled the bar and crossed as quickly as the rain-wet floor would let him to the round table he and his friend sat. It was their favorite, situated under one of the big neon beer signs for some German beer that no one he knew drank. It was their favorite because it gave the perfect vantage point to watch who entered the bar.

"Taras is at it again," Oleksander grumped. He set the drink in front of Kosma, who barely glanced up from his phone. "They're coming to get us, *blah blah blah*. He didn't even look twice in my direction. Do you think I made a mistake when I hooked up with him last year? I think that maybe—*Kosma!* Are you even *listening* to me?"

His friend jumped and slammed his phone down. He grinned sheepishly and reached for his drink. Kosma wasn't as fit as Oleksander. He was handsome, in a round-faced way, and wore square spectacles. He was too thin, as well, with closely-shorn hair that made his ears stick out a little. He spent too much of his time studying at university, and not enough of it at the gym, even when Oleksander invited him.

"Oi. Sorry, Sasha. I'm listening." Kosma took a sip of the drink and winced slightly at that first burn. Oleksander rolled his eyes.

"No, you're not. And don't call me Sasha—you know I *hate* that name." The two had known one another since their mid-adolescent school days, when Oleksander had been Sasha to friends and family. This was before they'd come out to anyone, even one another, of course. Kosma chuckled. Sasha had gotten more pretentious the older he'd gotten—trying to fit in with the urbane gay culture in Odessa, where they both attended university—but Kosma still really liked him. Even if he considered it his personal responsibility to not let Sasha forget where he came from.

"Who were you texting?" Oleksander asked, nodding at Kosma's phone on the tabletop. "Was it your American again?"

The geekier of the two blushed and snatched the phone off the table, as though he feared Oleksander might do so first. The other young man *tsk*ed. "Oh, God, Kosma. There are plenty of nice guys around here. Or at least chat with someone in Kiev or something like that. Why *America?*" Oleksander rolled his eyes and surveyed the bar. He sighed. Still dead.

"It's not about where he's from, *Sasha.*" Kosma emphasized his friend's nickname just to drive home his irritation. "He's nice. And he's studying to be an architect, just like I am. I've invited him to come and see some of the architecture we have out here, and he'd like to. Maybe this summer, he is thinking." He paused to finish off his drink. "And no, there aren't any nice guys around here. At least, none I like."

"Oh, what, you're too good for Odessa now? Three years ago, we couldn't wait to get out here." Oleksander fished a cube of ice out of his glass and flicked it across the table at Kosma.

Kosma winced, holding up his hands to ward off the icy projectile. He cursed as it plinked him right above where his topmost button closed his shirt and then, predictably, slid down his chest.

"*Augh!*" Kosma shoved himself away from the table and leaned forward, shaking out his shirt. Oleksander roared in laughter and thrust his fists in the air victoriously. By the time the rogue ice was gone—either dislodged or melted—they were both gasping with laughter.

"You're an asshole, Sasha."

Flipping him an obscene gesture, Oleksander leaned back in his chair and looked around again. Still no one, and the night was half gone. He suspected this was as good as it was going to get tonight. "Hey, let's get out of here. It's boring."

"Sure, if you like," Kosma said, glancing at the face of his phone. He probably wasn't even aware he was doing it, Oleksander mused. The bigger lad grinned when Kosma glanced up to find him regarding him coolly and slid his phone back into his pocket sheepishly. "Where would you like to go?" said Kosma.

"*Ugh.* I don't know. Nowhere, I guess. We already had dinner, and it doesn't look like this place is going to get any better. I bet the clubs are even worse. Stupid politicians. My father always said the one thing you can count on politicians to do is to ruin everyone else's lives."

"We can stop by the corner market and get a video maybe?"

"Ooh, and a bottle of wine. Yes, let's do that. We can even get an American movie, so you can practice your English for your red-haired architect."

"Well, okay," Kosma said, standing and tucking his shirt back in. They shrugged coats back on against the weather and headed for the door.

"Goodbye, Taras!" Oleksander shouted as obnoxiously as he could, hoping to interrupt his favorite bartender's night one last time. Still in conversation with the old timer at the bar—probably still going on about politics—Taras glanced up and nodded a parting, immediately returning to his chat.

"Prick," Oleksander huffed, and shoved open the door.

* * *

The route to the closest trolley stop was circuitous and wet. Both young men pulled up the hoods on their coats and started walking.

"I'm thinking about going to America," Kosma said after they'd been walking a little way. The Warwick was a part of town all but abandoned this time of night—only the few nightspots ever saw any people. Occasionally some came out to walk around the city, but not in this rain. They walked some more, until finally Kosma regarded Oleksander.

"Did you–"

"I heard you, idiot," Oleksander said quietly. Kosma kept watching his friend out of the corner of his eye until Sasha glanced sideways at him. "Why do you want to leave?"

"Well, I really like this guy."

The look Oleksander gave him could not have been more scornful. "But not *only* that, right? Tell me you're not leaving to become someone's mail order husband!"

Kosma chuckled and punched his friend in the arm. "No, stupid. That's not really why. It would be a nice addition, but I'd like to maybe study there. I've never lived out of the country. I think it would be interesting. And I've always wanted to visit there. I want to see New York City, like we've always seen in the movies, you know. All of those amazing *buildings*."

"*Ugh*, no. I can respect it if you're going to go there for a *man*, but if you're in love with buildings, our friendship is *over*." Oleksander returned the punch to Kosma's arm, this time a bit harder. The smaller man yelped, and both laughed.

They walked for a little longer, dodging puddles and sticking close to buildings, taking advantage of overhangs to protect them from the rain where they could. Oleksander reached over to wrap an arm around Kosma, glancing over his shoulder for a moment as he did so. "Well, it's probably for the best. It's probably going to get more dangerous here before it gets better, I bet."

"You could come with me, Sasha."

The bigger lad scoffed. "And do what? I am barely making passing marks right now. No schools are going to accept me over there. And I'm just not in love with any *buildings*, stupid."

Kosma leaned in to his friend, smiling. He looked up at him as they walked, crossing the street quickly to the side with the trolley stop. "You'll at least come and visit me, right?"

"Oh, I've seen all the movies, Kosma. I wouldn't miss those nightclubs for the world. Plus, thanks to the Czech porn companies, American gays all love Eastern European boys right now." Kosma broke out laughing again as Oleksander paused, glancing behind them again. He held out a hand, grabbing his friend and stopping his forward motion. Kosma halted and looked in the direction they'd come, and then back at Oleksander, whose brows were knit in concern.

"What's wrong?" Kosma asked.

"I think...I think someone is following us," his friend whispered. Gone was the silly affected Oleksander that lived and went to university in Odessa. This was pure Sasha, the Sasha Kosma remembered: strong, attentive, even cautious. A boy who grew up in the country, doing hard work with his parents and siblings, keeping his desires private. The Sasha who didn't like fighting, but knew all too well how to do it. "Something looks strange, though."

"Sasha," Kosma whispered. "It's...it's the streetlights." The bigger lad glanced upward, his hood falling back and rain collecting on his face. For a moment, he couldn't figure out what it was.

Oh. They were *dark*. Not all of them—just the bunch of them closest to them. They weren't out, either, it didn't seem—they were simply obscured.

Then, like a puddle of mercury running across a flat surface, the strange shadowy mass between them and the lights *moved*, its undulating motion unsettling in a lizard-brain way. Kosma gasped and took an unconscious step behind Sasha, pulling at his jacket, begging him to run. With only a moment—a precious moment they might have spent running, Kosma's thoughts shrieked—Sasha turned toward him and agreed, pushing him ahead.

"*Nelyud*," Sasha gasped, fear stealing his breath. "I think it's a *nelyud*, Kosma." The two boys broke into a run.

There is something primordial about being chased by an unknown *thing*. The mind rebels and refuses to accept it, babbling away all intention, reason and planning. Fear leapt all acid and hot from the pits of their bellies up their gullets, threatening to wrap itself around their necks and strangle until they couldn't breathe. Awareness of their surroundings collapsed to a pinpoint tunnel of pure, adrenaline-charged panic, and the need to escape became less of a choice and more of an instinct, a physiological reaction as uncontrollable as breathing.

Some dim part of Kosma's mind told him that this was what horror movies portrayed as their protagonists made stupid, frightened-hare decisions when the monster was on their tail. *I'm never making fun of those movies again.* The stupid thought swam into his consciousness, like some rational part of his brain doing its best to surface, gasping for air and control, only to sink again under the waters of panic once more.

Both boys periodically glanced over their shoulders as they ran. It was large, whatever it was that pursued them, and fast. Very fast, in fact, that nearly-drowning part of Kosma's brain insisted. It should have been able to catch them easily. Instead, it kept darting up around them and charging them, whipping behind them and somewhat over them almost as though...

"Sasha!" Kosma yelled, breathless. "It's *herding* us!"

A moment later, they rounded the corner to find *them* standing there. A quartet of thinly muscled young men in denim and leather jackets, all torn blue jeans and tall combat boots. Slogan pins and marker-writing adorned their denim; they all held weapons. Their heads were ominously shaven, as were their faces, laying bare sneering, contemptuous expressions. Kosma recognized at least two of them from some of the horrible videos he'd watched online recently, videos that he couldn't tear himself away from until it was to go vomit in the sink.

"Oh, shit." Kosma's voice trembled as he backed up a step, only to have Sasha slam into him. Both boys went tumbling to the ground.

"Oh, look," one of the skinheads said. "*Faggots*."

Kosma tried to get Sasha's attention, to direct him toward the imminent violence in the form of the four homophobes approaching them, but Sasha was too busy looking behind them, frantically searching high and low.

"Where is it? Kosma, do you see it? I don't–"

In a rush of air, Sasha—his Sasha—was *gone*, snatched up off the side street surface like a mouse in an owl's grip. He was hauled shrieking into the dark air above as the punks closed in on Kosma with fists and boots and truncheons. Bloody, red violence rained down on him from above (*how had he gotten on the ground? He didn't remember-*) and his blood was in his eyes and his mouth and on the ground beneath him. Wet concrete met his face again and again as someone snatched him by the back of his coat and slammed him into the sidewalk. He bounced on his last impact. He couldn't seem to catch his breath.

He was dimly aware of Sasha hitting the edge of the sidewalk with a sickening, meaty crunch, slumping down into the gutter. He was lacerated all over, his clothing and flesh shredded, his eyes wide and staring as his blood mixed with the rainwater before swirling into the gutter beneath him.

A set of boots landed between him and Sasha (*oh no, no Sasha, no*) as though leaping from a great height. They were military-style boots, a set of black military fatigues tucked into them. Sasha tried to lift his head to see who it was. The attempt made his head swim and his gorge rise.

Then, merciful blackness.

CHAPTER TWO

Portland, Oregon
April 19, 2013

>Hey. Im here.

On campus? Where at?<

>Big park in middle.

>Listening to street preacher.

>You should come save his life.

>Im DONE listening to his ass.

LOL Don't murder him. <

Class is almost out. OMW <

Rusty glanced up at the clock above the lecturer's head, trying not to be too obvious. Not that it did much good. He could usually count on eyes on him at about any point in the day.

It wasn't that he was all that good-looking. It wasn't that he was bad-looking, either—a redhead, with brilliant blue eyes and a patch of coppery scruff at his chin. His build bespoke a youth playing football, the one true religion in Texas, where he'd grown up. He'd given that up his sophomore year, though it had come with a habit for weight training he'd never quite abandoned. He usually wore t-shirts and cargo shorts—nothing altogether noteworthy.

No, they weren't ogling him. They were *watching* him. Like they expected something to happen. It would almost have been better if lust was their motivation, particularly from some of the hotter guys in the class. No, there was fear in some, fascination and curiosity in others. All manner of motivations at play, here.

Unsurprising, of course, considering everyone had their own opinions about Echoes. Everybody watched like they expected him to suddenly lose control of his powers, and they wanted to be ready to see it so they could either be first out the door or first to point a camera phone at him. When he'd begun reintegrating after the Gulf Event that gave him his powers, he'd decided to give them something to see. Not in a malicious way—he just remembered how stoked he was the first time he saw someone use their powers, and, frankly, thought having powers was something cool. Why wouldn't he share it with others who were interested, right?

That had gotten him thrown out of public high school. There'd been a literal panic, and meetings with the superintendent and chief of police. They used phrases like "zero tolerance" and "minimum safety range." The school district offered to pay for him to get his equivalency if that's what he wanted, or to have his parents explore private or home schooling. They'd even offered to help him get enrolled in a university somewhere.

He'd taken the hint, though his father had raged and wanted to sue. Instead, Rusty packed a bag and skipped town to stay with an aunt in New Mexico until he could "figure things out." It had taken him some time to get his head together, to figure out when he wanted to do, and he spent a lot of that time doing a solid impression of a stoner high school dropout. Hell, there was even the year in Los Angeles that was worse than that. It was like he was trying really hard to make a whole bunch of stupid decisions.

But he'd made it. It had taken him six years, but he'd gotten enrolled in school, a bit smarter and better prepared for it. Well, for all of it except the stares and the whispers. He wasn't sure if he'd ever get used to those. The university in Portland had offered to help keep his status quiet, but when they'd found out some of his choices during his post-high school years, they knew as well as he did that he'd eventually be recognized. They'd offered to set up as many of his classes as possible to take online, but he didn't want that.

The lecturer finally finished talking, and Rusty made a point to not dart right out the door. Even so, he was the first one out, and in a dozen yards or so, reached the autumn sunshine. The quad at the university did a credible impression of a city park, surrounded on all sides by old-looking buildings. He'd been applying himself to his architecture major well enough to recognize that a lot of the buildings on the campus were newer than they seemed—the university had invested in some stately facades to give it the impression of dignified age.

He knew right where to go, too. The Street Preacher, they all called the man. No one wanted to know his real name. Most of the students found him irritating or funny by turns. A few from more fundamentalist backgrounds found his loud proclamations comfortingly familiar, though even they didn't linger too long. Occasionally, some of the students, all afire from their latest social justice or philosophy course load, would try to engage his hateful rhetoric. They were always frustrated, though. The Street Preacher wasn't there to debate. He was there to *preach*, and by damn those around him were going to listen, even if just for the short time it took them to bustle past him.

Rusty recognized him right away from a distance, quickening his pace over the wet fall leaves towards the man. It wasn't so much the individual he recognized as the big sign he bore. Emblazoned with a massive cross and the words REPENT across its top, it was a graphic arts major's nightmare: every possible bit of white space on the board was taken up with (occasionally misspelled) phrases that laid out just which sinners the Street Preacher was talking at.

FAGOTS • LESBIANS • PERVERTS • DRAG QUEENS/TRANSSEXUALS • ECHOES • LIBERALS • ENVIRONMINTALISTS • ANIMAL RIGHTS • TATTOOED • DEMOCRATS • ATHEISTS/AGNOSTIS • CATOLICS • JEWS • MUSLEMS • ORIGINALS • ABORTIONISTS • DRUG ABUSERS • VIDEO GAMISTS • SWINGERS • FRAT/SORORITY • FREAKS/FREAK-LOVERS

It was dizzying to try to read them all, which is why Rusty generally didn't bother. The same could not be said for Deosil, of course. She sat on a bench, her jacket on the wet seat beneath her—this time of year, *everything* in Portland was constantly wet.

She wore a broomstick skirt the color of burnished copper and a sleeveless, pale green snug top that showed off her tattooed half-sleeves. It flared up around the collar into a wide hoodie, which she wore up to protect her head from the errant droplets falling from the big elm tree that stretched out above her. A seemingly half-forgotten shawl, in oranges, browns and gold, draped across her shoulders. Chestnut brown hair, curly and frizzy from the weather, spilled out of the hood and down either side of her face. Next to her was a simple military-green messenger bag, its strap slung across her torso. She cradled her chin in one of her hands, just *staring* at the man, an expression of irritation and confusion on her face.

She looked like she was trying to read his sign, and his refusal to stop bellowing and walking about was making that an aggravating proposition. Rusty snorted a laugh at her expression, and she turned to regard him quickly like someone surprised out of a reverie. With a huff of irritation, she lurched to her feet, shoving her bag around towards her back and pulling her hoodie back. She crossed to him and they hugged. "What are you laughing at?" she asked him archly.

"This scene," Rusty said, gesturing from her to the Street Preacher. "You two make a lovely couple."

Deosil rolled her eyes and flicked his ear, causing him to yelp. "Shut it. Let's get out of here." They found refuge a couple of blocks away at a falafel place. She laid claim to window seats while Rusty fetched their order, a falafel gyro and tall, hot chai for him, and a pot of mint tea for Deosil. He set their order on the small table between them, and then reached over to an empty table nearby, snatching up a sugar dispenser and setting it down in front of her.

Deosil grinned. "Thank you." She poured an obscene amount of sugar into her cup before filling it with steaming tea. She glanced up at him as she took her first sip and rolled her eyes. "What are you grinning at, ginger?"

"I just think it's hilarious how much sugar you use, is all." He nudged her ankle with the toe of his boot. "Aren't you required by the Grand Wiccan Council to only use like, stevia or fairy powder or whatever the currently approved non-high-fructose, non-refined sweetener is?"

She laughed, and kicked him in the shin. "Asshole," she said, wiping tea off her face and top. "Look, I don't smoke and I hardly ever drink alcohol. This is all I've got, man. I do feel terrible for the bastard who tries to take my sugar away. There's no one big enough to try in this cafe, I'll tell you that. You included, copper-top."

They both laughed, and Deosil fell silent, facing the big picture window, watching the rain, which had just started sprinkling outside again. Deosil stole some of the tahini-slathered cucumbers off Rusty's plate, and the two watched the world go by outside.

"Careful," Rusty said after a few minutes. "You're in danger."

The young woman arched an eyebrow, and glanced around her quickly. It was unconscious, an awareness that Rusty knew was a survival trait. She didn't seem to notice herself do it, but Rusty nonetheless felt bad for evoking it. "Of falling in love with Portland," he clarified, gesturing out the window. "I've seen looks like that before. You'll be eating granola and wearing big clunky sandals for..." He guffawed as she sheepishly shoved her feet under her chair. People turned to stare at the two of them, and he giggled into his tea.

"God, you suck. I already do those things." She glanced out the fog-edged window again, shrugging. "I've thought about it. I mean, I'd like to live close to you, for starters."

"Wait, seriously?" Rusty grinned. Deosil loved the way his face lit up when he was genuinely happy. Unguarded and sweet. "That would be awesome!"

Rusty launched into his own version of what their lives might be like if they lived in the same city, and Deosil rolled her eyes affectionately. Weekends in Seattle, hitting the mountains for hiking, and all sorts of other things featured in his narrative. She sipped her tea and listened. If there was one thing that could be said about Rusty, it was that his enthusiasm was contagious.

"Wow, sounds like you've got this all planned out for me, copper-top." She chuckled, setting down her tea mug on the table and nabbing another cucumber slice. She took a small bite and smiled. "We'll just have to be careful, is all. You know how twitchy the DTPA gets about overt friendships between us."

"I know," Rusty said, somewhat defensively. His face darkened and brow creased. Clearly, he hadn't remembered it. "I mean, they know we're friends. They've noted it at the Health Retreats before. I even had one of the counselors ask me about it last year."

One of the main undertakings by the Department of Transformed Persons Affairs were the annual Health Retreats—week-long events that everyone who benefitted from the DTPA's bureaucratic protection tacitly agreed to. If you were registered, you were expected to attend. An old military base in

Iowa called the Camp provided the setting, its barracks remodeled to provide a little more comfort than their original form.

For a full week, the Echoes who showed up were given all sorts of testing. The first few days were a battery of medical crap: extensive health screenings, updating records of any medical changes (well, any that hadn't already been noted), and testing to see what sorts of effects their powers had on their bodies. The days were filled with exercise intended to push attendees to their limits, and seemingly endless blood draws, MRIs, and swabbings.

After three days, they switched to field tests, in which DTPA scientists, along with Department of Justice flat-tops and lab-coats from the CDC, tested the capabilities and control of attendees. They organized sports-like competitions, a veritable Olympics of superpowers. There were team events, however; though no one ever commented on it, the DTPA was careful to discourage the notion of supers banding together. Though the world had embraced and even to some degree encouraged superpowered vigilantes in the early years after the Shift, those days were gone. These days, the only Changed who teamed up were criminals. Law-abiding Echoes who wanted to fight crime or defend the country joined law enforcement or the military, like everyone else.

It was a chance to show off, to really cut loose with powers in a way that was usually illegal, and everyone loved it. Supers didn't often mingle with one another, as it made law enforcement nervous when they did, so most Echoes only got to see their own abilities. The chance to witness other supers use their abilities was a rare opportunity, and half the reason Rusty even showed up to the damned things. Those who were interested or judged to need it by the DTPA science-types got one-on-one counseling, with the intention of learning how to control their powers. Half therapy group and half personal trainer, all overseen by a scientist in a field best suited to provide advice, these training sessions were often necessary for those who'd recently gained their powers. However, the sessions usually cut out just shy of teaching mastery of the talents; the goal was the ability to control their powers enough to know how to *not* use them.

Evenings in the Camp were fairly low-key. Social groups were either planned or simply evolved, from AA meetings to religious discussion groups to folks who shared interest in history, comic books, or whatever else. Hell, they'd even heard of a secret swinger group at the Camp, although that was more likely to be urban legend than anything else. It was at one of those events that Deosil and Rusty had met. Rusty, almost old enough for college, newly out of the closet and bitten by the activism bug, tried to put together an LGBT group. Only three people besides himself had shown up: Deosil, a gay terrakinetic named Tectonic, who was an Echo from the Mount Rainier Event, and finally Luminous, a lesbian photogenerative from the newest batch of Echoes out of the Anchorage Event.

It had, sadly, been something of a disaster. It became clear shortly into the meeting that Tectonic was just out to hook up, and Luminous was still far too freaked out by her recent Echo Event to even think about processing how or even if her new powers affected her sexuality. In the end, the two of them had left early—Tectonic in a huff at being rejected and Luminous in tears, apologizing. Rusty had no regrets, though. He and Deosil had sneaked off to share a joint, watch the stars, and get to know one another.

They'd been fast friends since, the Department be damned.

"But c'mon—it's not like we're *not* allowed to be friends or anything," he said. "They just don't want our friendships to turn into an attempt to be the newest group of dumbasses trying to be the Champions or whatever."

They passed the day the way they always did. Say what you like about what sort of "wild child" Deosil liked her routine. Every time she came to visit, they started the day with a tea-and-art crawl through the Pearl. The former waterside warehouse district had seen something of a renaissance, turning into one of the Portland's many centers of culture. It was still somewhat trendy, although deeply gentrified. Nevertheless, it held some of Deosil's favorite art galleries, and the inevitable art supply shops.

Deosil shopped cautiously. It frustrated Rusty to no end, but she agonized over every purchase she made, taking forever to contrast and compare the relative qualities and costs of every item she bought. Currently, she was comparing the bristle composition between two brushes whose difference in price couldn't have been more than a buck or two. She glanced up at his sigh and flushed.

"Sorry," she said. She threw both of them back on the shelves and made for the exit.

"Hey, wait!" Rusty said, surprised by her flight. He caught up to her as she stepped out onto the slick pavement outside, its surface plastered with wet, fallen leaves. He plucked at her shawl. "What's up?"

She whirled on him, anger in her face. "Look, we don't all live on Daddy's money, Rusty. Some of us have to struggle to make ends meet, to try and live out in the big bad world that doesn't have much use for us."

He snatched his hand back as though he'd been burned and shoved both his hands in his pockets. He turned away from her, not before she could see the heat in his face. Rusty stared at his pale reflection in the glass as though he were window shopping.

It was one of those moments of ugly honesty that Deosil hated so much, those liminal moments where something had shifted in a relationship. She wanted desperately to find something to say to lighten the mood, to take the emotional heat off both of them, but she knew better than that.

"I'm sorry," he said. "You're right, I don't know."

Thank the gods, she thought as she shoved herself into him, burrowing her arms up under his to steal a hug. For a heartbeat, she was terrified he wouldn't return it, but he did, wrapping her in friendship's embrace. He even sealed it with a kiss atop her head.

"I'm sorry. It's not fair to you that I can't just be honest and calm about shit like that," she mumbled. "And I know that while your family does cover stuff for you, it's not like you're rolling in it yourself. I know they're assholes about that. I don't mean to be a bitch about it, it's just–"

"No, money makes people weird, I know," Rusty said. "I know I've had it easy, and that sometimes makes it weird for me because I don't always understand other peoples' stresses, or it's weird for other people for the same reason."

"God, exactly," she said, sighing into his chest. She took a half-step back and stared into his bright blue eyes. "I try not to say anything because I'm a really, really proud woman, Rusty. When you grow up a poor kid, sometimes your pride is all you've got. And people want to take it away from you, because they've got this idea that when you're poor, you're supposed to be all fucking ashamed of everything you have to do to survive, you know? Collecting food benefits, driving a shitty car that barely runs, wearing hand-me-downs and charity handouts? It's not bad enough that you have to do those things, but people also feel like you're supposed to be in this constant state of apologizing for being poor." She clasped his hand tightly and pulled him into a walk alongside her.

He nodded. "Thanks for saying that. For putting it like that—I can understand it that way. I mean, you know I think my dad's the biggest asshole in the world, and he's exactly like that. He was *always* talking shit about 'welfare queens' and how you always supposedly saw 'those people' with phones and expensive cars while they were begging for handouts or whatever."

Deosil snorted. "Oh, believe me, I know. I've heard that narrative all my damned life. We're supposed to all be Dickensian characters, I think, begging for the favor and forgiveness of our betters. We're supposed to never have anything—no matter how inexpensive or small—that makes our lives better or more enjoyable in some way, mostly because being poor is a moral failing that you have to be constantly making amends for."

They walked for another block or two, headed for Powell's, the biggest used bookstore in the city. It was part of their routine. After the tea and art came the used books, the third part of Deosil's patented afternoon in Portland.

"You know, honestly, I never really thought of you as…well, as poor," Rusty said once they were inside. "I mean, it makes sense, I guess, but your life is so outside of my normal experience that I guess I just never attached any kind of regular ideas about lifestyle to you. I don't know many artist-witches who make part of their living by touring and speaking at witchcraft festivals and shit."

She chuckled and nodded. "Fair point. But that's kind of on purpose. I don't think I could live a normal life if I tried."

Their first destination, as always, was the cavernous room where the bookstore displayed its science fiction and fantasy novels. The smell of old, pulpy paperbacks filled the space, a scent that Deosil paused to take in like it was cathedral incense, the holiest of holies.

Rusty let Deosil lead the way. She slowly navigated her way down the tight aisles, scanning the alphabetical-by-author shelves. He knew from previous visits that trying to continue their conversation was a waste of time. She wasn't listening to anything. He followed along, glancing over the fantastical art that adorned the book covers, occasionally accepting a small stack of two or three books from Deosil as she shopped. Eventually he had to fetch a basket at one point as the pile grew beyond what was easily manageable.

By the time they reached the end of the section, she had nearly a dozen books tucked every which way in the narrow plastic basket, a riot of old yellowing paper and colored covers faded from their former glory. She steered over to a set of benches against a massive pillar in the middle of the space and plopped down next to an older gentleman engrossed in a magazine.

"This is one of those things, you know." She looked up at Rusty and patted the spot next to her.

"What things?"

"Luxuries." She took the basket from him and pulled out a book to skim through. "You're not supposed to be able to afford the luxury of shelves worth of books you love, even if they're secondhand. Poor people don't read. Everyone knows that. Or if they do, they use the library, you know?"

"Really? That seems stupid. Although, I do admit, I'm not much of a reader myself. I can't remember the last time I actually bought a book."

Deosil made an outraged sound. "Heretic. It's true, though. I used to get a lot of flak for that as a kid, even though it was money I earned. Hell, I know more big readers who come from disadvantaged backgrounds than I do any other source. I feel like a lot of poor people kind of make an art of escapism, you know? Like, it's a survival trait. For some people it's trying to show off rich things, like you're trying to deny your actual situation. For others it's drugs, or one shitty relationship after another, or television. For me, it was books."

Her system was straightforward. First, a glance at the cover. Title and author. Then a flip to the back of the book to skim its summary. Finally, a peek of the inside cover, to see the price. Eventually, she weeded her way through about half of them. Those she put in the basket, setting the others back on rolling carts to be reshelved. "Alright! Want to hit the rest of the place with me?"

"Lead the way." Rusty chuckled, picking the basket up. Once again, Deosil followed a somewhat predictable route: a stop off at the alternative spiritualities shelves to sneer at "fluffy" pagan books, and then a cruise through the LGBT shelves in sociology. She picked up a couple of books there, notably the biography of an early pioneer in trans activism and an anthology of steamy lesbian fiction. ("Wait, you mean people *read* porn?" Rusty asked, confused and obnoxiously loud. She shushed him and pushed him toward the elevators.)

The final stop was the art section, where they wandered, stopping occasionally to peer at the covers of big, colorful books, lithographs in plastic sheeting tacked up to the walls between shelves, and the small gallery of art at the front of the section. The art here constantly changed, a parade of evolving themes and mostly local artists. The current pieces were all photographs depicting various aspects in life in the former Soviet Union.

Rusty hesitated at one piece in particular, gazing at it with a frown. Deosil retreated to where he'd stopped, looking at him and then the piece curiously. It was a small gathering of youth—young men and women about their age, Deosil assumed—sitting around what was probably a diner table. School books and a laptop littered its surface, along with a smattering of food and drink. The young men and women were casual in one another's company, arms thrown over shoulders, one young man leaning on the shoulder of the woman next to him. The composition was murky, but it captured the camaraderie and the joy of young people the world over who'd just managed to get out from under the thumbs of their families and were trying adulthood on for size.

All in all, she really liked it. She glanced at Rusty, to see what he thought, and found him scrolling through his phone with a furrowed brow. "What's up?" she asked.

He looked at her, and then at the picture. "I don't know. I feel like I'm being stupid," said Rusty.

She wrapped his arm up in one of her own and dragged him to the benches in the middle of the display space. "Oh, good. Stories of you being stupid are some of my favorites," she said lightly. "What's going on?"

"So, I've been chatting with this guy."

Deosil chuckled. "Baby, all your best stories about you being stupid start this way."

Rusty sighed. "No, it's not like that. He's not local. Hell, he's not even in the U.S." He scrolled through his phone until he found a picture. The young man in it had dark hair, shorn fairly close to the scalp, with prominent pierced ears. His eyes were dark and intense, making him look older, though he was about their age. His face was rounded and he wore squared-off spectacles.

"This is Kosma. I met him on a Facebook group for gay guys in Ukraine. I'd been thinking about going there to see some of the architecture in Odessa during my break from school, and figured—well, you know. I'd want to check out the bars and stuff there, too. So I wanted to make some friends."

Deosil nodded. She placed one hand on his arm. He was worried, and that worried Deosil.

"Then, a week and a half ago, he just stopped messaging."

Deosil paused for a moment. "Well, is it likely that he's sick, or on vacation or something?"

"Well, maybe. I don't know. It's just that those are the sorts of things he'd have mentioned, you know? He'd have said something. We've been chatting for eight or nine months now, and he mentions those kinds of things. I don't know, maybe I'm just being paranoid. Like, I know as an American I've got a messed-up view of what life is like over there. He teases me about it, in fact."

"But?" Deosil prompted.

"But you see things. Especially lately, you know? You know how in Russia there's been all of these gays getting like kidnapped and tortured and stuff by gangs of skinheads, and no one is doing anything? I know he's not in Russia, but that kind of shit can spread."

Deosil sat thinking for a moment.

"Has there been any other kind of activity from him? Is he still updating Facebook or anything like that?"

"He's not, no." He flipped through his phone, coming to another photo, this one of two young men on the dance floor of a club or bar. One was Kosma, and the other was a young man with a tightly muscled build, curly hair and high cheekbones. "This is Sasha, Kosma's friend. We've never spoken or anything, but I knew his Facebook. I even tried sending him a message, asking about Kosma, but Sasha hasn't posted anything either. In about the same time frame."

Deosil sat back and thought, her gaze resting on the photo of the young Eastern European students. Something stirred in her gut, a low, roiling intuition she'd learned a long time ago not to ignore.

"I would reach out to the others in the Facebook group," she said. "If it's a group just for Odessa queers, then chances are good *someone* knows them, right?"

Rusty sighed and bit his lip. "Yeah, I thought about doing that. I just, I didn't want to embarrass him, you know? Or seem like I was stalking him or something."

"Hey. You're clearly worried about him. At worse, you embarrass yourself and have to apologize, but you'll at least know he's safe then."

Rusty pondered it and shook his head. "You're right. I'm going to do that really quickly, if that's cool."

Deosil smiled, ruffled his hair, and stood. "Totally. Do that. I'm going to go check out the rest of the gallery. I've been thinking about taking up photography."

Rusty grinned and lowered his head to his phone. He tapped furiously at his phone as Deosil wandered over to the matted prints along the gallery wall.

They had a sort of vibrant clarity that no one tried for anymore. Unsurprising, really, as they were a collection of photos from the late 80s and early 90s, most of them in Portland, from what she could tell. Whoever had curated them was clearly going for a sense of nostalgia of the time. Young people in flannel, busy streets with mostly new cars, construction and filled bleachers at a basketball game—all signs of the era's unrestrained prosperity, when it seemed like there could be no end to the economic climb of the day.

She'd been staring at one of them for a while when Rusty came up behind her, wrapping his arms around her and resting his chin on her shoulder, peering past her at the photograph.

"Hey," he said. "Look who it is."

The photo was taken from the ground, facing upward. It was raining, but a thin layer of sunlight filtered through the clouds and split itself into a brilliant wash of color over everything. It stood in impressive contrast to the scene of devastation: a collapsing building, one corner of it caught mid-crumble. The picture centered on two men, both in flight. To one side was Radiant, a thinly muscled man with a cowl, his suit matte black with white piping. His hands were raised before him, and he stared off to the side, where a twisted burl of metal with bits of concrete still clinging to it rose into the air seemingly of its own accord. People cowered beneath the debris, shadowed by its mass, but protected by Radiant's powers from being crushed.

The other wore a suit of blue and white, a marked contrast to his blue-black hair. In his arms, he carried a woman. She was battered and bloodied, but she'd glanced down and across the street at the photographer just as they'd snapped the pic, leaving the impression of immediacy in the viewer. She met the gaze of those viewing the photo, making them part of it. The half-lidded grogginess in her visage did nothing to disguise the sheer relief and gratitude present there—here was someone who'd been *saved* by Sentinel, a real-life hero.

"Wow," Rusty said after a moment. "That's—that's amazing."

Deosil leaned in to read the small paper label beneath the image. "It's called *The Old Town Rescue*. Looks like it's a photo taken during the Echo Event that happened in Portland's Old Town neighborhood in 1992. Sentinel and Radiant were in Seattle when it happened, so they heard about it and flew down to help with rescues and clean-up."

"That's the last time they were together," Rusty whispered. "Sentinel and Radiant."

The two of them were silent for a few moments, taking it in. Deosil glanced at Rusty, who was studying the image intently. "You'd better not have a boner pressing up against me, copper-top."

He flushed and shoved her away gently. "Bitch."

She giggled and spun around, stepping closer to hug him. "Seriously, you should see your face. It must have been a dream come true to meet him, huh? Think he knows how much you dig him?"

"Deosil, stop it, seriously." His blushing smile vanished, replaced by a furrowed brow. He didn't step out of her embrace, but he did push her to arm's length. "It's not like that. He's just…he's a *hero*, you know? A real hero, and he went through so much crap as a result of it."

"I know." She hugged him again before releasing him. "I know how you feel about him, Rusty. It's why I worked to get you that interview with him, you know?" She punched him in the arm. "But don't even try and tell me you don't have a thing for him. I'm a witch, bitch, and if I know anything it's when someone's in love."

Rusty barked laughter, clutching his arm and rubbing the spot where she'd punched him. "Witch my ass. You're a goddamned thug." He took out his phone, taking a photo not of the print, but of the label beneath it, capturing the information on where to purchase a print.

"So! I was thinking," Deosil said as they wandered away from the gallery. "Let's get some dinner and then maybe hit the town? That night club you took me to when I was here last year?"

He gave her a bit of dubious side-eye. "You *want* to go clubbing? You basically threatened my life if I forced you out on the town again."

She smiled as they got into the elevator. "Well, that threat still stands. But I'm the one wanting to go, and the drinks were alright at that place. What do you say?"

"I'm in, definitely."

CHAPTER THREE

Portland, OR
April 19, 2013

Fortunately for everyone involved, no one had to die that night.

"See? I told you. No dubstep." Rusty smiled as he and Deosil flashed their IDs to the man at the door, handing over their cash and wrists for stamping.

"Well, last time you tried to bring me here, there was dubstep all up in it." Deosil slipped her ID back into her bag. She took in the room and pushed him toward the bar. "Let's get drinks."

It was early, so there was still room to walk through the Synergy. A run-down place on the edge of Portland's downtown that had seen more than twenty years of service as a gay club, Synergy was showing its years. Hell, even its *name* was dated. The lights were lackluster, and its sound system could have used some upgrading. The place was mostly concrete, painted a flat black that had worn into a scuffed, chipped mess over the years. The tables matched, for the most part, although the chairs scattered here and there certainly didn't. Someone had attempted to class up the decor with little glass cups at every table, each containing a flickering LED faux-candle. Feeble, but points for trying, Deosil supposed.

In most respects, the place was basically a dive. But the cover and drinks were cheap, the music decent (fucking dubstep night notwithstanding) and

Portland's young gay scene loved it. Sure, there were classier clubs that catered to well-off urban professionals or the bear community or whatever, but Synergy was where those who had more energy than money or sense came to dance their faces off, hang out with their friends, and maybe even hook up with a handsome, sweaty stranger at the end of the night.

As they found their way to the nearer of the two bars, Deosil watched as Rusty got one of two reactions from other clubgoers. The majority who noticed him turned to whisper to their friends, calling attention to his presence there, none of them taking their eyes off his passage. They all looked like they had great stories to share with one another, and a salacious part of Deosil's curiosity was dying to know what they were saying.

Far fewer were those who waved to him and called out his name, each trying to be friendly or enticing in their own way. Hell, one scruffy-faced hottie who'd already shucked his shirt to show off a shredded body—the result of many hours in a gym, no doubt – stepped right into their path. He rested one hand on Rusty's shoulder and leaned in to whisper something, with a nod toward the dance floor.

Rusty shook his head, reaching up to push the young man's hand aside and avoiding making eye contact. With footwork that would have made a boxer proud, he stepped around the man, pulling on Deosil's hand. In short order, they were at the bar. Glancing behind them, Deosil watched Mr. Five O'Clock Shadow rejoin his friends, who all had something to say about that display.

"Man, you're a super shitty gay guy, you know that?" Standing next to him, Deosil wrapped an arm around his waist and headbutted his shoulder. He glanced down at her, trying his best to pull off a confused look, but there was the flush of embarrassment there. Ginger complexions don't lie, she remembered him joking. "He was into you, and hot. What gives?"

"What? Dude was a douche." He glanced back at the group and quickly looked away when he saw they were all still watching him. "I hadn't even gotten a drink yet."

Deosil snorted. "You're right. What an asshole. Imagine wanting to dance with you. At a nightclub. Jesus. How do those kinds even get in here?" Rusty shot her a glance, and then stepped up to the bar to order drinks for them both.

"Hey." The blond bartender, dressed in a black short-sleeve T-shirt, greeted Rusty. "Gauss, right? How's it going?" The young man—who looked only barely legal to serve alcohol—grinned at Rusty, who was taken aback for a moment. Rusty chuckled and leaned against the bar with a smile that was only a little bit forced.

Well, great, thought Deosil. Now he was going to be super-friendly to everyone all night just to prove her wrong. Well, it was better than the alternative, she supposed. In short order, he rejoined her, handing her a dark beer bottle. In the same hand, he held a folded-up piece of paper, which he showed her with a magician's flourish and then stowed in the front pocket of his jeans.

"That's more like it, goddamn it." She grinned and clinked his bottle with her own. "God, I can't believe you got me hooked on shitty hipster beer. I hold you responsible for the complete death of my personal integrity and dignity here." She took a swig from the bottle and pulled him onto the dance floor. Deosil barely noticed the music itself—it was some house remix, featuring plenty of repeated vocals from one diva or another.

It was the rhythm that Deosil fell into, aligning first body and then spirit to it. A small part of her mind cautioned her to *be careful, goddamn it,* but she sent that thought swirling away like a leaf down a spring-melt swollen stream. She wanted to dance, to lose herself, to not worry about her own problems, to not worry about her friends and family, to not worry about the state of the world. She wanted to find a drumbeat, glorious and ancient, for all that it came from a machine, and become part of it. Just for a little while.

Her senses expanded outward, an awareness of the world that she had no words for. It was an understanding that transcended reason and emotion, that was simply awareness writ large, without rhyme or reason. Deep draughts of cold air mingled with tiny, excited gouts of heat above the city of Portland like lovers, and in their commingling was born the eternal patter of rain outside. The soil beneath them was shot through with rich green life, a soil so rich that even that which lay beneath years' worth of concrete and asphalt still bore its touch, deep within its fragrant warmth. Somewhere to her left, she could sense the slow, steady heartbeat of the Willamette River, its surface placid and earth-hued, but its depths swirled with both life and filth, a mixture that felt a little like taking a deep breath of smog-tinged air.

As she fell into the flows of the elements that made up the world around her—transcending the club, and even the city itself, the land on which Portland was built—she could hear them. The strange voices that weren't voices, the excited whisperings of the skies over the city, the low sleepy grumble of the land that was the city's foundation and roots, the hissing disdain of the veins of fire deep in the earth. They all called to her, spoke to her. They were like kids trying to get her attention, pulling at her awareness, only they were ancient and powerful, each with their own desires that they tried to thrust upon her. She danced her awareness among them as surely as she danced her body across the dance floor, touching one, then the other, then off to a third.

She was pretty sure it had been two or three songs by the time she forced herself up out of it again. Her hands were empty, and she searched the room in mild, stoned concern. Rusty—now dancing with Mr. Five O'Clock Shadow, as it turned out—smiled at her, and handed both of their bottles to her with a wink. She took another pull on hers, and then gestured at the tables at the periphery of the dance floor. She took an unsteady step, then another, and then found her balance again—her normal, two-legged people-balance, so strange after dancing with the elemental powers all around her—and hunted for a table.

It was busier than when she and Rusty had taken to the floor. Maybe those two or three songs were more like nine or ten. At a table near the edge of the dance floor, a thin figure seated alone waved her over. A quick glance confirmed that there were no empty tables, so she smiled and crossed to it. She set Rusty's bottle aside, and took a long pull on hers while assessing her host.

He was a thin man, older. Deosil guessed he was in his early fifties, his meticulously combed hair thinning on top, shot through with grey at the temples. His cheeks were high, and had probably given him movie star looks when he was younger. Now they sheltered hollow shadows beneath them, matching those under his hazel eyes. He was dressed in a smart button-up and slacks, with a long elegant coat draped over the chair next to him. There was a drink in his ringed hands, an empty on the table. He watched her appraise him with a smile, and took a sip before extending one of those long hands towards her.

"Henry," he said. "Nice to meet you." Deosil smiled and took the hand, shaking it. He had a lightly effeminate air about him, in his speech, his handshake. Hell, even the way he sat the chair, leaned slightly over onto one hip, legs crossed, one hand or the other occasionally smoothing his pants, picking lint off his shirt.

"Jesh," she said with a smile. "Thanks for the rescue. I was afraid I was going to have to end up wandering all over for a table. Or worse, ending up crouched against the wall like some bum."

He chuckled and raised an eyebrow. "You dance beautifully." Henry gestured to the dance floor. "Most people get out there and do the minimum they have to in order to justify the space they're taking on the dance floor. Or they just music-fuck someone they're hoping to pick up." Deosil glanced at Rusty and his new dance buddy. "Music-fuck" was a good way to describe what they were doing. Rusty was pressed up against the guy, basically groping him to the beat, his head buried in Mr. Five O'Clock Shadow's neck like he was rubbing up against the guy's stubble.

God, boys are weird. Deosil took another drink.

"Are you trained?" Henry put his glass down and glanced over his shoulder, raising one elegant hand in the air, gesturing at himself and then Deosil, then raising two fingers. The blond bartender lifted his hand with a thumbs-up, and Henry turned his attention back to their table.

"Trained? Oh, in dance?" Deosil smiled and shook her head. "I'm not, no. Just feel it in my bones, I guess."

"Yeah, most people who dance like that are usually rolling or tweaking or whatever kids are calling it these days. You know, on ecstasy." He raised an inquisitive eyebrow in her direction, and Deosil chuckled.

"No, no. Not me. I mean, at least, not tonight. I've done it before, out at a Burn in the desert, you know. Never tried it, and the Playa is a good place to try new things."

"A Burn in the desert? The Playa? You've lost me, I'm afraid." He leaned back in his seat,.

"It's called Burning Man. It's a sort of festival, really artsy, where a bunch of people with alternative views—artists, queers, nudists, urban tribal types, sexually liberated people, all kinds—sort of escape the real world. At its best, it's a place to build the kind of culture you wish you belonged to, instead of the one you do." She took a last swallow on her bottle, emptying it.

"And at its worst?"

Deosil shrugged. "At its worst, it's a several-day party filled with other freaks like you where you can get laid and get high and run around in the desert naked if you feel like it."

Henry laughed, a quick guffaw that settled into a chuckle deep in his throat. A thin waiter with a pierced labret and hair gelled into short brown spikes brought drinks: another murky brown liquid in a glass for Henry and another bottle of beer for Deosil. He swept up the empty glasses and bottle from the table, as well as the bill Henry handed him—more than enough to pay for both their drinks, plus a fair tip, Deosil couldn't help noticing.

"Thanks for the drink," Deosil said, raising the bottle in salute.

"My pleasure. To Burning Man at its worst." He toasted, and Deosil laughed, clinking his glass with her bottle, and taking a swig.

The two of them chatted for a while. Deosil led the conversation, perhaps a little aggressively. It wasn't that she wanted to know about Henry so much as she wanted to avoid talking too much about herself. He was a fine conversationalist and a better storyteller. He'd come out when it was far less socially acceptable to do so and fled to San Francisco.

Rusty stopped by the table at some point, nodding a greeting to Henry when Deosil introduced them. He checked with her, to see if she was enjoying herself before shucking his outer shirt, leaving it on one of the empty seats, and returning to the dance floor in his undershirt. Henry watched him go with something like hunger and something like longing in his eyes before returning to his story. Deosil smiled at him and he winked at her.

"I was sure San Francisco was the Mecca of Our People, you know. And it was, to an extent—God knows there were lots of us there. I did all sorts of things to make a living there. I helped restore furniture in antique shops, I tended bar for a few years, here and there. My background was in theater, though. I mean, really. I'd been involved in the theater since middle school plays. I was *deeply* invested in it, so much so that today, thinking back on it, I consider it something of an affront that anyone had the nerve to be surprised when I turned out to be gay."

He took an indignant sip of his drink while Deosil laughed. "And now? What do you do these days?" she said.

"This and that," he said, gesturing vaguely. Deosil thought he just liked the way his rings flashed in the strobe lights of the club. "I do some volunteer work with the hospices and help with organizing fund raisers and other shows. You know—old fag stuff like that. But mostly, I just run this club."

"Oh, are you the manager?" Deosil asked, trying to remember if she'd made any disparaging remarks she might abruptly need to apologize for.

"Yes, but mostly because I'm too cheap to hire someone else to do it. I own the place."

"Oh!" Deosil perked up and glanced around the club again, though she wasn't sure why. She was pretty sure it hadn't somehow changed now that she knew its owner. "I *love* this place. I make Rusty bring me here when I'm in town for a drink and some dancing."

"Much appreciated, Jesh," he said, a hand over his heart. He held up his glass to her. "To the Synergy. Long may this old bitch of a club reign." Deosil laughed—practically giggled, really—and clinked his glass in another toast.

It was a tribute to how comfortable she'd gotten, sitting here chatting and drinking with Henry, that she didn't notice the trio until they were actually at the table. Their young ringleader was slender, not quite five and a half feet in height, with blond hair treated with plenty of product for a night on the town. He wore tight jeans and a white t-shirt that fit him like a glove. He slid into the unoccupied chair in between Deosil and Henry. His friends clustered around him, one of them standing behind his chair, leaning on his shoulders, and the other crouching at table-height next to him. Like the twink in the seat, they were young and thin and stylish.

Henry smiled welcomingly, but Deosil saw his eyes lose that fond sparkle. She sat back and watched Henry the gay club owner rise to the surface as he gave a fond if anemic hug to the blond kid, who leaned in to greet him with a kiss on the cheek.

"Henry, you haven't introduced us." His tone was arch, sort of catty and sort of playful, like he might chastise Henry but could play it off as just "being funny" at a moment's notice. He turned to Deosil with a smile and leaned forward, hand extended. Deosil was pretty sure he was wearing lip gloss. "I'm Matty."

"Matty, this is my new friend Jesh," Henry said. He was clearly put out by the interruption.

"Nice to meet you," Deosil said, shaking his hand. Matty gave her a questioning look, and then glanced at his cronies. He reached for his phone, unlocking it and flashing an image at her.

"Don't you mean *Diesel*?" He fairly crowed. His friends all *stared* at her, hungry to see her reaction.

Fuck. On his screen was her profile on the PHR: the somewhat-notorious website called "Post-Humans Roster." Though the site touted itself as a social media site dedicated to the phenomenon of the Changed, in reality, it was basically a stalkers' site. Users posted known supers, listing everything about them that public knowledge: cities of residence, known abilities, photos that users who'd encountered them had uploaded, plus space for users to contribute their own thoughts about them, which mostly amounted to inappropriate sexual commentary, stupid conspiracy theories, postulation about real names and backgrounds.

The Originals had too much pull to really show up on the site, aside from a handful here and there, and the Empowered never did, thanks to most of their top-secret government or corporate status, so the site was mostly fodder for info about Echoes. Deosil sighed. She'd heard that whoever ran PHR had updated it to include basic facial recognition software. It didn't work very well, but the photo that Matty had taken of her under the lights chatting with Henry was good enough to pick her profile out of the database's images.

"Oh, Matty." Henry sighed. "Don't be an asshole." He didn't seem angry, Deosil thought. He looked embarrassed and tired. Deosil let her stare on Matty waver, and she broke into a smile.

"No. In fact, I don't mean 'diesel'. Diesel is a kind of fuel. You probably think it's funny, because you're dying to make a 'diesel dyke' joke. Don't bother—I've heard them before, and from people who're cleverer than you are. We'd both be disappointed."

Matty blinked. His mouth gaped a little. He glanced at his friends, both staring at her with eyebrows raised and hands covering their mouths. Cute. Deosil smirked. They were all clearly used to being the important fish in their little ponds. "The word you're trying for is 'Deosil'," she continued, pronouncing it the Gaelic way: *JEH-shul*. "I'm also perfectly content with the pronunciation that most people who read English give it: 'Deosil.'" This time, she said it *DEO-sil*.

"I'm happy to meet any friend of Henry's he cares to introduce me to, but if you're just here to talk shit, make stupid jokes, and in general be a pain in my ass, then accept my cordial invitation to fuck all the way off. I'm not in the mood, little twinkie, for whatever Bitchy Diva Olympics you think you're playing."

There were a few tense moments of silence before one of Matty's friends snorted. "Oh, snap." Matty whipped his head around to glare at him. The friend burst out laughing and backed away from the table, waving the other friend along. Matty shoved his seat out from under him, again waving his phone in her face. "Fuck you, tranny freak," he said and stormed away.

A familiar tension spiked behind her eyes, like a storm blowing up from nowhere. Deosil pinched the bridge of her nose in a futile hope of alleviating it. She half-jumped when Henry put his hand on hers.

"Are you alright?" he asked. Something like shame played across his features, and she settled her other hand on top of his and smiled.

"Jesus, yes. If that's the worst I get during my typical day, it's been a good one, you know?"

Henry shook his head, casting the young men at the bar an unpleasant glance. Matty himself was ignoring them, his face buried in his phone, but his two cronies whipped their heads away, caught staring. Henry turned to her. "If you like, I'd be happy to have the bouncers escort them out. I don't tolerate homophobia—or transphobia—in my club."

There was hesitation there. It wasn't hard to suss out why. Stylish little Matty and his clique probably spent plenty of money here, and their presence probably attracted others as well—those who wanted to be them, those who wanted to watch them (and their little bouts of drama) and those who wanted to fuck them, Deosil guessed. Even now, Matty had a small crowd gathered around him, showing around her PHR profile, reading off choice tidbits of information and retelling their encounter, undoubtedly with a spin that didn't involve her handing him his head, she suspected.

"No way," she said. "Your bouncers would end up covered in glitter and hair gel, smelling of strawberry lip gloss, and I wouldn't wish that on anyone." Henry barked a laugh, loud enough to draw attention from the crowd over by the bar, including a death-glare from Matty. Deosil raised her bottle to him in salute.

One of the club's employees appeared at their table, a Bluetooth headset in her ear. She nodded a greeting to Deosil—she was pretty, honestly, with long straight black hair, and a killer figure under that jacket and jeans—and whispered something in Henry's ear. He perked up and smiled. "Go and open a few cases of good champagne, Denise, and let the bouncers and bartenders know."

He rose and drained his glass. "Jesh, I'm sorry I have to run. We've just had word that some celebrity types are headed this way. Usually a pain in the ass, but often worth the exposure in tabloids and the like, especially if you can get them drunk enough to do stupid shit." Deosil laughed and rose as well, hugging the man. He collected their empties and then disappeared into the offices behind the bar.

"What was all that about?" Like magic, Rusty appeared, worry on his sweat-streaked face. "I was hanging out with Miguel, and his friends were saying something about that little fuck Matty stirring up shit. Did he out you?"

Deosil nodded and smiled. She handed him his now-flat bottle of beer and took a swig of hers before speaking. "Yeah, he did. Outed times two, even. Someone's updated my PHR profile to include my boy-past, it looks like." She shrugged, though it bothered her how much it bothered her.

"Goddamn him," he said. He pulled a chair over, sat, and leaned his head in against hers. "I'm so sorry. He's the asshole who dug up all those old videos about me and showed them around the club. Hell, he probably saw us come in together, and that's why he searched for you on PHR."

Deosil winced. "Ouch. So, he's not just moonlighting as an asshole, he does it habitually. Professionally, even."

"Fucking understatement." Rusty put an arm around her, and for a few moments, Deosil let herself be in a place of comfort with a friend's care and concern. But she could only take so much of all that. She pushed him away, finally, wrinkling her nose.

"You smell like dance floor boy." She waved her hand in front of her face. Rusty chuckled and took a drink from his beer. He made a face, put it down, and stole a drink from hers. "Besides," said Deosil. "You're already developing some hellacious hickies, probably courtesy of Mr. Five O'Clock Shadow, and I don't want to know what else you got all on you. Spit and pheromones, probably."

Rusty laughed and tossed a wadded-up napkin at her. "Bitch," he said fondly, and stole another sip of her beer. "Wanna hit the dance floor again?"

CHAPTER FOUR

Portland, OR
April 19, 2013

Though they didn't see them right away, it was easy to tell when the movie stars showed up. A buzz swept through the people in the nightclub like a gust of wind through a field of tall grass. Heads turned, necks straining toward the front door. The dance floor cleared out as people abandoned it to get a better view of the celebrity arrival. Miguel and his friends were among them—the swarthy, scruffy hottie abandoned Rusty with a quick cheek-kiss of apology, leaving him standing by himself on the dance floor, like an asshole. Rusty raised his hands in an indignant gesture that signaled What the hell, dude?

Miguel—or Mr. Five O'Clock Shadow, as Deosil had started thinking of him—didn't even see it. Deosil danced her way over to Rusty. "Wanna grab our seats?" The redhead nodded irritably, and the two retreated to their claimed table before someone else decided to make it their own. After all, it did have a pretty good vantage of most of the club. It would be prime movie-star-gawking turf.

Luckily, they'd reached the table just in time. Deosil and Rusty practically threw themselves into their seats a couple of seconds before Matty and his crew—now augmented by six other assorted twinks and gym queens—could claim it for themselves. Without warning, the chairs nearest the group slid themselves under the table, and the chairs closest to the dance floor glided out as though welcoming Rusty and Deosil. Matty and a couple of his friends stopped with a gasp and a drink-sloshing step backward away from the animated chairs. One of them gave a little surprised yelp.

Rusty's laughter was loud even this close to the dance floor. Deosil threw him an admonishing smirk, but they were both thinking it. Sometimes, reminding people they were dealing with the Changed was fucking worth it. Rusty had no regrets. If you couldn't use your goddamned superpower to nab the seats you wanted in a club, then what was the point?

Matty paused for a minute, glanced at the knot of people at the edge of the club, and then made a decision. His face settled into that faux-friendly mask Deosil had seen on him earlier as he finished crossing the distance to the table.

"Gauss!" he said in a tone that was supposed to be bitchy-sweet, but that only stupid television characters on melodramas used. *Who the fuck talks like that?* Deosil wondered. *This queen has been watching too many soap operas.* "I'm so glad I got to see you tonight." He crossed to Rusty to give a little distance hug-and-air-kiss, one of these shows of camaraderie in which Matty was careful to not actually touch him.

"Hey, Matty," Rusty said mildly. He smiled up at the younger man. "Good to see you."

"I have a question for you." Matty leaned in as though they were old friends, but his volume rose. "There's a bunch of movie stars showing up, did you hear? Do you know any of them? I mean, I know you were a big movie star yourself, and all."

It is the curse of the redhead that no matter how cool their poker face, their skin will always give them away. Rusty'd told her that once, but Deosil didn't understand it until now. An angry flush shot up his pale neck and across his face, reddening his ears. He looked down and away as Matty and his cronies giggled. Though he tried to affect a bored disdain, from where she was sitting, Deosil could see Rusty trying to swallow a lump in his throat, and avoiding their faces so they couldn't see the angry tears in his eyes. Deosil stood, shoving her chair back with a metallic screech across the concrete floor.

Several members of Matty's entourage lurched backward with a gasp. Every one of them raised shocked faces to regard her fearfully. Deosil said nothing for a few moments, taking the time to regard each one of them searchingly, as though memorizing their features. Finally, her gaze fell on Matty, who raised his pointed chin defiantly.

"Why don't you boys fuck off, already?" She said it calmly, a contrast to the fury in her face.

Matty glanced behind him, gathering resolve from his friends' frantic gazes. He stepped forward. "Or what, *tranny*?" His retort was all bile and venom. Several of his friends gasped at him. Two of them flat-out turned and walked away as fast as they could. "Matty, *no*," another pleaded. One clutched his arm and tried to pull him away.

"You've got a shitty attitude, little man," she said, crossing to him. Rusty stood as well, looking anxiously around. Deosil ignored him and fixed her attention on Matty. "I know you think that you're hot shit right now, because you're young, and you're pretty, and you've got your choice of the pickings in most of the gay bars here. You clearly think you're enough to step to anyone who crosses you, because you're pretty sure all those things make you someone important. And they do. Here."

She pointed at the door and leaned in on him. "But out there? You aren't shit, little boy. It's why you stay in your little queer ghetto. You were harassed and tormented through high school, either because you were closeted but everyone knew anyway, or you'd come out and made yourself a target. And you're still hurting from all that bullshit, so you think the only way you can make it better is by becoming the new mean girl. You get to be the one on top of the social heap, and dish out the abuse to other people, and you're pretty sure that's how you get to feeling better. You're so busy reenacting your bullshit high school dramas that you don't realize what a lie it all is, though. You're still just a scared little boy who hides behind his hair product and his bar drinks and his gym membership and his one-night stands. The fact is, you're terrified of the world."

As she spoke, small gusts of wind rose around her, strange and unnatural. Even in the sweat-and-booze-and-industrial-cleaner scent of the club, they smelled of the loamy earth, of the Pacific Northwest rainforests in the height of autumn. Motes of witchlight rose around her, little sparks of innocuous luminescence so dim in the harsh club lighting that only those near her could make them out. Her face and bearing changed, and something ancient peered out at Matty from the hollows of Deosil's eyes. "And you're right to be," she said. "I *am* the world, Matty, and I don't have the time or patience for your shit."

Torn between terror and indignation at being so blatantly threatened, Matty froze. Deosil snapped a glance at one of his friends. He grabbed Matty and bodily pulled him away towards the bar. Another covered their retreat, hands held up as he backed away. "No offense, he's had *soooo* much to drink. He was just messing around, we'll keep him out of your way…" He kept babbling even after Deosil couldn't hear him, and she turned back toward their table.

Grinning at one another, Rusty and Deosil resumed their seats. "You are one scary bitch, you know that?" Rusty said.

"That's pronounced *witch*, asshole." She punched him in the arm playfully. She glanced back at the group clustered around Matty near the bar. Several of them typed furiously on smartphones, while Matty talked nonstop. "God. I'm sure they're tearing up the internets with how I threatened them or whatever."

"Bullshit. You didn't once threaten to do anything. You didn't even suggest it." Rusty held up his own phone and hit a button. Her voice came from it, tinny and weird-sounding, but comprehensible. Rusty clicked it back off triumphantly. "You avoided exactly the kind of things they warned us against in those Image Management workshops at the Retreat Weekends. You're in the clear, and I'll be happy to help you prove it if any of the spooks come around harassing you about it."

Deosil laughed and hugged him, kissing him on the cheek.

"Although," said Rusty, "I have to admit, as badass as you sounded, it was a little Lord of the Rings up in here for a minute. I seriously never thought I'd see you Cate Blanchett somebody."

She laughed and whapped him on the arm again. "Shut up! I love Galadriel. I'm taking that as a compliment. Now go and get me another shitty beer, before *I diminish and go into the West*." She furnished the quote with a silly, spooky tone and wide, creepy eyes.

He did his best to ignore the other people at the bar. Matty's crew, of course, were all whispers and stink-eye, though one of them was giving him that appraising, up-and-down, thinking-about-fucking-you look. Others at the bar noticed and started up their normal side conversations. It was worse by this time of night. Everyone was a few drinks in and not as subtle as they thought they were. They spoke louder, were more obvious in pointing him out to friends, and less concerned about being caught staring.

Jesus. If he kept up the mood swings of this ferocity, he was going to give himself whiplash. The cute blond bartender winked, passed him his drinks, and said, "On the house." Rusty smiled his thanks and winked back.

He had to cut his way through the crowd. The club's bouncers had already set up a semi-private cluster of tables against the back wall. Though the celebrity group's security formed a perimeter, the locals milled about as close as they were able, creating a knot of club-goers craning their necks and holding their phones up above their heads in vain hope of snapping a shot that wasn't blurry and totally off-center. As he pushed his way through, Rusty appreciated his height advantage and did a little rubbernecking of his own.

There were three of them. Ethan Carruthers, was a Hollywood regular. Yeah, he usually played sidekick characters in action films, the funny guy who bumbled his way through scenes of violence and danger, lovable and shriekingly afraid. Though he came off as shy and adorable in the films, he was reclined in his chair with a sour look, continually glancing at his phone. A sheen of sweat covered his forehead, and his hair was greasy and sort of thin on top.

Lara Dominguez, on the other hand, was real-life hot. She was one of the current crop of popular leading ladies, the sizzling Latina who preferred to work in action movies. She was notorious for refusing to use a stunt woman during fight scenes and didn't hesitate to strip it all off for love scenes. Tonight, she looked amazing in a bronze sheath dress that hugged her curves, set off with a pair of high-heeled sandals, straps wrapped halfway up her lower leg. Super fierce. Rusty approved and made a mental note to point her out to Deosil. He was sure she'd approve, too.

Rusty groaned when the third actor turned away from whatever he was saying to Lara, and scanned the crowd. He was a tall and well-built black man, a man making his mark in the action film industry. Easily the least-experienced actor present, he was the one with the most star power for one simple reason: his name was Optic and he was a super. Not an Echo, though, like Rusty and Deosil—Optic was one of the Empowered. The result of some Air Force program intended to create superpowered flying soldiers, Optic was one of the very rare Empowered who wasn't hidden away by layers of government top secret designations or corporate IP protection and NDAs.

Three years ago or so, he'd been drummed out of the military when he was outed. Though it looked like the Department of Transformed Persons Affairs was going to step in to force legislation through that circumvented Don't Ask, Don't Tell in the case of the Empowered, they never did, and Optic was discharged from the military under a great deal of public furor. His case became a rallying point between gay rights activists and legislators, and about a year and a half after he took off the uniform, Don't Ask, Don't Tell was repealed.

Though he'd disappeared for a year, he'd turned up at the Health Retreat that year, though he kept to himself. Most of the Echoes assumed he thought he was better than them, as someone who'd been given his powers instead of getting them accidentally. Shortly afterwards, his powers, charisma and military physique landed him a lucrative supporting role in a well-received action flick called *Full Burn*. His next role was a lead, and he'd been a media darling since then. Nobody seemed to know his full name—the Empowered in the military had their names classified, and Hollywood wanted a code-named movie star with superpowers, so he was just Optic.

He gazed across the crowd fondly when his eyes met Rusty's. He frowned, and rolled his eyes, turning his attention pointedly away. Likewise, Rusty spun and walked away from the little scene, shoving past one or two people on his way past. "For fuck's sake," Rusty said, practically dropping their drinks on the table. "As if I weren't having a shitty enough night."

"What is it?" Deosil rescued her bottle from tipping over and licked bit that sloshed over onto her hand before taking a big swig.

"Those movie stars? One of them is Optic."

Deosil whipped her head around, rose from her chair, and stood on her tiptoes, looking for him over the crowd. Shrugging when she couldn't find him, she slid back into her seat and regarded Rusty. "You okay?"

Rusty grimaced, sighing.

"Yeah. It's just the first time I've seen him since he blew me off. No, that's not true. It's the first time I've seen him since we hooked up at the Retreat. He never actually blew me off in person."

Deosil frowned. "That's a pretty shitty thing to do by text, I admit. Although, yes, you're right. I *did* say it was a bad idea. Summer camp hook-ups never work out. It's a law of physics or something."

Rusty lost himself in his phone, typing furiously. Deosil watched him studiously not glance up, although it was a fight to do so. "So, you going to get lost in your phone for the rest of the night, or what?" she said.

"Sorry," he said, clicking his phone off and slipping it back into a pocket. "I was just answering some replies on that Facebook group I was telling you about. The one searching for Kosma and Sasha."

"Oh, totally. Any luck? Has anyone seen them?" Deosil put her feet up in the chair next to her and settled in, sipping at her bottle.

"No. There's a couple of regulars at this bar they usually go to who said the police came in the other night, asking after them. Sounds like their school and their parents have both missed them, and that bar was the last place anyone saw them."

For a moment, Deosil envied Rusty. Not his situation, of course, who'd want friends to go missing? It was his openness. He wore his emotions frankly and unconsciously. His brow was furrowed, his gaze distant. He kept reaching up to his phone, like he was going to *do something right now*, but then just let his hand touch it. How long had it been since Deosil had felt like she could be that bald-faced about what she felt? In any capacity?

She reached over and took the hand that lingered on his phone. "Hey. I'm sure it'll be alright. College kids are college kids, right? Maybe they decided to take an impulsive trip into a bigger city and are getting into entirely age-inappropriate shenanigans there, you know?"

He nodded, unconvinced. "I just hate feeling like I can't *do* anything, is all." Deosil squeezed his hand and he smiled at her. "Thanks for putting up with me."

"God, I know. You're lucky you have me, you know." Deosil leaned over to kiss him on the cheek. "Seriously, though. I'm here for you, yeah?"

When she leaned back, they saw a pair of looming figures standing near their table. One was a sunglasses-wearing behemoth of a white dude, head shaved, dressed in black t-shirt and slacks. He was obviously the bodyguard for the other one: Optic. "Hey, you two," said Optic. "Mind if I sit for a minute?"

Rusty looked away in disgust and yelped as Deosil's clunky sandal found his shin under the table. She pulled her other foot off the chair and brushed it off, shoving it out. "Sure, Optic," she said with a smile. "Grab a sit."

"Thanks," he said and did so. His bodyguard waved over a waiter, who brought a bottle of champagne and some glasses to the table. Optic spoke as the man poured for them. "I hope you don't mind me bothering you guys. In the middle of all this, I kinda felt like celebrating this whole movie thing with people I already know, you know?"

Deosil smiled and took a glass, forcing Rusty to take it from her, and then took one herself. "Definitely! Seriously, Optic, you should be really proud of yourself—this is awesome."

They *tink*ed their glassed together—even Rusty did so, a little less grudgingly—and took a sip. Deosil shivered in delight. This was, as her momma would have said, the Good Stuff. Optic smiled at her over his own glass, and then lowered it to regard Rusty, who was intensely focused on the cheesy LED candle flickering on the table. "Hey, Rusty," Optic said. He set his glass down on the table and ran a nervous hand over his almost-bald head. Rusty looked up, and the actor leaned forward intently. "Look. I know I owe you an apology. I should have handled things after the Retreat better. Hell, I should have handled them at the Retreat better. I mean, I never meant for you to think that we…"

He sighed and took a gulp of his glass, almost draining it. "Look, whatever it was I intended, I obviously hurt you, and that was shitty to do. I've felt bad about it ever since it happened, but I haven't really known what to do about it, you know? I know neither of us is here tonight to rehash everything from the past, but it just—it feels like part of the problem was not talking face-to-face. And since we're both here, I just wanted you to know that I'm really sorry. I treated you like shit, and you deserved better than that. I don't expect you to accept that—Jesus, I wouldn't. But I treated you that way because *I'm* the asshole, not because anything you did wrong."

Rusty flicked his eyes up, just for a heartbeat, before his gaze slid away again. Deosil reached out and clasped his hand under the table, squeezing it. He held onto her grip like a drowning man.

"Well," Optic said awkwardly. "I'll leave you guys to it." He drained his glass and stood.

"Optic," said Deosil, just before he could turn away. "Thanks for the champagne. We're really happy for you, and hope this movie is a super success."

The actor nodded, and then smiled at her. "Thanks, kiddo." With that, he and his gorilla of a bodyguard slipped into the crowd.

Still gripping Rusty's hand, Deosil poured them more champagne. She took a couple sips of hers and then glanced at him. He took a deep breath, releasing her hand. She smiled and raised her glass.

"A toast," she said, in a tone that forbade him from defying her. (You know. Her normal tone.) "To horrible exes who come crawling back to apologize and acknowledge what douchebags they are."

Rusty laughed, then, almost in spite of himself, and snatched up his glass to clink against hers. He downed half the contents in a single swallow, and then laughed again. "He's right, though," he said. "I mean, I kind of knew that he was only after a short thing. Retreat romance, like you said. I was so needy, though, I wanted it to be more. I got pushy, and I was the one who set myself up to be hurt."

Deosil smiled at him gently. "Maybe. He could have handled it better, though. I mean, he could have at least spoken to you on the phone. Maybe you had unreasonable expectations, but he could have done better. He was the older seducer here."

Rusty snorted. "Seducer? Hell, I practically ambushed him in his bunk."

Deosil burst out laughing, setting down her glass. "Oh, fucking *redheads*." For a while, they both simply people-watched and checked their phones. Matty and his crew had indeed made scathing updates about both Gauss and Deosil on PHR. Bastards. After a while, both of them were drunk enough that the entries were hilarious.

By the time the bottle of champagne was gone, Rusty had created his own fake account on PHR and was posting ridiculous shit about himself and Deosil with unholy glee. Both of them were cackling, their sides hurt from all the giggling. Of course, that was when Optic walked by, his hand firmly around the waist of Mr. Five O'Clock Shadow—er, Miguel, Deosil amended. She saw it at the same time Rusty did. Rusty's eyes narrowed and he slapped his phone down onto the table. "Fucker," he said. Deosil wasn't sure if he was cursing Optic or Miguel. Maybe both.

Rusty fixated on the two stepping onto the dance floor, so much so that he didn't notice when the lissome figure clad in bronze slid into the seat by Deosil with a smile and what might have been a purr.

"Oh my God," said Deosil. She slapped her hands over her mouth. "You're Lara Dominguez!"

Rusty snapped his attention back to the table as the actress down an open champagne bottle with an impish grin. "You seem to be out of champagne," she said reasonably, and refilled all of their glasses. "That seems like a crime, if you ask me."

"I'm such a big fan, Ms. Dominguez," said Deosil. This time, it was Rusty's turn to deliver a wake-up kick under the table, and Deosil started. "Sorry, this was just unexpected," she said, abashed.

"No, no, I'm flattered." Lara laid a hand atop Deosil's. "I saw Optic over here chatting with you, and now that he's found a boy to go show off on the dance floor with, I thought I'd come and introduce myself. He was very cagey about who you were, so, well, you know."

"It meant you had to come see, didn't it?" Rusty grinned at her.

Lara's eyes practically danced with mischief. "You better believe it," she said with an excited flourish, like she wanted to reach out and pet them. She extended a hand to shake instead. "I'm Lara."

"I'm Gauss," Rusty said, and then gestured to his right. "This is Deosil."

"Ah, so you are supers, then," she said with a grin. "Ethan owes me fifty." Out of the corner of his eye, Rusty watched Deosil regain her composure.

"Yeah, we know Optic from the Health Retreats the DTPA makes us attend every year." Rusty found it comfortable to talk to Lara, who kept glancing at Deosil fondly. Was she interested? "He's a good guy. We're glad to see his success, you know?"

"We are," Deosil said. "He definitely deserves some happiness after all the crap the military put him through."

Lara nodded. "Such bullshit. And the worst part is that right after they kicked him out, they got rid of that stupid rule! They couldn't have hurried up with that? I would have been so mad."

"Well, honestly, a lot of the reason they got rid of it was because of Optic. Well, maybe not a lot, but he drew a lot of attention to it, you know, and gave a chance for the lawmakers and activists who'd been working to get rid of it to make it happen." Deosil glanced at Rusty as he spoke and shook her head. Even to him, it must feel like a little cognitive dissonance to be singing his praises.

"Did you know that they wrote him a letter asking him to come back?" Lara asked, taking a sip of her champagne. Both Deosil and Rusty shook their heads. Lara leaned in. "It's true. We were on set in New York, a couple of weeks ago. They said that since they're repealed the law, they wanted him to come back to work for them. He didn't even have to work with his old project if he didn't want to—he could be a liaison or publicity person or whatever."

"I bet he told them to get fucked, didn't he?" Rusty said with a slight, knowing smile.

"You better believe he did," Lara crowed. "Oh, man, you should have read his reply. I tell you, that one is *sharp*. I really like him." She scanned the dance floor and found him. Grinning, she raised her glass. Then, she turned back to Deosil.

"So, that dance floor is calling my name," she said, setting her glass down with finality. "Do you dance, Deosil?"

Rusty watched his best friend flush and nod. "I sure do." She stood and held out her hand for Lara's.

Before Deosil could get out onto the dance floor, though, Rusty leaned in. "Hey, I think I'm going to take off."

Concern knit Deosil's brow. "Are you sure? I'd rather stay here with you..."

"No way," Rusty said. He pushed her toward Lara, who smiled at him. "You guys have fun!" With a glance back at him, Deosil allowed Lara to lead her onto the dance floor. A crowd had started to gather at the edges, and the lights on the dance floor had gone a little strange. With some distance, Rusty could see why. The extra source of light was Optic himself. A photoassumptive, he'd started to glow and then actively strobe in time with the music. By the time Rusty got to the club's exit, the DJ had shut off the lights on the dance floor, and the club was treated to the brilliant display of Optic's power, a shimmering, unreal display of strobing, pulsing light, bursts of brilliant white accented with layered flashes of all different colors, all timed to the music and Optic's dancing itself.

Even from the door, Rusty could see Optic rising into the air, illuminating not just the dance floor but the whole club with the blaze of his lights. Making his way toward the exit, Rusty pushed past a wall of people, all staring, enchanted, at the display, most of them with phones in hand recording it.

The only one who was not, of course, was Matty. He caught Rusty's eye as he neared the exit. "Guess you're not the only one who can whore out his power, huh?" The venomous little cretin smirked before slipping off toward the bar. Shaking his head, Rusty glanced back one final time, and then left.

CHAPTER FIVE

Neza-Chalco-Izta, Mexico
April 27, 2013

The devastation reminded Blanca of the aftermath of the 1985 earthquake in Mexico City's slums. Tiny buildings—houses and small shops, many of them built of whatever materials could be scrounged from rubble and trash—lay shattered by taller neighboring buildings, the debris of too many unstable structures shoved into too-close proximity destroyed by shifting earth and collapsing walls. Fires burned out of control, raging through the flammable debris like something alive and hungry. But this was not the result of a natural disaster, and this wasn't Mexico City.

It was colloquially called Neza-Chalco-Izta, or just Neza. Made up of the municipalities of Nezahualcóyotl, Valle de Chalco, and Ixtapaluca, the area had the dubious honor of being one of the world's largest slums, with some four million people in its loosely defined boundaries. Its streets were comprised of tightly-packed houses and other buildings, crammed into rough grids. In truth, it didn't have quite the same degree of squalor that some of the world's worst slums suffered; Blanca still had nightmares about the conditions from one of her missions in Calcutta. But it was a place in the grip of crippling poverty, with at best sporadic access to basic living necessities like food, water, and medicine. The gangs who controlled the drug trade maintained tight grip on those resources as well, leaving only the meanest scraps for others.

When those gangs weren't squeezing what they could from their neighbors, they were warring over their little kingdoms, to the detriment of those who lived in them, of course. Blanca shook her head. Those sorts of conflict were bad enough when it was just *cholos* with their favorite weapons and a bit of pack-mentality-driven machismo. But when you involved one of the *adelantes*, as the government and media referred to those with powers? It was so much worse.

Many countries, Mexico among them, did not have Changed operating in law enforcement capacity. Oh, like most nations, they certainly had military assets with powers. But they couldn't spare them to come and deal with every criminal with a history in an Echo Event. Besides, just finding them was hard. There was a reason one of the slang terms for one of the Changed was *los escondidos*, the hidden. Echoes in Mexico tended to find themselves being recruited into either the military or the cartels whether they wanted to be or not, so a great many with powers hid them.

The Golden Cross briefing was light on the details, but she knew enough. Alacrán 22, one of the local gangs, managed to attract police attention by quickly gobbling up their rivals' territories and drug trade, wiping them out or absorbing them in equal measure. They clearly had someone who knew what they were doing, and at first the authorities assumed it was a new cartel sponsor or something of the sort.

As it turned out, however, it was an Echo.

His name was Luis Alcalá, an *escondido* who manifested during the Tampico Event in 2011. Though the authorities couldn't be sure, it was assumed that Alcalá had been a worker on the Huasteca oil field just outside of Tampico when the Echo Event occurred. Blanca knew there had been incredible loss of life that day, and the oil fields burned for weeks afterwards, doing untold environmental and economic damage to the area. Until today, she hadn't heard of any Echoes coming out of that Event, which wasn't unusual—particularly devastating Echo Events sometimes killed the Echoes they created, as they were often at the heart of the whatever devastation resulted. But Alcalá survived, and with good reason: he was a pyrotechnic.

The Alacrán 22 put his talents to immediate and deadly use, leaving horrible scenes of fiery murder as they dealt with their rivals. In a matter of six weeks, Alacrán 22 controlled most of Nezahualcóyotl's gang turf and were expanding into areas their rivals had been unable to conquer. It wasn't until they encountered Los Califas—another gang once well beneath Alacrán 22's notice—that they encountered some real resistance in the form of La Madalena. An Echo from the Flores Event of 2009, the mercenary who simply went by "La Madalena" was wanted by authorities on every level across southern Mexico and Central America. A violent and ruthless woman with the ability to cause explosive kinetic concussions, La Madalena sold her talents to the highest bidder in the criminal world, which often meant the cartels. Someone in Los Califas had the contacts and funds (or possibly the sponsorship of a cartel somewhere) to get aid from La Madalena, and Alacrán 22 and their pet pyrotechnic Echo had no idea what was waiting for them.

The results of that conflict, of course, were utterly devastating. Either Luis Alcalá or La Madalena could have leveled city blocks on their own. The two of them doing their best to kill one another and any of the rival gang who happened into their crosshairs? They cut an absolute swath of destruction across the landscape of Nezahualcóyotl, without hesitation or thought for those who might be in the way. Narrow streets and alleys filled with Alcalá's signature gouts of petroleum-stinking, greasy-smoked flame, which ignited particleboard and shattered cinderblock that so many tiny houses were constructed from. La Madalena's explosive fury left yards-wide craters in the old brick and packed-dirt streets, taking out supporting walls to use entire collapsing buildings as weapons against those she hunted.

At the end of the conflict, Luis Alcalá was dead and La Madalena lost beneath collapsing rubble. Though the local authorities were content to assume she was dead, it wouldn't be the first time she'd arranged situations to make it look like she'd died, only to appear somewhere else later. Of course, there were bigger problems to deal with. When the local authorities and emergency relief services like the Red Cross began having difficulties with the gangs getting in the way of rescue efforts, they did the only thing anyone did anymore in the fact of such overwhelming difficulties: they called in the Golden Cross.

In the large common tent where volunteers could rest between shifts and store their personal belongings, Blanca pulled away and folded the *rebozo* shawl she usually wore over her dark blue jumpsuit. The jumpsuit was one of the training uniforms the Department of Transformed Persons Affairs gave to their Echoes during their training weekends. Though it was a little more form-fitting than she liked (she kept telling herself, every year, that she was going to lose ten or so pounds, but you know how that goes), it had protected her well during more than one Golden Cross operation.

Over it she zipped up the grey jacket that Golden Cross Operations assigned them, the one emblazoned with the white and gold cross-in-shield that was the emblem of the rescue organization. Most people knew the symbol these days and knew what they were: an organization similar to other rescue and disaster relief organizations like the Red Cross or the Red Crescent, save for one detail.

Their volunteers were all superpowered.

"I worry that these jackets will make us stand out, in bad ways." The older man next to her shrugged off his own coat and folded it neatly. Underneath the heavy black wool garment, he wore a simple button-up shirt finished with the white collar of a clergyman. "Is that not a concern?"

"Not in my experience." Blanca smiled at him. "Even in situations like this, where people have been hurt by Echoes fighting one another, they usually see the cross first and recognize what we're here to do. Which is a good thing, no?"

The priest smiled, the lines that creased his face mostly hidden by his close salt-and-pepper beard. "That is so," he said. His Spanish was clipped and precise, with the diction of someone who spoke multiple languages. "If only the sight of the cross always inspired such faith in our world today. My name is Nazario."

She shook his proffered hand. "Blanca. But on-mission, I use Llorona."

"Ah, yes," he said with a smile and a slight flush. "Claviger is mine. Though I'm not entirely sure why we use them? Aren't these sorts of code names just a mask to hide behind?"

"Well, they are, yes." Blanca picked up her kit and slung it across her torso, shifting the strap so that it hung comfortably against her left hip. "We use them because it's necessary that we have the ability to come out and do this work without worrying about our private lives. The Golden Cross is a very public organization—usually by the time we get someplace, the media is everywhere. So we try and preserve as much of our identities as we can. There are also masks if you'd like one. Nothing complex, though. Just lower-face medical masks."

He chuckled. "Thank you, but that won't be necessary. When I'm not volunteering here, I'm an Antonine in the Church."

"I thought you might be," Blanca said. "Though I couldn't tell by the collar if you were Catholic or otherwise. I haven't met anyone from the Antonine order before."

"Well, Rome doesn't like to let us stray too far from Mother Church most of the time. We've got enough work to do within it, after all. In fact, I'm one of the first the Vatican has approved to volunteer in a capacity like this one. Good works are always worth doing, though."

Blanca found herself liking the priest. Unsurprising—she was comfortable around men of God, after all, even if she rarely attended Mass these days. There had been a time when the Church provided a very real sanctuary for her. And she'd been interested in the Order of St. Anthony—the patron saint of miracles—from the first time she'd heard about it. An ecclesiastic order within the Catholic Church comprised entirely of ordained Echoes who put their faith and talents into the hands of the Holy See, the Antonines weren't often found outside the faith structures of the Church.

Before she could ask the priest any questions, her radio crackled. "That's Grace calling us to meeting. Have you ever done this sort of thing before?" she asked.

"I admit that I'm rather new at it. What should I know?"

"Just follow me. The briefing will be short and sweet, we'll be organized into teams with specific mission goals, and then deployed around the disaster area."

He smiled at her kindly. "Thank you for the guidance. How long have you been doing this?"

"Me? Oh, I've been with the Golden Cross since it was founded. I was part of Cobalt's original recruits."

* * *

Blanca got plenty of opportunity to ask her questions; she and Claviger were paired up in a rescue team. While they waited for the empath Grace to detect the pockets of pain and fear that indicated the presence of living victims buried beneath rubble, the two talked. He admitted that while the

Antonine order didn't exactly maintain secrets of any sort, they were fairly private, in terms of their membership and undertakings.

"Even so, I have to admit that I was very proud to be a Catholic when I found out about the Antonines," Blanca said, pulling aside her mask. She poured a bit of her bottled water onto a scrap of cloth so she could wipe dust and ash from her face. "A lot of faiths either didn't know what to do with Echoes, or just leapt to the lazy 'spawn of Satan' route with us."

Claviger nodded as he swigged from a canteen and screwed the cap back on. "Oh, I won't pretend there weren't factions within the Vatican that espoused something similar. And under another Pope, it might have turned out differently, but–"

Their radio squawked for a third time that hour. Blanca and Claviger boarded a makeshift emergency services vehicle and gave them a location. Fortunately, the van was manned by locals who knew the area well. When the vehicle pulled to a stop, the priest crossed himself. He was doing his best to hide it, but the look that crossed his face bore a striking resemblance to hopelessness. "Are there really people still alive in all that?"

The building was a rarer two-story structure, built decades ago and housing a small neighborhood *tienda* on its bottom floor. From the looks of the destruction, part of the fighting between Luis Alcalá and the Madalena tore through the lower floor and something, probably one of the Madalena's blasts, took out a retaining corner. The sheer weight of the floor above it came crashing down, causing a chain reaction that leveled the building in moments, probably killing and trapping dozens of people inside.

"*Madre de Dios.*" Blanca crossed herself. "Okay. Just like the last time, only on a larger scale, yeah?"

The two of them walked to the edge of the crumbled structure, pushing their way through several rows of rubberneckers and those who'd lost people inside. Blanca stepped up onto some old plastic grocery crates. "Please, everyone listen!" She called out in Spanish, making sure her Golden Cross emblem was prominent. "We're going to attempt a rescue, but we don't know how stable the structure is. Please back away to a safe distance while we work!"

It took a few moments, but the crowd gave them some breathing room. Blanca thanked them and checked to make sure her heavy-duty phone was still in her vest pocket. "Alright, I've got plenty of battery life here. Ready?"

"After you." Claviger nodded to Blanca and stood back.

Whispering started in the crowd—they'd recognized her as Llorona. She turned to smile at them reassuringly and clicked on the small LED light on the front of her vest. Clenched fists at her side, Blanca began to hum. She let the sound build and grow within her, like some wild thing being born. When she finally opened her mouth, the sound was inhuman. It sounded like a slowly building keen, a wail so filled with grief it brought tears to the eyes of those listening nearby.

She raised the pitch, amping it higher. The higher it got, the more unsettling those watching found it: mothers clutched their children more tightly, older kids stepped protectively in front of younger siblings, and those already caught up in their own grief fled the scene.

It hit just the right pitch, and it seemed as if the very air was vibrating. The world distorted around Blanca, and in her white-and-grey outfit, she faded away to partial solidity. Blanca knew that something about this tonal vibration messed with the minds of people too close to her when she did this. Even those who knew the science of how she used sound to manipulate her bodily density found the desperate keening wail and her ghostly body unsettling. Blanca plunged into the wreckage, passing bodily through the wreckage like a specter. There was a gasp from those watching, and several of the spectators fled the scene with fearful glances behind them.

She passed through the debris in a hazy cloud. It was hard enough for light to fully interact with her eyes when she was phased, so it was already like moving through the world with cataracts in place. But there was no light but that which she carried with her, clipped to the front of her vest, when she passed bodily through piles of destroyed building.

From experience, she knew she could maintain her wail for several minutes. Even still, she moved quickly, passing through the rubble in tight, clipped lines. Just shy of a minute, she found a pocket within the debris with someone in it. She crouched and stopped the wail, regaining solidity. With quick movements, she shifted some smaller rocks off the woman half-buried in the rubble so she could check her pulse. As she did, the woman moaned and moved, then sobbed softly.

"Hold on," Blanca said. "We're here to help." She shifted so she was as far back as she could get from the woman, fishing out her phone. Getting as wide a shot of the small pocket as she could, she snapped several pictures. She checked its display and cursed. No signal, even with Operations running a booster for her. She'd prefer to send Claviger the photos that way, but she'd have to do it the old-fashioned way.

"Wait for me, auntie," she said, wiping some of the dirt and sweat from the older woman's brow. "I'm going to be right back." She wailed once more, pitching it so she could pass out of phase with her environment, and dove through the debris in a straight line, heading for the edge of the devastation. She emerged from the massive ruined building and paused to catch her breath.

Claviger came running up to her. "You alright?"

Blanca nodded and passed him the phone. He studied the woman and her environs in the photo. "It looks like it's just her lower body," said Claviger. "Might be lower spinal damage."

"No, I checked. It's just her legs. We can get her out."

The priest nodded. "Do you need a moment?"

Blanca shook her head and straightened, waving the medics over. "No, I'm good to go. Open it."

Claviger nodded, and waved her back. He straightened his posture and calmed his spirit, his hands before him, palms outward. To those watching, he seemed like a man in prayer, and in some ways, he was. The discipline he used to call on his power was a discipline he'd learned in devotional meditation. To those watching, it looked like a man of God prayed for a miracle, and God answered by throwing wide the gates of Heaven, flooding the area in strange, coruscating illumination. The field of light shifted and opened suddenly. The deep void within danced with pinpoints of light like the stars of the firmament spinning according to God's great plan, and those watching could not help but be caught up in the glorious display, frozen in awe.

"Go." Claviger's voice betrayed the stress it took him to open the gateway, and Llorona barreled through the portal. He was right on target. The rift opened into the chamber, filling it with dancing illumination like some benediction from on high. Llorona skidded to a halt, and found the injured woman within half-delirious from the lights. An added benefit of Claviger's power, in her estimation—it had some minor soporific effect, a blessing for those who were injured.

With a breath, and then two, she laid hands on the woman's shoulders, reaching up under her in order to haul her out of the debris. Though it was difficult from that awkward crouch, Llorona wailed once more, shifting not just herself but the woman in her arms out of phase. She pulled with all her might, shoving herself backward and the woman free of the debris. Without pause, she continued to pull, hauling the woman back through Claviger's gate and onto the street outside. Once there, she collapsed, her wail ending and both of them returning to solidity.

Claviger helped pull her aside, out of the way of the medics who sprang forward to treat the woman. Llorona took several gulps of air and shuddered—phasing someone else was hard on her system. Her wail always left her ears ringing, but the pitch necessary to alter someone else's physicality was exhausting.

"Here, drink," Claviger said, helping her to her feet and handing her an uncapped canteen. She thanked him and gulped the water while he helped her back to the shade of the van. "Good work," he said. "Your talent is truly a wonder to behold."

She smiled and thanked him. After another moment, she stood and got out of the van. "You ready to do this again? Grace's scan says there's another three people still alive in all that."

"Are you?" he asked. Concern creased his brow.

"Me?" She scoffed. "I can do this all day. I just need a break or two in between. I'm good to go."

* * *

That was what that day and most of the next looked like for them. It wasn't long before there were crowds waiting to see the ghost-woman and the gatekeeper of Heaven itself work their miracles. Local media interviewed them in between rescues. Llorona was careful to focus her interviews on the good the Golden Cross did internationally, per her training in media relations; Claviger spent most of his time emphasizing that while the Church considered all Echo powers to be gifts from God, his own abilities were not in fact miraculous, but simply a power like any other Echo's.

The mess tent was the last one to be taken down, as usual. Most of the volunteers and active staff had already gone home, other than those whose job it was to pack up the Golden Cross's temporary command center in Nezahual-cóyotl. Claviger had disappeared early, not terribly surprising, as this kind of work could take its toll. Plus, he didn't have to wait around for transportation, as he was capable of gating himself directly back to Rome.

Everyone having already gone home afforded Blanca some sit-down time with Grace to do their informal debrief and generally catch up. Grace was one of the few full-time Golden Cross employees. Her talents as an empath were supremely useful, both as a spokesperson and in the field. Blanca smiled up at her as Grace walked into the tent, eyes glued to the smartphone in her hand, though Blanca was much more interested in the bottle tucked under her arm.

"Is that what I think it is?" she asked as Grace sat down across from her.

"If you think it's *mezcal*, then yes," Grace said with a smirk. She clicked her phone into slumber and set it face down on the table between them as she took a seat. Blanca reached for a couple of cups. "One of the local officials gave it to me as thanks. Supposed to be pretty good."

Grace had a reputation among the Golden Cross Echoes as no-nonsense and even somewhat terse. Blanca knew that was because she saved the "sugar" for official work. The woman was not quite a decade younger than Blanca, herself forty-nine, though the rigors of the work she supervised showed in deep-etched lines of stress around her brow and hazel eyes. She wore her hair short, sprinklings of grey starting to make themselves known.

Blanca accepted one of the cups and raised it towards Grace. "To sixty-seven."

"To sixty-seven," Grace smiled and took a sip of the smoky drink. She made a throaty sound of enjoyment. "God, that's good."

"And well-deserved. You did good work, Grace."

"So did you, Blanca. As always. Honestly, knowing there are people like you running around and willing to come out to places like this to help us, for nothing more than our thanks? You literally make all of this possible, you know." Grace took another sip. "And the fact that you can remember how to talk to media as well? Priceless."

Blanca laughed, a bright sound. "Well, if I didn't have something like this, I'd probably go crazy. Or vigilante." She winked.

"Ugh, don't even joke like that." Grace refilled both of their cups. "Wait, you were connected to the Champions, right?"

"Connected to, yes. No Echo was ever part of the Champions proper—they're all Originals—but there were a lot of us who stayed on call in case they needed a hand. I used to help do stuff like that before the Denisov Measure. I'd help out the Champions who needed someone in Texas or Louisiana. But I also helped out the Houston PD when they needed some power to back them up. So, I wasn't purely a costumed vigilante."

Grace laughed, a barking sound that she tried to control, succeeding only in turning it into a snort. "Oh, my God. Did you actually have a costume? What did it look like?"

"You are enjoying this way too much," Blanca groused. She grudgingly picked up her phone and started thumbing through the photos on it.

"Oh, no. You have pictures of your costume *on your phone*?" Grace clearly thought that was either the greatest thing ever, or the funniest. Blanca couldn't quite tell which.

"Hey, now. I'm pretty proud of what I did during that time. Even if I did look a little ridiculous." With a sigh, she started to hand over her phone, but then stopped. "Just remember—I was one of the ones who helped stop the Fated Manifesto, alright?"

Grace nodded, making a grabby hands gesture. Shaking her head, Blanca handed the phone over. Grace's wide, goofy grin faded, and she got a thoughtful demeanor. She glanced up at Llorona. "Hey, this isn't bad. I expected more, you know, spandex or something."

"*Dios*, no. I don't know if you noticed, but I'm not an Original. I'm pretty sure they're the only ones to have the bodies to pull those sorts of costumes off. The rest of us have to deal with actual, real-world metabolisms and a refusal to lay off the sweets."

"Yeah, I'm kinda digging this old costume of yours. Even if it does look like Stevie Nicks helped design it." Grace giggled as Blanca launched out of her seat, snatching for her phone. Unable to steal it back, Blanca stole the bottle of mezcal as consolation.

"Seriously, though. These are great." Grace flipped through a few of the photos while Blanca shook her head, sipping at the liquor. Grace stopped scanning through the pictures and regarded her, suddenly serious. "Are these your kids?"

Blanca didn't look up at the phone. She didn't have to—the only photos of any children she had in her phone's gallery were of Rodrigo and Veronica. Her babies.

"Yeah," she said around a sudden lump in her throat. "They would be twenty-seven this year, if you can believe that. Old enough to have kids of their own, you know?" She took another sip of the alcohol. Grace clicked the phone closed and reached across the table to take her hand.

The two sat in silence for as long as Blanca could tolerate. She took a big breath and gulped the rest of her drink, slamming the empty cup onto the tabletop with a grimace. "Mezcal is the worst."

Grace smiled at her as she rose. "Well, I should go and get my bags packed. My flight back to Houston is in a couple of hours. It was good seeing you again, Blanca."

Blanca leaned over and planted a kiss on the younger woman's forehead. "You too." She walked toward the tent's exit.

"Blanca," Grace said. "It was sixty-five. You're losing your touch."

Blanca turned to regard her. "Sixty-five? Did we lose someone?"

"Nope. They were all good rescues. Just sixty-five of them."

Blanca pondered for a moment. "Are you sure about that?"

"I thought that's what the after-event report said. Let me double-check," she said, picking up her phone. They both knew that Blanca rarely misremembered the number of people she'd helped. "Yeah. Right here—sixty-five in all."

"That's weird. I was so sure that there were sixty-seven."

Grace shrugged. "Well, in any event, that's a lot of people you and the other volunteer helped. You should be proud."

Blanca nodded absently, wracking her brain trying to remember.

"How was working with him?" said Grace.

"With Claviger? Oh, very good. He's quite an asset—his help getting those people out was invaluable. We make a pretty good team, honestly."

"Good, good. He seemed a little flustered speaking to the media, but then I suppose anyone would, having to constantly reassure people that his power wasn't a literal miracle from God, huh?"

"Did you see it in action? Honestly, I had to look away after the first couple of times. There's a good reason why people walk away from an encounter with his ability feeling like they've just glimpsed Heaven."

"No telling if we'll be seeing him again, though. He seemed pretty shaken up by what he saw. Must not be used to seeing the ugliness out in the world when you live in the Vatican." Grace chuckled and started to pour herself some more mezcal, but thought better of it and screwed the cap back on.

"Hey, I should go," Blanca said. The two women embraced fondly and Blanca departed.

* * *

The command site was nearly taken apart by the time she left. Blanca did not go to the airport. Instead, she caught a cab to *Nuestra Señora de la Virtud*, the hospital where the survivors were taken after their rescues, calling her airline along the way to postpone her flight. Though she knew better than to bother the busy hospital staff, she found an ally in the hospital's chaplain, Father Federico. The two of them spent the next three hours visiting all of the survivors, ostensibly to check in on their recovery.

With that done, the good father was kind enough to help her make some calls to see if any of the other local hospitals had taken in other rescue victims. He didn't think any had, and as it turned out, he was right. All the survivors they'd rescued were brought to *Nuestra Señora*, which had even transferred non-critical patients to other hospitals in order to open up beds for those who needed them.

With the sun setting on her last day in Mexico, Blanca sat aboard her flight, unable to shake an inescapable fact—two of the people she'd saved were just gone. She could remember their faces: a young man, hardly out of boyhood, with too few tattoos to have been a cholo for long, and an adolescent boy who couldn't have been more than fifteen or sixteen. Neither of them had been badly injured; in fact, she remembered them because they'd both sat for so long in the Golden Cross command center, waiting for a ride to the hospital. The emergency team kept putting their transportation off in favor of the more critically injured. The young cholo was so traumatized that he wouldn't talk to any of them, but the teenager's name was Beto, and he kept asking whether each new person brought in was his mother or sister.

On consideration, Blanca never did see either of them taken to the hospital. It was within reason to suppose that either or both of them might have simply walked out of their own accord. That was the reasonable assumption, of course. But still, Blanca couldn't escape the thought that something strange was going on.

CHAPTER SIX

Portland, Oregon
May 3, 2013

Monday came too early, as usual. It probably didn't help that Rusty'd stayed up all night chatting with a friend of Kosma's. The guy—Yevgeny, according to his Facebook account—knew Kosma. Rusty had seen them comment on one another's posts and tag one another on photos at various nightspots. The guy was pretty hesitant to say it, but he implied that he was gay too, talking about some of the bars and clubs they both frequented.

Rusty glanced through the private message chat log again, for what seemed like the hundredth time, scrolling past all the introductory stuff and the weirdness of asking the questions he needed to ask.

> >So, you're a friend of Kosma.

> >No I haven't seen him. Not in days. We are worried too.

> >He's not the only one to go missing. I know of three from the bars who are disappeared too.

> >Some of the bouncers at the bars and clubs say there have been some of the skinhead gangs around like in Russia.

>You know the ones who attack gay kids? They
sometimes take them and torture them and post it to
vid sites for everyone to see them "punish" them.

>Its very scary. Ive been afraid to look on the
sites. I'm afraid I will see someone I know being
hurt or worse. They do very bad things to people.

>And the police don't care about it. Its just gays,
you know? They say: They're better off dead anyway,
so they don't embarrass their families.

Rusty veered off-course in the hallway, finding a small side lounge, and forced himself to sit down and take a few deep breaths. It didn't help to dislodge the knot in his stomach, but it did clear the sharp spikes of fear in his chest. He glanced at the message log again, and then forced himself to click his phone screen off. *I've got to stop looking at it,* he tried to tell himself. *I've got class.*

His mama said his imagination got the better of him sometimes. She'd always supported his weird flights of fancy, saying that creative people needed room to dream. But he also tended towards the two bad habits of people with strong imaginations: an inclination toward escapism, and letting his imagination conjure up the worst possible scenarios, sending him spiraling into near-panic.

Just take a breath, baby, she'd always told him, gripping his hand tight.

The last time she'd done that was in the hospital after the Gulf Event. He'd been so terrified when he woke that the metal in the room started to shake and shiver almost in perfect time with his own trembling. The nurse came in with a sedative, but his mama waved her away, clutching his hands and talking soothingly to him.

The shaking stopped, on both the inside and the outside. They'd worked to find something to distract him when he was feeling stressed. Absentmindedly, Rusty reached into his messenger bag, into the pocket there, and palmed the two large steel ball bearings there, spinning them around in his grip. Another of his mother's ideas. It had started with a pair of those cheap metal balls, with the little chimes in them, that you could find in bad import stores and on the sales floor of martial arts supplies shops, all decorated with jewel-toned enamel, bright dots of silver and gold here, and Chinese symbols.

They'd made a pleasant sound as he spun them, and he discovered something else. The more he manipulated them, the greater a magnetic charge built up in them. The buzz of it against his skin, cycling in a soothing pattern, helped calm him. The buildup of the charge had eventually been too much for the cheap pair she'd gotten him, causing the hollow spheres to dimple and then rupture along their construction seams. But he found that solid steel ball bearings of a large size not only could resist the charge he inevitably built in them, but also transmit it to him better.

The spheres made no sound as he spun them in his left hand, but the magnetic resonance—so even, pulsing with a sort of orderly sound and sensation—did a lot to calm him.

"Dude, that's badass!"

Rusty started out of his reverie, glancing up. Two students were standing over him, watching his hand. At some point he'd stopped manually manipulating the ball bearings and started doing so with his magnetic power, resonating with the motion and the sensation on a deep level. He closed his hand around the ball bearings and flushed. Standing, he gathered up his bag, virtually fleeing.

"Hey, wait!" One of them skipped over to catch up to him. "Sorry, I didn't mean to freak you out or embarrass you or whatever. I'm Albert, this is Sid."

Albert matched his pace to walk alongside Rusty. Sid lagged behind, voicing a half-hearted objection, suggesting that they leave Rusty alone. Rusty took a deep breath and stopped at a vending machine. He turned and smiled at Albert, who had bright blue eyes and broad shoulders. The guy was pretty cute, he had to admit. He had that frat-bro thing going on.

"Uh, sorry. I'm Gauss," Rusty said, stowing the spheres in his bag, and then shook hands with the young men. "I was just sorta lost in thought a little, and…well, the Department kinda drills it in our heads that we're not supposed to show off our powers. Kinda freaks some people out."

"Lame asses, maybe," Albert scoffed. "As long as you're not hurting anybody, I think you should totally be able to use your powers, you know?"

Rusty smiled. One of those guys, then.

"So, are you like telekinetic or something?" Albert asked.

"Nah, dude," Sid said, stepping up. He wore a t-shirt with the logo of some band Rusty'd never heard of, and had glasses and hair like he'd just woken from a nap. "Gauss, like a gauss rifle, right? Magnetic?"

Rusty grinned. "Busted, yeah. How'd you know?"

"Sid reads shit loads of sci-fi and stuff. He always knows shit like that." Albert was clearly used to being the alpha dog in their relationship, pushing back into the conversation. He leaned in, conspiratorially. "Do you smoke, dude?" He held up his thumb and index finger, miming pinching something.

Rusty snorted. "Uh, not often. Very occasionally."

"We're headed back to my dorm. You want to come?"

Rusty glanced back down at the phone in his white-knuckled hand, then back up at the two of them. "You know what, I do. That cool?" He glanced at Sid, ignoring Albert's reassurance that it was. Sid seemed to consider it for a moment, and then smiled, nodding.

* * *

Rusty hated the weird cottony texture in his mouth, the burning in his lungs, and the strong smell the he knew was all over his clothes now. But even though Albert's pot was some low-grade skunky stuff, the spiraling thoughts in his brain slowed down, and the panic in his belly receded a little. And it was apparently noticeable.

"Now you're feeling it, huh?" Albert chuckled and took the pipe from Rusty. "You look way less fucked up about whatever it was."

Rusty laughed, a freeing sound. "Yeah, I am. I'm feeling much better."

The three of them sat on the floor, with their backs against Albert's bed. The place was a wreck, though not as bad as some of the dorms Rusty'd seen. To Rusty's right, Albert leaned against his bed, slowly rubbing the back of his head against the sheets, clearly enjoying the sensation. This guy was like a bad stereotype when he got stoned, drawing his words out, and using lingo Rusty was sure only people in stoner movies ever actually used.

In contrast, Sid—seated to Rusty's left—closed off even more when he was stoned. He was deeply involved in reading something on his smartphone, gazing at it unblinking through bloodshot, half-lidded eyes. He'd pushed his glasses up onto the top of his head and was pretty much ignoring them.

"Dude." Albert's tone changed, the sound of someone who was both blazed and having The Best Idea Ever. "Okay, I know you're not supposed to, but…"

Rusty sighed at the pause. Here it came.

"Can you show us how your power works?"

That got Sid's attention. "Albert—you're not supposed to ask that, man. They're not allowed to use their powers like that. You could totally get him in a shitload of trouble." Sid looked upset on Rusty's behalf, which was sort of endearing.

Rusty patted him on the knee reassuringly and turned to Albert. "He's right. I mean, my control is way better than when I first got my powers and shit. It's been years since I've had a surge I couldn't control, so there's not a lot of danger of me losing it or anything."

Albert laughed—really, it was almost a giggle. "Are you telling me why you can't do it, or convincing yourself that you can?"

Rusty snorted. He glanced at Sid, once again looking offended and upset on his behalf, but also decidedly curious.

"What do you say?" Rusty asked him, and then glanced back and forth at both of them. "If you guys promise not to tell anyone, I'm down."

Albert snorted. "Dude, that sounds like the opening of a bad porno."

Rusty blinked, and his high plummeted for a second, before he chuckled.

"We're in, yeah," Albert said. "We won't say shit, man."

Rusty glanced at Sid, who seemed way more torn over it than he did. "Sid?" Rusty asked, and got a nod in return.

"Not a word," Sid said, and lowered his glasses back onto his face, scooting away from the bed and settling down directly in front of Rusty. Albert whooped and joined him. Rusty pulled himself up to a seated position on the bed, planting his feet firmly on the ground in front of him.

"Check this out," he said. Both boys looked down at his feet. Rusty routinely wore steel-toed boots, the style that construction workers often wore. He held his hands out over his feet—this was all for show, he didn't need his hands to use his powers—and focused. There was a snap, a sound like a tiny firecracker, the sort of sound that a quick burst of static discharge makes, and then his bootlaces came to life. They twitched like worms having a seizure, twisting and writhing, untying themselves to extend upward like someone stretching after a long nap. They swayed in time to the music playing on Albert's computer.

The two boys stared. Albert's mouth was hanging open. He looked up at Rusty like he was trying to figure out what he was seeing.

"There's steel filaments in the cores of my laces," Rusty said, smiling. "I've found it's pretty useful to have stuff like that with my power set, you know?"

He raised his hands to show the dull burnished steel bracelets locked around his wrists. "I can do some basic levitation and shit when I'm wearing all this stuff."

"That's badass!" Albert crowed. "Can you levitate right now?"

"Uh, it's probably not a good idea," Rusty said.

"I bet it fucks up electronics like crazy in a small space when you do that, huh?" Sid said, suddenly interested.

"It sure does. I fuck up my phone all the time. They won't even give me insurance anymore, so I have to buy backups and shit at pawn shops." Rusty grinned, showing his powered-down phone's beaten-up case. "Also, it kinda hurts. I'm not made of steel, so I can't control my actual body, so in order to lift myself, I sorta have to pull upwards on my boots and the bracelets. I need a better design, though, because the bracelets bite into my wrists like crazy."

"That's cool as fuck, dude," Albert said. "Is that all you can do in here right now, though? Not that dancing shoelaces aren't dope as hell."

Rusty grinned. "Nah. I was saving this for last." He reached out a hand—again, more directing their attention than anything else—toward the wall next to the doorway, where he'd dropped his bag.

The bag moved a little, and then again, this time with more force. Only it wasn't the bag itself—it moved like something was trying to get out. Then, with a pop, one of his side pockets snapped open. A collection of marble-sized ball bearings flew out of it, lazily drifting in and out of formations as they crossed the room. The small mass of them—maybe a dozen in all—split down the middle to wander around Sid and Albert. Both of them stared agog as the small steel orbs floated past their faces on their way to Rusty.

"This is why I went with the codename Gauss." Rusty reached out with his hands. The orbs split into two groups and began to orbit his hands slowly. He spun them in slightly faster patterns, making them weave around each other and his hands. He made them adhere to his bracelets, and then dropped them by reversing the charge, catching them with his power just before they hit the floor, and floated them up to orbit his head like a tiny solar system.

"I can move them faster—lots faster," Rusty said. Albert and Sid were stock still. Sid was clearly fascinated, while Albert had the biggest grin on his face. "I can reverse the attraction they have with something. Usually myself, or my bracelets in particular. I can change the magnetic charges in them relative to the metal around my wrists, so that they repel one another so hard and so suddenly, the ball bearing shoots away really fast."

"Like a bullet from a gauss rifle," Sid said.

Rusty nodded. "Of course, it's dangerous, and I don't do that sort of thing casually. It's basically a gunshot, and I can get prosecuted as though I had fired off a gun, so it's something I only ever really use in the camps, you know?"

"I've heard a little about the Health Camps," Albert said, settling in, his elbows resting on his knees, his chin propped up on his hands. "What are they like?"

Rusty glanced over at Sid, who was going through his phone again. Rusty didn't think Sid had snapped a picture; he collected the ball bearings in his hands and set them on the ground. Probably best to stop showing off now, just in case. "Uh, they're pretty shitty. Imagine summer camp, except you're in the barracks of an old military base once a year. Half the time, you're undergoing every goddamned medical test under the sun. The other half, you're either being tested on the limits of your powers, or are grouped with other Echoes with similar abilities, in theory so you can all learn to better control them."

Albert looked at Rusty like he was crazy. "Are you kidding me? That sounds awesome! I mean, the medical shit sounds weak as fuck, but the rest of it? It's like a sports training camp, except there's superpowers involved, man."

"Well, it's not quite that." Rusty shook his head and got up, fetching his bag. He slid the ball bearings into the pocket as he returned to his seat, settling his bag on his lap. "Most of the training isn't about using our powers. It's about *not* using them—control and avoiding accidental triggers is at the top of the list, and it's all any of the trainers really care about. Even once you've got a handle on it, there's zero interest in learning better or stronger control. They put us into high-stress situations to make sure we're not going to accidentally trigger. You kinda win by not using your power."

Rusty had never really thought about how much he disliked that part of their training. He was grateful for the Department's Health Camps at first, quite honestly. It took him a while to lock down control of his power, and the sessions there served a purpose. But now?

Albert pulled a sour face. "That's such bullshit. You guys should be in training to use your powers for badass stuff." Rusty chuckled, agreeing, and glanced over at Sid. He wasn't paying attention to the conversation at all, engrossed in his smartphone. Albert rolled his eyes and reached over with the kind of calm assurance possessed by one friend who routinely harasses the other, and plucked the phone out of Sid's hands.

The geeky guy squawked and started snatching at the phone. "Give it back, you asshole! Give it!" Albert guffawed, turning his back on Sid and hunching over to keep the device out of his buddy's hands, and to give him a chance to see what was on the screen. Sid fought like he was trying to prevent his friend from seeing something embarrassing on the screen. Rusty chuckled, watching the interplay.

"Holy shit." Albert glanced up at Rusty. He had a gobsmacked look on his face, so much so that Sid had no problem snatching the phone back.

"Rusty, I'm so sorry, I didn't mean–" said Sid.

"Dude, you did porn? Like, gay porn?" said Albert.

Shit. Rusty went pale, and he couldn't really think. Sid was standing, clearly embarrassed and angry.

Albert was outraged, it looked like, if he was being honest. "Are you fucking serious?"

Rusty stood quickly. "I did, and it's none of your business. Fuck off." He pushed past Albert, but it was Sid who pursued him out into the hall.

"Dude, wait. I'm sorry, man—"

Rusty whirled on him, angry. The fact that traitor tears escaped his eyes just made him angrier. "Were you fucking Googling me? While I was in the goddamned room with you? You could have at least had the decency to wait until I was fucking gone!"

Later, when Rusty told the story to Deosil, he'd say he stormed out of the building. She knew that meant he'd fled before anyone else could see him shaking and crying.

* * *

"You reached Deosil's phone. I'm not making any promises about when or even if I return your call. Project that expectation onto me without my consent at your own peril."

"Bitch," Rusty said. At least he didn't sound like he was actively crying any more. "Why the fuck are you out in the boonies of Washington sacrificing goats or whatever it is you do? I just managed to embarrass the fuck out of myself to some frat bros who found out I did porn. Wish you were here. Bye."

His dorm room was comfortable and dark. Once again, he lit his phone, and scanned through social media. Just like before, he skimmed the chat log with Yevgeny. He dialed Deosil and got her voice mail yet again.

"Also, I think my friend Kosma may have been kidnapped by skinhead homophobe gangs, who are probably torturing him for being a fag. I really fucking wish you were here." He opened up his social media app and found a new notification asking to befriend him, from an Albert Morris. It was accompanied by the message: "DUDE. So sorry about today. I was high as fuck and a jackass, and Sid really feels like shit."

He clicked his phone off, and sighed, letting it fall onto the bed. With a thought, Rusty extended his awareness of the subtle magnetic fields around him, homing in on the disruption in that field caused by the metals in his lamp. With another, he gave those fields a slight twist—hardly more than a nudge—and his desk lamp clicked on.

The bulbs illuminated his workspace, a messy arrangement of books, papers and an empty water bottle or two, with only a small cleared space for his laptop. Above the desk was a corkboard. He'd purchased it with the intention of using it to get organized, or whatever other freshman pipe dream he had at the beginning of the school year. Currently, it held a lot of photos and printed-out articles of Sentinel, from last term's project about him. He sighed and turned away. He was pretty sure Sentinel would never have taken the offer to do porn, even if someone had built up the nerve to approach him. Rusty didn't know him personally, but he'd met the man last year and felt comfortable making the generalization.

He grabbed his phone and read the waiting invitation from Albert, then looked once more at his conversation with Yevgeny. He narrowed his eyes and glanced up at the corkboard again. What would Sentinel do with this information? If he knew that gay kids were disappearing, being kidnapped, beaten and some even killed, and the local police didn't give a shit?

What would *he* do?

In Rusty's fantasy world, he'd jump back into that blue-and-white costume he'd worn as one of the Champions and go make it right himself. He was familiar enough with the man to know what he'd actually do, though—advise Rusty to leave it to the authorities. Maybe take some awareness-raising action to get media focus on it. Something like that.

For a moment, Rusty almost wished he was Sentinel. No way he'd sit idly by and let these guys be hurt and murdered. He'd *do* something about it, damn it. Well, do something more than leave it to the authorities. Rusty chewed his lip, glancing at the conversation with Yevgeny and then back to the corkboard, and back and forth a couple of times.

Finally, with the air of a man with a mission, Rusty rose from his bed. He threw some things into a bag, dug out his old welding goggles from a trunk, pulled them down around his neck, and walked to the door. He looked around, smiled, and closed the door, clicking both the lamp off and the lock shut with his powers as an afterthought.

CHAPTER SEVEN

Central Washington State
May 4, 2013

Being a guest of honor at a pagan and witchcraft festival meant never having to put up her own damned tent. Sure, there were a handful of responsibilities that came along with it, mostly in the form of remaining in the public eye, being pretty much "on" the entire time, meeting new people and doing her damnedest to remember their names. Well, and there was the ritual and the speaking events, but those were hardly chores.

"You guys know you don't have to do this for me, right?" Deosil smiled at the three volunteers, empty hands extended in front of her, as though to prove she was ready and willing to work. "I bought that tent because it was easy to put together."

"It's the least we can do," Monica said, glancing up from hammering in a stake. "You're supposed to let us provide accommodations, but if you won't take a spot in the guests' cabin, we'll put this together. No big deal." She smiled a genuine smile and then bent her head back to her task. Deosil had to admit that the whole bohemian skirt and actual-ribbons-in-hair thing that Monica had going on were kinda doing it for her.

"Well, I appreciate it," said Deosil.

"Besides," said Gavin, a cute blond kid with a slight Southern twang. "The opening ceremonies are in twenty minutes."

"Hmm. Okay, point taken." Deosil dumped her big duffel bag down near the site. "I'm just going to drop this off here and go find somewhere to change, if that's alright?"

Monica looked up with a smile again. "Sure thing. Feel free to use my tent." She pointed. "It's the old canvas one, on the edge of the meadow over there. The one with the crescent moon banner out front."

Deosil turned to follow the woman's gesture. "Is that a coven banner?"

"Not a formal coven, per se. More like a study group that occasionally gets together for full moons. Stuff like that."

"Gotcha. Thanks for the lend." Deosil leaned over and picked up her backpack. "See you at opening ceremonies?" Monica nodded and waved her off.

The walk across this part of the campsite was pretty typical for an event like this one: a collection of pagans, late-model hippies, earthier occultists, animists, and all sorts of similar folk, come together for a three-day event to celebrate Beltane. There would be workshops, rituals, and similar events held during the day, big communal meals, and evenings of drumming and hanging out and sometimes even dancing around bonfires long into the early morning.

Most of the festival-goers who recognized her and nodded or waved their greetings were younger. Not terribly surprising, given that Deosil got her place in this community online first, through what started as a set of video blogs exploring the nature of her powers as they aligned with her own practice of neopagan witchcraft. Commenters left questions, which she began answering, and before she knew it, she'd turned her couple-of-times-a-month video diary into an instructional blog on her take on witchcraft.

In short order, some of the publishers who specialized in pagan topics asked her to write for them, first some articles for periodicals and calendars, then pieces for their websites, and finally, they wanted her to write a book. A book which was, as of this morning, something like five months late. It became hard to figure out what she wanted to say. It wasn't a writer's block thing—oh, no. If anything, she had *too much* to say, and didn't know what to include.

Not only was she, as a lesbian and a trans woman, a big advocate for LGBT inclusion and safe spaces in constantly growing modern paganism, but she was also an Echo whose powers were intricately tied to her own witchcraft.

Shortly after the Playa Event in Nevada that made her what she was, she'd talked about the idea that her powers weren't superpowers but were in fact actual magic, but that had mostly been her toying around with the ways in which they overlapped.

Somatic Manifestation was what the DTPA medical sorts called it: that thing when someone used a form of ritual or action that wasn't actually tied to how a power functioned, but the Echo in question needed it as a crutch to control their power. They assured her that she would outgrow the need for it eventually, and that was the big topic on her blog that gained her all the notice—she didn't *want* to outgrow it.

She reached the canvas tent—a little water-stained here and there, and sunbleached besides—and ducked inside. Monica knew how to camp. She'd brought a wide futon mattress with her and basically turned the floor of her tent into a big bed. She had some pendants, amulets, and strings of beads and tumbled stones strung across the tent, and a small gay pride flag hanging up just inside the entrance.

Well, well.

Deosil stripped out of her traveling clothes and put on some of the garb she liked to use for ritual. She wasn't a high ritual theater sort—she didn't maintain special robes or anything for the purpose. She did like to dress comfortably, though, and in something that made her stand out a little. Who doesn't want a little flash when they're doing the thing they love best?

She slipped into a dark green broom skirt with tiny flashes of gold all across the fabric. She thought about going barefoot as she did sometimes, but she wanted to get a feel for the area before she did that. Instead, she slipped a pair of simple leather sandals on, wrapping the straps halfway up her calf and knotting them tightly. She shrugged out of her coat and shirt, stuffing both into her bag, and removed the folded brocade from within.

She slipped the vest on, buckling it up the front. It was her favorite piece of gear—light, but kinda swank, and with a generous hood on the back of it. It always drew compliments when she wore it. It was sort of talismanic for her, in fact. It was the first article of clothing she'd worn when she'd taken the plunge to start presenting as her genuine self. She'd worn it to school her freshman year. Though the decision to attend her freshman year as herself (rather than the boy everyone else kept telling she was) led to a whole onslaught of harassment—even from teachers and school staff—it had been her first steps into something like authenticity of self.

This simple vest was her armor, its hood her veil when she needed it.

But she didn't need it today—not for that. Today, she didn't need to hide and she didn't need protection from anyone. She was a guest partially because of who she was and the journey she'd gone on. Repacking her bag, she dug out her phone, and in lieu of a mirror, snapped a quick selfie. Perfect, she thought, and uploaded it to her social media. Or tried to, at least.

"Fuck. No service, of course." The event's website had warned her of the spotty service. Oh well. It was showtime.

* * *

The opening ceremony was a tradition at these events. A time to get everyone attending together to discuss the basic rules of the event, to introduce the guests of honor (mostly so the attendees could recognize them by sight), and to get things underway. The ceremony usually closed with an invocation of some sort, and the organizers had asked Deosil to do the honors. She'd agreed—it was something she was known for, to some extent. Everyone wanted to see her powers, after all, and it gave her a chance to do a little demonstration that was in alignment with her beliefs and show why she was invited to speak at these events, to show that even a talent as rare as superpowers can still be applied to a witch's devotional work.

"And now, we end the opening ceremony with an invocation by our guest of honor, Deosil!"

Deosil nodded and thanked the speaker who introduced her, and stepped up to the center of the circle. She smiled at all the faces that watched. She turned to the eastern portion of the setup, where a small wooden column stood, with a set of beribboned wind chimes on it. A similar pillar stood in each of the cardinal directions. This particular symbolism was ubiquitous among many modern pagans, standing in for the four quarters of the world, the four elements, the four winds, and almost every other set of symbols that came in fours. Fortunately, the event's organizers kept the symbolism simple and elemental.

"We thank the spirits of air," Deosil intoned, her voice strong and sure, pitched in what her acting teacher in high school had called her 'back row voice.' "Bless this gathering with curiosity and insight, with wisdom and knowledge. Hail!"

"Hail," the crowed intoned around her as she lifted her hands and gave herself over to her power. A chill ran up her spine as she reached out with her awareness, feeling the currents of wind around them. The sun warmed the air, which rose rapidly as a result, causing a small blanket of rippling winds just below cloud level above them. With a silent invitation, she twisted a small ribbon of those winds, pulling them down to her. A gust of warm air arched down, blowing through the gathering, carrying the scent of summer with it. The wind chimes tinkled merrily, and the ribbons blew outward dramatically.

She repeated that style of invocation at each of the cardinal directions, causing the small charcoal brazier in the south to flare up in a dancing, spiraling ribbon of flame. In the west, she caused a copper basin of water to swirl within its boundaries, its edges arching up as she formed a small whirlpool in the center, and then abruptly reversing the direction of the flow so it spiked upward in a thin cone that sprayed those nearby with a light, cooling mist.

Finally, she set the softball-sized globe of marble spinning in the north, turning it in its indentation in the top of the pillar. She wished her control over earth were a little stronger, but she'd always had the hardest time with that one. She smiled as everyone pointed out its movement. They seemed as impressed with it as with the others. Monica stepped up to her then, handing her a chalice half-full of wine, with a wink and a touch of their fingers.

"We thank the spirits of this land," Deosil said, pouring the wine out on the ground around her. "You who are our true hosts this weekend, who bear up under the burden of our presence here, who were here before us, and who will be here after us. Hail!"

With that, the festival was underway. There was half an hour before the workshops and myriad rituals started, just enough time for some of the attendees to gather around, asking her questions.

* * *

By midday, Deosil was grateful the event was large enough to have dedicated space for interviews, a pavilion divided into a couple of niches with backdrops for video interviews, all tucked away under the shade of a big old red cedar tree.

Deosil rested on a large, comfortable cushion. She stretched her arms above her head and then flowed downward, keeping her legs tucked under her and bending at the waist until her forehead nearly touched the rug floor of the pavilion. She arched her spine and was rewarded with a slight pop in her lower back, and she groaned with relief.

"Hello, sorry to interrupt," a voice said.

Deosil straightened quickly. "Hi there," she said, letting her interviewer settle into place in front of her. "Sorry. Just stretching a little."

"No problem—it must get exhausting, talking to people all day," the young woman in front of her said. Deosil judged that they were about the same age. She had chestnut brown hair, and wore a simple summer dress and sandals, with a modest triple moon pendant set with a bit of moonstone. "I'm Cathy. I'm not professional media or anything, but I do run a video blog called *Around the Cauldron*. They said they weren't sure if you were alright talking to me." She trailed off, as though she expected to be refused.

Deosil clapped her hands in delight. "I'd be a hell of a hypocrite to refuse, considering that a vlog is how I got my start, you know?"

"Oh, thank God," Cathy said with a relieved sigh. "They told me that they couldn't guarantee me anything, but I went ahead and paid the media membership rate, and—yeah I'm rambling. Sorry."

Deosil grinned. "Why don't you go ahead and set up your camera, and we can start?" Cathy nodded and set up a simple digital recorder on a somewhat rickety-looking tripod. Deosil took a swig from her water bottle while she waited.

"Okay. I think we're good to go," Cathy said finally. She'd set up so that they were both facing the camera, seated side-by-side. She went through the typical introductions, speaking to her viewers casually, explaining where they were filming from, who Deosil was, and the like.

"So, what do you think about the popular theory in pagan circles that the Playa Event—which you were at, right?—was more of a manifestation of magical energy being raised there than some scientific thing like the other Echo Events?"

Deosil blinked. "Wait, is that a thing? I'd never heard that before."

"Yeah, it is! I saw an interview with Groove, and he was talking about his experience with the Playa Event and how different it was from so many other Echo Events, you know? Like, he said there was a weird sense of union and transcendence right before it happened, that a lot of people there—even those who didn't get any powers—experienced. Can you corroborate that?"

Oh, God. Of course something like that would come from Groove, one of the other Playa Event Echoes. He was a DJ spinning at the big alternative desert retreat when the Playa Event happened. She'd heard him claiming to have "amped the power" at the event, practically taking credit for causing the damn thing at a DTPA Health Retreat last year. Obnoxious.

Of course, that meant that her response was going to be compared to his. Though he wasn't a pagan, he was in touch enough with the alternative counterculture that billed itself "urban tribal" that if she said something disparaging, it would reach his ears. *Especially* if she dissed him, honestly—the pagan and alternative spirituality communities loved their scandals and rivalries.

"If I'm going to be honest," said Deosil, "I don't remember a lot of exactly what happened. I mean, the earth went totally nuts at the Playa Event, and I was psychically hooked into that because of my power manifestation. Groove's an empath, so he's probably better able to speak to what people's emotions were doing at that time. I was too busy freaking out at the two tornadoes that touched down, the geysers, and the spontaneous combustion of the freaking *air* around us."

Cathy regarded her with wide eyes. "Wow. That's nuts. Was it really that crazy? It sounds dangerous!"

"Well, not to put too fine a point on it, but twenty-three people were injured by the event, and six of them died. Honestly, we were lucky that Llorona was attending the event, you know? She got lots of people to safety—thank the gods for her training and experience with the Golden Cross. It could have been so much worse."

"So, what is your opinion on it? Like, was it caused by magic, do you think?"

"I don't, no. But by the same token? Science can't really figure out Echo Events either, you know?" said Deosil.

"I thought they knew enough to artificially induce Echo Events. Isn't that how—what do they call them–"

"Empowered? Yeah, Empowered are created through artificial Events, but the thing is that every one of them has been an accident to date. They can't replicate them. They're just poking around in the dark trying to figure out how to harness the power that Echo Events generate, and they're no closer to figuring them out now than they were when they first started." Deosil was thoughtful for a moment. "Here's my honest opinion. You know I believe in magic. I don't believe my powers are themselves magical. Well, that's not the right way to put it, obviously. What I can do isn't the result of magic. I've had a couple of people approach me before online, kind of bummed out because they thought that practicing magic would eventually let them do what I do—with my powers, I mean."

Deosil hesitated, searching for the right way to put it. "My powers don't come from magic, but they can be used *for* magic. Just like someone who has a great singing voice, someone who is really good at making candles or pendants or whatever, or someone with a good understanding of building rituals. These are all natural abilities that aren't innately magical, but they can be used to make magic. My powers are just one more tool in my tool chest when it comes time for me to work magic as a witch. I don't think that the source behind the original Event, or any of the Echo Events, is magical. But I don't think it's necessarily scientific, either. I think there's a primal source—something that is the building blocks of the universe, you know? And I think that science can help figure out some of those building blocks sometimes, and do things with them, and that magic can do the same thing. It's my opinion that said source used to just sit there, quiet, waiting to be tapped into occasionally in the past, but it's awake now. It's active—not sentient, really, but more like water. It used to just be there, room temperature, but now it's been brought to a boil. Echo Events are that source blowing off steam."

Cathy was nodding, glancing back at the camera every so often, her lips pursed. "Wow. That's a lot to think about!"

Deosil tried not to sigh. That was a brush-off phrase if ever there was one, and she wouldn't be surprised to find that bit edited out of the final vlog. Cathy turned her questions to more immediately personal topics to Deosil: her spiritual and magical practices, what kind of training she'd had, and if she was involved with any established groups.

As they were nearing the end of their allotted time, the questions came that Deosil always dreaded. "So, can I ask—what was your name when you were a boy?" Cathy was grinning, like they were besties sharing fun gossip.

"Excuse me?" Deosil kept any tremor out of her voice. Almost as if summoned, Monica appeared behind the camera, off to one side. Deosil doubted Cathy could see her, but Monica had a sour look on her face.

"You know," said Cathy. "From before you were a girl."

"Okay," Deosil said with a sigh. "Let's be super clear here. I was *always* a girl. My body may not have always matched that, but I was never a boy. I was given a boy's name, but it was never mine, so I don't see any use in bringing it up."

"Oh, okay. Sorry if that's a touchy subject," Cathy said with saccharine sympathy, like someone who sees a cute puppy in the window and wishes they could take it home with them. "Can you tell me about your transition? Your registration with the DTPA—you get medical coverage with that, right? Is that what paid for your surgery?"

"Holy shit," Deosil said, taken aback.

Monica stepped around the partition, into Cathy's sight, and reached past her to click the camera off.

"Hey!" Cathy objected.

"You've got some nerve," Monica said. "Take your harassment of my guests and shove it up your ass. You're done here."

Cathy squawked, a piercing sound of indignation.

Deosil shook her head. "Monica, no, it's, well, it's not alright, but–"

"You're damned right it's not alright. The fact is, you are not the only trans attendant we have at this festival. I appreciate that you might feel forgiving about it, Deosil, but I have a responsibility to my other attendees as well." She turned back to Cathy. "I wish you'd read our code of conduct a little more carefully. I'm going to need you to pack your things, per the agreement you made when you signed in."

Cathy stared at her, open-mouthed. "Are you fucking kidding me?"

Monica narrowed her eyes. "Please don't make me call security. They're loud and embarrassing people and have as little tolerance for this kind of bullshit as I do."

"You know this is going to be all over my vlog, right? You can't be serious."

"Tell anyone and everyone you like. I'm proud that our event has a zero-tolerance policy when it comes to this sort of thing. Tell as many people about it as you can. I appreciate the free advertising." Monica stood aside, gesturing for Deosil, who rose, grabbed her bag and walked out of the pavilion in a daze.

"I'm so sorry about that," Monica said.

The more Deosil walked, the angrier she got. "Look, it's not that I don't appreciate it, but you know that you just basically white knighted me back there, right? I don't need someone to come to my rescue here. I've been dealing with those sorts of questions—and much, much worse—since the Playa Event."

Monica stopped and winced. "I know. And I'm sorry. But I meant what I said. I have full faith in your ability to take care of yourself and deal with that kind of bullshit, Deosil. I mean it. But I also have a responsibility as the organizer here. I hope you can see that."

"No, I can. I do. I just, I'm a little sensitive about that kind of thing, you know?"

"I do. I should have handled it better. I can't help it—my Mars is in Aries."

Deosil stared at her for a moment, and then burst out laughing. "God, I cannot believe you just trotted out 'the stars made me do it.'"

Monica laughed as well. "Okay, okay. Guilty. Let me make it up to you? I have some awesome tea with me. It's super soothing, back at my tent. Peace?"

"Well, alright. But only because I *really* like tea."

* * *

The rest of that day passed more smoothly. Monica flirted with her outrageously, but Deosil made a point of toeing the line between flirting and actually sleeping with festival folk. That never ended well.

That night she stayed up far too late drumming around the fire. When the fire dancers started spinning, she joined them, snatching up live flames from the bonfire to dance with. She needed neither poi nor chains, and the fire darted and swopped around her like a living thing. She was the fire goddess Pele that night, the fire hungry, and she gave it the sacrifice of herself, dancing and whooping long into the night as drummers pounded out a rhythm, until she was too tired to keep the flames safely focused. She snuffed them, to wild applause, and retired to her tent. Monica walked her back, and they said their goodnights.

The Playa Event haunted her dreams that night. Roaring, dust-filled winds. Geysers of scalding water exploding from the deep places of the earth. Flying shards of flint and clots of hard clay. It wasn't surprising—she had dreams of her Event sometimes. All Echoes did. Sometimes the dreams caused her powers to manifest, as though trying to recreate the Event. She would sometimes dream of an apocalypse, remembering the Event, only to wake to a scaled-down version of one, as though her powers were trying to make her nightmares reality. It didn't happen often, especially as her control grew, but it did happen. It was always terrifying.

These days, it wasn't as bad. She was in better control of her powers, and her post-trauma therapy made her less susceptible to the primal panic those dreams used to cause. Still, she woke drenched in sweat. She did not wake with a cry, as she did sometimes, but that was because there was something echoing in her ears, the sounds of something loud and distant. She got up quickly, throwing on the heavy wool cloak over her t-shirt and yoga pants. She usually brought it to colder events with her, and was grateful for its weight right now.

Stepping out of the tent, she looked around. Others were emerging from their tents as well.

"Did you hear that?" someone asked. Everyone was milling about in confusion. Most of them had been asleep, but a flushed couple—obviously in the middle of not-sleeping in their bed—said, "It was an explosion. We heard it."

Deosil clutched her cloak around her and closed her eyes, counting her breaths. In for four, hold for four, out for four, hold for four, repeat. The sounds around her fell away, and other, more primal senses took hold. The land was cold with the night air and the moisture was building high, waiting for the proper moment to fall as morning dew. No animal moved within the range of her senses—they were hiding in nests and burrows, beneath fallen logs and wherever they could, all of them startled by the strange sound. Deosil could almost *feel* the last vestiges of the sound, like a memory she couldn't place, a word that was on the tip of her tongue.

She expanded her senses further and found it—the strip of asphalt that cut through the land like a foul-smelling, sticky ribbon. She sensed the heat first, its presence as obvious as a spotlight in the darkness. Twisted metal and spilled gasoline, and the unmistakable presence of shed blood and tears. She opened her eyes. "There's been an accident on the highway. About a mile and a half from here. Someone get someplace and call 911. I'm going to go help." She stepped up to the dwindling embers of the fire.

"Do you need a ride?" Monica asked, as others scrambled for phones and car keys. Deosil extended her hands over the fire, into the outpouring of rippling heat that rose quickly into the chilly darkness of the sky.

"I don't. Thank you."

Monica stepped away as Deosil's hands began to glow, reaching the same hue as the cherry-red remains of the fire at her feet. The low, dark luminescence spread over her body in streaks until her eyes began to glow with the same hue. Deosil's best-known power was what she called elemental evocation—the power to reach out to the elements in her environment and cause them to move, to shift, and to change according to her will. But it wasn't her most potent power. This was.

Elemental *invocation*, the act of taking the essence of power in the environment around her, of merging her own essence with it, transformed her bodily in a fashion the scientists at the DTPA were still trying to classify. She could invoke stone to her body, becoming strong and hard to injure, or reach out to the green life around her to heal her injuries and feed herself with sunlight.

Or she could breathe in the power of a hot fire, and its ability to rise quickly on the night air. Looking like nothing so much as a phoenix, she rose, her feet dragging the earth until her last bare toe left it, and then she was off like an ember on the cold dark winds. Her cloak spread out against the dark sky and for a moment, Deosil glanced at the others on the camp below her, their wonder-filled faces turned up to her. And then she was gone.

This power wasn't full flight. Its movement wasn't that of a jet, but that of a hot air balloon. She rose, seeking the strong winds above them. They pushed her in the direction she sought, toward the bright burning light at the edge of the darkened terrain. They carried her quickly, and as she neared the accident site, she began to release the fire, cooling and dropping at a dizzying but safe rate. She released the last of the invocation of fire when her bare feet touched down on the asphalt littered with glass and pieces of metal.

Fuck. Now she wished she'd remembered to put on shoes. Her teeth chattered, and she pulled her cloak more tightly around her shoulders. One of the benefits of DTPA registration was that she was trained and registered as a first responder volunteer. She surveyed the scene. It was two vehicles. One was a massive tanker truck, a semi with a payload of fuel. It had clearly hit another vehicle—an old beat-up sedan, from all appearances. The impact had turned the truck on its side on top of the sedan, which was all but crushed beneath it. The windowed portion of the car was crunched down like so much tinfoil, glass shattered, and doors buckled beyond hope of opening.

A fire had started beneath the sedan and was slowly rising. It would soon be high enough to hit the fuel leaking from the tanker above the sedan's point of impact.

Great.

There were people in the sedan, from the sounds of the screaming and the pounding on the doors. She looked around and found another body beside the road—the truck driver, as far as she could tell. She quickly crossed to him, hoping he might help her. He was already moving and groaning when she found him, though, clearly in no shape to do any such thing.

"Hey. Don't move. You've been in an accident," she said, kneeling beside him with a glance up at the truck and car. "I need you to lie still. Help is on the way, okay?"

The man breathed hard—an ugly, rattling sound—and nodded. Deosil pulled her woolen cloak off and bundled it up under his head. She stood and crossed to the wreck, rapping on the sedan to get their attention. "Hey! Try to get away from the door. I'm going to see if I can get it to open, okay?"

"Help!" A young man's voice called from inside. "My friend is bleeding really badly."

"We can smell smoke!" another voice cried, panicked.

"I'm here, and I'm going to do my best to get you out. More help is on the way." Deosil stepped back and extended her primal senses. No good sources of water nearby, save in the upper atmosphere, and the conditions weren't right. She'd never be able to turn it into a strong enough downpour to kill the fire in time. Besides, who knew exactly what was burning—water might make it worse.

She opened her eyes and surveyed the scene again. She had zero control over metal. If her affinity with earth was stronger, she might be able to do something with the metal, but she did well to move rock and dirt. Plus, fire was licking up all around it. That she could do something about. She closed her eyes and found the flames in her primal senses, the sun-brightness of the flame and its hungry desire to consume. Fire made her nervous—that hunger was so all-encompassing sometimes. Not malicious, but dangerous, the way a large predator in nature is. She steeled herself and breathed gulps of cooling air, calming the hunger of the fire. The fire's ardor diminished, but she couldn't extinguish it entirely. She'd found that she couldn't control a fire enough to make it snuff itself—she always needed another element for that.

Her best control was air, but that wasn't helpful right now. Not for getting them out of that damned car.

Alright. Time for brute force. She closed her eyes and breathed in the essence of the stone and earth beneath her feet. She vaguely heard the sound of cars pulling to a stop behind her. When she opened her eyes, her flesh was the color of dark basalt, lit by the headlights behind her. She turned and saw several of the festival attendees—including Monica—rushing toward her.

"Get back!" she yelled. All of them skidded to a stop. "If anyone has first aid training, there's a man over there who is injured and could use some help. The rest of you keep back—there's fuel in this tank, and a fire. I've gotten it down low, but it's not going to stay there, so everyone keep back."

Monica stared at her. She seemed like she might argue for half a second, but she was turning and backing everyone away as Deosil turned to the car. "Goddamn it, Rusty," she said. "I sure could use your power right about now."

She stepped up to the car and pulled on its door. As she suspected, the handle came off in her hands. The door was tightly wedged, buckling with the weight of the tanker. She growled and drove her basalt-strong hands into the metal at the edges of its frame, punching through to grip the door. She set her feet, tightened her grasp and leaned back, pulling with all of her might.

The metal gave a horrible groaning sound, almost like a shriek. She stopped, losing her basalt invocation. She felt tears prickling at the edges of her eyes and wiped them away furiously. Goddamn it. She didn't have super-strength in that form, just super-resilience. She was focusing on the problem, pacing back and forth and occasionally shouting reassurances to the people inside when the fire truck arrived.

"Oh, thank the gods," she whispered. She crossed to them as they began unloading gear. "My code is Deosil, TP-010392. I'm a trained first responder, though this is a bit beyond my ability to manage. I'm an elementalist—I've been keeping the fire from climbing too high over there, but can't figure out anything else to do to help. I'm an elemental manipulator as well as elemental assumptive."

The leader looked her up and down. "Captain Ripley. Glad to have your help, ma'am." She quickly told him the situation, focusing on the fuel, the fire, and the buckling caused by the weight of the tanker.

"What we need to do is to get some of the weight off of the car, if we can," said the leader. "We've got spreader-cutters here that can do the job, but if we try to use it while the weight of that tanker is bearing down on the frame, it'll likely jackknife it outward, hurting someone. Plus, it might weaken the frame of the car holding the truck up."

"Which would result in it coming crashing down on top of them. Got it. So, we need to relieve some of the pressure on top of the car."

"We've got rams that can exert the force needed to get the tanker off, but if it comes crashing down, it's likely to not only crumple the car on that side, but to spill fuel everywhere. If that hits the fire…well."

"Gotcha," Deosil said, examining the scene. As firemen donned fire-retardant gear around her, she walked around the wreck. "Okay. Sorry to say, this is going to use the power I'm weakest at. Can you set up rams to push it from this side, so that it rolls away from the door where the passengers are?"

"Sure. But again—"

"Crushing car plus spilled gas, I know," Deosil cut him off. "I'm going to give it something soft to roll over onto. Wait for my word." Deosil walked to the back of the wreck while Ripley organized the setup of the rams.

She normally sought out the strength of stone when she used her evocations of earth. This time, she closed her eyes and sought the gorgeous, soft black loam of the Washington countryside, rich earth that had gathered with the push of glacial forces thousands of years ago. Beneath their feet, chunks of basalt rumbled, and three mounds of earth rose. A cry of alarm came from the other side of the wreckage as fire fighters retreated. The sudden shift in the ground beneath the wreckage caused the whole mess to move slightly, with the sound of groaning earth.

"Everything alright?" Captain Ripley asked as he came around the back of the vehicles. Deosil nodded as she concentrated, raising the last of the earthen mounds to a height about level with the car's roof. The mounds were high, with a steep slope facing the car, but a long and gentle one facing away from it. Getting the truck off the car's chassis and onto those slopes would cushion it enough to avoid spillage or additional damage.

She hoped.

"So, we're going to use the rams to roll it back off of the sedan and onto those?" he asked. Deosil nodded while he examined it. "Could work. Let's do this. They ready to go?"

"They are," Deosil said. She backed away while the fire fighters put the final touches on the footing of the hydraulic rams on the other side.

Monica found her and gave her a big hug. "You're goddamned amazing," she said.

Deosil shook her head. "I'm just a helper. I know people who could have rescued them in nothing flat. But I can't do a damned thing but play with the dirt here."

"Hey," Monica said, pulling up Deosil's chin to look at her. "Stop. What you're doing? Your instincts to immediately come and help? That's amazing. You're amazing."

Deosil nodded, and closed her eyes, breathing deeply. She took a moment to ground and center herself. When she evoked earth in a strong way, it made her melancholy. She wanted to crawl under her covers until the world was okay again, but right now, she knew she couldn't.

"Alright, we're ready," the captain yelled. Fire fighters took up positions. He clicked the controls for the hydraulic rams, which slowly began extending, exerting incredible pressure. The tanker moved slightly, groaning. For a moment it seemed like it would work. Then one of the rams punched through the truck's side with a hollow *whoomp*. Part of the tank's structure that had been damaged by the wreck gave way, incapable of supporting the force on it. The whole hulking wreck tilted crazily with a shearing shriek of metal, a sudden movement that splashed fuel in an arc as the thing jolted backward. The fire at the base of the wreckage rose toward the sky as the fuel fed it, and it was hungry for more.

"Back!" screamed the captain. Fire fighters dove away as the whole tanker shifted sideways, crumpling part of the car. The back half skidded away from the car, but the front half swiveled toward the gathered crowd, spraying fuel everywhere. The fire roared toward the fuel container, licking hungrily. Suddenly winds screamed in their midst, knocking down the crowd. The wind snatched up hats and light equipment, poorly-moored plants and bits of earth and loam as it whipped around.

The fire reached for the fuel, but the tornado snatched the fuel into the sky overhead and sucked the fire with it. Air pressure fluctuated, stealing their breaths. A couple of the bystanders blacked out, slumping to the ground. The fire rose like a terrible dragon into the air, giving a triumphant roar as the tornado sucked the fuel up and away from the ground level. It lit the night sky with a great flame cyclone, twisting and bucking like a living thing.

Then it was over, the fuel dispersed and burnt up in the air, pressure returning to normal. The area filled with a sudden rain of dust and ash, and the caustic stench of burnt petroleum. Everyone stared for a heartbeat, unable to believe they were all alive. Captain Ripley yelled "Go! Go! Go!" to three of his men, who ran to the side of the car. Two others ran to prop up the tanker—now extended out over the car sideways, at a ninety-degree angle—to steady it while the three men with the cutter-spreader sheared open the side of the door.

Deosil didn't realize she was on her knees until she threw up. She didn't realize she was crying until Monica was hugging her close, wrapping her cloak tighter around her. "You did it. You did it, Deosil. You saved all of us. It's okay now. Oh, God, you saved us."

Deosil snuffled and inhaled a shaky breath. Her training told her this was a natural reaction to the spike of adrenaline that came with a life-or-death situation, but she couldn't stop crying and shaking. She glanced up to find a number of people—festival goers mostly, but also a few of the firemen—standing around her, watching her with different demeanors of gratitude, relief, concern, and shock.

A paramedic stepped up to her and knelt beside the two of them. "Are you okay?" She shushed Monica, who tried to answer for her, and asked Deosil to look at her. "Can you answer me? Are you alright?"

"Ye-yeah. Yeah, I'm not hurt."

The EMT handed her a bottle of water, instructing Monica to keep her warm while she checked on the others. A few on the edges of the tornado had flash-burns, but nothing serious. Once Deosil was breathing again, she found Captain Ripley next to her.

He smiled, a hand on her shoulder. "I've never seen anything like that in my life, kid. If that fire had reached the fuel in that tank, we'd have all been dead—you saved the lives of not only the people in that car, but my men and all these people here as well. I hope you know that you're a hero."

Deosil laughed, a gasping, uncontrolled sound, and then wiped her eyes and nose. She nodded gratefully. There was a lot of rescue that still needed doing, but Monica took Deosil back to the campsite, insisting she needed some food and rest. Deosil was too confused and fog-headed to complain or object, even if she'd wanted to. A beep sounded as they rode in the car, and Deosil fished out her phone. It had a pair of messages from Rusty. "You asshole," she said. She knew she should be concerned about what Rusty was planning, but she just couldn't focus enough to do so. Maybe tomorrow. She let Monica get her back to the camp, feed her some peanut butter crackers and what had to be a gallon of water, and then tuck her in to sleep it off.

"Thank you," she said to Monica as the woman stepped toward the tent. Monica stopped and turned back to regard Deosil.

"Gods, Jesh," she whispered, shaking her head. "Thank *you*."

Deosil faded off to sleep, somewhat disconcerted at the unabashed hero worship in Monica's eyes. She found that she kind of missed the casual flirtiness from earlier.

CHAPTER EIGHT

The Rails from Portland, Oregon to Boulder City, Nevada
May 4, 2013

Dusty wind blew over Rusty as the train whipped past him, thundering the earth with its length of cargo cars. He coughed and pulled his dust mask up over his mouth and nose. Shutting his eyes tightly, he yanked the welder's goggles on his forehead down over his eyes, struggling for a moment with the tight rubbery strap. By the time he got them in place enough to open his eyes, the last of the cars was roaring past him.

He sighed and looked down the track at its rapidly diminishing shape, now a block of vague silhouettes in a nimbus of dusty light. In a few heartbeats it was gone, and he was left in the dark once more. Rusty buttoned up his pea-green bridge coat. He suspected he'd be glad for its warmth before the night was out.

Truth be told, he'd tried this trick before. Though a fair-sized city, downtown Portland quickly emptied of people at night, at least in the area around the university. The streetcars had tracks all over the place there, embedded railings that let him practice this little trick. His own research into electromagnetism had wandered, as such things do on Wikipedia, on to an article on mag-lev trains—crazy-fast bullet trains and the possibilities for their future.

The concept was simple: the train was suspended above the track itself, held in place by electrically generated magnetic fields. The magnetic field also provided forward motion, in essence providing both lift and thrust, allowing the train to run both more smoothly and quietly than typical wheel-and-axle mechanisms.

He stepped up onto the track's raised bed, and then positioned himself over one of the rails, straddling it. Cautiously, he extended his awareness to the earth's magnetic fields and homed in on the thin line that was the track's presence in that field, distorting and attracting it subtly the way most ferrous constructions did. He pulled that awareness back, zooming out and examining the line up and down its length. He found the train that had just passed him, a warping bullet along the thin line of the track, and then searched in the other direction as well. The next train along the track was maybe a half hour away and heading in his direction.

All right, then. His awareness shifted effortlessly into control, and he reached out to seize up the coruscating power covering the whole world. With a bit of effort, he aligned his own body to that power and rose up, wobbling as he fine-tuned his control, until he was hovering steadily above the track. Though in theory he didn't need them, the big steel bracers and steel-toe boots he wore eased the transition, giving him something to hold on to while he got everything lined up. Taking a deep breath, he focused his mind as he cinched the backpack shoulder straps and buckled the strap around his waist.

He crouched like a runner at the starting line, waiting for the pistol shot. With a thought, he shifted the polarity of the field around him subtly, moving from "vaguely levitating" to "pushing away from the track." His heart leapt into his throat as the magnetic field reacted, thrusting him away from the earth while shoving him forward at a running pace. He checked the fit of his dust mask and goggles, and then poured on the teslas. He shotgunned away down the track, carefully riding its subtle turns and shifts in grade. Rusty grinned like a madman beneath his mask.

* * *

It was a trip of just over a thousand miles from Portland to the Hoover Dam in Nevada, although the train tracks didn't take direct routes. He figured it would take him about four hours or so to get there.

It took much longer. In an ideal world, with just him and the tracks, he could have managed that distance quickly. But the trains actually on those tracks were much slower than he was. He could avoid those coming in his direction easily enough, dropping off the track to give them room to pass. But he couldn't dart around those moving in the same direction as he was when he had only a single track. He spent a frustrating amount of time with his speed throttled, waiting for a second line of track on his route.

Which was frustrating as hell, generally speaking.

Though he'd figured he'd be there by midnight or so, dawn was greying the eastern sky by the time he arrived in Boulder City, Nevada, just down I-93 from the dam. He slowed as he saw the lights of the town ahead, skidding to a halt in a cloud of dust. The next train was fifteen minutes away or so, but he hurried off the track and onto the road nearby, thrilled to be done with rail-riding for a while.

He shook himself off on the side of the road, kicking up dirt. Waving the particulates of most of California away from his face, Rusty pushed his goggles up onto his forehead and lowered his mask. He took a few moments to breathe the chill pre-dawn air and reached into his coat pocket. Thumbing the power on, he started walking. A few minutes later, the screen still hadn't lit up.

"What the hell?" said Rusty. Cautiously extending his awareness to the rectangle of electronics in his hand, he confirmed his fears—the phone was fried. Normally, just shutting off his phone was enough to keep from EMPing it. Of course, he rarely used his power to the extent necessary for his transportation out here, or for nearly as sustained a length of time.

"Fuck." He wondered if he could find a phone that included Faraday shielding. He had his doubts, really—he didn't remember that among the options offered by any major cell providers. Fortunately, the walk into town was relatively short, though it took him a couple of tries before finding a place that was open, a mom-and-pop roadside gas station called DOUGETT'S GAS. He stripped off mask and goggles, stowing them in his pack, undid a couple of buttons in his coat and beat the hell out of its front, trying to get as much rail dust off it as he could before walking in. The kid behind the counter was cute, in a redneck kind of way, and Rusty smiled as he approached him. "Do I need a key to use the bathroom?"

"Uh, well, you need to buy something," the cashier said, reaching up to remove the earbud from his ear. He had shaggy brown hair, and eyes the kind of hazel that Rusty really liked. He wore a ribbed sleeveless undershirt under the open short-sleeved button-up that had definitely seen better days. On the plus side, it showed off some ink down one of his arms. Definitely cute; definitely redneck.

"I promise," Rusty said, crossing his heart. "I just really need to use the bathroom first."

"Sure, man. Here you go." He slid across the counter an old wooden ruler, its length worn and splintered, with a key attached to one end of it. Rusty thanked him and exited the store, wandering around to the side of the building.

Rattling the door open, he flicked on the light and got a good look at himself in the streaked mirror. Well, no wonder the dude inside had given him the eye, and not in a good way. He was doing a great impersonation as an extra from a post-apocalyptic movie. Dust (and other things, he thought, shuddering) caked his red hair, turning it into a dirty dun, a color extending down most of his face and body.

"Great." He stripped off his shirt. His bladder demanded he tend to it, and he did so with a sigh. There's only so long he could piss out in the dark wilderness beside train tracks before he started to feel half-feral. The water from the sink didn't smell like anything he'd want to drink, but it got the dust off his face well enough. He dipped his head under the faucet a couple of times and scrubbed out as much of the dust-to-mud from it that he could. It was a good thing he kept his hair short.

Unzipping his backpack, he hauled a clean shirt out. He'd wanted to wait until he could get an actual shower before changing, but there was no way he was going to his meeting wearing a shirt this caked in dust and bugs. He rubbed his hair as dry as he could with a handful of rough brown paper towels and stepped back to regard the mirror. Well, it would have to do.

The bell over the door rang as he walked back in, twirling the ruler-and-key. "Hey, man. Thanks for–"

The man in front of the counter whirled and pointed a pistol at him with a shaking hand.

"No, no! Look, look, it's right here!" The cute kid behind the counter was frantically shoving money from the register into a plastic bag as the man looked between them with panic in his eyes, swinging the gun in big, exaggerated arcs as though he could keep them both covered at the same time.

Rusty knew that face. He'd seen more than his fair share of tweakers in the scene during his day. And this wasn't *party-til-you-drop* tweaking, either. This was *pissed-off-fuck-the-world* tweak-face.

"Who the fuck are you?!" the trembling robber shouted, spittle flying. The guy seemed to be in his early forties, though he was probably younger. Rusty grimaced as the dude showed off the rotting teeth in his meth-mouth. "Hey, shit. No trouble, man," Rusty said.

"Your wallet! Now!"

"Sure thing, man." He reached for his dusty pants pocket. The meth-head's focus was on him, and the kid behind the counter began to crouch, reaching for something under the counter. Rusty shook his head, trying to call him off, but the cashier was only watching the robber.

The same could not be said for the robber. Seeing Rusty's head-shake, he whirled on the kid behind the counter. "No!" Rusty shouted as the man squeezed the trigger and hell erupted.

Later, he'd have a vague recollection of the network of metal in the ceiling of the place, and magnetically reaching out for them in his panic. In the moment, though, there weren't decisions so much as instincts. With a simple act of will, faster by degrees than even the simple physical act of pulling a trigger, Rusty filled those old metal beams with raw teslas, twisting the fuck out of their polarity until they were basically supermagnets.

Doors on the freezers swung open, trying to shoot upward, while metal shelves not bolted to the ground tumbled from floor to ceiling, spraying packaged food and bottles of soda everywhere. The cashier shrieked as a hundred different little pieces of metal bullshit behind the counter—from bottle openers to cheap mobile phones to the entire fucking register—flew upwards as though someone had reversed gravity. The gunman cried in terror and pain as the tightly-gripped pistol was wrenched from his grasp, the metal guard abrading his knuckles on the way out of his hands. Likewise, the shotgun the cashier was reaching smacked into the lip of the counter and flipped up towards the ceiling.

For a moment, they all stood there, staring upward as a store's worth of metal objects hung trembling on the ceiling. Then the gunman and cashier focused on Rusty. He smiled as the lights in the building flickered under the magnetic assault.

That did it.

The tweaker bolted for the door, tearing ass for the car idling in the parking lot. It didn't take much multitasking to reach out and slam the doors shut on his car, sealing them to the frame the way he'd stuck half the shit in the store to the ceiling here. The tweaker wailed piteously as he tugged on the door handle to his car. With a glance back at the building where they stood, he took off at an awkward, panicked run, disappearing down the road to the rest of the town, now painted with the colors of the dawn.

"Holy shit," said the cashier.

Rusty turned to the guy behind the counter. This was the moment of truth, generally speaking. When someone realized that a person near them was one of the Changed, there was no telling what their reaction was going to be. Fortunately, the cashier was young, and like most people of Rusty's generation, had grown up in a world whose media was obsessed with superpowered folk.

"That was *awesome!*" Adrenaline and the after-effects of terror for his life mixed with wonder, and the guy practically leapt over the counter to high-five him. Rusty chuckled and slapped his hand with a grin.

Lights flashed into the parking lot as a sheriff's deputy car screeched to a halt in the parking lot. On the road behind it, another car swerved away from the turn-in and sped up, heading down the road where the gunman was running away.

"Oh. I hit the button when that dude first came in here," the cashier said. Rusty sighed, and then knelt, putting his hands behind his neck. "Wait, what are you doing?" said the cashier. s

"Just get on your knees, and put your hands on your neck, man," Rusty said.

Two deputies rushed into the store, pistols at the ready. They'd obviously seen the mess in the store—it was hard to miss a couple hundred pounds of metal sticking to the ceiling even from the parking lot—and were following their training.

Since the advent of the Originals, the Department of Transformed Persons Affairs had taken great pains to train law enforcement on every level in TPT (Transformed Persons Tactical) training. Generally speaking, it meant that this incident had already been called into the DTPA's central database, a clearing-house with twenty-four-hour access to law enforcement officials on every level across the country. The database provided details about the Changed who were registered with the DTPA, particularly as many details of the functions and weaknesses of their powers as the Department's scientists had managed to measure and confirm.

From what Rusty knew, these yokels had already broken the first rule of TPT: do not engage. Generally speaking, even local law enforcement was supposed to wait for a SWAT or equivalent backup. They probably had an ass-chewing coming to them, so the least he could do was make their lives easier.

"Get down!" one of them barked. "Hands behind your head!" The cashier, blinking in confusion, complied quickly, faced for the second time in less than a few minutes with firearms pointed in his direction.

"Identify yourselves," said the same deputy, a broad-shouldered man with dark, squinty eyes and a dusting of facial scruff. The other deputy, a thin man without much chin to speak of, skirted the edges of the store, doing his best to avoid being underneath any particularly heavy chunks of metal adhered to the ceiling.

"Sam...Sam Waller," the cashier stuttered. "Jesus, Jim, what's..."

"Shut it, Sam," Deputy Jim snapped, turning his weapon wholly on Rusty. "You. Identify."

"TP-009813, DTPA Code: Gauss," Rusty said, enunciating carefully like he'd been taught.

"Not your Jolly Pirate nickname, junior," the other deputy sneered. "The one on your ID."

For a moment, Rusty panicked. "Uh, sir, my real name? I don't—"

"Shut it, Miller," Deputy Jim said. "Were you not paying attention during the last Department refresher? We're not allowed to ask for their real names. What was that number again, kid?"

The deputy relayed this information into the radio speaker at his shoulder, careful not to take his pistol off Rusty. Thank God one of these guys was up to snuff on his code. The Department of Transformed Persons Affairs had long ago established the right to allow Echoes who'd registered with the Department to use only code names, even in legal situations.

As the deputy communicated with his dispatch—who was undoubtedly in communication with the DTPA—Rusty glanced at Sam and shrugged. "It's a glamorous life," he whispered with a rueful grin.

"Quiet, you two," said Deputy Jim, though his voice had lost the hard edge. The other deputy returned to report that there was no one else in the building. Deputy Jim ordered Sam to his feet and out of the store. It was another few minutes before the chatter on the radio back and forth ceased, and the cops gave the all clear.

"Can I stand up now?"

"Yeah," Deputy Jim said, though there was some clear hesitation in his voice. "Go ahead."

"Thanks," Rusty said. Through the window outside, Sam was all worked up, nearly yelling at the confused older couple beside him and the deputy who was doing his best to be patient.

"So, can you do something about this?" The deputy nodded upward, taking off his cap.

"Well, I can, but it's probably going to make a mess. I mean, I'm not entirely sure where everything *goes*. It won't fall, though. Just get set down." The cop wandered over to where the robber had been standing and glanced upward at the pistol. Reaching over the counter, he hauled a plastic bag out and shook it open, then stood beneath the pistol, bag extended. "Go ahead."

Rusty closed his eyes and found the metal in the ceiling. Gently, he unraveled the artificial magnetic field he'd infused them with, letting up on it so that the objects in the shop lowered themselves from the ceiling. Everyone outside the shop watched, eyes wide.

Once he'd snared the gun in the bag, the cop glanced over at Rusty. "Magnetism, huh?"

"Yes, sir." He didn't really know what else to say. The DTPA would have given him the rundown on his abilities. The cop tied the bag off, slipped his cap back on his balding head, and gave him an appraising look. "Not a damned thing we could have done against you, is there?"

Fuck. He hated this kind of thing. He knew that it was smart. He knew that given the number of suddenly superpowered assholes out there who'd decided to use their power for shitty, selfish reasons, it only made sense that law enforcement had to think first of how to respond to a situation involving someone with powers in terms of quickest takedown. It still made him queasy to think that every cop he met who knew about him was trying to figure out the best way to kick his ass, if not flat-out kill him.

"Not true," said Rusty. "Your guns wouldn't have done much good, and depending on my environment, I could have made it hell for you. But if you get the drop on me with baton or bare fist, I'm just any other guy."

The thought seemed to make Deputy Jim content and he waved Rusty out the door.

Right into a very indignant Sam Waller. "That was total bullshit, Jim! This guy kept us from being shot by that piece of shit tweaker!"

The deputy rolled his eyes and squared his stance, jaw tightening.

Rusty intervened. "Hey, Sam—it's cool, man. He did the right thing. He had no idea what was happening, and a guy with powers is always a higher security priority than even the tweakingest tweaker with a gun. It's cool."

Sam was incredulous. "You're *okay* with all that?"

"Dude. I've been trained to expect it, just like him. With great power comes great government oversight, man." Rusty grinned, trying to defuse the situation. Though, if he had to be honest, having the cute young cashier coming to his defense in such an indignant way did make him feel better about it. He knew he wasn't allowed to be pissed off by the treatment. They'd drilled that into him at the DTPA. It just did him good to have *someone* be pissed off by it on his behalf.

It was another hour or so until everyone's statements were taken. By that time, the deputies reported that the tweaker had been picked up. Unfortunately, the store's video feed was more than a little fried by Rusty's trick, but the deputies thought they had more than enough for a conviction. After giving his own exhaustive statement to a fearful deputy who wouldn't, for some reason, meet his gaze, Rusty finally left.

Not a half block away, a shitty old land-yacht of a car pulled up next to him, and Sam threw open the door. "Get in, dude. Gauss, right?"

Rusty gratefully climbed in, grinning when Sam handed him two bottles of sports drink.

"Jim said the spooks told him you get low electrolytes when you use your ability," Sam said.

Rusty chuckled. "That's exactly what I was going to buy when I walked back in the store, actually." He took a big gulp from one bottle, stowing the second in his backpack. "Thank Deputy Jim for me, yeah?"

"I still think it's bullshit."

"Seriously, dude, I'm used to it. It's why most of us don't use our powers very often. And really, they handled the situation wrong. Most law enforcement who aren't SWAT or other tactical types aren't even supposed to engage us directly. Those deputies were cool—I mean, getting cuffed by SWAT is a shitty way to start the day—but they should be more careful. There are some real assholes out there."

"So, can I drop you somewhere?" said Sam. "I called my girlfriend and left her a message that I'm coming home early, but I don't have to be anywhere immediately. She'll be in bed for another hour or two."

Ah. A girlfriend. Oh, well. "Yeah, do you know where the Firehouse Cafe is? I'm supposed to meet a friend out there."

"Yeah, definitely," Sam said.

They'd driven for a few minutes before the silence became uncomfortable. Rusty chuckled. "Alright. I know you've got questions. Hit me."

Sam shot him an abashed grin. "You sure? You must get asked this shit all the time."

"Nah, it's all good. The least I can do for the ride and drinks, right?"

"So, what…kind are you? Wait, sorry. I don't know if that's the right way to put it."

"No, I get you," said Rusty. "I'm an Echo. Most of us are. I was at the Gulf Event, back in 2008."

"The Gulf Event? Not familiar with that one."

"Not surprising—the oil company that owned the rig did their best to keep it out of the media. It happened on an oil rig in the Gulf of Mexico. My dad works in the oil industry and he was touring the rig. I was with him, because he wanted me to start taking an interest in the business. I was sixteen."

"So, what happened?"

Rusty looked out the window. "It wasn't terribly different from a lot of Echo Events—it started with the ringing in the ears, and then the nosebleeds, like usual. Then—*blam*. The whole world was suddenly fucked up."

He thought back to the ringing in his ears that made him nauseated with vertigo. About half the crew had gotten it, to one degree or another, and a few moments later, they all got the nosebleeds. By that time most people in the western world knew what the warning signs of an Echo Event were. Normally there would have been a massive panic to get out of the area. Only so far you can run on an oil rig in the middle of the Gulf of Mexico, though.

He remembered the bright, pulsing lights. The sudden rising of massive waves from all sides of the rig, threatening to swamp it, pounding on it over and over. The shrieking as the structure twisted, trying to turn itself into a building-sized fucking pretzel.

"How many were affected?" Sam seemed hesitant to ask.

"Depends. Lots of injuries. A dozen people died from the Event phenomena, including two of those who were developing powers. Five of us Echoed, but only three of us survived—me, a hydrokinetic called Tidal, and a radiant called Heatstroke."

"Oh, shit. I heard about Heatstroke," Sam said. "Wasn't he arrested like two years ago for hurting a bunch of people?"

"Yeah, he was. Real asshole—one of the roughnecks who had always been jealous that not everyone had to work as hard as he did. Kind of an alcoholic, too. I think I heard that he was torn up on tequila when he did all that. He's still in prison for it."

They rode in silence for another moment or two. "Yeah, tequila makes me mean, too," Sam finally remarked. They both laughed. It felt good. "So, you're gay?" Sam asked, wiping his eyes.

Rusty knew it was stupid that this question shocked him more than anything else Sam had said so far. "Uh, yeah," he said, trying to be nonchalant. An uncomfortable moment of silence fell. "How did you know?"

"Patch on your backpack," Sam said, gesturing at the bag on the floorboard at Rusty's feet. "I saw the pride rainbow patch thing on it, with the pink triangle. That is a pride thing, right?"

Oh. *Dumbass*, Rusty chastised himself. "Yeah, yeah it is."

"Cool." Sam pulled the car into a parking lot that looked and smelled recently re-surfaced. "Well, this is the Firehouse."

Rusty opened the door, pulling his backpack out as he got out. He closed the door behind him, and the window lowered. Rusty leaned over and peered back in. "Thanks for the ride, man."

"Shit, thanks for the save, dude," Sam chuckled. He opened his glove box and dug through the crap in there. He pulled out a napkin and old sharpie and with square, blocky handwriting, wrote a phone number and then his name at the bottom. "If you're going to be in town, and want to grab a meal or hang out or something, give me a call, yeah? I'm sure my girlfriend would love to meet you."

Rusty smiled and stowed the napkin in a side pocket of his backpack. "Sure thing, man. Thanks again." He watched as Sam pulled back out of the parking lot and drove back towards Boulder City.

CHAPTER NINE

Boulder City, Nevada
May 5, 2013

When he walked into the Firehouse, there were already a few customers seated at tables. Folks on their way to early jobs, for the most part, and they ate with the speed of people watching the minute hand tick past. The Firehouse was a good place for this sort of crew, Rusty thought. Though it was your average greasy spoon, they were fast and efficient. He'd been here once before, hanging around mornings and evenings for the research on his final paper last semester, and he'd gotten to like the place.

He glanced at the clock above the bar. Not quite 6:30 a.m. Perfect. Maisey, the blonde, round waitress behind the counter, smiled at him casually, the glance someone with years of customer service gives a newly-entered patron, and then did a double-take. She barked a laugh and rested her hands on her ample hips for a moment. "Well, I'll be." She smiled, waving him over to the abandoned front counter, its row of stools bolted to the tile floor. She poured him a coffee. "If that isn't my boy Rusty."

"Hey, Maisey." Rusty upended the sugar canister over the mug and glanced at the time again.

"He won't be in for another ten minutes or so," said Maisey. "You want your usual?"

"Yes, ma'am." Though he'd only been in the area for a week last time he was here, he'd eaten nearly every meal here.

Maisey bragged that she never forgot a face and or the order that went with that face, and quickly proved it. "Chuck!" she called out, sliding a hastily-scribbled ticket across the hot-shelf at the old ragged cook who squinted up at her from the grill. "New Mexico scramble, no onions, add salsa. Biscuits instead of toast."

She arched an eyebrow at him, and Rusty couldn't help but laugh. Truth be told, he understood why the man he was looking for came in here. It was a simple place, one that did its best to evoke an old-timey atmosphere when people knew each other, noticed each other. Rusty had no doubt that alone held an appeal to the gentleman he was hunting.

He didn't have to wait for the full ten minutes. The mirror behind the counter gave Rusty a great view of the front door, and at 6:24, the doors opened and in he walked. Rusty couldn't help but admire the figure he cut. He was tall, with a full head of dark hair that was only now starting to go grey at the temples. His face was lined from too many years in the sun, and he'd grown a goatee with a sprinkling of salt among the pepper. Those deep green eyes—so intense they never failed to make Rusty catch his breath—glanced around the room negligently. His shoulders were broad, and his build was thick and sculpted, like the Platonic ideal of a strong man. He wore a thin cotton button-up shirt tucked into the wide-belted waist of his clean but well-worn blue jeans, the cuffs of which neatly covered the top of his steel-toed workman boots.

For a moment, Rusty thought the man was going to walk right past him, but sure enough, he slid into the stool next to Rusty at the counter like that was where he'd been heading the entire time. "Rusty," the man said by way of greeting. He nodded to Maisey and nodded as she gestured at him with the coffee pot from halfway across the room. Only then did he turn to Rusty. "I thought I asked you not to come back here, kid."

"Look, Sentinel, I know, and I–"

"I also asked you not to call me that. You're a pretty terrible listener, all things considered."

Rusty barked a laugh and held up his hands in admission of this bit of truth. "I know, I do know. Sorry. *Mitch*." He couldn't keep the hint of sarcasm out of his voice. "But in my defense, Mitch is a stupid cover name." Rusty shrugged as Maisey set a mug of coffee in front of Mitch and topped off Rusty's.

"It's Mitchell. And it's my middle name." He took a sip of the coffee, straight up. Rusty shuddered—black coffee, no cream and no sugar, was part of his definition of what it must be like to hate the world so much that you had to make some of the best things in it terrible.

As though reading his mind, Mitch snorted and took another sip. As an act of rebellion against a world of black, bitter coffee, Rusty dumped more sugar into his drink. *Heaps* of sugar. Mitch shot him a fond glance, smiling behind his coffee cup. "It's good to see you, kid. Thanks for sending me a copy of that paper."

"Definitely," Rusty said, grinning. "Did you read it?"

"I did. Didn't understand most of it."

Rusty side-eyed him. "Bullshit. You're like three times as intelligent as I am. I know you get used to playing dumb blue-collar grunt, but c'mon."

The older man grunted, the closest he ever got to a laugh. "Alright. I think your conclusions were a bit biased, at least. You were reading into me what you wanted to get out of your topic, and you conveniently ignored the parts that didn't match up to it."

Rusty mulled that over as Maisey set his plate down, reassuring Mitch that his usual was coming up. "Yeah, well, you suck. Forget what I said earlier—I prefer it when you're acting dumb." He dug into his food.

"Professor said the same thing, huh?"

"Almost word for word!" Rusty exclaimed, throwing down his fork in exasperation. "How did you know that? Are you a telepath now, too?"

"Quiet down with all that," Mitch growled, not turning to face him, but narrowing his eyes dangerously at the younger man in the mirror. "I've told you. You're the only one who knows me like that here, and I'd like to keep it that way. If you can't respect that, I'm happy to let you finish your meal from across the room, and let that be the last we have to say to one another."

"Okay, okay. I'm sorry. Not trying to be a dick, I just don't think of you as a normal guy."

"That's the problem, Rusty. Once they know who I am, no one else can, either. And right now, I…I just need normal guy, okay?"

Maisey set a wide platter of food in front of Mitch, refilling his coffee. She winked, smiled her most winning smile at him, and walked away with an extra swing in her step. She had the look of someone who was crushing on Mr. Working Man here, and probably had been for a long time. Not that Mitch was anything but oblivious, most likely—or at least, that's what he pretended to be. Rusty's time out here last time made him perfectly cognizant of just how aware the older man was.

But then, even in a world populated (however sparsely) by superpowered freaks, the Originals were something special. They were the first, of course, and were still the most powerful. The sudden storm of terror that grew up around the appearance of their power in late April of 1974 left its mark on history as surely as any other major event in the last hundred years. Suddenly and overnight, the world woke up to strange reports from all over the globe of weird phenomena. For a few days, the stories were dismissed as hoaxes, the use of hallucinogenic chemical warfare, attributed to miracles or supernatural origins and any number of things other than what they were.

It didn't take long for the truth to come out, though. By early May, all everyone was talking about were the "Changed," as the Western media started calling them. Reports came in from all over the world, revealing others had undergone similar transformations. In all, the media spoke of almost a dozen such individuals; history would remember there being twenty-two of them in all.

Now they were simply called the Originals, and given almost urban-legend status. Though a handful of them had gathered to form an honest-to-God superhero team who called themselves the Champions in the mid-'80s, it was the most public any of the Originals had ever been. When the Champions broke up in the early '90s—a result of ideological and political conflicts within its membership—most of them withdrew from public life. Several of them simply left for less developed parts of the world, to help shape societies they wanted to see exist, or to simply use their abilities to help societies get a leg up against the exploitation of the so-called First World.

Others founded companies or organizations where they felt they could contribute the best part of their talents to the betterment of the world (and their own bank accounts, occasionally). Others, like Sentinel—the man who sat next to him enjoying a farm-boy's breakfast—simply disappeared. Conspiracy theorists love to talk about where they might have gone, particularly since the advent of the internet. If their stories were to be believed, they'd simultaneously taken over the governments of the world, founded elite terrorist organizations, transcended to another level of existence, gone into exile to seek spiritual evolution, and a whole bunch of other crap.

Rusty was pretty sure no one assumed that even one of them was now working in construction.

Not that he blamed him. Even without the research he'd done, Rusty knew that the member of the Champions who used to be called Sentinel had been through a lot. Lots of historians said that his coming out was the first step towards the dissolution of the Champions, and it always sounded to Rusty like people were bitter about that. Even to him as a kid, it had seemed stupid and unfair that despite the development of superpowered people in the real world, there had only ever been one team of actual superheroes. Of course, people who said that were missing the fact that it wasn't Sentinel's coming out of the closet that undid the Champions. It was the death of Radiant.

Radiant had always been one of the most popular members of the Champions. He was handsome and charming, with a roguish attitude that made people think of that bad boy they knew in high school with the heart of gold that everyone was sure he had. He loved giving interviews and the camera worshipped him. In many ways, he was the lifeblood of the Champions' public image. Sentinel came off as a bit dour and holier-than-thou for the '80s, an old-fashioned boy scout that no one could really measure up to. Marque was all military, from the cut of his team uniform to the buzz-cut, to say nothing of acting as the main point of contact between the Department of Justice and the team. Alchemy was too smart, really. He intimidated people to the extent that it was rumored his actual power was super-intelligence, though everyone today knew that no one had yet manifested any kind of boosted intelligence. Dryad seemed distracted half the time and intent on castigating society for the environmental damage they caused the other half. Of them all, Cobalt came the closest to being the team's media darling alongside Radiant, and Rusty suspected that was because she was only too happy to play up the superheroine-in-revealing-garb angle. To be fair, she routinely shredded uniforms that constricted her too much when she assumed her metallic form—but even Sentinel had said that she was good at turning a limitation into an advantage.

Still, Radiant was the face for the team, and the one who withstood the most public scrutiny, which was why he and Sentinel had been very, very careful to never reveal their relationship to their teammates. Radiant earned himself a notorious reputation as a womanizer, being seen at the grand openings of big night clubs and dating one Hollywood starlet after the next. In contrast, everyone knew Sentinel was a stick-in-the-mud, a rancher's kid from Montana, raised Methodist, the favorite hero of that portion of the country that needed higher moral fiber in its heroes.

They got it from Sentinel in spades. But even the junkies and party-goers couldn't help but respect Sentinel, whose morals and ethics were as invulnerable as his heavily-muscled form. He was the team's moral compass, and the one who insisted that innocent bystanders be rescued first, and that killing wasn't something heroes ever did, no matter how despicable their foe. Hell, it might have been better if there *had* been some hint of impropriety between the two. Some idea, some juicy rumor for the tabloids to speculate on. But there wasn't, which was why no one could really understand why Sentinel fell apart when Radiant was killed in the early '90s in battle with the woman who called herself Mata Hari, another of the Originals.

Bereaved and inconsolable, Sentinel came out on national television during an interview with the journalist Miriam Land, expressing his regret that he and Radiant were forced to live in such isolation and fear. Though his request for a life of dignity for gay men and women became a powerful weapon for gay rights activists in the Western world, there were just as many who refused to believe him. He was accused of besmirching the reputation of a dead man who couldn't defend himself, of projecting his unrequited love into a fantasy to suit his own political agenda.

Sentinel might have withstood such an onslaught any other time, but he was grieving. Worse still, rather than rallying to his side, the Champions cracked from within under the weight of the examination of the scandalized public. Alchemy and Marque nearly came to blows over Marque's vehement homophobia and outright rejection of Sentinel as a friend and teammate. Cobalt, who had always fought rumors that she was a lesbian, took pains to distance herself from the Champions, eventually becoming the first of its members to quit, followed by Marque. Dryad disappeared one day as well; rumors said she'd wept terribly during the entire ordeal of infighting, eventually fleeing for the sanctuary of the temperate rainforests of the Pacific Northwest.

In the span of a year, the Champions went from the premier defenders of Western society to completely disbanded. Sentinel did his best to try to find a purpose for himself in its aftermath, taking up work with the Golden Cross until their religious backers threatened to withdraw support if they didn't disassociate the organization from working with him. He volunteered for a short while with a handful of gay rights organizations, but when the help they seemed to need from him involved dredging up his relationship with the now-dead love of his life over and over, he quit working with them and vanished entirely.

Rusty had found Sentinel through Deosil. He knew they'd met when she was working during a hurricane in the South at some point. She hadn't even known Sentinel was there until he suddenly was, and he'd gotten her out of a situation that could have killed her. After she and Rusty had been friends for a year or so, she mentioned knowing Sentinel and offered to introduce them. A year and a paper discussing the Changed as the movers and shakers in popular culture later, here they were, Sentinel calling himself by his middle name while working on the refurbishments of the Hoover Dam, an anonymous grunt laborer for a contractor that was—if you followed the corporate shell game—owned by his old teammate Alchemy.

"Look, I'm sorry, man," said Rusty. "It's shitty of me to just show up like this and act like an asshole. You've been a better friend to me than that."

Mitch shook his head and chuckled. Catching the young man's eyes in the mirror in front of them, he smiled that dimpled smile of his, the one that made Rusty's belly flip-flop. "Has anyone ever told you that you curse way too much?" Mitch laid a hand on the redhead's shoulder. All forgiven, then.

Rusty roared with laughter. "Oh, man. You and my mom, yeah."

The two went back to eating their breakfast. Eventually Mitch waved away the offer of a fourth cup of coffee. He turned in his seat to regard Rusty. "Alright. So. Why are you here? I know you didn't ride another Greyhound all this way just to pay a social visit, and I've got to get to work soon."

"Well, not exactly the Greyhound. I rode the train tracks."

"You took a train out here? There aren't any passenger trains that—ah. Not the train. The tracks. Good lord, Rusty." Mitch shook his head, but his dimples—Jesus, those dimples—showed his amusement at the idea.

"So, the thing is, I'm not sure it's something we can discuss here, Mitch," Rusty said, his look pointed. "I mean, I know you've got to get to work and all, but do you think you'd have some time to chat afterward?"

Mitch regarded Rusty thoughtfully, scratching the rough goatee on his chin. "Do you have a room in town?"

"I don't, no. The thing is–"

Thankfully, Mitch interrupted him. Rusty was grateful Mitch knew he was perpetually broke, despite having a rich dad who paid for his education (but not much else). "Alright, here," he said, fishing his keys out of his pocket. He unthreaded one key from the ring and held it out, point up. "Let's get you over to my place and get you a shower and some rest. You seem like you could use both. I'll grab some Chinese on the way home tonight, and we can talk about it. Will that work?"

"Definitely. Thanks, Mitch. You know I appreciate it."

"Sure, sure, kid. Just don't make a mess. Come on—I've got just enough time to drop you by there and still make it into work on time."

The big lug wouldn't even let Rusty pay for his own breakfast.

* * *

Mitch's apartment was right at the edge of Boulder City, not more than three miles from the cafe. It was pretty plain. Three rooms, basically: a living room/kitchen combo, a bedroom, and a bathroom. The living area had a single recliner, no sofa or any other furniture that suggested a social life. A couple of well-stocked bookshelves, including one where a television ought to be. Mitch was a big reader, Rusty recalled, with a huge variety of interests. Classical literature shared shelf space with Reader's Digests, textbooks covering a bewildering array of subjects, and along the lowest shelf a complete collection of leather-bound Encyclopedia Britannica.

He had a CD player—a bit beat-up, probably purchased from a pawn shop—and a small stack of CDs by people Rusty had never heard of. If he remembered correctly, it would be a mix of big brass bands, jazz, and classical music, most of it without lyrics. Rusty flipped the switch over to the FM function and sure enough, nothing but static. Mitch avoided the general broadcast media. Originally out of pain and a desire to remain ignorant of what was being said about him, but these days more out of habit than anything else. No one was talking about Sentinel, Radiant or the Champions these days outside of history classes and Wikipedia.

His kitchen was tiny, but clearly stocked by someone who'd grown up on a ranch. A tiered wire basket of tomatoes, peppers and onions hung beside the stove, and a sack of potatoes rested on the floor beneath them. The air smelled strongly of citrus, and opening the refrigerator, Rusty found a big pitcher of lemonade cooling in there, waiting for Mitch's return.

Eggs, cheese, real butter, milk, a smaller carton of buttermilk—all kinds of the ingredients someone who actually cooked might use filled the fridge, with a small beef roast thawing in a bag in the bottom. No beer or other alcohol to be seen; hell, no soda, either, for that matter. Rusty poured himself a small glass of the lemonade and drank down the sweet-and-tart in a single gulp. He gave his glass a quick wipe down with the soapy sponge before rinsing it and setting it to dry in the rack beside the sink, taking care to be far neater than he ever was in his own dorm.

Rusty hefted his backpack and slowly walked through the rest of the one-bedroom apartment. The pictures on the wall were cheap prints, laminated rather than framed, and none were personal in any way, landscapes and photos of rural Americana, mostly. Rusty was sure it reminded Mitch of his roots without having to bear the pain of actual faces of old friends and estranged family. They used to call Sentinel "America's Favored Son" back in the days of the Champions, and they'd been right. He was a big Boy Scout, all "mom, baseball and apple pie" in a real way that you just didn't find any more. Rusty found himself tearing up to think that even though they'd turned their backs on him, Mitch had never turned his back on them and their legacy.

It was fucking unfair.

Shaking it off, Rusty found his way to the bathroom. He turned the hot water on and stripped, piling his dirty clothes nearby. Adjusting the temperature of the spray, he climbed in and dunked his head under the just-this-side-of-boiling water, vigorously washing the trail between Oregon and Nevada out of his hair and off his body. He soaped and scrubbed and rinsed and repeated, until he was good and clean. He thought idly about doing something else to help himself unwind, one hand almost unconsciously cupping himself. Spending time around Mitch did that to him—he didn't know if it was hero worship, or just the fact that the man who used to be Sentinel was still a stupidly hot, if older, guy in a rare all-American way or what. But he decided against it. It just seemed wrong, somehow, to masturbate to thoughts of the man in his own shower.

Rusty wasn't sure why—he didn't hesitate to stroke one out thinking of any of his other acquaintances he found casually attractive, or to celebrities. It was just different, somehow. Tacky.

Jesus Christ.

He finished up in the shower and twisted the knobs until the water ceased to spray, somewhat irritated. Obviously he was exhausted from riding the rails all night and needed some sleep. Wrapping a towel around himself, he found Mitch's bedroom. He grinned, thinking about the last time he'd been in here alone. He'd been intent on bursting the good-boy image Mitch had, and so he'd gone searching for the man's pornography while he'd run to the store. What guy didn't have porn, right?

Total bust.

The morning was proving to be a bit warm, so Rusty turned the bedside fan on. He draped his towel over one shoulder, letting the strong air play over his wet skin, sending goose-prickles up and down him. After a few moments, he scrubbed at his body vigorously with the towel before laying down on the bed. He just needed to lie there for a moment. He knew he ought to get some clothes on, but the air felt so good, he was content to just enjoy his rest for a few.

* * *

He woke groggy and confused, the light in the room shaded and sort of weird. He looked around, and found Mitch standing in the doorway. Realizing Rusty was awake, the older man quickly turned his head and cleared his throat. "Good morning," he quipped, and walked out of the room.

Starting, Rusty realized he was still lying on the man's bed naked. Oh, not just naked—sporting morning wood like nobody's business. Even though Mitch was no longer in the room, Rusty turned and covered himself up, feeling his flush reach his ears. *Goddamn it.* He sat up and found his backpack, putting his clothes on after yanking them out of his dusty bag as though they'd personally wronged him. By the time he was fully clothed again, he could smell the Chinese food from the other room.

He emerged from the room clutching his backpack. Mitch was sitting in his seat, dishing up from the little white folding boxes into a couple of bowls sitting on the small coffee table before him. He was very intent on what he was doing, not glancing up at Rusty as he walked into the room. Great. He'd embarrassed arguably one of the most powerful men in the world.

Rusty sat down cross-legged on the pillow on the other side of the table, and cleared his throat. "So, uh, sorry about that," he said. Idly, he noticed that there was a bottle of cold soda, the brand he preferred. *Huh. He remembered.* "I grabbed a shower, and then was just drying off. I didn't mean to nod off without—I mean, I didn't mean for you to—" Belatedly, Rusty realized the man was trembling with barely-contained mirth. "You asshole!" Rusty laughed, snatching the pillow out from under him to hurl at the bigger man. The pillow smacked Mitch with a *flumph* and that was all it took for the laughter to break loose. Mitch howled, leaning back in his seat.

The redhead waited impatiently. What the hell was he laughing at? Had he found something about Rusty's naked body funny? Did he think he was trying to seduce him, and that idea was somehow hilarious? What the *hell*, already? Belatedly, he realized there was a part of him that didn't care, because Sentinel was laughing, and given what he knew of the man that seemed awesome, no matter how personally humiliating the impetus.

After a moment or two, Mitch caught his breath, and wiped his eyes. "I'm sorry, Rusty. I shouldn't laugh, I know. You just looked so serious."

"Well, yeah." The younger man sighed, frustrated. "I mean, the first time we met, I totally threw myself at you like an asshole, and I just didn't want you to think that I was trying to, you know…"

"No, I do know. And I know you weren't." His dimpled smile was back, and Rusty *hated* how much better seeing it made him feel, even when he was pissed. "You just, if you'd seen what I saw, there was no doubt in my mind it wasn't an attempt to seduce me, alright?"

"Ah, Jesus," Rusty said, and buried his hands in his face, chuckling despite himself. After a moment, he sighed and glanced up. "I was drooling, wasn't I?"

"Like my pop's old basset hound." Mitch handed him a bowl of broccoli-and-beef with a couple of egg rolls on top. Rusty took it, his pride pricked, but still able to find the humor in it.

"And I'll have you know that you 'throwing' yourself at me was one of the best feelings I'd had in years," Mitch said after they'd both taken a couple of bites. Rusty arched an eyebrow at him, chewing. Mitch nodded, and held up a hand. "Don't get me wrong. I still don't think I could go there. I've been through too much and, well, you know all my reasons. But I'm human enough that a really attractive young man expressing interest in a man my age still feels good."

"Jesus, Mitch," Rusty said, after a swallow of his soda. "You say that like you're decrepit or something. You've got the Originals physiology, man. I know you're in your *sixties* and all, but you barely look like you've made it out of your early thirties, and that's only because of the salt-and-pepper. Did you know that medical researchers are estimating that the Originals probably have a two-hundred-year lifespan, and that you won't seem much older than your mid-thirties for *all* of it? You're going to still look as good as you do now when I'm the old decrepit one."

Mitch blinked at him and seemed to sober. He took a thoughtful bite of his food.

"Hey, c'mon, man." Rusty put down his bowl and scooted around the table to sit beside the older man's chair. He rested a familiar hand on Mitch's leg. "That's like a godsend for a gay man."

Mitch ruffled Rusty's coppery hair fondly. "I know. I just hadn't heard that. It's like, I can't help but think about what that life is going to be like for us, you know? The other Originals and I. All we'll have is each other after the first hundred years or so. A world full of people, but the only ones who really know you are a small handful of people that you can't escape from. Who remember every mistake you've made."

"Hey, man. People already have to deal with that. They're usually called 'family,' right?"

Mitch contemplated the idea as he ate, and Rusty did likewise, leaning back against the side of Mitch's recliner. Finishing up his bowl, he glanced around to find the older man regarding at him thoughtfully. "And just so you know," Rusty said, rising and dusting himself off. "That offer still stands. Any time."

This time it was Mitch's turn to flush a little, and he lost that faraway look. "Rusty, you know that…"

"No. Shut up." Rusty reached down and took Mitch's empty bowl. "I know all of your reasons. I'm the one who tried to find a way around them last time, remember? I understand. I'm just saying that if any of that ever changes, I'm not going to be changing my mind about this, that's all. I'm going to put these in the sink."

Grateful for the quick excuse, Rusty exited to the kitchenette and spent a few moments changing out the once-soapy water for some fresh hot water, and then washing the bowls. On some level, he'd forgotten how being around Mitch made him feel. He hated that he felt like he was constantly throwing himself at the man who'd made his lack of interest clear. But it felt like he had no choice—like feeling like a fool constantly was worse than the idea that Mitch might ever be interested and think that Rusty no longer was. Finishing up the few quick dishes, Rusty washed his hands and walked back into the living room, drying his hands on a kitchen towel.

Mitch glanced up at him, flipping through his CDs. "Thanks for taking care of those."

"No problem. Seems only fair after you letting me crash here for the day and all. Plus, you know, breakfast and dinner."

Mitch set the stack of CD cases down, holding one of them. He flipped it open and carefully lifted it out of its case and into the open CD player. A button-click later, orchestral strings started to play. The older man glanced across the room at Rusty and smiled. The redhead smiled back. "So," Mitch said, returning to his seat. "What was it you wanted to talk about that we couldn't discuss in the cafe?"

Rusty resumed his cross-legged seat and took a swig of his soda. "I've got this friend named Kosma. He's this Ukrainian kid—really nice guy, a total sweetheart. Wicked cute, too. He's studying to be an architect, like I am. So the thing is, Kosma has gone missing. Just sort of disappeared. At first I figured he just got really busy or whatever. But someone posted something to the Facebook group I met him on that the police were searching for him and his friend Oleksander. But those friends said the police weren't looking too hard at all, because Kosma and Oleksander were pretty publicly gay."

Mitch furrowed his brow. "Alright, go on."

"So, I started talking to that friend of theirs, Kilina, and she said that lots of the people in the gay community there were worried that some of the crap that's been happening in Russia had spread to Ukraine, too."

"Wait," Mitch said, holding up a hand. "What crap in Russia?"

Rusty sighed. "I swear to God, Mitch, I'm getting you a newspaper subscription. So, over the past year and a half or so—almost two years now, I guess—there's been a shit-ton of anti-gay sentiment in Russia. Like, they passed a bunch of shitty laws saying that gays could never adopt, that gays couldn't have any kind of civil or legal connection to each other, making it illegal for teachers to 'teach about' homosexuality, shit like that."

Mitch shook his head. "Assholes."

"Well, it gets worse. So, right at about the same time, these groups of skin-heads and other punks started hunting down gays there. Like, going out of their way to bust up gay bars, and hunt down individuals and beat the shit out of them. Really horrible bashing stuff, too. The police, of course, not only ignored them but sort of unofficially encouraged them.

"Then, it got really bad. They started doing stuff like kidnapping gays and trans people and filming them while they tortured them, then posting those videos on the Internet. Mitch, there's videos of these motherfuckers raping some of these people with bottles."

He hated seeing Mitch's reaction. The older man paled visibly, and turned away as though he couldn't quite grasp the horror in Rusty's description. But on the other hand, Rusty was gratified, because when he turned back to him, the anger in the set of his jaw wasn't Mitch.

That was pure Sentinel.

"And you're afraid this has happened to your friend?"

"I am."

"And you're planning on going there, aren't you?" It wasn't really a question. Rusty met his eyes. "I am. And I'd like you to fly me over."

Mitch frowned.

"Look, you don't even need to stay or anything. I just, you know how hard the DTPA makes it for us to travel out of the country. I can't wait the weeks it would take to get the okay."

"Rusty, you can't do this," Mitch said. Even though he'd known to expect this, Mitch's tone pissed Rusty off. "It's illegal. Hell, it's more than illegal—it could cause an international incident. You can't just hare off and go vigilante even in the United States, man. You going to another country and doing it is worse! You need to leave it to the authorities there."

"Haven't you been listening?" Rusty's anger pushed him to his feet, and his volume rose with him. "The authorities don't fucking give a *damn* that they're torturing and possibly killing queer kids, Mitch. Do you have any idea how many of these kids just disappear *entirely*?"

"Hey, lower your voice." Mitch hissed. "I've got neighbors."

"*Fuck* your neighbors, Mitch." Nonetheless, he lowered his volume, and ran his hands over his face and through his hair. Mitch couldn't miss the tears he was trying to surreptitiously wipe away. "I'm sorry. IMitch, they're torturing and killing gay kids over there, and *nobody* gives a damn. Nobody is doing *anything*. These are all young people—teens, and people my age—who are trying to push their society the way *you* helped push ours. Don't you see that? But they don't have super-strength or invulnerability, Mitch. No one could step up to you when you came out, but these kids don't have that. All they have is each other and a whole lot of bravery. And they're *dying* because of it."

His lower lip trembling, Rusty crossed to the window that looked out on the parking lot, his hand over his face. Though trying his best to contain it, the tears ran down his face.

A moment later, Mitch wrapped those big arms of his around Rusty. The younger man turned and buried his face in Mitch's neck and wept. For a moment, he could imagine what life might be like to have someone to hold him like this – hell, not someone. To have *Mitch* hold him like this. He let himself unwind in his arms, and find a little comfort.

But not for long.

"Sorry," he said. "Thanks. It's just, you don't know what it was like, Mitch. I'm not trying to make light or diminish or whatever the horrible experience you had coming out, but you came out as an adult. One of the Originals. I know what it's like to be just a stupid, normal kid who comes out. Like, the only reason I was on the oil rig—the Gulf Event, the one where I got my powers—was because I'd come out to my dad recently because I kept getting beat up in school. I was fifteen and he wanted to toughen me up. To see how 'real men' lived and worked, or some bullshit. I don't really know."

Still silent, Mitch cupped his hands over both sides of Rusty's jaw, placing his hands on either side of his face and lifted his gaze up to his own eerily green eyes. Rusty hadn't even been aware that he'd been avoiding his eyes, and the simple gesture almost made him cry again.

Mitch's response was simple, his eyes shaded in equal parts sadness and that steely refusal to accept injustice that for a generation defined the hero called Sentinel.

"So, let's go find them."

CHAPTER TEN

Boulder City, Nevada to Portland, Oregon
May 5, 2013

"Alright, I think I'm ready to go." Mitch wore a thick hoodie, zipped up to his throat, and a backpack slung over one shoulder. He patted himself down, checking his pockets—wallet, keys, that sort of thing, all there—while Rusty buttoned up his knee-length bridge coat. Surreptitiously, he noted that Mitch was fidgeting, continually tugging at the zipper of his hoodie, smoothing it down, and shifting his backpack around.

Rusty abruptly stopped what he was doing. "Oh my God," he said. "You're wearing it, aren't you?" Mitch—the man who bore the dubious honor of being one of the most powerful men in the world, a man in his sixties, a man who'd saved thousands of lives in his ten-year time as an honest-to-God superhero—blushed like an adolescent and looked away. Rusty dropped his bag, his coat hanging half-open and forgotten. He crossed to Mitch slowly, like he was approaching a skittish animal. Mitch glanced up as he did so, warily.

"Can...can I see it?"

Mitch pondered for a moment, and then nodded, a quick jerky motion. With one hand he grasped the bottom of his hoodie, and with his other, he unzipped it.

The hoodie parted down the middle, and Rusty caught his breath. Lines of deep navy blue and brilliant white clung to Mitch's tightly muscled torso.

They delineated the almost inhuman curve and valley of muscle that made up his broad chest, swooping tightly down to his ridged belly and then…

Rusty quickly lifted his eyes, but Mitch hadn't noticed. He was looking away, over Rusty's shoulder, biting on the inside of his cheek.

"Hey," Rusty said gently. "Are you alright?"

Mitch closed his eyes and made a sound like he was swallowing tears. "That look scares me, Rusty."

"Uh, what? I mean, I'm sorry, I didn't–"

"No, no. Not you specifically," Mitch said. "In general. People get this *look* when they see the uniform, you know?"

"It's hard not to, man." Rusty shook his head, hardly believing he was seeing it in person. The thought that Mitch might still have it had never occurred to him. He took a step closer and raised his hand hesitantly, then glanced up at Mitch. "Do you mind…?"

The bigger man considered for a moment, then shook his head. Rusty reached out and touched him, laying his hand—just the tips of his fingers, really, splayed out like he was trying to encompass as much of it as he could—in the center of Mitch's torso. The material was tough, denser than he'd thought it would be. He traced the lines of blue and white, thinking of how many times he had, as a kid, traced those same lines on action figures, photos, comic books.

Sentinel. Right here, in front of him. *Sentinel.*

"That's the look that scares me most," Mitch whispered. Rusty shifted his gaze back into Mitch's face and pressed the whole of his hand against the man's wide chest, a gesture to steady and support. Mitch looked away from Rusty and went on. "It's the look that says people *need* me. That they want to put their safety in my hands, but not just that: they want me to be a container that holds their ideas about justice, about power, about responsibility. I'm not big enough to contain all of that, Rusty."

"Hey." Rusty caught his eyes, and tried not to note the tears there. "You listen to me. You don't owe people that. My sociology professors say we live in a 'post-superheroic world,' whatever that means. And I'm going to be honest with you: people looked at you like that because you already did all of those things. It wasn't something you had to set out to do—you just did them, Mitch. You weren't a hero because you set out to try and be—you just *are.*"

And just like that, Mitch was all around him, wrapping him in those big arms and squeezing. He laid his cheek against the top of Rusty's head and rested there. Rusty's arms were wrapped as far around the big man's torso as he could get them, under the open hoodie. They stood there for a few heartbeats, just breathing.

Finally, after a moment, Mitch kissed the younger man on the forehead and stepped back, glancing down at the space between them. Rusty was altogether too aware of the effects that sudden, wonderful closeness had on his goddamned pants.

"I much prefer that look," Mitch said, a wicked gleam in his eye, and let him go.

Rusty's face burned, and he barked a laugh. "Asshole," he said. Mitch laughed and zipped his hoodie back up. Both of them picked up their packs.

"Ready to do this?" Mitch asked. "I'm going to tell you right now—flying is cold as *hell*." Something leaped in Rusty's chest, and he was twelve again. Cold be damned—he was going flying with *Sentinel*. He nodded, and they walked out the door, shutting and locking it behind them.

* * *

They kept the Rockies to their left for most of the flight. Initially, it was awesome. All that crazy magical shit Rusty thought it would be. Tucked tight into Mitch's arms, their bodies pressed together, soaring over the world. For the first fifteen minutes or so, Rusty had a hard-on that wouldn't quit, and though he would have denied it, totally took the opportunity to grab on tight to the big man's frame.

If he was a creeper for the first part of the trip, he considered the unpleasantness of the last part of it to more than make up for it. He was glad he'd brought goggles and a coat. Admittedly, they were going fast. The Rockies and the desire to avoid being seen from the ground forced them higher than he'd assumed they would need to ride.

Still, even if he'd known, it wouldn't have prepared Rusty for just how bone-chillingly *cold* the trip was. He'd also had this idea that they'd be able to chat along the way—kind of like snuggling and whispering with someone you were really into, only just slightly below the speed of sound, right? Not so much.

Even with the telekinetic field Mitch extended over them both in flight, there was no sound but the roar of the wind. By the halfway point, Rusty was basically curled up against Mitch, burying his head in the bigger man's neck, shutting his eyes as tightly as he could and hoping desperately for an end to the flight.

He blinked his eyes open as he felt them slowing. Below was a vast swath of rocky terrain, covered in patches of vegetation colored grey-green by the dim moonlight. They were miles and miles from any settlements, from the total lack of lights in any direction, except for a few tiny roaming pinpoints that it took Rusty a minute or two to identify as cars on a distant road.

They'd slowed down significantly, and seemed to be circling slightly, dropping in altitude. "Wh-what's wrong?" Rusty asked through chattering teeth.

Mitch smiled at him. "Nothing. Let's take a break for a moment." Spotting a low point in the terrain, Mitch descended smoothly toward it. It was a precision that only telekinetics in flight could manage. Gently, he set them both down, but retained his grip while Rusty found his legs again. However long they'd been aloft had been enough, Rusty could barely feel his legs, and his muscles ached from clutching Mitch so tightly. He rubbed his shoulders and stomped his legs, coaxing feeling and warmth back into this body.

He glanced over at Mitch, who simply smiled at him. "God, you don't even feel that, do you?"

"It's part of why I wore the suit," Mitch said with a shrug. He found a large, flat boulder and leaned against it, unzipping his hoodie. "It retains warmth pretty well."

Rusty snorted, and walked around the clearing a bit, gazing off into the distance with his hands shoved into his pockets. After watching him for a moment or two, Mitch started digging through his bag, hauling out a bottle of water and a couple of energy bars. "Hey," he said, tossing them to Rusty, who caught them gratefully and dug in.

"It is not just the suit," Rusty accused him, chewing the last of one of the bars, and unwrapping the other. "It's the Originals physiology, isn't it?"

Mitch nodded absentmindedly. "It is, yeah. The first couple years after the Shift, they did so damned much testing to see what our limits were. At first, it was hard to separate what our individual powers were, and what were just part of the changes that happened to us all. Last time I talked to them, the full extent of their findings were still considered a national secret."

"Really?" Rusty was intrigued, the power bar in his hands forgotten. "I mean, we all know that you stay super-healthy, and it's become obvious that you guys don't age the way everyone else does. What else is there?"

"Lots of stuff, actually," Mitch said. He dug another energy bar out of his bag and opened it, peeling back the crinkly wrapping and taking a bite out of it. He chewed thoughtfully while Rusty joined him up against the boulder. Mitch gestured with the power bar. "Food and water, for instance. As part of the initial testing, they checked to see how long we could go without it."

"Yeah? Long time?"

"Two weeks without water. Close to two months without food."

Rusty goggled. "What?! Are you kidding me? You *starved* for them?"

Mitch grinned and shook his head. "Don't get me wrong—it was terrible. More like torture than testing. Horrible hunger pangs, an overwhelming thirst. But none of us started to even show the first signs of deprivation until about the midway point. Metabolism slows way down, and by the end of the testing period we were sleeping between twelve and eighteen hours a day. The docs said they thought we could have probably gone longer than that, too."

"That's insane. What else?" Rusty polished off the energy bar and washed it down with a swig of water. Only about half of it was unfrozen, and it was teeth-achingly cold.

"Lots of weird little stuff. Better-than-average senses. Most of us can hear stuff going on for blocks around us with no effort, and a little farther than that by concentrating. Our bodies—bone, muscle, skin—it's all denser than other people's. Even without my telekinetic shielding, it takes a hit from a professional fighter or someone using a weapon to really injure me. Still hurts, but actual injury is hard unless they're really strong, really skilled or really lucky."

Rusty shook his head and grinned. It was pretty obvious that Rusty loved this kind of thing, and for some reason, Mitch liked being able to share it with someone. "Healing, too. I haven't been sick since the Shift, and I heal injuries really fast. I mean, not like some 'heal while you watch' kind of thing. Just a much faster recovery—a wound that might lay a guy out for a week getting better would only put me out of commission for two or three days at most. We can push through the sorts of injuries that send other people into shock, too."

He reached over to Rusty and took the bottle from him, taking a sip of it himself. He started to take another, but paused, bottle halfway to his mouth. "You guys—Echoes, I mean—must have something like that, too, though, right? I mean, maybe not to the degree we do, but something?"

"No way. I wish. No, we're basically totally regular, except for our specific powers. Heck, I've even heard of people who have a power but whose bodies aren't adapted to help them survive that power. That's actually the reason why at any Echo Event, there's often one or two who gain powers but don't survive. They get a power that kills them."

Mitch furrowed his brow. "That's horrible."

They sat there in awkward silence for a moment. "Thanks for stopping and letting me warm up a bit. I don't think I realized how cold it would be. I might have to rethink this whole flying to the Ukraine thing." Rusty sounded worried.

"Maybe not," Mitch said, clapping a hand on the younger man's shoulder. "We'll be able to do some of our flying during the day, and stay lower near the surface of the sea. You'd be amazed how much difference that makes. Plus, you'll make sure to dress warmly for the trip. A bigger question, though—do you know what sort of measures the military has set up to detect fliers? In my day, they didn't have the technology to do so worth a damn, which was a big security concern. I haven't exactly kept up with that sort of thing, though they must have developed something like that by now, right? Do you know of anything?"

Rusty shook his head. "No, sorry. The DTPA and military keeps all of that kind of thing pretty strongly under wraps."

"Hmm. Damn it. I'd really rather not have to try to outrun fighter jets." He pondered for a few moments.

"I know someone who might know, actually," Rusty said. "I don't really like the guy at all, but do you know Optic?" Mitch shook his head. Not surprising—as big of a star as Optic was, it wasn't terribly likely that Super-Hermit had heard of him.

"He's a super. Not an Echo, though—he's Empowered. Some USAF-backed project of some kind *gave* him his powers. He's a photoassumptive but not a photogenerative." Mitch just gave him a look. One of those patented *what the hell?* looks. Rusty chuckled. "So, the DTPA loves its words. I think they probably employ half the English majors in the United States. Let me see if I can remember. Kinetics are people who can control stuff, Generators can create it, and Assumptives are people who become it. They have another word for people who completely become something else, but I don't remember that one. So, they add a prefix that says what the stuff is, and use one of those that says what they do with it. Optic can transform his body into light. So, he's a photoassumptive."

"Okay. So?"

"Oh. Yeah. So, anyway, he's kind of a big media figure—he's been in some action movies and stuff like that—but he used to be in part of the military that acts as first responders. They're all really fast fliers and they specialize in intercepting other fliers. But I figure, they have to find those other fliers somehow, right?"

"That makes sense, sure. You said you know this guy? Would he talk to us?"

"He's in Portland right now, filming a new movie. He doesn't exactly like me much, on account of the fact that I've basically got a big mouth and think he's sort of a douchey sell-out. But I bet he'd talk to you."

"Good at making friends, aren't you?" Mitch shook his head, smiling slightly. "Okay, then. We'll be getting back into Portland before sunrise. Let's head that way, shall we?" Rusty nodded and gathered up his stuff, stowing away the empty bottle and trashed wrappers in his backpack. He excused himself to take a quick leak and came back buttoning up his coat. "So, the airport is on the north side of town, out near the river that runs east-to-west."

"Gotcha, good to know. I meant to ask that, so I can avoid it. It's about the only time you encounter aircraft at the altitude we'll be flying," Mitch said. He stepped up and pulled Rusty close to him again. He smiled down at Rusty, who took a deep breath. "You know, you don't have to hang on to me as tightly as you have been. As long as you're in physical contact with me, my telekinetics will hold you safe."

"Oh." The redhead paused and met Mitch's green eyes again. "Maybe I just want to, though."

Mitch snorted, and shook his head. Rusty pulled in close to him, and despite all that, Mitch wrapped his arm tightly around the young man. They left the solid ground far below them once more.

* * *

The city was a blaze of light when they landed just south of Portland proper. I-5 roared with cars to their left, and the brilliance of the gas station that lay between them and the highway provided the perfect patch of darkness away from the road in which to make a covert touch-down.

"Ow, ow, ow," Rusty said, hopping slightly, favoring one of his legs.

Mitch shot him a sympathetic look. "Cramp?"

Rusty nodded, kneeling in the tall grass to massage his calf. "Man. This was not the superhero life I was imagining." Gingerly, he raised himself to his feet, extending his aching leg, flexing it back and forth to work out the kinks. Mitch just watched him with a bemused smile. "I must seem ridiculous to you, mister superhero," said Rusty.

"Not at all." Mitch shook his head and then glanced behind them. He seemed perpetually aware of his surroundings, always aware of little sounds, changes in air pressure and temperature, noticing the small visual changes in their environment. It was pretty cool. "I admit, I'm not accustomed to long-distance flying with someone who isn't an Original. I don't think I really appreciated how tough it must be on someone before now."

"Yeah, tell me about it." Rusty straightened and started the short walk to the back side of the gas station. "I'm sort of worried, actually. Not sure how we're going to make it across the freaking ocean."

"Well, we're here to get you some better travel clothing, first of all. Layers, most likely. I suggest we get you a wetsuit, for starters. It should help you retain heat the way my uniform does."

"Not necessary," the redhead said. "I've got one of the uniforms they give us at the DTPA Health Weekends. Based on some of the same technology yours is, only more mass-produced. Armored slightly, but also really, really warm. Should be perfect." Rusty chuckled. "You know, we always joke about costumes—sorry, uniforms—at the camps. *You're not a superhero til you've worn spandex.* That's the joke. Guess I'm about to become the real thing, huh?"

Mitch furrowed his brow. "It's not, it's not spandex," he said. Rusty laughed and stepped in front of him. He reached out and closed the distance between them, slipping his hands up under the bigger man's hoodie, and running it along the taut muscles of his torso, grinning up at Mitch the entire time. With a look of consternation, Mitch caught his wrists, and stepped back. "I'm sorry, Rusty. I'm just not…"

Rusty blushed, running a hand through this coppery hair. "Shit, sorry. I just got—it was the flying, and the being close to you. I kinda forgot myself."

Mitch tugged on the bottom of his hoodie, unconsciously smoothing it down. He mumbled something about it being no problem, but he was clearly upset. Not angry—just distressed a little. Embarrassed, it seemed like.

"Hey, I really am sorry. I didn't mean to be the asshole again." Rusty turned to stump through the tall, dry grass toward the gas station, walking like he could leave his embarrassment behind them. After a moment, Mitch caught up with him and matched his stride, and the two walked in silence to the gas station.

Rusty sighed to find that it was closed, a sigh that stretched out into a yawn. Man, he could use some caffeine. He turned to Mitch, standing in front of an old beat-up pay phone, digging through his pockets for change. "Sorry I fried my cell, Mitch."

Mitch glanced up at him and grinned, shaking his head. He ducked it once more, scanning the advertisements plastered along its side. Finally finding what he was after, he fed the machine some coins and dialed. "Hi, yes. I need a cab, please." He listened for a moment, then furrowed his brow. Glancing somewhat helplessly at Rusty, he covered the mouthpiece with one hand. "Uh, where are we?"

Rusty chuckled and walked over, gesturing for the phone. Mitch seemed inordinately grateful. The big man leaned against the phone as Rusty gave them their location, scuffing his work boots against the dingy sidewalk.

Finally, Rusty hung up the phone. "They'll be here in about twenty minutes or so." Mitch nodded, and sat down on the edge of the sidewalk. Rusty did likewise, glancing at him occasionally.

After the silence drew out as long as he could stand it, Rusty sighed and turned to face Mitch. "Look, this is making me crazy. I really am very sorry. That was totally inappropriate, and I just–"

"Hey, hey, no." Mitch held up his hands, imploring him to stop talking. Rusty gulped a breath and regarded him, waiting for him to talk.

Goddamn it, he *would not* cry.

"I'm not mad. Seriously, I meant what I said in Boulder City." Mitch tiptoed over his words, like he was unsure of what to say or how to say it. Finally, he took a deep breath. "It's that I feel guilty, Rusty. I feel terrible about this dynamic, you know? I meant what I said: you're really handsome, and anyone would feel lucky to have your attention. It's just that I'm kind of damaged goods."

He paused for a moment, his head bowed and facing away. He couldn't see them, but somehow Rusty just *knew* that he was hiding tears.

"I don't know who I am anymore. Who I'm meant to be. I get through it day by day, just get up, take care of work, go home and try to avoid any kind of emotional entanglements. It's been, Jesus, it's been *twenty years*, Rusty. Since that bitch Mata Hari killed Craig. And I'm not over it. I'm a long, long way from over it. Sometimes it feels like I died that day, too, as stupid and, I don't know, melodramatic as that sounds. It sits like a lead weight in my gut, Rusty, and I don't know how to make it go away."

He buried his face in his large hands, hiding shameful tears. His shoulders shook, and Rusty's heart broke. He hesitated for just a moment, but not much longer than that, before scooting closer to him and wrapping as much of his arms as he could around the man's hulking shoulders. With a desperate urgency, Mitch clutched at Rusty. And he wept.

His grief was like a storm—terrible, elemental, unexpected. Rusty could only hold onto him, not even trying to steady or comfort him. He knew the best he could do in the face of this was be an anchor, something to hold onto, and so that's what he did.

Which was just as well, really—he was pretty sure it was all he could have managed to do, the way he was feeling. Something shifted in Rusty, something intrinsic and so foundational that he couldn't have even identified it before now. For the entirety of his life, he'd *needed*. Needed someone to look up to, someone to rescue him. Someone to make the world better, to be a figure to remember and be inspired by when things were at their worst. But here, holding in his arms the weeping figure of his very first real hero, that changed.

"Hey," said Rusty. Mitch's weeping abated, and in the corner of his mind, Rusty was grateful for tardy cab drivers.

The bigger man took a big, shuddering breath, and chuckled a little. "Sorry," he said, shaking his head. "I told you. Damaged goods."

"Bullshit," Rusty said. "You're invulnerable, and super-strong, and you can fly. You're everybody's hero, Mitch. But you're still a normal guy, you know? You're still human. You're allowed to be vulnerable, you're allowed to be hurt, and you're allowed to grieve."

Mitch stared hard at him, then. Shit. Even though red and puffy, the man's green eyes were startling and powerful. Just then, headlights turned into the parking lot, briefly illuminating them. Rusty bounced to his feet and reached out his hands. Mitch took them and stood, nearly hauling Rusty down with the power of the pull.

"Jesus!" said Rusty. "I take it back. You're a goddamned ox."

They got into the cab, and Rusty gave the man an address. They'd only just merged onto I-5 heading into Portland when Mitch reached down and clasped Rusty's hand. The younger man turned and grinned, squeezing his hand.

CHAPTER ELEVEN

Portland, Oregon
May 6, 2013

It was still an hour or so before sunrise when the cab dropped them off on the campus of Portland State. Mitch paid the driver, who regarded him oddly, like she recognized him for a moment. She must not have placed his face, though; either that, or she elected to give him his privacy. Either way, Mitch was grateful. Rusty was standing on the sidewalk, fiddling with his destroyed phone with a sense of petulance. The sight amused Mitch to no end—kids these days couldn't resist constantly dinking with those damned things, even when they weren't working.

"You're not going to be able to get that thing going again, you know," he said, stepping up onto the curb as the taxi pulled away into the light early-morning downtown traffic.

Rusty shot him a glare both irritated and embarrassed. "*Pfft*. Says who? I can do some crazy shit with my powers." The redhead was playfully defiant. In one hand, he held up his phone in front of his face, and squinted at it, like he was concentrating at the rectangle of plastic, glass and metal before him.

Mitch watched him for a moment. "Mostly because if you could, you'd have done it before now." He shifted his bag to his other shoulder and grinned.

Rusty sighed and slipped it into his pocket. "Tell me about it. I *hate* being without a phone. Do you think we ought to get me another one really quickly before we go?"

Mitch shook his head. "I wouldn't. You can be tracked by phones these days."

Rusty rolled his eyes. "Did you learn that from watching literally any cop show in syndication?" he teased, and took the lead. Mitch snorted and followed him through an open space between two of the big, stone buildings that made up PSU's central campus. They passed through the breezeway and onto the wide park block that cut straight down the middle of the school. Rusty pointed ahead at the tall building that housed his dorm.

Mitch spoke up again. "Unless something has changed drastically, a lot of Eastern Europe maintains an organization called Vigilance. It's a paramilitary group funded by its member countries, with a small core of supers who act as its primary strike team. They respond to any reports of powered law-breaking or other trouble. They're pretty good trackers, too—in the Champions, we were pretty sure they had someone in their group who was either precognitive or possibly had some ability to detect the use of superpowers. Alchemy thought they might even just have someone who could detect people who possessed superpowers, without those powers being in use. Not sure."

"So we're going to have to be subtle."

"Yeah, until we can't be. Then, we're going to have to be *fast*." Mitch smiled. He couldn't miss the telltale gurgle of Rusty's stomach. He glanced down at the younger man's gut, which Rusty saw. The redhead slapped his hand over the offending belly, coloring quickly.

"Let's stop and grab something to eat first, why don't we?" Mitch said.

Rusty sighed. "Man, I can tell hanging around someone with super-hearing is going to get old fast." He led Mitch toward the small campus dining hall. It was a broad room, scattered with tables, and a double handful of various food franchises along the walls. Even at this hour, a handful of students and faculty wandered its length, scouting their breakfast options. The greatest number of them clustered around the two little coffee stands.

Rusty purchased a couple of breakfast tacos and a carton of orange juice from a Tex-Mex place while Mitch got them coffee. The bigger man was clearly uncomfortable, even in the dilute crowd of the early-morning dining area. He pulled the hood of his hoodie up and slouched while he waited. Even so, he couldn't help but draw attention—it's not often people see a man of about six and a half feet built like a professional bodybuilder.

When they met back up, Rusty smiled at Mitch, and elbowed him in the side. "You alright?"

The older man just nodded. "Yeah. I hate it. I feel like everyone is staring, and knows who I am. I know I'm being paranoid, but I can't help it."

"Well, they sort of are staring." Mitch snapped him a worried face, and Rusty winked at him. "You're going to have to accept the fact that you're a stone-cold hottie, man. I mean, if they recognized you, the reactions would be very different, you know? But you're just flat-out being checked out. Three-quarters of the women in here have given you the once-over like you wouldn't believe, and I'm pretty sure half that table of frat boys you passed on the way over here just gave some very serious consideration to that whole 'experimenting in college' thing."

Now it was Mitch's turn to blush, his neck and ears reddening. Goddamn, he was attractive, Rusty mused. Glancing around for a table, Rusty spied someone, and then turned back to Mitch.

"Hey, do you mind if I introduce you to someone? Like, introduce you as you? She won't draw attention to you or anything."

"Who is it?" Mitch said hesitantly. Rusty pointed with one corner of his food tray at a lady in her late 40s or so, sitting in a back corner near the door. She was dressed in a pant suit of charcoal grey, and a somewhat ratty coat hung over the back of her chair. She sat alone at her table, glancing down over the top of her glasses at the newspaper spread in front of her while she nibbled on a bagel.

"That's Professor James. She taught the class I wrote that paper for, the sociology one that was about superheroes and stuff. She's really helped me out a lot in the time I've been here—there aren't many people I can talk to about the crap that comes with being an Echo, but she's always been willing to listen."

Rusty watched Mitch consider, his expression warming as the younger man spoke. He nodded, and the two headed toward Professor James' table.

"Hey, Prof," Rusty said as they neared it. The academic smiled at the sight of the young redhead. "Mind if we join you?" The professor nodded, trying to swallow a mouthful of food, but gesturing for them to seat themselves.

"Professor Donna James," said Rusty, "this is–"

"Oh my God," the professor said, her hand half-extended toward Mitch and promptly forgotten. "Senti…er, Robert McCann, isn't it?"

Mitch seemed surprised and took the woman's hand gratefully. "Yeah. Yeah, it is. Though I just go by Mitch these days. Nice to meet you, professor."

"Good lord, please call me Donna." She grimaced at Rusty, who was having far too much fun watching her reaction. She turned back to Mitch. "It truly is an honor."

"Any friend of Rusty's, as they say," Mitch said. He sat down and popped the lid off his coffee. Black and bitter, Rusty noted. He hadn't even thought it was *possible* to find plain black coffee in Portland.

Professor James turned to regard the smirking Rusty. "You know, I admit, I only half believed you when you said that you knew Mr. McCann here. I mean, I had no doubt that you'd talked to him, but I assumed you'd just conducted a phone interview, or something. And yet, here you are."

"It's true," Mitch said. He reached up absentmindedly and scratched at his beard. "I'm a little surprised you recognized me, though. Most people don't, with the beard."

The professor smiled and shook her head. "Oh, it's not the beard, Mr. McCann. It's the lack of the costume. Studies have shown that when presented with iconic appearances that are easily identifiable—like your old uniform—most people don't actually register much of the actual appearance of the one wearing it, though they think they do."

Mitch's eyebrows arched. "Huh. Interesting. That still doesn't explain how you knew me, though. I'm curious what I'm doing to give it away."

"Oh, well. As to that." She paused. Rusty saw something strange there. Something he'd never seen before and didn't really have words to describe. She took a deep breath, and glanced around. They were still secluded. She exhaled with the finality of someone who'd made a decision. "I recognized you because I've seen your face before. In person, I mean." She glanced at Rusty, a glance that said she was about to go into personal things, and she was hesitant to do so around her student.

He stood suddenly. "So, I think I need to get–"

"No, no, Rusty. Please sit down. God knows you've shared enough about your personal life and difficulties with me." She regarded Mitch fondly, and then took a sip of her tea. "In 1992, there was an Echo Event, here in Portland.

In the Old Town district. You and…you and Radiant were in Seattle when it happened, and came immediately to help."

"Wait a minute," Rusty said. "You're the woman in the photo. The Old Town Rescue, right?"

She picked up her phone, flipping through its gallery until she found the photo. She slid the phone across the table to Mitch, who picked it up. His eyes lost their hard, stressed edge, and the wrinkles in his brow vanished. He stared at it, hard. After a few moments, Rusty realized there were tears in his eyes.

Professor James continued. "I lived here in Portland at the time, but my mother and my sister were visiting us. A for-the-girls sort of holiday, to celebrate my mother's fiftieth birthday. We were in Old Town when it happened."

She was now regarding Mitch with an almost teary-eyed fondness. He finally glanced up from the photo.

"I remember this. I remember *you*," he said in a grief-harshened voice.

She smiled at him. "There were these weird waves of force that kept rippling through the area. You couldn't see them, but you could see its effect on everything else—stone, trees, buildings. My God, I remember the *asphalt* was rippling in waves. Part of the street collapsed and caught me as my mother, sister and I were running—they were ahead of me, so they were fine, but they watched as the earth basically swallowed me up."

Her lower lip quivered, and she smiled. "But then there you were. Like some guardian angel, you literally dove out of the sky, and caught me before I could fall, and you bore me back up out of that sinkhole." She laughed a little then, and wiped at her eyes self-consciously. "I remember thinking, in that moment, that I'd never felt so safe in someone's arms. I also remember thinking how angry that made me, self-assured feminist that I am!"

Mitch looked away, suddenly uncomfortable. Professor James waited until he met her eyes again. "You never forget the face of the person who saves your life, Mr. McCann. Not ever. The man who saves your life and that of your mother and sister."

Rusty half-wished he had excused himself earlier. Mitch seemed so uncomfortable, but he could tell this was also an extremely important meeting to his professor.

"I know you've retreated from public life, and I know some of why from

Rusty's paper. More than anything, though, I just wanted to thank you for what you did."

Mitch's gaze dropped to the table in front of him, as though he were ashamed.

"Mr. McCann," Professor James said, reaching out and placing her hand over his. Mitch shifted and clutched her hand tightly, almost desperately. "You saved my life that day. I know you've lived a life where people expect things from you, and I don't wish to add to that burden. I pray that my gratitude comes across as simply that: gratitude. You did an amazing thing that day, and you changed my world for the better, and I shall never forget it. My family still talks about you as though you were a member of our little clan."

She smiled, and Mitch broke a little. He laughed, a quick chuckle, but tears overwhelmed him and he lowered his gaze, raising a hand to forehead to shield his reaction from anyone else in the room. Professor James smiled affectionately. "You are entitled to your privacy, Mr. McCann, and I hope you've found some peace. An act of bravery should carry with it no obligation or expectation of future acts. During your career, you saved thousands of lives. But even if you'd only ever saved one, that would have been one more than would have been saved without you there. So, thank you, from all of us."

Rusty laid a hand on his shoulder. Professor James seemed somewhat discomfited with Mitch's silence.

"Rusty, thank you for the introductions," she said, gathering up her things. "Mr. McCann, it was a singular pleasure. I hope my woolgathering hasn't upset you too much, and I hope you gentlemen have a fine day."

With that, she turned and walked out of the dining hall. Rusty sat quietly for a few moments, then bumped the bigger man's shoulder with his own. Green eyes turned to meet his, and Mitch smiled at him.

"Sorry," Rusty said. "I thought her interest in you was academic. If I'd known–"

"No, no. God, don't apologize." Mitch rubbed the edge of his hand over his eyes quickly, with a smile. "I think I kind of needed that, you know? I'd already been second-guessing my decision to go and do this, but that was exactly the right time for that. Message received." He covered Rusty's hand with his own and smiled warmly at the young man.

Don't get used to this, Rusty told himself as he felt a warm flush wash over him. It was an awesome, easy companionship, a sweet intimacy that he knew Mitch didn't have room for in his life long-term. Not really. But for right now? For right now he was going to enjoy it, and he smiled back at him.

"If you give me the address where they're shooting the movie, I can go down and meet up with Optic while you get ready," Mitch said, leaning back in his chair. The change of subject was obvious, but it was alright. He'd been through the emotional wringer the past couple of hours, and Rusty knew he was the kind of man that needed to *do* something, something useful, when he felt like that.

"Cool. That sounds like a plan," the redhead said, gathering up the remains of their breakfast. "I admit, I kinda wish that Deosil was available to come with us. I suspect this would be a lot easier with her help."

"Probably," Mitch agreed. "Although I'd have a tough time flying two people there."

"Fair point. She can fly, sometimes, but she can't get the distance and speed you can." He pushed the doors open and shoved his hands into his coat pockets. The two men paused outside of the dining hall. "So, see you back here in a couple of hours?"

"Let's call it noon, just in case I have a tough time getting to see him. He is a movie star, right?"

Rusty chuckled. "He is, yeah, but I'm going to say you probably won't have a lot of trouble seeing him." Rusty gave him the address for where the movie was being shot. The production needed lots of extras and hit up the university student population for a lot of them, so it was pretty well-known where they were filming for the couple weeks they were on-site. He also explained to Mitch how to get there from the university—it was a little over a mile away.

"Great. Easy to walk, then. I kinda wanted to see the city some," Mitch said, and turned to head off. Rusty watched him go with a weird ache in his belly and chest. He realized he really wanted to go with him, not because he relished the idea of seeing Optic again (frankly, he was good if they never laid eyes on one another again), but because he flat-out didn't want to be parted from Mitch.

"Jesus," he said, walking toward his dorm building. "You've got it bad, Rusty. Pathetic."

* * *

For a little while, Mitch watched the filming. It seemed weird to him: so many people, so much stress and so much money being spent, generally for just a few minutes of footage at a time. It seemed extravagant—maybe even a little wasteful—but there was still a kind of magic to it. He wore his hood up, but that wasn't unusual in Portland, he discovered—hoodies seemed to be the preferred outerwear here. He also slouched a little, and stood down on the street rather than up on the edge of the sidewalk with the rest of the gathered crowd behind the barrier constructed. Both helped disguise his height.

After maybe forty-five minutes of watching, he caught a glimpse of Optic. He was a tall African-American man, with a distinctive, frankly heroic-looking chin. He still had the demeanor of a career military man, and it was clear that the crowd loved him. A production assistant hung out near the assembled crowd, asking them to keep quiet while filming was in progress, handing out occasional "prizes" as incentives. They were choreographing a fight scene. It was obviously tedious work, shooting the same move over and over from different angles, using different combinations of actors and stunt men. Finally, after about an hour and a half, the director called a break.

"Excuse me," Mitch said to the production assistant. The young woman was chewing gum, and had a ring through one of her eyebrows. She was obviously listening intently to the massive set of headphones that covered her ears. For a moment, she ignored him, and Mitch thought she might not have heard him. Before he could repeat himself, she gave him an exasperated look.

"Yeah?" she said, pulling the small headphone mike away from her mouth.

"I'm an old friend of Optic's. Is there any way I can speak with him during this break? Or could you at least pass him a message from me?"

She regarded him dubiously. "Okay, no offense, but I'm pretty sure half the people in this crowd would love to chat with him, too. I can give your name to his assistant, and he'll pass it on."

Mitch paused and glanced around. Some of the people near him had taken an interest in what he was saying, and watched the exchange pretty closely. He sighed, and leaned in.

"Please, I'd like to keep this as private as possible." He all but whispered. "My name's Robert McCann."

She narrowed her eyes, like the name rang a bell, but she couldn't quite place it. Not terribly surprising—she was young, and it had been nearly twenty years since his real name was a household term. "Just a sec," she said, and stepped away from the crowd, ostensibly where he couldn't overhear her conversation. "Can I get Lincoln on the mike, please?" she said. She waited, surreptitiously fishing her smart phone out of her pocket.

Damn it.

With two hands, she typed something into the phone, glancing back at Mitch briefly. "Hey, Lincoln, I've got some guy who says he's an old friend of Optic's, and he'd like to see him? Yeah, says his name is Robert McCann." She stared at her phone, clearly waiting for it to do something. "No, I'm not sure why he is showing up here if he really does know him. He's kinda built, though. Maybe he's a military buddy or something that–"

She stopped speaking, staring down at her phone in near-shock. Slowly, she raised her head to regard Mitch, he mouth hanging open slightly. "Lincoln. Lincoln!" She all but yelled into the mike, and Mitch sighed, hoping she wasn't about to get loud. He shot her an imploring look.

"Dude!" she said. "I'm bringing him back. No, no—don't you know who Robert McCann is? I thought I recognized his name, and his face a little. I'm bringing him back. I'll tell you there." With a smile, she waved him over, and he crossed to her sheepishly. He glanced behind at the people in the crowd trying to figure out what was going on.

"Right this way, sir," she said, all professionalism in their earshot. She raised the barrier and waved him in, and then closed it up again. She turned back to the crowd. "The director called a break, so we're looking at about a half-hour or so before we get started again, everyone."

With that, the two of them walked away, heading for the cluster of trailers that occupied a small pay parking lot at the edge of the set. "I'm sorry to keep you like that. I should have recognized your name," she said.

A kind of kid's excitement brought the youth back to her face, he thought, and he smiled at her. "Honestly, I'd prefer that people forgot my name entirely. I grew out the beard for a reason. Thanks for being willing to listen anyway."

She winced as the headphones squawked in her ear, and she shoved the mike back in place. "Yes, Lincoln. That's exactly who it is. Now shut up about it, will you? Give the man some privacy. I'm bringing him over to Optic's trailer."

Toward the back of the parking lot, past a handful of other trailers, one was set apart with a security guard standing nearby. The big man clearly recognized the young woman walking next to Mitch, and he nodded as they walked past. She fished a set of keys out of her pocket, jingling them, and stepped up the short steps, unlocking the trailer.

The interior was frankly lavish, with plenty of room for relaxing in style. A large, seating area, finished in leather, was against one wall, curving around a coffee table next to it. Half of the table's surface was swiveled aside to reveal a cunningly crafted mini-bar inside.

A desk with a tall-backed chair was to his left, and opposite that desk was a couple of overstuffed chairs with a table between them. Beyond those was a door marked "Private" that led to the back half of the trailer. The young production assistant shoved her headphones down around her neck, and unconsciously smoothed back her hair. "My name's Olivia, by the way. It really is nice to meet you, Mr. McCann."

"Please, just call me Mitch," he said, stepping into the trailer. She gestured at one of the chairs near the desk, and he seated himself. Yes, just as comfortable as it looked. Nevertheless, he sat on the edge, leaning forward with his hands clasped in front of him.

"Can I get you something to drink? Wine, or beer?" Olivia said, the desire to ingratiate herself very strong in her delivery.

"Uh, it's a little early for me," Mitch said. "Thank you, though."

"Oh. Uh, yeah. I mean, of course it is. Sorry," she said, and then basically ran out of things to say. She glanced at the door, and then at him. "Make yourself comfortable. I'm sure Optic will be here shortly."

With that, she all but fled the trailer. Mitch felt bad, but he was also a little relieved. He leaned back in the chair.

"Fuck, Olivia. 'Wine or beer?' So fucking stupid." The young production assistant castigated herself outside the door, quietly enough that he shouldn't have been able to hear.

He smiled.

* * *

Rusty crossed the wide park at the center of the university. Even as he was opening the door to his dorm building and making his way up to his room, he was mentally figuring out what he needed to pack. A lot of it was the same stuff he'd already packed for his rail-trip out to Nevada, but there were other things to–

He stopped, two doors down from his own dorm. The door to his room was cracked open.

He'd never given a key to anyone. He looked around. It was life as normal in the dorm hall, with people half-studying in the nearby lounge, others rushing to or from classes. Tentatively, he crossed to the door and slowly pushed it open, making a point of remaining in the hall.

A man and a woman were in his room, both in dark charcoal business attire. The man was balding and thin-shouldered, professional-seeming with wire-rimmed glasses. He was seated at Rusty's desk, with several windows on Rusty's laptop open—his calendar, a couple of folders with documents in them, and his email program. The woman stood in his closet, going through the boxes and other things on the shelf above his hangars. She was younger than the man, with dark brown hair pulled back into a braid. She held a phone in her hand, taking photos of whatever it was she was going through in his closet.

"What the fuck?" Rusty said, stepping through the door. "Who the fuck are you people?"

"Ah. Mr. Adamson," the man said, standing smoothly. He left Rusty's laptop where it was, though he did step away from the desk. The woman smiled politely, like someone he'd just met at a party instead of rifling through his possessions, closing the closet door behind her.

"I'm Agent Elliot Roman, with the Department of Transformed Persons Affairs," the man said, quickly flipping open his wallet to show a flash of badge. "This is my partner, Flora Maldonado."

"Um. Oh." Rusty closed the door behind him.

"Mr. Adamson–" Flora began.

"Rusty. Just call me Rusty. Or Gauss."

She paused for a moment and smiled wanly at him. "Mr. Adamson, we're here because we registered a law enforcement check-in on your DTPA number from a sheriff's department in Nevada."

Rusty blanched.

"Is that accurate?" Agent Roman prompted. "The report was within the last twenty-four hours, Mr. Adamson, which seems strange, given that we find you here at school. If someone is misreporting, using your number–"

"No, no." Rusty shook his head and sighed. "No, it was me. I was out there visiting a friend, and was in the wrong place at the wrong time. 'Wrong place' being a convenience store, and 'wrong time' being when some crackhead decided to hold the place up." He glanced between them with some concern. "Look, I did everything I was trained to do, and followed all the procedures that I was taught to do. I mean, I *think* I did. I'm sorry if I missed something or whatever, but in my defense I'd just been almost shot by the crackhead and was kinda freaking out, and–"

"Mr. Adamson!" Agent Maldonado's voice whip-cracked. Rusty shut up, his jaw clenched. She smiled at him. "According to the report from the authorities, you did everything correctly. They even asked to log a commendation for your actions—they have reason to believe that your quick thinking saved the life of the cashier."

Rusty exhaled and slumped against the door, shoving his hands into his pockets.

"Mostly we were concerned," Agent Roman said. "We hadn't registered an intent by you to do any major traveling, so it seemed strange that we'd be receiving such a report from so far away."

"Uh, the suits at the Health Weekend said that kind of reporting wasn't mandatory." Were they trying to entrap him somehow? What the hell was going on here?

"It isn't," Agent Roman said, shaking his head. "It's just that most registrants with the Department *do* let us know, for situations just like this one. It was unusual for us to get a contact that indicated you were hundreds of miles from what we knew to be home."

"We also didn't register any flights or other travel arrangements to Nevada for you," Agent Maldonado said casually. "And we know you don't own a vehicle or have a driver's license."

Shit. There it was. That's what they were digging for. Rusty looked away from them quickly.

"Mr. Adamson, did you use your powers to travel to Boulder City, Nevada from Portland, Oregon?"

Rusty bit his lip, and nodded.

Agent Maldonado threw her partner a glance. *I told you so*, it said. "May we ask how you did it?" she asked.

Rusty hesitated for a few moments. "Train tracks," he mumbled.

"Excuse me?"

"I rode the train tracks," he said. He hated this feeling—this feeling of being interrogated, though they were doing their best to keep it from being apparent. "Magnetically. I suspended myself above them via magnetism, and moved along them magnetically by repelling myself away from them at an angle. Like a mag-lev train does. It's completely safe, doesn't affect the tracks in any way, and I'm in complete control of my momentum the entire time."

"Mr. Adamson," Agent Roman said, attempting to inject concern for Rusty's safety into his voice. So this was Good Cop, then. "We're worried for your safety when it comes to stunts like that. You could have been hit by a train."

"No, I couldn't have," Rusty said shortly.

"Why is that?" The agent sounded like he was talking to a twelve-year old.

"Because he can detect any trains coming. Probably long before he can see them. Isn't that right?" Agent Maldonado said, favoring him with a critical stare. "His file says he's aware of anything that distorts the magnetic field around him, for some incredible distances. A big metal train definitely qualifies, I think. How close am I?"

Rusty smiled at her. "One hundred percent on the nose. I've studied mag-lev technology extensively. I even consulted with one of the physics professors here at the university on it."

Agent Roman sighed. "Well, at least you're doing your due diligence."

"That's all well and good," Agent Maldonado said. "But Mr. Adamson, you need to be aware that this sets off some warning bells. It's a bad precedent to get into. We're not trying to imprison you or anything. We just want you to work with us when it comes to situations like these. Even if your magnetic rail-riding trick is one hundred percent safe on your end, you aren't in control of the whole world. You could have caused an accident, your passage could have thrown off sensitive electronics too close to the rail line, you could have startled lots of people. If you feel the need to do this kind of thing again, we reiterate what you've heard a dozen times now: contact us. Work with us. Let us know, so we can make sure you stay safe and the public stays safe. It's what you agreed to when you signed up—all we ask is that you honor that agreement."

Rusty sighed, nodding his head. "Sure," he said meekly. "Sorry."

With that, the two agents departed, Maldonado without a backward glance, and Roman with a firm handshake and a hope he had a good day.

* * *

Mitch didn't have to wait long. He heard Olivia greet the movie star, noted his total lack of response, and then the door swung open. Mitch stood as the man entered, and Optic stopped, poised in the doorway to stare. The two men locked gazes, both of them questioning. Finally, Optic turned toward the open door. "Thank you, Olivia. Could you let Bill know I'm going to need a little extra time on the break?" Outside, the production assistant assented and then walked away, already speaking into her headphone mike.

"Sentinel," Optic said once he'd pulled the door shut, the tone a greeting. "I admit, this is a hell of a surprise." He ran his hand over his head of close-shorn black hair.

"Thank you for taking a moment to meet with me," Mitch said politely, stepping forward to offer his hand. Optic took it quickly. "I know you're a really busy man on set, and if it were anything that could wait at all, I wouldn't have–"

"Jesus, no," the actor said, chuckling, waving him back into his seat. Mitch sat gratefully, and Optic took the chair opposite him. "Frankly, I could use the break."

Optic just stared for a few moments, almost as though he were trying to reconcile the presence of the big man in his trailer. After the regard drew into awkwardness, Mitch looked away and cleared his throat. "Shit." Optic catapulted himself out of his seat, crossing to the mini-fridge behind his desk. "Can I get you a juice or something? I can have someone run and grab a coffee, if you'd prefer."

"Ah, no, thank you. I came here from breakfast," Mitch said. "I'm sorry to get right to things, but time is sort of pressing on this." Optic waved him on as he fished a plastic bottle of orange juice out of the fridge, and popped the lid off, taking a swig that drained half the little bottle.

"I think you're in a unique position to help me. I know that you've got a past in the USAF, and in one of its special projects, before, well."

"Getting my ass kicked out for being a homo, yeah." Optic tried to keep the tone light, but there was a bitter note under the surface, pain in the man's eyes.

"Which was wrong. So damned wrong." Mitch shook his head, and Optic laughed. Mitch squinted, not sure what was so funny.

"Sorry, man—it's just if you'd ever told me I'd be sitting here with Sentinel himself telling me about how wrong it was to get *Don't-Ask-Don't-Tell*ed out of the Air Force, I'd have told you you were crazy."

Mitch smiled. "Well, it *was* wrong. Though, if you don't mind, it's just Mitch these days. That other name has got some real baggage to it."

Optic's grin softened, and he examined Mitch's face. Then, he nodded slowly. "Yeah, I imagine it does. You got it, Mitch. I'm Wendell."

"What I'm about to ask is probably illegal. If you don't feel comfortable telling me things you learned while on active duty, you just say so and I'll–"

"Hey," Wendell interrupted him, and returned to his seat. "The fact is I left a hell of a team behind. A bunch of good guys who stood by my side the entire way, from when we were all just nobodies that signed up for Project: Seraphim, you know? We were basically brothers after all that specialized testing and training, and we only got closer after they started the process, and some of us starting *dying*. That kind of thing builds family. So yeah, I'm loyal to those guys, but not to the people who took me away from that family, you know? The upper brass, and the fucking bureaucrats. The irony, of course, is that since they repealed DADT a year and a half ago, it wouldn't even be an issue any more today. Just like that, overnight, it's not actually a big deal anymore."

"I hadn't heard that, actually," Mitch said. "So it's legal now to be gay in the military in the U.S.? Like, openly gay?"

"Sure is," Wendell said, not bothering to hide the bitterness there this time. "Don't get me wrong—I'm so fucking happy for those guys who're still in there, you know? I mean, I fought hard on that lobby. Contributed and gave speeches and everything. It sounds like you've been hidden away under a rock somewhere, so you probably weren't aware, but the lobby to end DADT basically turned me into their poster boy for all of that." He shrugged, and then regarded Mitch thoughtfully. "Of course," he said. "I was still basically walking a path you'd already blazed years ago, huh?"

"No," Mitch shook his head, and leaned back in the chair. He looked Wendell in the eyes. "I never had to sit in front of a military tribunal. My judge was the court of public opinion. I was never in danger of serving prison time for who I loved, as difficult as the media made everything. Don't take away from what you accomplished—that victory is all yours, man, yours and everyone else's who fought."

Wendell glanced away, shaking his head. He drained the rest of his juice.

"And let me tell you this," Mitch continued. "You did what I couldn't. You stood out in front of everyone, as a gay man who wouldn't be shamed, and you fought for other gay men and women. You pulled yourself up by your bootstraps, and then kept the fight going for people who didn't have the means of fighting the battle you did. That's an act of outright heroism, Wendell. Don't ever downplay that."

"Thanks, ah, thanks for saying that." Wendell was clearly uncomfortable with the thought, and something Mitch couldn't decipher crossed his face. He almost visibly shook it off. "So, you were saying?"

Mitch sighed, almost regretting having to ask. "I need to be able to cross the U.S. border in flight. I know that Project: Seraphim was dedicated to creating Empowered whose first and foremost talent was flight, and fast flight at that, in order to intercept other flying supers who crossed into our airspace. But in order for that to do the military any good, they'd have to be able to *detect* a flying threat, wouldn't they?"

Wendell winced and looked away. "This could land me in trouble, yeah. Like, a lot of trouble."

"I wouldn't ask if it weren't necessary, believe me. I know what you're risking here," Mitch said, trying to keep his tone neutral.

Wendell shook his head and studied Mitch. "You know, if it were anyone else—even a member of my own family, Mitch—who came to me with this question, there's no way. I'd assume that they'd been sent by the government to see how well I was keeping the information I walked away from Project: Seraphim with. Anyone else. But not you. I know you don't go by that name anymore, but if anyone else in the world other than Sentinel had come to me with this, I'd have bounced them out of my trailer by now."

Mitch lowered his gaze, abashed. "If you're not comfortable–"

"Hell, no, I'm not comfortable." Wendell snorted. His hands played with the empty juice bottle nervously, absent-mindedly. "Just tell me it's for a good cause."

"There are kids—gay kids—who are being kidnapped, tortured and even killed in Eastern Europe, Wendell."

The movie star arched an eyebrow. "Are you about to go and become a gay superhero?" He smiled at the thought. It did sort of conjure a ridiculous image, all rainbow-patterned cape and big pink triangle on the chest.

"Nothing as flashy as that, I hope," Mitch said. "You know Rusty, right? Gauss, that is. He's got a good friend that has gone missing."

"Oh, lord. That one," Wendell snorted again, and shook his head ruefully. He rose from his seat, every tic of his body language suggesting his distrust of the kid.

Against his will, Mitch found himself bristling. "It doesn't matter who prompted me. The fact is that I've buried my head in the sand an awful long time, telling myself that all the government and law enforcement teams that accepted and included supers had made my old responsibilities null and void. There were now legal officials who could do what I used to." He also stood. "But Rusty was the one who pointed out to me that no one was looking out for those kids. No one—not even their own government. Hell, especially not their own government. And yeah, it was a friend of his that made the situation immediate and personal, but that's no less real. So we're going over there to see if we can't find this kid, and maybe some of the others like him."

Wendell watched Mitch rant, stone-faced. Then, slowly, he broke into a widening grin. "Oh, it's like *that*, is it?" Wendell laughed, and winked, and all of a sudden Mitch realized the implication of what he wasn't saying. He sat down, furrowing his brow, not sure what to say to that. It wasn't the point, but it also felt *wrong* to try and deny that Rusty…well. Rusty.

Goddamn it.

"Okay, okay!" The actor chuckled once again and raised his hands in front of him, a surrender. "You're right. I can't sit in my trailer bragging about what an awesome gay icon I just became and then ignore this, can I?"

"You don't have to get involved. All I need is the information on how to get past whatever the sensors are that the military uses to detect fliers. I know we're too small for conventional radar and the like."

Wendell took his seat again, leaning forward. "The fact is simple: there is a way, but it's not as good as the military likes to claim it is. Most of their ability is based on simple sightings by people who report it, along with a whole series of satellites that are set up with some equipment that lets them pick up weird energy signatures, like radiation, temperature, pressure systems and things like that down to about a hundred yards or so. Most fliers use *something* to let them fly, so if it's air control or fire or whatever, those satellites can often pick it up."

"Can they detect me?" That really was the million-dollar question, wasn't it?

Wendell shook his head. "Nope. Not a chance in hell. As long as you keep it subsonic, there won't be anything to detect. There isn't any technology that can detect the psychic ability to move shit with your mind, man."

Mitch was so relieved. "Thank God. So as long as we keep out of the vantage of any potential spotters, we're golden."

"You are." Wendell was thoughtful. "You know, I admit, I kinda had a little fantasy when I was on my way to the trailer, after Lincoln told me who was waiting for me here."

Mitch raised his eyebrows, and Wendell laughed. "No, not that kind of fantasy. You're not really my type." He winked, and seemed to take a great deal of delight in Mitch's blushing embarrassment.

"No, no. I thought, for a moment, that maybe you were coming to invite me to join a team. You know, of supers."

Mitch's jaw all but dropped. "Oh, God. I didn't...I mean..."

"I know you're not, of course," Wendell hastily added, still smiling. He looked away, and his voice and face turned thoughtful. "I guess I didn't realize how much I missed working like that, with other guys. Other supers, you know? Missing that purpose. Entertainment is great, don't get me wrong. I'd be an ungrateful asshole if I pretended I didn't love what I do now. I guess I just miss it sometimes."

"I know what you mean," Mitch smiled, standing. "I'm in my sixties, and sometimes I feel like the whole of my life was basically summed up by my time in the Champions. And everything after it has just been, well, has been sort of hollow. Like I was really alive then, and just trying to figure out how to be whole again once I lost that."

Wendell nodded. "Yeah, kind of like that. So, are you in contact with any of the others? Your old teammates?"

Mitch shrugged. "Sort of. Not really. Alchemy is a big dog in the corporate world. He's tried to make contact occasionally, through the DTPA, but it never felt right. Nobody's heard from Dryad in years, as far as I know, and Cobalt stays busy with her position in the Golden Cross. I've done some work for them before, when she's asked me, so we stay in contact a little, but it's mostly professional. She and I never really developed much of a friendship even when the team existed. As for Marque, well."

"Yeah, I know all about that asshole. He was at my hearing. He's involved with DTPA pretty tightly, usually as their military liaison, and so when he gave a big speech about how being gay made you unfit and a liability to military service, even if you did have powers, well, it made a hell of an impression on the committee. My lawyer said that they'd been talking about the possibility of coming up with an exception to Don't Ask, Don't Tell for those of us with powers before that, simply because we were so damned rare. But he really changed their minds, and they got to milk all that in the media talking about how no one—not even a super—is exempt from the 'moral standards of the U.S. Military,' as they put it. I got so damned tired of that clip."

Mitch shook his head. "Asshole is right." He sighed and shook his head. "Anyway. I should let you get back to work, Wendell. Thanks. If there's anything I can ever do to repay you, please let me know."

They shook hands and Wendell smiled. "Are you kidding? As far as I'm concerned, knowing I could help in some small way get the Sentinel back to saving lives? That's payment enough right there." Mitch rolled his eyes, but appreciated the man's sincerity.

He opened the door, and Mitch clambered down the stairs. "Mitch," Wendell said from the doorway, and the bigger man stopped and turned to regard him. "If you reconsider that whole team thing, let me know." With a grin, he closed the door and Mitch pulled his hood back into place, shaking his head.

CHAPTER TWELVE

Portland, Oregon to Odessa, Ukraine
May 6, 2013

Rusty was geared up and ready to go by the time Mitch found his way back to the campus in the late part of the morning. He was still wearing jeans and his long bridge coat, with his big steel-toed work boots. His burnished steel bracers peeked out of the edge of his coat sleeves, and he hoisted the backpack on his back a little higher.

"You ready to do this?" Mitch asked, and Rusty nodded.

"Yeah. I'm wearing an extra layer or two for warmth, and I've got some food and water for the trip over." He paused, a little hesitant. "So just how high up are we going to be flying, anyway?"

"I'm sticking fairly low to take advantage of cloud cover while we're in U.S. airspace. Once we're beyond that, though, I'll take us upward. The thinner atmosphere will reduce drag and let me get a speed boost, but I'll drop back down into the thicker atmosphere occasionally so you don't get lightheaded or anything. Just let me know if you start to feel dizzy while we're flying."

"Will you be able to hear me?"

"Definitely. We'll be flying just behind a cone of telekinetic force, shaped like the nose of a plane. It'll cut wind drag, but also provide a small pocket of calmer air. That's what we'll be breathing most of the time, and though we won't be able to have conversations or anything mid-flight, I'm able to hear things someone in the pocket with me says."

Rusty shook his head and looked thoughtful.

"Having second thoughts?" Mitch asked.

"Is this stupid?" Rusty asked. "I mean, am I just signing us up for a world of trouble here?"

Mitch laid a hand on his shoulder, squeezing it. "Might be. But that doesn't mean it's also not the right thing to do. But if you want to back out…"

"No way. We're doing this." Rusty offered his open backpack to Mitch.

The older man fished his wallet out of his pocket and dropped it in there, and then tossed his powered-down phone on Rusty's dorm bed. He followed Rusty out of the room and onto the roof of the dorm. The roof was wet from the rain, but that was good—it meant most people weren't watching the sky, and gave them low cloud cover to reach quickly.

"So, I called Deosil from the dorm phone."

"Yeah?" Mitch's reply was carefully neutral.

"I kinda felt like I had to tell her what we're doing. She didn't want us to go. She's worried we'll get in trouble with the DTPA and Vigilance."

"Vigilance is definitely a concern, but the DTPA doesn't have any legal authority over us."

"Well, maybe not you," said Rusty. "I signed up with them right after the Gulf Event that gave me my powers. I agreed to certain things, among them that I wouldn't go playing hero."

Mitch hesitated. "There was no law about doing such things when the Champions got started. No one dreamed anyone would actually get out and do something like this, like something out of a comic book. I mean sure, there were laws dealing with vigilantism, but not on the scale the Champions operated at. It took them years to draft up legislation that even covered the idea."

"Of course, the Department's authority really only covers those of us who sign up with them, and even then, it's only in the U.S. Still, they won't be happy."

"You sound like you're trying to talk yourself out of it."

"I kinda am." Rusty zipped his backpack closed. He handed it off to Mitch, who shrugged it on, adjusting the strap lengths and buckles. "It's like, if I can manage to talk myself out of it, then it's for the best, because my everything isn't in it, you know? If I can psych myself out before we leave, then it was never important enough for me to actually do it. I wasn't doing it for the right reason—I was just doing it for the thrill, or whatever."

Mitch smiled at him as the younger man met his gaze. "Not having much luck talking yourself out of it, are you?"

Rusty shook his head.

"Alright. Let's do this, then." Sentinel shrugged out of his street clothes, revealing his iconic blue-and-white uniform from his Champions days. It clung tightly to his build, all curved lines and sleekness. It was made of a weird composite, created by Alchemy two decades ago. A version of that composite saw all kinds of use today, replacing Kevlar as the preferred cloth body armor in use by law enforcement. Reaching out, Rusty touched Mitch's chest, resting his hand in the center of that broad expanse. Mitch looked down at the hand, and then at Rusty, with an eyebrow raise.

"Shut up," Rusty said, hating the flush he got at ears and neck. "I'm not perving on you. You're right, though—I can feel the fibers of metal used to create the composite. It's only by touch, though. It doesn't register as ferrous to my magnetic senses at all. This is so weird. This is not the same stuff we use today."

"Will it suffice for our purposes?"

"Sure will." Rusty began to shrug out of his clothing. He, too, wore a tight uniform underneath—all black, though, less of a "superhero uniform" and more like compression workout gear. It was the gear the DTPA provided during Retreats, allowing them freedom of movement and some minor degree of protection from accidents while working with their powers. He bundled up his civilian clothes and walked around Sentinel to get to the backpack.

He definitely didn't try to sneak a peek at the view from back here. Mostly.

"All set!" he said. He had his goggles on his head, and was fitting them in place over his eyes. Sentinel spun around and stepped up behind Gauss, who leaned back into him. For a moment, Gauss was distracted as the bigger man hesitantly placed his hand on his hip, then shifted upwards to hold him around his torso. He was facing outward, this time, like a concession to the distance Mitch seemed to need even though they were about to be very, very close physically once again. Gauss leaned his head back, resting it against his chest, and extended his magnetic senses through the multiple points of contact.

"Ready?" Sentinel whispered, and Gauss shivered a little. He licked his lips.

"Up, up and away," the redhead whispered back, and Sentinel groaned. Suddenly they were in flight, the sudden movement snatching the laugh right out of Gauss.

Sentinel's grip was loose around his chest, just firm enough to hold him steady and in place. The flier didn't hold onto Gauss—Gauss held onto him, attaching himself in a tight magnetic field to the reactant fibers in Sentinel's costume. They rose quickly into the low clouds. Though it was raining, the droplets didn't touch them, thanks to the thin cone of nothingness resting above them, courtesy of Sentinel's telekinetic power.

"Wow," Gauss said, and glanced back at Sentinel, craning his neck to try and see the bigger man's face. He felt rather than heard the chuckle and the two spun lazily in mid-air, simply drifting for a moment.

"You're sure you can do this?" the bigger man asked.

"You mean keep velcro'd on this way? I can do this while asleep."

"No, I mean navigate. I can't really do it on my own for long distances. I always flew with guidance from a dispatch agent in my day."

"Oh, yeah. Totally." Gauss nodded and paid attention to the distinct patterns of the Earth's magnetic field around and above him. "Each place has a unique magnetic signature, as distinct as fingerprints. I can not only recognize them, but I can also tell where areas I'm familiar with are, relative to my current position, from anywhere in the world."

"You're your own GPS, then."

"Kinda, except that I don't need a satellite system to do it. It's sort of instinctual at this point, though it took me a little while to figure it out. Another magnetic, Borealis, taught me how to do it my first Retreat weekend. She also taught me to 'spectrum paint' and how to use my powers to generate an electromagnetic baffling field. It'll fuck up our radar profile as we fly, keeping us off radar systems that might be good enough to pick me up using my powers."

"Sounds like we're a go, then. I'm going to keep us mostly in the cloud cover, so let's practice this navigation—can you get us to that spot on the coast you were telling me about?"

"Let's find out!" Gauss extended his senses, allowing them to ride the patterns of magnetic energy across the world's ionosphere, finding a location he knew well. He pointed the direction, and they took off fast, but not fast enough to disturb their cloud cover. It took about ten minutes, and they left the cloud cover behind as they arced up and over the Coastal Range mountains along Oregon's western edge. To compensate, Sentinel rose even higher, putting them beyond the visual range of most people to identify them as anything but spots in the air. Oregon's coastline came to a sudden end, and they landed atop one of the tall outcroppings of monolithic rock that thrust up out of the water there.

Gauss grinned. "This is one of my favorite places. These are the Needles." He spoke loudly in the high coastal wind, gesturing to the rock they were on, and to similarly-shaped outcroppings. He pointed to another monolithic formation, broader and squatter, with a distinctive hole in it. "That's Haystack Rock. I usually use this site as my ground zero for magnetic navigation. I just wanted to get another quick feel for it before we go."

"Makes sense," Sentinel said and held up his hand, his shield blocking off part of the sea-breeze, and reducing the noise. "Are you going to be warm enough in that?"

"This?" Gauss touched his DTPA uniform. "Oh, totally. As long as your shield traps some of the warmer air, I'll be fine. They're meant to compensate for alterations in temperature. And I brought my gloves, so I'll be good." He rescued them from the backpack, and slipped them on as Sentinel prepared. He glanced up at the sun and turned his back to the sea. Gauss followed his gaze back toward the shore. "Wait," he said. "Are we flying east?"

"It's actually a shorter distance across the U.S., the Atlantic, and Europe than it is to span the Pacific and Asia, if we're headed for Ukraine," Mitch said.

"That's about two continents and the Atlantic Ocean worth of flying ahead of us," the younger man said with a whistle. He playfully punched Sentinel's shoulder. "You up to it, old man?"

Sentinel snorted. "You just hold on, junior. Try and keep up. And you trust me not to drop you or get us lost?"

"No. I mean, you'd totally get us lost. That's why I'm navigator."

"You know what I mean."

Gauss grinned. "Yeah, I trust you. You're Sentinel."

The older man shook his head. "That used to mean something. Not so sure it does any more."

"Hey." Gauss waited to speak until Sentinel turned to regard him, backlit by the afternoon sun. "It still means something to me. I know you kinda hate that, or are weirded out by it, or whatever, but it means something to a lot of people. I trust you. Completely."

Sentinel sighed and nodded. "Alright. Shall we test out the warming properties on that uniform of yours?" He stepped up behind Gauss once more, this time pulling him close and clasping him tightly, and the two took off, arcing high and far.

* * *

They were a few hours into the flight when Gauss realized he hadn't really thought this whole thing through. Oh, the mechanics of the flight were practically perfect. They couldn't have made a better team if they'd tried. Sentinel got some height somewhere over eastern Oregon, up to a level below what most planes cruised at, but still plenty high enough and then poured on the speed. Even protected by Sentinel's power, Gauss felt it when they broke the sound barrier, a shuddering in his gut and head.

Gauss remained magnetically adhered to the field around Sentinel's suit, even altering the charge of the metals in the suit to make them stick better. Neither of them had to exert much effort to maintain the connection. Despite that, Sentinel kept one arm around Gauss. It made sense, to some degree. After all, what else was he going to do with that arm, right?

It's just that Gauss hadn't anticipated what being that close to Sentinel was going to do to him over the long term. Which was stupid, of course. He knew he was attracted to the man, but he was flying across continents! Surely that would be distracting, right? Turns out, intercontinental flight is dull whether you're in a big metal tube or being flown there by one of the fastest flying superpowered men on Earth.

Well. Not dull, in the latter instance. Gauss couldn't help himself, but when they got nice and high up, and the air around them got thin and cold, he worked himself a little closer in to the human furnace that was Sentinel. It didn't help that Sentinel pulled him closer in those instances, and Gauss let himself imagine what it might be like to be like this in other situations.

Man, fuck everything about compression suits.

As twilight colored the eastern horizon, they reached the opposite edge of the North American continent. When they landed on a small island off the east coast to let Gauss warm up and stretch his legs, Sentinel didn't say anything. Of course, he was the kind of guy who never would say something, even if he did notice.

"We're making good time," Gauss said, facing away from the man in blue and white. He was doing some of the stretches he did before working out at the gym. Keeping limber, getting the blood flowing in his limbs, and giving his body time to knock it off with all that "finding the big dude really hot" thing.

"Yeah, not bad. It's good to know I haven't lost the touch," Sentinel said. "Good job noticing those planes, by the way. I think it's best to keep steering us out of their vicinity."

"They're hard to miss. On the ground, metal and terrain messes with the magnetic field, but up here, if there's something distorting it, it's a plane. Since I can detect that kind of stuff from a long way off, it's easy enough to keep out of their path." Gauss straightened, in control enough of his body to turn back to regard Sentinel. "Especially since we don't want to get spotted by pilots."

"Oh?"

"Yeah, since about the early 2000s it's been mandatory that all U.S. pilots report any sightings of superpowered fliers. The DTPA liaises with the aviation networks, and they track sightings. If there's a flier somewhere they shouldn't be, they send a team to investigate."

"Huh," Sentinel said. "It's been a while since I've been out flying, I guess."

Gauss took a sip from the water bottle on a rock nearby, screwed the cap back on and stowed it away in the backpack again. "Ready to make this leg of the trip?"

They both gazed out over the vast dark waters of the Atlantic, which reached to the horizon.

"I am. Are you? That's an awful lot of water."

"I'm not worried. You got this. I'm just along for the ride."

Sentinel chuckled. "So, we'll be flying through the night. If I'm right, we should be arriving in Odessa by mid-morning or noon at the latest. What are the chances of you being able to sleep?"

Gauss regarded him dubiously. "Uh, pretty slim, if I'm being honest. I mean, I set the charge between your suit and my own magnetic field so that I don't have to pay attention to it at all, so if I did there wouldn't be any issue. But I guess I hadn't thought about the time difference. We're going to be hella jet-lagged, aren't we?"

Sentinel at least had the grace to look embarrassed. "Well you will be."

"Sorry?"

"Originals physiology. None of us need all that much sleep—I can go something like four days before I start to feel fatigue. I've gone a week before without much more than a headache for the effort."

Gauss shot the older man a disgusted look. "Fucking Originals. You're the literal worst." Sentinel chuckled and Gauss sighed. "Alright, let's do this."

Sentinel stepped up behind him, and Gauss enmeshed their respective magnetic fields. Without noticeable effort—and about as much warning— they were airborne once again, climbing in an ever-higher arc.

The sonic boom disturbed the seabirds on the rocks where they'd been and left a slight contrail in the darkening sky, and then they were gone.

* * *

To his distinct surprise, Gauss found that he could sleep while in flight. Of course, it wasn't a very deep sleep. But he hadn't had any decent rest since his day in Sentinel's bed in Boulder City, so it wasn't surprising that his body insisted on some form of unconsciousness. When he woke again, it was to the pleasant sensation of a bearded chin rubbing back and forth over the back of his neck, the scruff there rasping pleasantly. Gauss shuddered awake and Sentinel jerked back.

"Sorry." He leaned down to whisper in Gauss's ear. "Habit."

"Hey," the younger man said, reaching up to wrap his own arm around the arm Sentinel was using to keep hold of him. "No complaints, big guy."

They dipped down low again, and the rush of fresh air did a lot to wake him. He watched as they raced over long, green swaths of land beneath them. The terrain was somewhat hilly, streaked with all shades of beautiful green, occasionally shot through by the sparkling of water, or the long black ribbon of a road. "Where are we?" said Rusty.

"France, I'm pretty sure," Sentinel answered. He pointed at the smudge of rising grey on the horizon. "Pretty sure those are the Alps way out there, though. I figure they'd make a good place to stop for another rest. It's been a while since you've eaten anything."

"Yeah. I also kinda need to piss."

Sentinel snorted. "Gotcha. We'll be there in no time." They rose again. Sentinel poured on the speed, and true to his word, they were landing in Alpine pastures in under fifteen minutes.

"Wow. It's really beautiful up here," Gauss said when he returned from taking care of business to find Sentinel laid out in sweet-smelling clover, stretching his limbs as though trying to soak up as much morning sunlight as he could. Gauss grinned at the sight.

"I know. I love it here," Sentinel said without opening his eyes. He sat up, wrapping his arms around his knees and resting his chin on his huge arm. He squinted into the distance, like he was considering something, and Gauss let him. In the meantime, Gauss sat and unzipped the backpack to retrieve the small bags of jerky and dried fruit to munch on. He sat next to Sentinel and chewed, watching the bigger man.

Sentinel turned back to regard him, laying his head along his arm and then said, very quietly, "Craig loved it here. He was the one who showed it to me."

Oh. Shit, of course. Craig Velasquez, code-named Radiant. One of the Originals, founding member of the Champions, and Sentinel's murdered partner. Gauss had studied the old Champions enough and interviewed Sentinel enough to know that if there was one defining person in Sentinel's past, it was Radiant. Though he was deep in the closet, he was the one who figured out that Sentinel was gay also, and the two were lovers for nearly the entire time they served with the Champions. Something like eight years before he was murdered by Mata Hari, another Original.

"I can see why," Gauss said lamely, filling the uncomfortable silence.

Sentinel shook his head like a dog shaking off the rain. "Sorry. I try not to do that as much these days."

"Hey," Gauss said, clasping his shoulder. "There's nothing wrong with good memories. I know it's important to recover from grief and all of that, but

I don't think that means getting rid of the good memories, you know? Those are fucking important."

Sentinel chuckled. "He had a mouth like a sailor, too." He stood and reached down a hand to Gauss. The younger man fumbled with the bag of snacks he was working on and took his hand. Sentinel lifted him to his feet effortlessly and took the bag of jerky and dried fruit away from him. "The faster we get back in the air, the faster I can introduce you to the wonder that is *pyrizhky*." He tossed the bag into the backpack, zipped it back up, and shrugged it on.

"Uh, what exactly is a...peer...peereez..."

"*Pyrizhky*," Sentinel repeated slowly. "Baked buns filled with tasty meats and other stuff. Great food." He stepped up behind Gauss, who snapped their magnetic fields together.

"Alright! To Ukraine–"

They shot into the air with a speed that snatched the words out of Gauss's mouth, and were a mere dot on the horizon within a few minutes.

CHAPTER THIRTEEN

Odessa, Ukraine
May 7, 2013

Gauss was forced to concede the point: pyrizhky was damned tasty.

Of course, he didn't get to find that out right away. The day was bright and sunny, with a brilliant blue sky. On such a day, Odessa's beaches drew plenty of folks, and its parks tended toward sparser attendance, which is why Sentinel chose one of the many swatches of green in the middle of Odessa's cityscape to land in. There was no guarantee that they wouldn't be seen, but they quickly dressed in civilian clothes upon landing, and then wandered out of the park as tourists.

The city was magnificent. Sure, it had poverty-stricken pockets, places of old Cold-War era construction groaning under the weight of the proliferation of billboards and advertisements that came with capitalism's late march through those neighborhoods. But there were also parts of the city that were older—much, much older in some cases. More than once Mitch had to grab Rusty to keep him from wandering off to see the entirety of some building's facade or study the interlocking stonework of a cathedral's main arch.

"I knew you were an architecture student, but you really like this stuff," Mitch said, only half teasing. "Let's stop for lunch here, yeah? You need some real food." They took tables at a small sidewalk bistro-style eatery that clearly catered to tourists, as the waitstaff spoke some English.

"God, I do love it, yeah." Rusty's enthusiasm was disarming. "This is why I know Kosma, in fact. He's an architecture student, and he posted some amazing photos of sites around Odessa in his profile. I met him through a queer group on—what?" Rusty couldn't help but notice the look on Mitch's face.

"Sorry, it's weird to hear someone using that word to describe themselves voluntarily."

"What word? Queer?"

"Yeah. When I grew up, that was the go-to homophobic insult," Mitch said quietly, shoving his hands into the front pockets of his jeans. "Nobody ever used it on me, of course. Nobody ever suspected me. But it sure did get thrown around a lot by some of the others."

Rusty nodded. "It wasn't as bad as all that for me, even though I was out. I mean, sure, there were assholes, and the few of us in my high school that were out got harassed by them a lot. But nobody went for that as a default insult, you know? Except the jocks. Those dudes always seemed obsessed with calling other guys faggots and gay and stuff."

"Take it from me—it's probably because more than a few of those jocks are gay themselves," Mitch said humorlessly.

Rusty side-eyed him. "Please don't tell me you were one of those awful homophobic jocks in high school."

"No, no, not me. I played baseball, but I was so scared people would figure out that I liked guys I avoided the topic of gayness entirely. Everybody knew me as a good Christian boy. So, I could sort of dodge having to prove my manhood by harassing people, but there was also no possible way I was gay. Worked out pretty well."

Rusty snorted. "Man, I bet my mom would have way preferred to have had you as a son than me."

"I find that hard to believe."

"Oh, no. No, trust me. I came out really early on. I told her when I was in eighth grade. Told everybody else when I was a freshman in high school." Mitch got so quiet that Rusty stopped, and turned to face him. "You okay?"

The big guy looked poleaxed. He chuckled, though, shaking it off. "Yeah, yeah. Sorry. I can't actually imagine what it would have been like to have everyone in school know I was gay."

"Ah, c'mon. It couldn't have been that bad. It's not like you were in school in the fifties or something."

"Near enough. I was a freshman in high school in 1963, Rusty." Mitch glanced at him sideways and watched the redhead try not to react. He mostly succeeded.

"Hmm. Okay, fair point."

"Plus, this was out in Montana. It might not have been such a big deal if I'd run off and hung out with the free love crowd and all that—though I heard it wasn't even accepted there all that openly then. But where I was? That was farming and ranching country."

"Oh, believe me, I understand." Rusty shook his head and sighed. "I grew up in north Texas."

"Is your dad a rancher?"

"My great-granddad was. We still own the ranch—stables and pastures, and all of that—but my granddad got into oil as soon as he graduated college. Dad did it, too. Hell, I might have also, if I hadn't Echoed." Something caught Rusty's attention then, or at least he acted like it did. Unsurprising, really—in the time Mitch had known him, he'd always avoided talking about the Gulf Event where he gained his powers. Echo events tended to do a lot of property damage, so he could only imagine the devastation that an event occurring on an oil platform in the middle of the Gulf of Mexico might do. He remembered the months of clean-up in 2008 all along the Texas and Louisiana coastlines.

"So, you were talking about Kosma earlier?" said Mitch.

"What?" Rusty turned back to regard him, barely managing to pull his attention away from the buildings that lined the square across from them. "Sorry. Architect-nerding again."

"Kosma. Tell me more about him."

"Oh, yeah. Keep in mind that I don't really know him very well. I mean, we met online, in a group for gay guys in Ukraine." He chuckled at Mitch's confused face. "I was planning on taking a summer trip here, to check out the architecture; I wrote a paper about some of it for one of my classes, and it caught my interest. I figured I'd get to know some of the local queer community, so I'd know some people when I got out here, you know? I met Kosma, and he was an architect, too. We hit it off pretty well."

"And then he disappeared."

Rusty nodded, his eyes dropping to the table. "Yeah." He shredded the edge of his napkin.

"Hey," Mitch said, pulling Rusty's gaze back up at him. "We'll find out what happened. I'm going to warn you now, though. I'm not going to beat up a bunch of skinheads in retaliation, even if the worst has happened, Rusty, and I'm not going to stand by and watch you do it, either. If that's why you came out here."

"We should probably have had this conversation before we left," Rusty said, shaking his head. "But relax. I'm not here to hurt anybody. I just want to find him. If he's being held by someone, I'm getting him free. If he's in a hospital somewhere, I want to know where. And if, how did you put it?" His voice dropped to a whisper. "If the worst has happened, then I want to find out who did it, and get some proof in the hands of the people who knew him. That's all."

"Alright. Let's do this, then," Mitch said. He turned to their waiter and rattled off something in not-English. He turned back to find Rusty staring at him, eyebrows raised. "What?"

"What the hell was that?"

"Ukrainian," Mitch replied, all sass and unspoken 'obviously'.

"You speak Ukrainian?"

"Rusty, I speak Ukrainian, Russian, and just over two dozen more languages."

Mitch was sure the redhead's eyebrows were going to crawl into his hairline.

"Seriously? Is that an Originals thing, too?"

Mitch chuckled. "Sort of. I mean, it's an Originals gift—it's just not *mine*. There is an Original who goes by the name Savant. He's a telepath, extremely high grade of precision, but none of the overt mind-reading and stuff. His power works primarily on the parts of the brain that have to do with learned skills, languages, and the like. He can not only read someone's mind and give himself their exact level of skill in just about any field that person knows— including muscle memory, by the way—but he can also put a willing subject to sleep and 'sleep-teach' them those skills. He retains every ability or knowledge he gains in that way. The Champions got tired of having to deal with language barrier issues, so we paid him a fee to teach us most of the major languages of the world."

Rusty narrowed his eyes. "Are you fucking with me?"

"Nope."

Rusty pondered it for a few moments. Mitch dug a few bills out of his wallet and paid for the meal. Thankfully, they got enough tourists in here that American cash was just fine.

"That is the dopest shit I've ever heard," said Rusty. "Seriously. Why have I never heard of this dude?"

"Savant is probably one of the most highly skilled individuals in the world, Rusty. He's got entire vocations and professional skillsets locked away in that brain of his, and he uses them. I know for a fact he's had access to some of the best spies and other people who specialize in not getting noticed. He left the United States when they proposed the Denisov Measure. He had some pretty solid ideas about what the government might be willing to do to recruit someone with his talents, and he's probably not wrong. Haven't heard anything about him in years."

"Yeah, no kidding. Damn." The two of them stood and left the bistro behind. Mitch led them across the street, to the square Rusty had been ogling from their table. They had a few hours to kill, and he was finding Rusty's enthusiasm for old buildings a bit infectious.

* * *

Their plan was simple, up front. Rusty had already contacted some of the people he knew from the Odessa MSM social media group and asked them to meet him at the Warwick Bar, where Kosma was last seen. Most of them refused out of hand. One of them, Oleksander, never replied, though Rusty thought someone had said that Oleksander was missing, and might have been hanging out with Kosma the night he went missing as well.

Two, however, had agreed. Lyov, one of the admins of the group, had replied enthusiastically. Rusty knew he was one of the people most concerned with the disappearances—not just of Kosma, but of some others in Odessa's large but underground gay community. The other was Foma, who was not quite as enthusiastic. In fact, Rusty had been forced to push more than a little to get him to agree. Rusty and Mitch stopped at an internet cafe so Rusty could check the messages on the group to let Lyov and Foma know that they were still on, and to give Foma another push if necessary. It was, but Foma promised he'd meet them there.

"So, what do you know about this bar? It doesn't sound like a Ukrainian bar," said Mitch.

"The Warwick? Oh, no. It's a hotel bar, actually. The hotel sees a lot of Western European and American tourists and business types, so the management goes out of their way to make sure it's an okay place for queer patrons to gather. All those world-traveling queens who've watched too much porn with Eastern European guys in it apparently prefer to stay there. It's one of two bars attached to the hotel, but it's not the bar that's actually in the hotel. It has an independent door, anyway."

"So, is it a seedy place?"

"The hotel is pretty upscale, I guess. Not sure about the bar. It's on the edge of the city's center, though, so it can't be too bad. Kosma said it was kind of a pain to get to—lots of hopping around on public transportation and shit—but that it was totally worth it for the drinks, the music, and the safety." Rusty couldn't help but notice how uncomfortable Mitch was. "What's up?"

"Confession time—I've never actually been to a gay bar." He paused. "Rusty, stop looking at me like that."

"I'm sorry! It's just, really? Never? Not once?"

Mitch sighed and shook his head. "I mean, to be fair, I never really went to straight bars or clubs, either. It's not like I've been avoiding it, it's just never come up. Craig and I were totally undercover the entire time we were together, and then after that I kinda perfected the art of being a hermit."

Rusty logged out of the computer and grinned at him. "So, promise me something. We're here on a mission and everything, but promise me that you'll have one drink and one dance with someone you don't know."

Mitch frowned and pushed open the cafe door. It was a block or so before he spoke again. "Why? Why is that important?"

"Because if you never do something like that, I think it should be because you choose not to, rather than because you've never had the experience."

"I'm not going to have some disco epiphany, Rusty."

Rusty burst out laughing and seemed like he couldn't stop. Mitch's face warred between embarrassment at the stares his guffawing companion was drawing, and pleasure at provoking such a reaction. Finally, Rusty took a breath. "Oh, God. I'm sorry. Disco epiphany. I feel like that should have been some Andy Warhol art piece. Or a super whose power is like hypnotic light effects or something." He paused. "Oh, shit. I know someone with that power at the Retreats, I think. I'm going to suggest she make that her code name."

Mitch shook his head. "You're ridiculous."

"No, seriously, though. I know you're not going to suddenly become a circuit queen or anything. I'd be a little freaked out if you did. I guess I just kinda would like to think that after all this is done, maybe I could talk you into coming out to have a drink and a dance or something, you know? To hang out. I know Deosil would dig seeing you again."

They walked for a while. The sun was sinking low in the west, and it painted the city gold and bronze. Finally Mitch spoke up, a little more quietly than before.

"I don't really know about all of that. I mean, I'll have a drink and maybe a dance, that's fine. Though I can't dance *at all*."

"Holy shit, I've discovered the only weakness the Originals have."

"Shut up. It's a Mitch-weakness. Craig could dance like nobody's business, and so could Dryad." He grinned at the memories and then sobered back up. "What I'm saying is that I have no idea what this little trip is going to do. For me, for how I interact with the world, or whatever. I'm doing my best not to think about it, because it's kind of scary to think about. So, I'm just focusing on the here and now, for the moment."

"Hey." Rusty reached out to grab Mitch's hand, leaning into him. "It's cool. I understand, really. No obligations. Play it by ear, right?"

Mitch craned his head sideways, to rest his cheek atop Rusty's head, and then stepped away, shaking his hand free from Rusty's grip. Rusty was pretty sure he didn't even know he did it, but he saw Mitch glance around, like he was making sure nobody saw that moment of public affection between the two of them.

Old habits, and all.

"Why don't we catch a cab over to this Warwick hotel?" Mitch suggested. "I could use a shower, and you can catch a nap."

Rusty groaned at the thought. "A hot shower and a bed sound like gifts from Jesus right now."

Mitch snorted and started hunting up and down the street for a taxi.

* * *

The shower was hottish, and the sheets had way too much starch, but despite all of that, Rusty was dead to the world by the time Mitch got out of his shower (by which time the water couldn't even be called hottish, but he'd known the risks he took when he insisted Rusty go first). He padded over to the window, drying his hair, wearing only a towel. Pulling aside the curtains, glancing over at Rusty with a wince to make sure the clacking things didn't wake him, he hauled one of the fake-leather-upholstered chairs over to the window. He dried his hair absentmindedly as he sat and *listened*.

His hearing was obscenely sharpened, like all Originals. It was the most crippling thing he'd experienced after the Original Event, aside from the headaches that came as his telekinetic power manifested. It had taken him weeks to learn to allow the things he heard to filter into the background as white noise. But in moments like this, he closed his eyes and focused on those details.

Closest to him, he could hear very tiny details. The sounds of not just Rusty's breathing, but his heartbeat. He could hear the conversations of nearly everyone on this floor, and those of people on the floors above and below this one if he tried. And it wasn't like normal hearing, with sounds floating out of the air with no real discernible way of knowing where they came from. He and the other Originals could pinpoint the source of a sound precisely; Marque had more than once fired at targets he could only hear, right through walls, with an aim as true as if he had perfect line of sight.

He could hear other, louder sounds out to about a block radius. Not conversations, but raised voices, certainly, the ringing of alarms from clocks and phones, the slamming of doors, the sounds of teenagers listening to music too loudly in their bedrooms. Dogs barking, dickheads on the street catcalling women walking by, the precise location and movement of every vehicle by its engine noise. Mitch knew it wasn't meditation, per se, because from what Dryad had explained to him, that was all about blocking out distractions. What he did was sort of anti-meditation. It calmed him to sit and listen, to immerse himself in the noises of the world and to pretend for a little while that he was just another part of it.

He listened to the sounds go on around him and took comfort in the fact that they happened and kept happening wholly unaware of who he was, of who he'd once been. The world spun on, and it didn't need him to be Sentinel. It had no interest in talking about who he slept with, or who he saved, or how he used his power. Families squabbled, lovers loved, kids played, and he was neither responsible for it nor necessary to its continuation.

It was the closest to peace he'd found since the Original Event.

One hundred and seventy-one minutes later, Mitch realized that Rusty's breathing pattern had changed, and he glanced at the window to see himself reflected in it. It was dark outside, and the room's light turned the window into a mirror. Rusty was lying in bed, on his side as he had been while sleeping, but his arm was tucked under the pillow he rested on and his eyes were open, just watching him.

"Sleep well?" Mitch asked, the smile in his voice evident even if Rusty hadn't been able to see it in his reflection.

"Yeah. You?"

"I wasn't sleeping. I was just listening."

Rusty laid there for a moment, without saying anything. "What did you hear?"

Mitch considered for a moment. "There's a couple above us—I think they're Swiss or Austrian—who flew out here to attend a big business dinner of some kind, but the wife isn't feeling well. The husband sounds angry, but from his heartbeat, I'm pretty sure he's just scared to go to the dinner by himself. I don't think she knows how much he relies on her in unfamiliar social situations."

He paused again. "Across the street, a family just got home from a funeral, I think. Everyone is quiet, and most of them went to separate rooms to have a good cry. The teen daughter is still singing one of the hymns they sing at Eastern Orthodox funerals, which is why I think that."

Rusty shifted so that he was on his back. "It amazes me what you can do sometimes. Not the stuff everyone knows you can do. You're Sentinel, right. Super strong, super-fast flyer, super tough. Stuff like that. The other stuff, like this, or how little you need to eat or sleep, and the rest of it."

Mitch grinned and swiveled in his chair so he was facing the bed. He flushed a little, acutely aware that both of them were chatting while naked—Rusty beneath the covers, he still with a towel wrapped around him. "Want to see my greatest secret? The power I've never showed anyone else before?"

Rusty looked wary. "Uh, you totally know the answer to *that*."

Mitch reached out to the table beside the window, with its vase and silk flower, and a nondescript ashtray made of thin plastic. He held his hand out over it, focused his eyes on it, and then concentrated. Hard.

For a moment, Rusty was sure Mitch was making fun of him. But then, it happened. The thin plastic tray shifted, as though the table had been bumped. Mitch kept focusing while Rusty's mouth fell open.

Then, with a scraping sound, the ashtray slowly crept across the length of the table and flung itself off it in more of a fall than a throw.

"No way!" Rusty sat up in bed, pulling the blankets more securely around himself. "You moved that! Telekinetically!"

"Yup," Mitch said with an embarrassed little grin. "Sad, isn't it? I mean, I was the first telekinetic in the world, but literally everyone but me can move things with mind alone. So, I knew it was possible."

"I thought you had to physically touch things to affect them with your telekinetics. How long have you been able to do that? Have you always been able to?"

"Oh, God, no. That's the best I've done to date, and that's taken about two years to get to that point. Ever since the DTPA discovered that my powers were telekinetic in origin and not actual physical super-strength and everything, I've been pushing at them. Not much progress, but it's more than I was ever able to do."

"That's seriously amazing. I mean, every other TK I know—I've met Whisper and Cascade, both—can't lift anywhere near your level of weight. If you can learn to freaking move that without touching it…" Rusty's eyes practically boggled as he no doubt brainstormed long list of the things that could be done with such a feat.

"Well, let's not get ahead of ourselves." Mitch chuckled and stood to pick the ashtray up. He gestured with it. "For now, this is as good as it gets."

"Still, that's nuts." Rusty threw himself backward in bed and stretched languidly. "I just wanna stay here and do this. I just want to hang out, in a hotel in Odessa, and geek out about your powers and my powers, and maybe eat a bunch of Ukrainian food, and not—you know." He sighed.

"Hey." Mitch sat on the edge of the bed next to him. "That's what you're supposed to want. You're not supposed to want to be in another country illegally, trying to find a friend of yours who has gone missing, and maybe facing down the possibility of seeing some really awful things in the next few hours. It's not bad to not want to do it. In fact, I'd be worried if you were excited. It'd tell me you weren't taking this seriously."

Rusty sat up, which brought his face close to Mitch's. He just stared at him for a few moments, blue eyes searching Mitch's own green. For one half-panicked moment, Mitch was sure that Rusty was going to kiss him. The fact that he wasn't sure if he would actually mind rounded out the panic nicely.

But instead, Rusty threw up his hands. "You're right! Let's do this!" With a whoop, he threw himself backwards and kicked his legs up in the air awkwardly, doing something vaguely resembling a clumsy somersault off the other side of the bed, in a flurry of rough blankets. He hit the ground with a thud, and then sprang up, already walking to the bathroom, without a stitch on.

"Woo!" he whooped, smacking his own naked right ass cheek triumphantly before closing the door behind him, leaving Mitch laughing.

* * *

They left the main entrance of the hotel, wearing their civvies once more, with uniforms underneath. It was a simple walk down half a block and then over half a block to get to the Warwick Bar, attached to the same hotel, but with its own discrete entrance. It was a Tuesday night (*wait, is that right?* Rusty wondered, and tried to count his weekend full of weird travel and sleep patterns, failing hopelessly), and almost no one was in there. Rusty held open the door, and said, "Now, don't freak out when you walk in there."

Mitch stopped cold, with a suspicious glance. "Why?"

"Because you look the way you do, and you've never been into a gay bar. If it's anything like any other gay bar on Earth, you're going to be cruised *hard*. There may be *actual drool*. No, don't look at me like that. I'm not fucking with you. Just don't let it weird you out. That's all."

Of course, they walked in, and Mitch snorted. The place was all but empty, with two people seated at a back table who glanced up and then away when they walked in, and the bartender.

"Well." Rusty scanned the room in profound disappointment. "There would have been drool. If there were anyone to drool. Oh, shut up." He stalked to the bar, leaving Mitch grinning at him in the foyer.

The reaction the bartender gave Mitch more than made up for it, however. *You see,* the look Rusty threw Mitch back over his shoulder seemed to say. Mitch rolled his eyes. The bartender said something to them in Ukrainian, as Mitch sat down at the bar next to Rusty. Mitch replied, and the bartender grinned even bigger. "Americans, yes?"

"That's us," Rusty said. "Can I get a beer?"

"Of course, my friend," he said jovially, in delightfully accented English. "And for you?"

"Club soda, please," Mitch said. The bartender shrugged, and served them up quickly.

"Apologies for my not-so-good English," the shaven-headed server said, setting the glasses down. "I am Taras."

"I'm Rusty, and this is Mitch. And your English is better than my Ukrainian, so nothing to worry about." Taras left them to their drinks for a few moments. Rusty swiveled in his seat to view the bar.

"So when are your friends supposed to be here?" Mitch asked, taking a swig from his glass.

"They didn't actually say. Tonight is all they told me." Mitch glanced at him sideways. "Yeah, I know. I could barely agree to get them to meet me, man. People are kinda on edge here lately with stuff that's been happening."

They waited an hour, and then two. As the night wore on, a few people did trickle in. Foma never showed up (though Rusty would find later that he sent a terse apology), but Lyov did around nine. He was a tall kid a little older than Rusty, with fashionably cut wavy brown hair and a bit of thin chin scruff. He pulled up short when he saw Mitch (*told you,* said Rusty's knee-nudge), and then grinned and greeted Rusty. Rusty ordered him a drink, and the three wandered away from the bar to take a table.

"So," Lyov finally said, after some awkward and weird pleasantries. "Do you think you can find Kosma and Oleksander?"

Rusty glanced at Mitch. "We hope so. I don't know what good we're going to be able to do that you guys can't, of course, but."

"No, you misunderstand. There's no one searching for them." He said that somewhat shamefacedly, looking away.

"What do you mean?" Mitch's question pulled his gaze back to them. The young man's face guilt-ridden.

"No one is inviting whatever danger found them. We're all friends, but people are afraid. They're not the only ones to disappear from around here. From this bar, in fact. Seven or eight people, I think."

"And the police aren't doing anything?"

Lyov shook his head. "They start investigating. But by the time their research brings them here to ask around, they lose interest, you could say." He paused to finish his drink, then leaned forward. "It's like, with Kosma. His family had not heard from him in a long time. So, his family went to the police. Their investigations led them here, and the police asked Taras just enough questions for them to know that he was gay, and then they stopped asking."

"Why? What kind of sense does that make?" Rusty asked. Mitch glanced at him and rested his hand atop Rusty's own.

"They think, 'Ah, one more faggot, that's what happens!' Best not to embarrass the family by making them hear any of the details of how our lives may have gotten us killed, they think."

"So, they seem to be of the opinion that this is just what happens to gays here, then? You just disappear one day, and it was because you chose to be this way, and you probably had it coming?" Rusty was clearly doing his best to keep his voice down. His neck and ears were flushed with anger. "How does that even make sense?"

Lyov smiled at him sadly, nodded, and shrugged.

"It used to be like that in the U.S., also," Mitch said, gripping Rusty's hand. "Hell, it still is, in a lot of the country. For them, being gay is not just a choice, but it's a selfish choice you make, turning your back on decency, church and family, no different from being a drug addict. They see it as a bad lifestyle, one that will only inevitably get you killed."

It wasn't until everyone at the table had been quiet for a moment that Taras stepped in, swiping away empty glasses, and delivering fresh drinks. "It seems like you could use some refills," he said, carefully neutral.

"Taras knows," Lyov said, catching the bartender's attention. "He's the one the police usually talk to." The big man sneered and muttered something. Rusty didn't speak Ukrainian, but didn't need to. Taras arched an eyebrow at Lyov, who caught him up to speed on Rusty and Mitch's goal.

"You're searching for Oleksander? And his friend Kosma?" said Taras.

"Kosma is a friend of mine. From online, of course, but when I heard what was happening…" He trailed off because of how ridiculous he knew it sounded, but Taras clearly didn't think so. He clasped Rusty's shoulder and seemed like he might cry.

"We should all have such good friends," he said finally. "I have a friend, who works with the…" he paused, and said something in Ukrainian.

"Police dispatch," Mitch translated, and Taras nodded.

"Yes, police dispatch. When some of us go missing, I sometimes ask him if there were any crimes or anything reported in the area. Sometimes there are."

"Was there something on the night that Kosma and Oleksander disappeared?"

"Yes. Two different households called to report what sounded like thugs mugging or beating somebody. One of them, an older lady, said she saw something very strange. When they asked to talk to her, though, her caretaker said that she was just seeing things. The report said that they lived in an apartment right above the alley where it happened."

Rusty regarded Mitch questioningly, and the bigger man nodded and turned back to Taras. "Can you give us the address of the alley?"

* * *

Rusty was quiet on their way over, and Mitch didn't push it. They'd said hurried goodbyes, promised to send word if they found anything of use, and left. It was still early in the evening—no later than ten—but the route was all but abandoned. This downtown area mostly cleared out at the end of the workday, and even those who lived here pursued their nightlife in different sections of Odessa.

Finally, they reached the mouth of the alley. "Hold up," Mitch said. Rusty stopped and glanced back at him. "This may be a total bust, okay? We might not find anything at all here. If it was a crime scene, I'm sure the local police have already cleaned up any evidence."

"I know," Rusty said, clearly unhappy with the thought. "Hell, I know this whole damned thing has had the possibility of being just wishful thinking powered by some good intentions, right? But we've got some advantages the police don't."

With a nod, Mitch led him into the alley. The space showed signs of having been combed over by the police recently. Most of the debris was pushed away from its center, leaving a cleared space in the back of the alley that suggested if something had happened, it had gone on there.

"Let me look around first," Mitch said, and Rusty nodded. Glancing around, Mitch stepped into the air and hovered there, flying just high enough off the ground to avoid touching it, while keeping the motion subtle. He propelled himself in the center of the cleared area and began to examine its edges.

"There was definitely blood spilled here," he said. "They've scrubbed it away, but I can still smell it. No gunshots, though, or anything like that, near as I can tell." He stood over a drainage gutter. "Yeah, I can still see it here, down on the concrete along the sides of the gutter."

Rusty walked into the space then, slowly. Mitch glanced over to him, about to wave him over, when he saw that the boy was walking with his eyes closed and his head tilted. "Rusty?"

"There's..." The young man scrunched his face up in concentration. "There's something *weird* here." He paused again, like he was seeking the right words. "Like static? Electromagnetic static that did something weird to the local field. It's fading now, but there was clearly something."

Rusty got to the wall over the gutter where Mitch stood, nearly running into him, before putting a hand out to steady himself. He glanced upward, brow furrowed, studied the view for a moment, and then pointed up. "It's stronger up there."

Mitch nodded, looked around, and grabbed Rusty around the waist, silently gliding them up the two stories. "Yeah, holy shit," said Rusty. "Something really fucked up happened up here. There's the weird static up here from whatever that was, but there's also something else." Mitch put him on the roof of the building, and Rusty paced its length while Mitch knelt at the corner.

"Yeah. Right here," said Rusty. "There's something wrong with this area. Not just 'wrong-like-weird-static' but like, the field here is off."

Mitch didn't look up from where he was studying the edge of the building. "Off how?"

"You know how I've said that the electromagnetic field of the Earth is pretty distinctive, right? Each location has its own fingerprint, shit like that?" Rusty looked around and closed his eyes. "Yeah, that's definitely it. It feels like this location has been exposed to the unique magnetic field in another location entirely. Like, the field is showing signs of being affected by another place's EM field, without actually being next to each other. Like finding one fingerprint overlaid another." He opened his eyes. "Mitch, I think someone was using a power up here. Maybe more than one. I think this is from–"

"A teleport," Mitch said. "And yeah, definitely more than one power at work here. Look at this." Rusty walked over, and Mitch pushed him out of the sparse lighting. "See that?"

The edge of the building was cracked, spiderwebbed with terrible impact. Blood was spattered darkly there, along with some stray hairs glued in with the red-brown mess. Rusty swore and backpedaled.

"Something was slammed into the corner of this building, and then dropped," said Mitch.

"But they were at street level. Weren't they?"

Mitch nodded, glancing around them. "Which means that something snatched someone up from ground level, and…" He stopped mid-sentence and stared across the street from the alley. Rusty followed his gaze just quickly enough to see a curtain fall back into place on the third story window with what had to be the best view of the alley.

"An old lady," Mitch said.

"I bet that's the lady Taras was talking about, the one who called the police when it was happening." Rusty looked at Mitch, who brought them both back down to street level.

"So now what do we do?" Rusty said.

Mitch pointed across the street. "We go ask an old lady some questions."

* * *

In another apartment in that building, a man picked up a phone with trembling fingers and dialed.

"Yes," a man's voice said on the other end, his Ukrainian accented with the sounds of Scandinavia.

"Someone is here. Examining the alley. They…" The speaker paused, and swallowed noisily, a repugnant sound. "They flew. Up the building, to look at the roof."

"Good," the voice on the other end said crisply. "You will be paid, as we agreed," and then hung up.

CHAPTER FOURTEEN

Odessa, Ukraine
May 7, 2013

Though the apartment building was protected from entry by a simple lock at the front door of the building, Rusty easily tumbled through the locking mechanism until he found the configuration that clicked the lock open . He let Mitch lead the way up the stairs. They encountered only a single old man who was slowly tromping down the stairs with a bag of trash. Rusty was pretty sure that Mitch was about to offer to take the trash out for the geezer, but they had pressing business. He chuckled at the thought.

"Something funny?" Mitch said as they reached the third-floor landing. Rusty shook his head, smiling, and gestured Mitch ahead.

With a minimum of guesswork, they figured out which door was most likely attached to the window they'd been spied on from, and knocked. Mitch stood there, concentrating carefully. "Someone just walked to the door and checked through the peephole," he said in a low voice. "Damn it, she's walking away now."

"To be fair, it is after ten at night. It's probably a little shady to be knocking on strangers' doors."

"You might be right. Maybe we need to…hold on," he said, turning back to the door. Rusty could hear the loud clacking lock slide in the door, and then the door was open. Standing there was a tiny elderly lady. She was thin, with bony joints and a dark-toned skin that hung loosely off her frame. Her face was friendly, with deeply-carved lines from a life of smiling and shouting and loving people. She wore a pair of ratty green slippers, a flannel nightgown and a fraying bathrobe.

She regarded at Rusty, and smiled when he smiled, and then her glance strayed to Mitch, who greeted her in quiet Ukrainian. She paused for a moment and began digging in the front pocket of her robe. In the meantime, a woman's voice called out sharply. A young woman with long dark hair past her shoulders, and a simple t-shirt and track pants appeared in the hallway behind her.

"*Babusya!*" The shout was castigating and tinged with fear as she practically ran to her grandmother, who stood in an open doorway with a pair of large male strangers outside. Not to be deterred, her grandmother finally fished a pair of glasses out of her pocket and put them on. She gasped when she saw Mitch, and her face went from pleasantly smiling to positively beatific.

The younger woman shouldered past her grandmother, which meant stepping across the threshold of the door. Mitch raised his hands and spoke in calming Ukrainian. The older woman said something, over and over, and actually clapped her hands once or twice.

"What's going on?" Rusty asked Mitch, who seemed overwhelmed and even a little embarrassed.

"I think that, uh," he said, and the younger woman turned to regard Rusty.

"I speak English," she said, as though it were some kind of warning. "You need to leave! Or we will call the police!" She was leaning against the doorframe, seemingly to block the two strangers from barging in, but it also appeared she was struggling to keep her grandmother inside the apartment.

Rusty held up his hands, placatingly. "Whoa, whoa, sorry. Look, we just want to talk for a minute."

"Olena!" her grandmother said. "You let them in this minute! These nice gentlemen won't hurt anyone—this is the hero Sentinel!"

Rusty's eyebrows rose. Mitch glanced around, clearly hoping no one heard the commotion. Olena glanced over her shoulder, where her grandmother was shoving at the middle of her back, trying to get her out of the way, and hissed something in Ukrainian.

"Uh, no ma'am. She's actually right," Mitch said. "I used to be Sentinel."

Olena stopped struggling just long enough for her grandmother to shove past her and into the hallway. She nearly fell over in the doing, but Mitch was there, gently helping her catch her balance.

She smiled up at him then, and took his hand in her own, patting it a few times and then wrapped her arm around his forearm. Mitch seemed more embarrassed than anything else, and glanced at Olena, who stood there staring at him intently, like she was trying to see that iconic hero past the scruffy beard and blue-collar get-up. Mitch held up one finger to his lips, winking at her grandmother as he worked his arm free from her grip and then undid the top two buttons of his work shirt. He pulled it open to show her the very edge of the iconic blue-and-white that was his costume.

The younger woman raised her hand to her mouth and looked around. No one had come to investigate the fuss in the hallway, but she clearly anticipated them doing so at any moment. Without another word, she waved them in. The little granny smiled—a victorious little *I told you so, I am very right and you are as usual terribly wrong* sort of smile—and led Mitch in by the arm. Rusty followed sheepishly.

"So who are you?" Olena asked him, shutting the door behind them and locking it. "His sidekick?"

Rusty snorted. "We are really sorry to bother you. We just need to ask some questions, and then we'll be out of your hair. Five minutes tops."

At least, those were their intentions. Bohdanna—Olena's *babusya*—had other plans, however. In short order, there was tea being made, and Olena was forced to dig out the good china set. Bohdanna even threatened to make fresh cakes for the tea, but Mitch insisted they'd had a very large dinner and couldn't possibly. Rusty helped Olena make the tea while Bohdanna did her best to monopolize Mitch.

"So he speaks Ukrainian," Olena said, setting the kettle on the stove top. "That's surprising. He's always painted here as the ultimate in naive American icons, you know?"

"Really? That's hilarious," Rusty said, leaning against the counter. Olena pointed to the cupboard next to him, and he opened it and began gathering up some delicate teaware. "I'd always kind of wondered how he was thought of elsewhere."

"Well, the old government used to really want to turn him into a symbol of all that was wrong with American values, but they had their work cut out for them. When he showed up, saving lives, stopping criminals, and being polite the entire time? The people loved him here." She paused for a moment. "Of course, when news of the scandal reached us, there was a great deal of crowing from the upper tiers. Proof that even the best the West had to offer was decadent and corrupt."

Rusty shifted uncomfortably. Olena glanced up at him with her dark eyes, and smiled. "Of course, my grandmother wouldn't hear of it. She used to work at the American Embassy here, you know. It's why her English is so good." She handed him a box of teabags—weird little pyramid things, with no strings or tags—and he plunked one in each of the mugs. "She wouldn't hear of it. She never went as far as to approve of all of that or anything, but her point was that who he loved was none of our affair. We were not his friends or his family. He was only a hero to us, and just because we knew some part of his private life that we had no right to didn't mean he was any less of a hero. We were the ones who were lessened by that knowledge, and our thoughts about it, not him."

Rusty blinked and turned to look back into the living room. Bohdanna was gleefully showing him the contents of a photo album, and Mitch seemed genuinely interested, pointing at photos and asking questions. He realized he was a little misty-eyed at the thought of someone, so far from him, standing up for Sentinel in that way.

"Wow. She's pretty amazing," he said, and Olena smiled sadly.

"She is. You've made her year, I hope you know. Though she may not remember it all." She took the kettle off the stove and poured tea in each cup. "She has dementia. It's not always bad, but those bad days are getting more and more frequent."

Rusty glanced back out at the living room. He crossed his arms, leaning against the door frame. He watched the two of them until Olena had prepared the tea and nudged him in the arm with the tray she was carrying. "Oh!" he said, straightening. "Sorry. Guess I wasn't much help making tea. At least let me carry this in there." Olena nodded as he took the tray from her, and the two went into the living room.

Mitch straightened in his seat, cleared the table in front of them to make room for the tray, and everyone settled in. "Bohdanna was just telling me about her days in the Embassy."

Once he had a mug in hand, Rusty walked over to the window in the living room. Overlooking the street below, it clearly wasn't the window that looked out onto the alley; from here, he could only see the very forward part of the alley.

"So, what is this about?" Olena asked. Between Rusty and Mitch, they explained why they were there.

"Oh, those poor boys," Bohdanna said. She turned to Olena. "You see? I told you there was something strange."

"Something strange?" Mitch asked. "In what way?"

"The lights outside, they were doing strange things. I looked outside, thinking I must call someone to repair them, but the fault wasn't with the lights. There was something outside. On the roof of the building you talked about. I could not see it properly, it was too large, and when it moved into the light, rather than being able to see it properly, the light itself seemed to be blocked!" She crossed herself.

"She called out to me when she saw it," Olena explained. "When I got to her window, I couldn't quite make out the strangeness of the shadow she was talking about, but I was there to see several thugs—some of the local trouble-makers—just as they attacked the two boys. We're far away and couldn't see very well, but they were brutal. I watched for a moment, hoping they'd get away, but then I saw one of the boys disappear."

"Disappear?" Rusty asked. "Like what?"

"Not disappear," Bohdanna said. "He was *grabbed*. By the shadow thing, on the roof above him. Snatched up like a bird might snatch up a fish!"

"I didn't see that, I was paying attention to the other boy. I ran to get the phone, to call the police, but by the time I got back, it was over."

"I saw it, though," Bohdanna said, sadly. "There were lights like stars, spinning, like all of the sky had come down to touch the roof of that building. It was like God himself was looking down, and you could *feel* his gaze." She crossed herself again. "Sometimes, the homilies and stories of the saints talk about the ecstasies they felt in the presence of God. It was just like that. I was overwhelmed, and felt I might faint from just seeing those lights."

"When I came back, *babusya* was sitting on the edge of her bed, crying and praying. It was very disturbing."

"I was sure I was dying," Bohdanna all but wailed. "It was like I'd seen into the gates of Heaven and was being called into it. I hope to never see such a thing again, until I am dying in truth."

"Hush, don't speak so," Olena said, sliding down the sofa's length to put an arm around her grandmother. "You will outlive us all."

"Rusty, what do you—what's wrong?" Mitch said, turning to where the young man stood beside the window. He wasn't paying attention to the conversation, but was standing, slightly swaying, with his eyes closed. Mitch had seen him do that before when he was studying the magnetic field of an area.

"I don't know. It's something weird, like that static? I think that—"

"Down!" Mitch shouted, just as he heard it. The sound was like a groaning, like the noise of an old building settling, but it continued for too long, the sound of stress on the structure increasing rather than decreasing, until the crumbling of its facade made it too obvious to notice. Mitch snatched up a cushion from the chair he was seated and pushed it down over Bohdanna and Olena, where they sat on the sofa. With them secured as best he could, he reached under the sofa and lifted as he pushed himself forward and away from the window where Rusty stood. Using the sofa—wrapped protectively in a telekinetic field—as a battering ram, Mitch broke through the front wall and door of the apartment, landing with the sofa in the hall outside.

Behind him, some horrible, elemental force ripped off the front of the building, shattering plaster and wood and brick with a sound like a giant screaming. The front end of the living room fell away from the third floor and plummeted to the street below, taking several chairs, a wall full of mementoes, and Rusty with it.

"Rusty!" Mitch screamed and bolted back into the room. A room that was cast into terrible darkness. Though Mitch could see in even the darkest natural darkness, this was different somehow. It felt alive, and Mitch was aware that there was someone...some*thing* in it with him.

Something slammed into him then, a cracking, searing pain. Mitch lashed out with fists and connected with nothing. He waited while whatever it was attempted to strike him again and again. Thankfully, now that he was aware of the danger, he could lessen its blows by means of his power. Still, even when he caught hold of the thing striking him—it felt massive and sinuous, like a serpent bigger around than his thigh, and *fast*—it ceased to be solid. Even as he stumbled from the sudden shift in balance, the darkness receded and collapsed into the body of a man.

He was pale-skinned, with long black hair that hung down in his dark-circled eyes. The strange shadows covered his body and rose up from his back like writhing wings made up of tentacles. His expression was cruel and focused. The shadows lashed out at Mitch viciously enough to shred his clothes, revealing his costume underneath. Mitch gritted his teeth, arms up and crossed in front of him, feet planted to avoid being shoved back by the assault.

"I've always wondered how this fight would turn out," he said with a sneering Scandinavian accent, and the darkness in the room receded even further, as though he was gathering it in, forming more and stronger tentacles. The room was a shower of sparks from sheared electrical lines, and invaded with cold night air three stories above the streets of Odessa.

"Shittier than you might think," Gauss snarled as he rose up above the edge of the shattered apartment wall, a field of small burnished steel spheres orbiting him like planets around a sun. The strange shadow-man turned in surprise as Gauss fired a volley of the ball bearings at him in rapid succession. At the last minute, they went wide, and Sentinel saw why. Behind him, Olena and her grandmother were in the line of fire for any of them that missed. The shadow-man leapt, his tentacles seizing the edge of the roof above, and hauled himself up out of sight.

"You have to get these people out of the building," Rusty said. He was trembling from the adrenaline. "I'll keep this asshole busy." He stepped out of the building, and shot upward toward the roof in pursuit of the man, magnetically adhering to the steel in the building's construction and repelling himself away from the ground.

"Goddamn it," Sentinel said. He knew that his power set was better suited to getting people to safety, especially with his speed. *Be careful*, he wished after Rusty, and then turned toward the two women in the quickly filling hallway. "Everyone out!" he yelled in Ukrainian, and started listening for the sounds of people in distress.

* * *

When Gauss got to the roof, there was no sign of the shadow-man, though the static whine of his presence in the magnetic field told him he was close. There was, however, another man standing there. He was older, with a dark Mediterranean cast to his features and a head of white hair. He was dressed in the clothes of a priest—collar and everything.

"Ah. You're no doubt seeking Kaamos," the man said in an accented English that betrayed an upper-class education. "I'm very sorry for this, my boy."

He raised a hand, but Gauss was faster, slinging a hail of ball bearings at the man. It was uncanny—he'd never used them against real people before. He still wasn't using them at their full possible speed; he was a little afraid of the harm he might cause if he did so. Though he had no idea what the man in the priest's robes could do, he wasn't going to throw everything he had at him. Not yet.

Even so, he used the force he'd always used in training scenarios at Retreat Weekends, and that seemed sufficient for his purposes. It was always weird to fire the ball bearings. People are accustomed to things moving at such a speed being accompanied by a sound of some kind: the twang of a string or cord, the crack of gunfire, something like that. Not his attacks—they were utterly silent, and difficult to anticipate because of it, until they started slamming into their targets.

The priest spun, his cassock flaring out around him. Though he was clearly physically fit, it wasn't a superpowered maneuver in the least, and he stumbled as several of the ball bearings slammed into him. It sounded like hail falling on a side of beef: rapid, staccato, meaty thumps. The older man fell and did not get up. Gauss focused on the shadows, searching them for this Kaamos fellow. He used eyes, ears, and magnetic senses, and found something odd—radio chatter, coming from the rooftop. Unsure what it meant for a moment, Gauss realized it was communication. They were in contact with someone else while they did this, and if there were two of them, there might be more.

With the snap of his fingers, he laid down a blanket of electromagnetic static over the area. "Just you and me, Kaamos," he said aloud, gloating. "I don't think I want you–"

He wasn't ready for the man to coalesce out of the shadows and barrel into him, shoulder first. Both of them slammed to the rough rooftop, Kaamos riding Gauss like a bodyboard while the redhead took the road burn of the skid along its surface. He stopped when his head and shoulder slammed into the lip at the edge of the roof.

"Augh!" Gauss howled. "Get away get away get—" He reached out with his power, anxious for anything to get this jerk off him. He latched onto the power lines just above their heads and yanked them down, slamming their sparking ends into Kaamos's spine. The man shrieked and disappeared, his body dissolving into a broad, wide field of shadow, blinding Gauss for a moment.

He took that moment to kneel up and gesture, pulling his ball bearings from where they were strewn across the roof. They shot toward him and entered a rapid orbit a few feet from him, spinning faster and faster. Protected for a moment, Gauss stumbled to his feet and extended his magnetic senses. *There you are*, he thought as Kaamos re-coalesced from shadow on the other side of the roof. He flung his hand outward, sending a tight spiral of ball bearings streaking toward Kaamos, who once again lost physical cohesion, blinking out of solidity long enough for the projectiles to miss and pepper the wall behind him.

Someone without Gauss's senses wouldn't have known how he did it, but Kaamos's darkness registered as a strange static in the EM spectrum. To someone else, it would have seemed as though Kaamos had simply leapt fifteen or more feet into the air, crossing the distance between them in a single bound. But Gauss saw how he solidified the shadow above him, creating tentacles that lifted and threw him forward.

Kaamos was clearly not used to fighting someone who could see through his darkness. Gauss knelt into as tight of a ball as he could, shoving the rapidly oscillating steel spheres outward, giving them a spin as he did so. Kaamos slammed into the protective edge of that barrier and took a rain of ball bearings blows to face, body and arms. There was a sickening crunch as he did, and he flew aside.

The darkness faded around him just in time to give Sentinel a view of the rooftop. He streaked up from behind the building, rising quickly from the street the building's residents were fleeing to, and then arced downward, a grin on his face to see Rusty standing there victorious.

In a flash, though, Gauss's joy turned to horror. A shimmering field of darkness appeared, its interior spangled with gleaming, spinning starlight. Gauss felt a strange sensation wash over him: a mixture of awe, terror, and deep soul-wrenching guilt that knocked him to his knees. He glanced to one side long enough to see the priest rise to a kneeling position, opening the portal directly in Sentinel's path.

And to see Sentinel, unable to stop quickly enough, fly right into it and disappear. For just a moment, Gauss sensed the magnetic fingerprint of some other place that was far, far from Odessa, and then it closed with a snap.

Sentinel was gone.

CHAPTER FIFTEEN

Odessa, Ukraine
May 7, 2013

"You son of a—" Gauss screamed. The priest rose to his feet as the younger man pulled his ball bearings toward him in a wide arc. Doing so gave a recovered Kaamos his opening. He rose to his knees, throwing his arms out wide, and inky tendrils of darkness sprung out from behind him, flying like spears at Gauss.

Though he twisted, throwing himself aside, the horrible writhing things scored deep lines across his right side, laying open bloody furrows across his shoulder, arm, ribs, and hips. Uncontrolled ball bearings flew off in all directions, pinging off hard surfaces and arcing over the lip of the roof. Gauss landed hard, tried to pull himself to his feet, but buckled back to the rooftop. Pain burned white-hot across his body, and the young redhead wept with the pain, breathing raggedly. In no way had even his most arduous training sessions at the Retreats prepared him for this kind of hurt and exhaustion. He could feel the effects of using his powers at this intensity, muscle cramps, body-wide fatigue, and a slight dizziness.

"I'll take care of him, Claviger."

Gauss realized the tall shadow-man was standing over him prepared to strike, shadow-tendrils rising up behind him like horrible snakes preparing to leap at their prey.

"No, Kaamos, hold," the priest said. "The principals will have use for him. We can take him—"

Gauss had no intention of letting the man finish that thought. With a scream he rose to his feet, shunting himself upward more by his power than his muscles, which screamed at the sudden movement. He magnetically pulled himself toward the most potent source of metal nearby, the exposed girders of a neighboring building. Someone had clearly intended to complete construction there, but never had, and Gauss knew the open steel would give him some measure of advantage.

He sprang off the roof and slingshotted across the small alley separating him from the unfinished building, adhering to the vertical girders by bracelets and boots. He dropped to the half-constructed floor below it and caught his breath. Glancing up, he saw Kaamos and Claviger reach the edge of the roof they were on. Gauss flipped them the bird and turned to run across the building. Even as he did, Kaamos's tendrils were reaching up and across, clinging to the structure to so he could swing himself across the gap. Finding a long length of exposed girder in the floor, Gauss kicked his magnetic field in and poured on the juice, maglev-ing inches above the metal as he had on the railroad tracks a few days earlier.

Kaamos reached the building's edge and landed just in time to see Gauss speed away like a bullet train, crouched to lower his center of gravity, one arm out in front of him to control his velocity and the other at his side for balance. Kaamos leapt into the air, his brachiating tentacles moving him quickly across the old construction site, but nowhere near the speed the young redhead managed.

Gauss heard the shadow-man swear. Unable to keep up, Kaamos began to climb, probably to keep an eye on him. Too late, Gauss realized that he'd stopped focusing on the radio static, though he could hear what they were saying over the radio transmission. He paused, concealed for the moment behind some of the tattered plastic sheeting that was all over the construction site.

"Home base, this is Claviger. We need Velocity. Engagement is too fast for Kaamos and I."

"Received, Claviger. Velocity and crew inbound."

"Fuck that," Rusty muttered, and laid down more radio static. Then he magnetically snatched up a pair of three-foot sections of steel girder and shot them at Kaamos. The shadow-man leapt off his perch, throwing himself into a fall, but one of the girders clipped him, striking him in the leg. He grunted as his tentacles caught him once more, but the sudden jolt looked far from easy or painless. He slammed into the half-constructed wall. It collapsed out from under him, all weather-exposed cinderblock, and he tumbled to a position of cover and looked around frantically.

Gauss slid around a half-built wall, skate-sliding over a girder some twenty feet above Kaamos, and gestured. A volley of spear-like rebars, each almost six feet in length, arced down, slamming into the rough construction at Kaamos's feet, punching into the flooring like nails hammered into place with a single blow. It was an impressive strike, but none of them really came anywhere near him. Just as rapidly, Gauss followed with a typhoon of rivets dropped down on him from above. The real attack, rather than his feint of rebars. Gauss poured everything he had into the attack, wave after wave of steel and iron construction material peppering Kaamos. He even dropped the radio static again, reaching for that extra bit of power.

Gauss's magnetic senses screamed again as Claviger opened his damned gate.

"Portal is open," Rusty heard Claviger say over their radio, the strain evident in his voice. "Velocity is through. And so is Mercy."

"Fuck," Gauss said, and turned to get the hell out of there.

* * *

Sentinel emerged at full speed from the strange celestial portal, only a few feet above a vast body of what turned out to be saltwater. He plowed into it at immense speed and force, and even his telekinetic cone didn't save him from a thorough soaking. Momentarily stunned by the unexpected impact, Sentinel righted himself, rose to the surface, and gained some height above the water.

Water in all directions. He could see coastline far in the distance, but he had no way of knowing what coast that was. For all he knew, the coastline was as likely to be California as Sri Lanka. He quickly oriented himself. Knowing what direction he was facing at any given time (another sensory trick all Originals shared) didn't precisely tell him where in the world he was, but he had a better idea of what to look for. The coastline was to his north and west.

Fortunately, he spotted a fishing boat by its running lights, several miles distant. He sped in that direction, building speed to just shy of the sound barrier. As he did so, he glanced down at his clothing, now well-shredded. He extracted his wallet, stored it away in a slot on the inside of his boot, and shrugged out of the rest of the tattered garments.

He arced downward toward the boat, coming even with it some fifteen or so feet away, floating over the water. "Hello?" he called out, startling the men aboard it. Someone replied in Russian. He switched to that language. "Where am I? How far to Odessa?"

One of the men pointed in a general direction, babbling with something that sounded a little like awe and a lot like terror. Even so, he heard one of them tell the other who he was, and he lifted a hand in thanks, rising out of sight.

With some distance between him and the water level, Sentinel poured on the power, diverting as much as he could safely shunt of his power into flight. His telekinetic cone was left with just enough potency to avoid crumpling under the force his flight was generating, but that was all he needed. Within a moment, he reached Mach 1, gritting his teeth at the sheer pressure he was generating against his own body. He set his direction toward where the fisherman had said Odessa was. The sonic boom echoed in the open sky over the ocean, and he became a streak of sound and motion in the air.

"Hold on, Rusty," he whispered.

* * *

Gauss and Kaamos played a deadly game of hide and seek through the half-built tenement apartment building. First Gauss would pepper Kaamos with high-speed metal projectiles, slinging anything he could find and easily lift with his magnetic abilities. Kaamos was slippery, weaving and dodging, batting hurled debris out of the way with tentacles. Even those that did make it past his defenses didn't always land—his body could become partially made of an insubstantial shadow stuff, like a tarry black smoke.

Then it would switch, and Gauss was skating past, trying to put obstacles between himself and Kaamos's barrage of shadowy tentacles. Gauss used the last of his ball bearings mostly defensively, keeping them orbiting him quickly. If he was focusing on other things (like maglev movement or slinging rebar), the tentacles could get through, but when he focused on his defense, the high-speed whine of the ball bearings shredded any of the tentacles physical enough to reach out to him.

It wasn't long before Gauss realized he was going to need an escape, however. He had no idea where Sentinel was, or when or if he'd be back. He might be able to hold his own against Kaamos and Claviger—mostly because Claviger didn't seem to have much in the way of offensive capability—but they were bringing in two more code-named allies. Two more of the Changed that he was sure were ready and willing to at least kick his ass, if not worse.

He wondered who the fuck these people were to begin with, but fought himself back into focus quickly. That was the kind of shit you worried about once you survived something like this. For the first time since arriving in Odessa, he was seriously reconsidering his opinion on superheroing. A lot less glamor, a lot more blood and bodily contusions, it seemed. He reached a corner of the building. He'd lost Kaamos somewhere behind him and to his left. The shadow-man had eaten more than his fair share of ferrous projectiles tonight, so he was moving a little more slowly and a little more cautiously, which gave Gauss the minute he needed. He closed his eyes and focused on his magnetic senses.

The magnetic field encompassed and surrounded him, and he could feel details of his environment mostly by the distortions they caused in the field. He could discern the static of strong and weak electrical sources, and out to a few blocks could mostly tell the structure of the world by the way its metals warped the field—ferrous metals creating stronger impressions, but less magnetic ones registering faintly as well.

Bigger metal features showed up strongly, practically beacons to those senses. Bigger features like...ah, there it was! A railroad track, about four blocks over.

Gauss opened his eyes, glanced around, and stepped off the side of the building, slowing his descent by adhering to the system of girders that ran down the side of the construction, more elevator than maglev train. Still, his descent was quick. He landed softly and stumbled a little. He pressed a hand to the ugly slashes that marred his right side. He was still bleeding, and standing still for a moment, he was overcome with nausea and dizziness.

Damn it. At this point, he wasn't sure if it was blood loss or the electrolyte depletion his power caused. Whatever it was, he felt like shit. Glancing about, he broke into a run, moving as silently as he could, homing in on that length of train track. If he could just get to it, he was pretty sure that–

Sudden blinding impact threw Gauss multiple feet in the air, slamming him into a garbage dumpster with a hollow metallic thud. Gauss shook his head and looked up to see what hit him.

The woman had a slight Asian cast to her features and wore a composite bodysuit much like his own, in a simple green-and-gold design. She was removing a pair of goggles, their lenses shattered by his protective field of rivets and ball-bearings. She was also holding her side. The outfit left her arms bare, and already bright bruises in the shape of Gauss' defensive debris bloomed on her fair skin. She tossed aside the goggles.

"That was my best pair," she said, in American-accented English and threw herself at him. She was *fast*—insanely fast, in fact, and she came at him with a boxer's lunge.

Gauss was ready for her charge this time. He half-pivoted, focusing his power on the large but mostly empty green dumpster behind him, and swiveled. Trash bags and other alley debris went flying as the big metal thing shifted its position with a metallic screech of protest, interposing it between himself and the woman. She slammed into it with enough force to not only dent the hell out it, but to shove it back into Gauss, slamming him into the wall. It didn't quite knock his breath out of him, though it did crack his head against the brick of the wall behind him.

Brick and steel wall, that is.

With no physical movement from him at all, Gauss not only boosted the magnetic potential of both dumpster and girders in the wall behind him, but he shifted them to radically opposing charges. With a horrible sound, the dumpster shot away from the wall, slamming into the woman. It bull rushed her across the open space and crunched her up against the wall on the other side of the alley.

Gauss quickly got to his feet and ran. Two more blocks. Just two more blocks.

He never made it. With less than a block to go, another woman found him. She wore a simple composite bodysuit of white and dove grey, and a pearlescent white mask that covered her forehead, cheeks and nose, its lower halves dipping down to her jawline. In a half-moment she was in front of him, wincing as his defensive barrier impacted her, peppering her with high-speed debris.

Then, in a literal heartbeat, she was *inside* his field.

Gauss wasn't entirely sure what happened then. He knew she laid him into a grapple of some kind. There were pressure points involved, and joints being forced to cartilage-grinding directions. He shrieked in sudden pain, forced to his knees, and then with a pivot, his face was ground into the sidewalk concrete. Things popped and snapped inside his body and he gasped and then mercifully lost consciousness.

* * *

Gauss' debris field clattered to the ground like so much junk, and the masked woman smiled down at him. In a blur of green-and-gold, the speedster caught up to them and skidded to a halt.

"That's always impressive as hell to watch, Mercy," Velocity said with a grin.

Mercy held up a finger and tilted her head, listening intently. Then her gaze snapped to the air above them.

"Velocity, can you carry us both?" Mercy asked.

"What, you and the kid? No way, sorry."

"Alright, just me, then." She stepped up to Velocity, who hefted her up. Mercy spoke into their earbud radios. "Claviger, portal out at the ready. Sentinel's found us. Extraction time; we leave the kid."

Velocity sped off in a streak before Claviger could respond.

In less than a minute, Sentinel arced down out of the sky. He landed beside Rusty, and looked down at him for half a moment, fear threatening to paralyze him. Shaking it off, he knelt beside the boy. There were broken bones, he could tell, and ugly slashes along the right side of his body. He was breathing, though, if shallowly, and Sentinel could hear that now familiar heartbeat, though it was weakened. He glared in the direction he'd seen the attackers flee, then gingerly scooped Gauss into his arms and took to the air.

CHAPTER SIXTEEN

DTPA Cascades Medical Facility, Washington State
May 18, 2013

In the hour she'd been waiting in the overly-white lobby, Deosil fidgeted in her seat, bounded to her feet to walk some of the anxiety off, returned to her seat when her pacing clearly began to aggravate the nurse on duty at the desk, leapt to her feet again to go glare at the vending machines, found another seat where she could curl her legs up under her, popped outside to get some fresh air and stare at her phone, and then come inside to reclaim a seat.

She was so damned restless that she was sure the desk nurse was going to call an orderly and have her sedated, so she was relieved when someone called her name.

"Deosil?" the man in the blazer asked. He peered at her owlishly through his round glasses, his hair slicked back as usual with some kind of god-awful smelling hair product.

"Dr. Ryans." She stood to shake his perpetually sweaty hand. "It's good to see you again."

"Likewise," he said effusively. The last time they'd seen one another was last year's Retreat. Doc Ryans was responsible for giving her the annual psych eval. "How are you? Is everything alright?"

She grinned at him and flicked the VISITOR badge clipped to one of the strings of her oversized hoodie. "Yeah, I'm not here for me. A friend of mine was being treated here and he's being released today."

"Ah, you must mean Gauss," he said, with the look people get when they put two and two together. "There's been a lot of talk around the facility about him and how he got here, yeah."

Which of course made sense. But still, knowing that Rusty's exploits were the talk of the DTPA's Cascades Medical Facility? Not her favorite bit of trivia. "Yeah, I imagine so."

The doctor kept nodding and just *looking* at her, the way he did during their previous session. She wondered if it would be terribly rude to remind him that they were having a *conversation*, and that he needed to hold up his end of it. Fortunately, he seemed to realize that on his own. "Ah, well. Will we see you at the Retreat next month?"

"I'll be there, definitely," she said warmly. "Will you be doing the eval for me again this year?"

"Ah, there's no telling. They usually like to mix such things up, you know. Although, I am based out of here, so if you'd ever like to schedule some sessions—you know, outside of the Retreat—I'd be happy to do so."

She meant to say *In your dreams, motherfucker.* Instead it came out like "I'll definitely keep that in mind. Thanks."

Fortunately, he ran out of things to say, couldn't justify hanging around the lobby chatting, and went on his way. Deosil collapsed back into her seat, which made an annoying squeak as she slid against the...pleather? What was this stuff? Nothing natural, anyway.

Finally—mercifully—the elevator doors opened and a nurse emerged, pushing a wheelchair with a wan Rusty in it. Despite the fact that he still had hints of how badly damaged he'd been, mostly in weird pale green-and-yellow mottling where big ugly bruises used to be, he was talking to the nurse very animatedly. "I'm not even saying I have to walk, really. Like, I can push myself in the wheelchair. It's all metal—I can just move it along with my power. No physical exertion for me, and you can get back to your...nursing... things..."

The nurse ignored him studiously, but she did seem relieved when he stopped talking, having seen Deosil. "Jesh!" he exclaimed, giving every indication that he was going to leap from the chair.

"Sit," the nurse said gruffly, and Rusty shrank in on himself, nodding.

Deosil crossed to him and bent down to give him a big hug. "You ready to get out of here?"

"Jesus, am I." He craned his head back to regard the long-suffering nurse who clearly wanted nothing more than to *please* get this wheelchair out the door. "Is there anything else I need to sign or do or whatever?"

"I just have to wheel you out the door," she said with a pointed look to Deosil, who took the hint and sidestepped so she could walk beside them. She did reach down to grab his hand, and he smiled warmly up at her.

Despite this, there was some final bit of red-tape that needed managing. The nurse pushed the chair into a small alcove between some of the seats in the lobby, and walked purposefully over to the nearby desk. Rusty groaned, and looked at the big glass doors beyond which waited the light of day and no smell of antiseptic whatsoever.

"So close," he whined. He scanned the lobby like he was hoping to find something, but caught himself doing so and stopped.

Deosil frowned. "Did he still not come and visit you?"

"No," he said quietly. Deosil slid into the chair next to him and held both his hands. He looked like he might cry. "I know I'm stupid to expect anything. To hope for something like that."

"Hey," she said, gripping his hands tighter. "I'm sure he's got a damned good reason for not coming to visit you. Sentinel wouldn't just abandon you here, you know?"

"I know he felt really bad about everything. Maybe he just feels too guilty or something? He's a really nice guy."

"He is. And yeah, maybe he's wallowing in stupid guilty man-pain or something. If he is, though, I'm going to kick his ass for him, Original or not. But whatever it is, I'm sure it's not because he doesn't want to see you, or is avoiding you, or whatever else bullshit self-loathing story your fucking brain is telling you right now."

Rusty laughed, but she didn't miss the quick tear that spilled over onto his cheek before he wiped the treacherous bit of moisture away. "Ugh. Pain meds are making me so moody." He looked out the window for a moment, and then glanced back over where his nurse was filling out some sort of paperwork, chatting with the nurse on duty. He did that thing where he chewed the inside of his cheek for a moment, and Deosil let him. She knew he had something important on his mind.

"I think I'm kinda in love with him, Jesh," he said finally, and studiously avoided facing her, turning to watch the window again. "It's stupid, I know, but…"

It was. Of course it was.

"Hey, stop it, no," she said anyway. "Love is supposed to not make sense. You can't control it, and it's totally unreasonable."

"I mean, it's probably something all wrapped up with what happened in Ukraine, and I just–"

"Okay," Deosil said. "Let's not bullshit here—you've been in love with him since you met him. Probably since before you met him. You literally know dozens of Changed, and yet he was the one you went to in order to get help with this? So, no. What happened was awful, but he was there for you, which I'm sure has definitely cemented how you feel, but it's not why. You already were in love. You're just super shitty at figuring that stuff out."

He laughed again. "God, you're the worst."

"Shut up. I'm amazing. You only barely deserve someone as awesome as I am." She scoffed and rubbed his hair like she was threatening to give him a noogie. He winced, though, and Deosil belatedly remembered something about a head injury. "I just think that–"

"All done here," the nurse said, beside them again. Without another word, she wheeled Rusty out the door, with Deosil beside them.

"Well, well, well," Deosil said in that God-awful smug way she had sometimes.

Mitch was standing just under the overhang, watching them emerge with a face full of anxiety. He'd clipped away his beard, though he still had a light dusting, like he was doing everything in his power to avoid looking like the clean-shaven face of the Champions. Deosil didn't miss the nurse pausing to regard him, and then glancing back inside. She sniffed and helped a frankly poleaxed Rusty out of the wheelchair.

"You came," Rusty said. If he actually knew how much he'd said with just those two words, Deosil was sure he'd be very embarrassed, but he had other things on his mind right now.

"Of course I did," Mitch said. He stood there for a moment, as though he weren't sure exactly what to do. If his six-and-a-half-foot of wide-shouldered muscle being all awkward and weird weren't so sad, it would be endearing.

Fortunately, Rusty had no hesitation and wrapped him into a hug. Mitch seemed relieved, and returned it warmly.

Deosil rolled her eyes. "Okay, I'm going to let you two get caught up while I go get the car. Stay right here. Don't fly away to save any more people until I get back. Assholes." She pointed to the bench and Rusty laughed and thanked her. He shuffled over to the bench, leaning on Mitch, who greeted her belatedly, embarrassed at not registering her presence. She snorted and set off for the parking lot.

Rusty and Mitch watched her go, almost as an excuse to avoid talking, it seemed like. Finally Rusty leaned his head into Mitch's shoulder affectionately and said, "I'm crazy glad to see you."

Mitch rubbed his cheek against the top of Rusty's head, and said, "Me, too."

Rusty straightened, and shifted slightly on the bench. His movements were ginger and cautious, with the physical hesitation of someone who's just recovered from extensive bodily trauma and a couple of weeks in bed. Rusty bit his lip like he wasn't sure what to say.

"What's up?" Mitch asked, brow furrowed.

Rusty sighed, frustrated. "Well, not to be shitty, but why is this the first time I'm seeing you, man?"

Mitch blinked at him, confused. He glared back at the doors to the facility, jaw clenched. "Did they not tell you?"

"Tell me what?"

"Rusty, I'm so sorry—I assumed they would at least tell you," Mitch said, voice full of anger. "I tried to come visit you. The Department banned me from the facility."

"What?" Rusty's voice raised in outrage. "They wouldn't let you in to see me?"

"I tried twice, and they made excuses each time. The third time I came back, they had a DTPA security team on premises, who told me I wasn't allowed in at all." The frustration in Mitch's voice at what must have been a humiliating face-down with a team of DTPA Echoes was palpable. "I'm so sorry. I hate the thought of you being in there this entire time, not knowing, thinking that I wasn't coming to see you for no reason."

Rusty hugged him again, and the bigger man returned the embrace. They were still hugging when a woman cleared her throat deliberately. Mitch pulled away first, glancing at her out of embarrassment and then did a double-take that was all clenched jaw and narrowed eyes.

"We're leaving," he said curtly. The woman was in her late thirties or early forties, dressed in a women's suit, navy blue jacket and skirt in razor-sharp, perfect lines. She held in her hands a tablet computer. Behind and to her left stood Caustic, someone Rusty recognized from the Retreats. Rusty nodded a greeting to him, but Caustic's gaze was focused on Mitch.

"This isn't about that," said the woman. "You're fine here, and you've respected the limits we requested of you. We have no problem." Though her tone was conciliatory, she appeared to be here in some official capacity and had no intention of lessening her established authority in their relationship so far.

"Then what is this about, Director?" Mitch's tone was curt.

Rusty shifted uncomfortably; she smiled at him. "My name is Belinda Veracruz, Rusty. I'm the Director for the DTPA in the Pacific Northwest."

He recognized the name. It was often all over the various pamphlets, letters, and emails he got from the Department. She was one of the six Directors, the ones who made all the decisions. "Nice to meet you," he mumbled, and stepped out of the way. Only then did Caustic glance at him, and then away at Mitch again.

"I've been asked to take your statement about the incident in Ukraine, Mr. McCann," she said to Mitch, that smile etched unwaveringly on her face. "Both the DTPA and the State Department have some questions that we'd like answered, if we can take up a moment of your time. Rusty has already been kind enough to give us his account."

Rusty felt a little sick to his stomach. They'd come in shortly after he'd regained consciousness, post-surgery, his doctor and a man in a suit from the Department, with an hour's flurry of questions. He'd been solicitous in his concern for Rusty's health, and firm in his condemnation of his and Sentinel's actions, but overall pleasant enough. Despite that, after they were done, there was no question in Rusty's mind that it was an interrogation, and those answers were going to some important people.

"Not interested," Mitch growled. Director Veracruz continued to smile, but behind her Caustic scowled and unconsciously clenched his fists. Belatedly, Rusty recalled Caustic was one of those Echoes who felt like he had something to prove. Jesus, he wouldn't be stupid enough to try something against Sentinel, would he?

"Mr. McCann, you and Rusty were returned to the United States by Vigilance. The Department managed to smooth things over with the Ukrainian government and Vigilance, but part of our deal is that we share our debriefing information with them. We'd like to offer them as complete an account as we can, as a sign of good faith and no bad intentions, and we'd appreciate it if you would do the same by sharing your perspective with us."

"You've got to be kidding me," Mitch spat. Rusty was shocked at the heavy contempt in his tone. "You don't have any legal authority over me. I've never signed up with your organization. If the United States government has an issue with me, they can come and talk to me directly. In fact, I'll be happy to go to them. But I'm not dealing with Marque's organization. You're out of your mind, Ms. Veracruz."

Rusty was genuinely afraid that Caustic was just going to pounce, but Director Veracruz held up a hand. He relaxed, though he did throw a warning glance at Rusty. The Director sighed. "I'm aware of your past troubles with Marque, Mr. McCann. And I knew to expect some degree of reticence from you, in terms of your cooperation with us because of it. What he did back then was inexcusable, particularly by today's standards. But he's only the Chairman of our organization, with no authority other than when the Board of Directors is deadlocked—a situation we take great pains to ensure never happens, I might add.

"The fact is, Sentinel, he's our founder and the primary liaison for the Department with the U.S. government, thanks to his military and political contacts. But we're not all like him. Some of us are just trying to keep everyone safe, and this is one of the ways in which we do that."

Deosil's clunker of a ride pulled up then, and Rusty glanced back at her. She got out of the car, and stood, driver's side door open, staring across the roof of the old rusty station wagon, concern on her face.

Mitch never took his eyes off of the Director. "Let me tell you something. You say you're trying to keep people safe? That might be the case in the United States. But there are people who *aren't* safe. Who don't have *anyone* to watch out for them. If you want to send my report back to Ukraine and Vigilance, you can tell them this: when they start treating everyone in their population like human beings worthy of respect and protection—including the gay ones—then people like me will butt out." He turned and started to guide Rusty to the car, but paused to turn back to regard the carefully controlled face of the Director. "But until then? No promises."

It wasn't until Rusty was safely ensconced in the passenger seat, and Mitch about to fold himself into the back seat that the Director said something. "Mr. McCann." Her voice shook a little, though her control over it was iron-like. "I hope that I don't have to warn you not to do anything foolish. Vigilantism by the Changed is a federal offense. It would grieve a lot of people to be forced to arrest you, Sentinel, but we will do just that if you force us. Don't think we don't have the means of making even you obey the rightful laws of our nation. You aren't above them, no matter what you might think."

Mitch gave no indication of having heard her, instead sprawling into the back seat.

"Get us. The fuck. Out of here," Rusty hissed at Deosil, who did just that.

* * *

The silence in the car as they left Olympia in the late afternoon was unbearable, and stretched on until they were firmly on the I-5, headed back to Portland. Rusty leaned his seat back a little and kept shifting, trying to get comfortable. He closed his eyes.

Mitch glared out the window. He was in a backseat that was too small for a man of his stature—he knew it had to be nearly comical to see him folded into it. He leaned sideways, his temple resting against the driver-side window, the right side of his face bathed in the light of the setting sun. Rusty reached back with one hand, inquisitively, and after a few heartbeats, Mitch took it.

For her part, Deosil focused on the drive. Eventually, though, the silence got the better of her. "So, what was that all about?"

With a sigh, Rusty told her. She nodded throughout the re-telling, and then sighed. "She's kinda right," she said. Mitch glanced up, a frown on his face, and caught her watching him through the mirror. "Not about you, per se. I mean, you're an Original—you guys have always kind of been your own thing, you know?" She glanced sideways at Rusty. "But you broke the law, Rusty. That's a big deal. I know that Sentinel doesn't need them, but if it weren't for the DTPA, you'd probably be in some fucked-up gulag or something. At the very least, you'd be dealing with some crazy legal bullshit, you know?"

"I know," Rusty said miserably. Mitch squeezed his hand. After a few more moments of silence, the redhead shifted in his seat so he could regard Deosil better. "But you know what? I was fucking right to be concerned. I mean, I know that everyone is all worried about what Vigilance is going to do, politically or legally, and all the rest of that. But seriously? I was *right*. Not only did Kosma and Oleksander fucking disappear without a trace, but when we started putting our noses into it, we got attacked by Echoes, Jesh. Mean motherfuckers, too. There's something shady as hell going on."

Deosil nodded. "It's kinda different outside the U.S., Rusty. Other countries don't all have something like the DTPA, so it's still kinda dangerous cowboy Wild West territory out there. It's not surprising."

Rusty narrowed his eyes at her. "So, what, we just shrug? These dudes are snatching up queer kids in countries that don't give a *fuck* about whether or not those kids go missing. Vigilance literally didn't even *hear* me when I told them that. You should have seen the reaction of that big one—"

"Medvedka," Mitch supplied.

"Yeah. He just smirked when I told him, and then walked out of the room. Like, not only did he not give a damn, but like he was *happy*."

Deosil bit her lower lip while she drove. Rusty turned back in his seat to watch the Washington countryside fly by out the passenger window. He rubbed at his eyes.

"I know," she said quietly. "And I hate it. I do. But you also have to take care of yourself. You have to be careful. Getting yourself imprisoned or fucking killed doesn't do anyone any good. You're not one of the Originals, Rusty. You're just a dude, with some powers."

She glanced back into the mirror, and Mitch's gaze was there waiting for her. He held it for a moment and nodded. She blamed him for this, Mitch knew, and she was right. If he'd refused to help, Rusty wouldn't have even had the ability to try something like this. Mitch was the first to look away, shamefaced. He suddenly very much longed for his small apartment and his simple construction job.

After another twenty minutes or so, Deosil glanced back at the mirror. "You okay back there? You've got to be crammed up into that tiny seat. There's a diner I know of just ahead. You boys want to get out and stretch a little?"

"I'm alright," Mitch mumbled.

Rusty looked back at him. "I'm not," he said. "And some non-hospital food sounds awesome right now. I could kill like three burgers."

* * *

They arrived at the diner, Rusty swearing the entire way that he was going to eat three burgers all on his own. Mitch was smiling when they all got out of the car, but he paused beside the old beat-up station wagon.

"Hey, Rusty, can you go grab us a table? I need to steal a second with Jesh."

Deosil and Rusty glanced at one another—one of those looks to see if the other knew what the hell this was all about—before he grinned and warned them that he was probably going to get started without them. Deosil lingered beside the vehicle, not sure what was going on, but trepidatious nonetheless.

Once the redhead had retreated indoors, Mitch leaned against the car. "Hey. I just wanted to apologize."

She squinted. "Uh. What for?"

"You know what." He sighed, exasperated. "For getting Rusty into trouble. I know he's a good friend, and means a lot to you. I just—I don't know. I don't have a good excuse."

She hesitated, and then leaned against the car herself. "Thanks," she said. "Yeah, he does kinda mean a lot to me, the idiot."

"I don't..." Mitch paused, searching for words. Or maybe a touch of courage. "I don't want to hurt him."

"Ah," she said. "Has he said anything to you himself?"

"No. He's just not terribly subtle."

Deosil cackled. "Isn't that the damned truth?" She sobered and fixed him with a look. "Thing is? He's kind of fragile. When he falls, he falls hard."

"So, how do I do this? I'm not going to lie. I'm in my sixties, and am treading entirely new waters here. I've only ever been involved with one person, Radiant, and he did all the pursuing. He knew what was what, and I could just follow his lead, if that makes any sense."

"It does. Just him, huh?"

Mitch nodded, as though it took every ounce of his strength to do so. "I know it's stupid. I do. He knew who I was on the inside, and I was so much more of myself when he was around. I know it's not healthy or sane, even, but I feel like the only time I was ever truly me was when we were together, and when he died? I did, too. The real me, at least."

Deosil reached out to lay a hand on his arm. He regarded her with an expression full of pain. "Am I too messed up to even be thinking about something like this? If he's as fragile as you say he is, I don't think I know how to be the strong one in a relationship, Deosil."

She shook her head sadly. "I'm going to level with you—I don't think anyone's ever the strong one in the relationship. I think we're all just different degrees of broken people, and we do our best to figure out how to make the people we love hurt a little less, while trusting them enough to let them make our hurt a little less."

He smiled—goddamn, that winning smile, that iconic smile that was almost literally the face of America for a decade and change—and hugged her. "You're pretty wise for someone your age."

She laughed and hugged him back. "Well, I can dish it out pretty well. But I'd really be wise if I could figure out how to take my own advice. Now let's get our asses inside before he follows through on his threat to eat himself sick, and we have to pull over every ten minutes on the way back to Portland."

"Hey, before we go in." Mitch stopped her and glanced back at the diner window. Rusty was seated beside it, doing his best not to show he was watching them. For a moment, Deosil was glad Rusty wasn't an Original. "When some people I know found out what was going on with all of this—it's not exactly in the news or anything, but I still know some people from my Champions days—they contacted me and some things about Rusty came up."

Deosil's spine straightened.

"Is it true that he's done–" he paused, searching for a way to put it. "Adult movies?"

Deosil fixed him with a pointed regard. "You haven't looked online for yourself?"

He shook his head. "I mean, I know how, if that's what you're wondering, but it seemed like it would be an invasion of his privacy."

"Even if it's all on the internet?"

"*Especially* if it is."

Deosil hesitated, and then sighed. "So, here's the thing. By all rights, I should be telling you to ask him directly if you really want to know. He deserves that kind of honesty, especially if you're concerned about it in any way."

Mitch at least had the decency to look abashed.

"But," she said, with a raised finger. "Here's the thing. It's true, he did some very high-profile porn, about two years ago. He was eighteen and had no idea what was ahead of him. He got all wrapped up in the party lifestyle, because when you've gotten shit from family as a kid, the kind of enthusiastic acceptance you can find at clubs and bars is practically addicting. Yes, he ended up doing porn. In fact, he made some bank from being the first Echo to do porn. I met him at the Retreat shortly after he did it, and he was getting all kinds of attention—none of it the kind he wanted. He was a broken kid that nobody wanted to help get his shit together, and cute, so there were plenty of people interested in taking advantage of his fucked up-ness."

She fixed Mitch with a very severe look. "If this isn't something you can handle—I know you grew up in a different time and place or whatever, so I'm not judging you if it's the case—but if it's a little too much of a freakout for you to possibly be interested in someone that's done porn? Say so now. Don't you fucking stretch it out, because his past isn't going to magically go away."

Mitch nodded. "I know what everyone thinks of me. And I'm seriously not that uptight. I mean, I was a big celebrity hero on the world stage in the eighties. If I learned anything growing up a closeted queer kid, it was that I don't have a right to judge. I've kind of earned my reputation as something of a prude, but that's all on me. I don't expect other people to hold to that.

"I'm asking because I wanted to know if the stories I'd heard were just slander. He hasn't said anything himself, but I can't imagine how you'd bring something like that up. To me? I don't give a damn. I just needed to know, not for my opinion of him, but for my opinion of the people who felt the need to tell me."

Deosil paused. "Huh. Well, aren't you a little bucket full of surprises." She glanced at the window. "Let's go inside already."

Their lunch offered the kind of greasy satisfaction that only roadside diners can provide, and despite his threats, Rusty ate less than any of them. "Hey, some of us are recovering from extensive injuries, you know," he said.

"So, what all was the final tally in that department?" Deosil asked around a grilled chicken sandwich.

"God, I don't even remember. I've got some gnarly scars from where Kaamos laid my side open in about six places—three along my ribs, one at the hip, and two more along the top of my right leg. Lost a lot of blood from those. Whoever the masked woman was who got ahold of me really messed me up, though."

"Was that the speedster?" Deosil asked.

"No, that was Velocity, I think. The one I'm talking about was the one in grey and white, with the weird mask. I didn't see her use any powers, actually, unless it was the power to kick the shit out of me. She was fast, but not like speedster fast. Just quick and agile. She got inside my shield and like, tried to *murder* me. She dislocated one of my shoulders and the elbow on the same arm. She kicked me in the knee and displaced the cap a little and broke a rib. She drove the damned thing into one of my lungs, in fact—deflated it, straight up."

Deosil goggled. "Are you fucking *kidding me*? How are you even up and walking around right now?"

"Oh, one of the Vigilance supers. He apparently had healing powers of some kind. I was in rough shape when Mitch got me to the hospital there in Odessa, but by the time I was on a flight back to the U.S., it was mostly ugly bruises and a world full of soreness."

Deosil shook her head and smothered the urge to kill Rusty right here. It seemed rude to do in the wake of someone actually trying to do so. She thought a change of subject was in order. "So, you remember telling me about that portal guy?"

"Yeah. You said his power seemed familiar?"

"It did, and it was bugging me. I found where I'd read it before." She turned to Mitch to include him in the conversation. "You know the volunteer work I do with the Golden Cross? My elemental powers are useful when it comes to natural disasters and stuff. So, they have an online forum for their volunteers to talk about their experiences, share 'battle stories' and generally form a sort of community, encouraging and congratulating one another on their successes, and stuff like that."

She turned back to Rusty. "So, I was on that forum, and someone was asking some questions. She described someone who used powers just like you describe—not just a portal, but all disco lights and woo-woo endorphin rush and everything. The post was kinda cagey, like she was trying not to say too much, but I got the impression there was something else going on."

"Do you know who made the post? What it was about?" Mitch asked.

Deosil shook her head. "I do know her, but she didn't say why she needed to know. Her name's Llorona. She's based out in Texas, and does almost full-time work for the Golden Cross. She apparently worked with the Champions back in the day, and when Cobalt formed the GC, she asked Llorona to join. Worked with them ever since."

"Llorona," Rusty mused. "Isn't she the one who was there at the Playa Event? Where you Echoed?"

"That's her. Honestly, she saved so many lives that day. She also talked me down—she figured out that someone onsite was making the elemental storm worse through their powers. She could have just kicked my ass to knock me out or something, but she talked me through it instead. She's pretty awesome."

"I know her," Mitch said. "I occasionally do some emergency work in big situations the Golden Cross deals with—earthquakes, typhoons, stuff like that."

"Really? You still go out heroing these days?"

"Not in costume or anything. And it's not really Champions-type stuff. I'm not beating up superpowered jackasses—it's rescue work, and phenomenon mitigation."

Rusty squinted. "Phenomenon mitigation?"

Deosil grinned at him. "That's what the Golden Cross calls it when they get one or more supers out to use their powers to stop natural or unnatural disasters with their powers. I'm shit at rescue ops, but I'm really good at most mitigation work." She smiled up at the waitress who brought her dessert, and waited till she left. "Anyway, I've pinged her to see if she'll tell me some more about what that post was about. But *only* so that we can pass that info on to the DTPA, alright? No more vigilante bullshit."

Rusty nodded with a smile, and stole a bite of her ice cream and brownie, ignoring her protestation. "Yeah, honestly, I'm down for laying low for a while. The term is ending soon, I've got some make-up work to do, and I could use some more sleep."

Mitch's clenched jaw was like stone. "Agreed. Those people were clearly trained killers. And I have no intention of letting them use that little trick on me again."

Deosil turned to blink at him. "Again? You're going after them again?"

"I'm going to keep hunting for them, yes. I'll happily take that information to the authorities, assuming the authorities give a damn."

"Is this a payback thing?" she asked, cutting right to the heart of it. Rusty winced.

Mitch hesitated. "Truth? Maybe. I don't know. But there was a lot of blood on the side of the building, Jesh. A lot of it. If this is a regular thing for them, I have no intention of remaining idle. I'm sorry if that upsets you."

Rusty smiled, and focused on his French fries some more, studiously ignoring Deosil's warning glance in his direction.

"I just think that—Damn it, hold on," she cursed, answering her phone. Rusty took that opportunity to catch Mitch's eye and whisper something he knew the bigger man would be able to hear, but Deosil wouldn't.

"Count me in," he said. Mitch gave him a warning glance. *Let's talk later,* it seemed to say. Rusty smiled and ran his foot along Mitch's calf.

"Holy shit, okay," Deosil said, hanging up the phone. "So, that was Optic."

"What?" Rusty grimaced. "What the hell did he want?"

"Well, he said he tried to call you, but couldn't get a message through," she said, taking a last bite of her dessert. "He heard we're getting back into town, and he'd like to chat with us about some things he's heard. He wanted to know if we'd have dinner at his place in Portland?"

"What did you tell him?" Mitch asked.

"I told him I'd check with you two, and text him." She thumbed through her phone, bringing up her messaging app. "So, yea or nay?"

Mitch glanced at Rusty. "He could have some useful information. And he did help us out earlier."

"Oh, God," Rusty sighed. "Alright. Let's do it."

CHAPTER SEVENTEEN

Portland, Oregon
May 18, 2013

Deosil's old clunky beater got them into Portland early that evening. The sun was low in the west, though it wasn't quite dusk. "You okay back there?" Deosil asked Mitch as they left the bridge over the Columbia River. "I'm sorry it's so cramped, especially for someone your size."

Mitch smiled up at her in the rearview mirror. "I'm fine, thanks, Jesh."

Rusty reached back and squeezed his knee, craning his neck around to see him. "I'm surprised you didn't just fly out. Meet up with us at Optic's."

Mitch responded by capturing his hand and giving it a squeeze in return. "I wanted to ride with the two of you. It's been too long since I've gotten to see you. I want to make sure you're okay."

Deosil shot Rusty a smug look, but he was too busy grinning like a loon. "Okay, so make yourself useful. Optic texted me the address," Deosil said, shoving her phone at Rusty. He clicked through it a bit, and then whistled.

"What is it?" Mitch asked.

"Oh, I just should have known," Rusty said, rolling his eyes. "Of *course* Optic would get a place up in the West Hills. It's a super-swanky part of town. God, the map-cam view of his house from the street is just ridiculous."

He flashed it to Mitch. It was an expensive home, with a prominent wrap-around deck made of fieldstone that extended out over the view of Portland from a high hill. It was all tall windows and artist's angles.

If the phone view was noteworthy, then actually standing in front of the place was flat-out memorable. It was bigger than the picture made it seem, and Optic had done some renovations to suit his taste that the maps app hadn't updated yet. The paint job was a darker color, and the massive windows were fitted with electronically controlled tinting.

When Deosil's old rattling car pulled up in his driveway, Optic stepped out onto the front porch. He was barefoot, wearing a set of blue soft cotton workout pants with a simple white short sleeved t-shirt that showed off his tattooed arms.

"I'm not sure this is a good idea," Rusty said, half-turning to Deosil as she shut off the car. "Maybe I should just go. Tell him I've got school or something?"

She fixed him with a glare, unbuckled her seat belt, and shifted in her seat so that she was facing Rusty directly. He couldn't seem to meet her eyes.

"Nope," she said with authority. "That idea is, as usual, terrible. You're staying. You're having dinner. And you're not going to be a freak about it, because you're a grown-ass man that has investigated murders and fought supervillains, and you sure as hell don't have to worry about whatever summer flings you might have had with our host. Got me?"

Rusty couldn't help but grin. "Loud and clear," he said.

"Good," she said, opening her door. "Now get your ass out of the car." She took her own advice, slamming the door behind her, and crossed the small distance to the threshold of the house.

"She's a firecracker," Mitch said, reaching his hand up to rest on Rusty's shoulder. "She's right, though. You can do this. Do you *want* to do this?"

Rusty unbuckled his belt and in his seat to face Mitch. "I so do. Let's go."

Optic greeted Mitch enthusiastically, and he returned it. Rusty was pretty sure that Deosil's immediate kidnapping of Mitch was on purpose; he just wasn't sure whether to thank her or murder her for the favor of leaving him and Optic alone.

Once it was just the two of them on the front porch, Rusty squinted at the house that loomed above them. "Nice digs," he said.

"I appreciate you coming, Rusty," Optic said. "I know you didn't have to."

Rusty nodded distractedly, as though the man's house were far more inter-esting than anything going on between them. He should say something, he knew. He just wasn't sure what. He knew a peace offering when he saw one, but to be honest? He wasn't sure if he wanted a peace offering from Optic. If it was possible to get comfortable holding onto a grudge, Rusty realized that he'd become very at-home with that resentment. He'd spent so many hours discussing it with Deosil—how could he let it go cavalierly?

Especially without an actual real-life apology?

"Let's go inside," Optic finally said, with a sigh. "I've got some stuff to put on the grill."

After giving everyone the tour of the six-bedroom house, which proved to be as unbearably nice as Rusty had expected, the small group retired to the back deck to enjoy the last warmth of the day and watch night settle in over downtown Portland. They gathered in a cluster of wooden chairs. A folding door opened in the wall of the house behind them, displaying the deck's bar and mini-kitchen, and Optic wandered from it to the ridiculously large grill a little further along the deck, cooking up a handful of steaks and foil packets of veggies and small red potatoes.

"That's a hell of a grill," Deosil said as Optic returned to the chairs and sat down again, taking up his bottle of beer. "There's no way in hell you actually put it to full use. I mean, a big celebrity like you? Like, if you had that many people over, you'd just have it catered or something, right?"

Optic chuckled. "Let me tell you something. I am from Alabama and grew up all around the South. I don't trust anybody in this town to grill up some-thing the right way. And I'll have you know I put this grill to very good use."

"Do tell." She smiled up at him.

"Nothing much to tell, honestly. I like to invite the cast and some of the production and crew over when we get a couple of days off. Most of us don't really know anyone in town, and there's only so much bar-hopping you can stand. It's not really rest when you've got to keep an eye out for paparazzi and shit. So, we come hang out here, drink a little, burn a little meat, and just relax."

Deosil nodded, and absentmindedly tucked her lap blanket in around her legs. "Nice thing about this set-up—it's gotta be hard for camera-wielding stalkers to get the drop on you up here, I guess."

"Well, you'd be surprised, but yeah, mostly." He pointed with his beer bottle at a neighboring property. "Our neighbors don't live here full time. At our last party, one of the grips saw someone taking photos over the wall there that separates our places. Trespassing, just to get a couple of good shots."

"That's insane," Mitch said, shaking his head. "I swear, I could handle the natural disasters, the unforeseen tragedies, and the bands of superpowered cretins trying to make a quick buck at others' expenses. The worst part of the Champions was dealing with the cameramen lying in wait wherever we went."

Optic chuckled. "Yeah, I'd never had to deal with them before. One of the benefits of being a military unit, I guess—the media isn't altogether interested, mostly because Uncle Sam says so." He stood, setting his beer bottle down and returned to the grill. Rusty rolled his eyes, and Deosil glared murder his way.

Be nice, she mouthed.

"Everyone alright with salt?" Optic called.

"Definitely. I kinda need to make sure I get plenty, in fact," Rusty said. Optic eyed him curiously as he worked the salt mill over a portion of the grill for an extra moment.

"Why's that?"

"Electrolytes. When I use my power, it's like a normal, particularly sweaty workout. Upsets my electrolytes balance a bit. When I push it, though—like I kinda did in Ukraine—it can screw me up. Muscle cramps, nausea, blood pressure goes through the roof. When I was first using my power, I used to even get seizures, but it doesn't hit me like that anymore."

"Huh. Weird," Optic said. "Even this long after you pushed it?"

"Yeah. The doctors told me that I probably passed out as much from over-pushing my power as from getting my ass kicked by that bitch in the white mask."

"Any idea who she was?" Optic was poking at some of the meat on the grill, examining it, but was mostly focused on Rusty.

"Over the radio, they said they were bringing in two others to help them— Velocity and Mercy. One of them was a speedster, so I'm guessing that was Velocity."

"Which would make the other one Mercy," Mitch said. He stood and walked over the railing, turning his back to it and leaning against it. "There was something familiar about her. Can't quite put my finger on it, though. I just got a glimpse of her from up in the air. Never seen the costume before, though."

"So, these guys were full-on costumed, huh?"

"Sorta," Rusty said. "Kaamos was just in all-black. Pretty form-fitting, but he was all shadowy and weird, so it's hard to tell. Velocity and Mercy were definitely in costumes. I'd swear it was the composite material we use in the DTPA. The priest was, well, wearing a priest-robe thing."

"Like, a Catholic priest?" Optic asked, and Rusty nodded, taking a sip from the bottle of cider he was nursing.

"Claviger. At least, that's what Kaamos called him."

"Huh. That's a weird costume choice," Optic said, shaking his head. He unloaded the contents of the grill onto plates, passing them around. He shut the grill and everyone settled in to eat. All four of them simply enjoyed the meal for a few moments before Optic spoke up again, with the air of someone who clearly couldn't help himself.

"Okay, so I'm going to come clean." He leaned back in his chair. "I heard from some of my old unit buddies that there was a dust-up between two American supers and some unknown assailants in Ukraine. I couldn't help but remember your visit, Mitch, and that was an easy little math problem to solve."

Mitch chewed carefully, his face guarded. Optic continued. "I want in," he said forcefully. "I know you said that you weren't putting together a team or anything, but c'mon—this is a little too much coincidence, you know? I know a shadow op when I hear about one, and I know who was responsible, even if the rumor-mill doesn't."

"What?!" Deosil glared around the gathering as though she'd discovered herself in the midst of madmen. "A team?"

Mitch sighed. Rusty seemed delighted. "There's no team, now or in the future," Mitch said. "It was something one-off, a thing I did because Rusty was worried about a friend."

"Putting together a team is illegal, Optic," Deosil interrupted. "As in, against the law."

"I know what the word means, Deosil," Optic said irritably. He glanced back at Mitch, embarrassed. "I'm sorry, I just sort of assumed that—I mean, given what happened and everything–"

"No, that's my fault," Mitch said. "Look, I know what people think of the Champions and that legacy. The media and historians have romanticized the hell out of that era, and everyone thinks it's great. I get that. But even if it weren't illegal? No way. That life took too much from me already, Optic. I never could. Not again."

Optic winced and nodded. "Fair enough." He stood and gathered some of the grilling gear, along with his half-finished plate. Excusing himself, he bussed them all into the kitchen indoors. No one missed the fact that he could just as easily have taken them to the sink in the bar. It was an obvious retreat, and Rusty felt kind of bad for him. "Poor guy," he said quietly.

"He's nuts," Deosil hissed at him. "Why would anyone even think that way?"

"He misses the camaraderie," Mitch said, watching him busy himself in the kitchen inside. "You form very close bonds with people you go into those sorts of situations with." He glanced almost unconsciously at Rusty. "They become like family after a while, and Optic had that taken away from him. Can we please not judge him too harshly?"

* * *

The rest of the evening was a great deal more relaxing. They sat out on the deck as the cool night descended on them, and eventually pulled their chairs around the warmth of a little clay chiminea. Their conversation pretty broadly, from shared stories about DTPA Retreats (including the only one Optic had ever attended), to Deosil telling them about her festival and the accident she assisted with, to Mitch regaling them with his experiences as part of the Champions. At one point, when Mitch rose to carry some empty bottles inside, Rusty followed him. Optic watched them go, waiting until they were inside before turning to Deosil. "Kid's got it bad, huh?"

"For Mitch? Oh yeah," she said. She grinned impishly at him. "I mean, you have to admit—it's got to be irresistible."

"What's that?"

"The unique experience of someone he's interested in treating him decently."

Optic winced. "Damn, girl, you don't pull any fucking punches do you?"

She shrugged. "Sorry. I'm just protective."

"No, no. It was a solid hit," Optic waved her off. "And one I had coming, I know."

Deosil raised her bottle in his direction, and took a swig. He grinned at her. "What about you?" he asked. "Anyone special in your life?"

"Me? Gods, no." She turned away, shaking her head. For a moment it was as though she couldn't bring herself to meet his gaze, but then she forced herself to. That impish look was back. "Why, you interested?"

The gaze he returned to her was heavy with playful challenge. "Maybe I am."

Deosil laughed, shaking her head. "Please. I'm not your type."

"How do you know what my type is?"

She leveled a halfway intrigued gaze in his direction. "So, you're what—bi now?"

"Now?" He scoffed, taking another drink. "Always have been. Ain't nothing changed there."

She sat up in her chair. "All kidding aside, are you serious?"

Optic nodded, not really able to meet her gaze. "Yeah. I mean, I lean more toward dudes, in general. But I also kinda don't feel like I can admit that to anyone. Isn't that weird?"

"It *is* weird. Why not?"

"Well, it's like this. When the military discovered I was into guys, that was all that mattered. The fact that I was also attracted to women? Irrelevant, because I was attracted to men."

"It's kind of like you're tainted, right?" Deosil said, crossing her legs under her, setting her empty bottle beside her chair. "Like it's a purity thing. You don't get to be heterosexual unless it's a one-hundred percent thing."

"Yup. But it's always like that. I mean, with every minority." Optic stretched his long legs, shifting over to sit in a chair next to Deosil. "It's like, that's how majorities keep their power—by policing purity. You have to be totally masculine to be a 'real man'. Even a drop of black blood in your family's past makes you not-white. Suck a dick once, and *bam*! You're out of the straight-guy club."

Deosil threw her head back and guffawed. Optic grinned at her. "Seriously, though. It's gate-keeping. Those who have the power—the privilege—they keep it by making sure that people are excluded from their group. They create bizarre cultural and physical requirements in order to belong to that group, and to hell with anyone who doesn't meet those criteria."

Deosil nodded. "No, I get that. I have to admit, you're pretty up on all this social justice stuff."

"Hey, I wasn't the poster boy for the anti-Don't Ask, Don't Tell movement just because of my good looks."

Deosil giggled. Like, *actually* giggled. Time to stop drinking, she noted. "Seriously, thanks for sharing that. But for the record, even if I am your type—and I mean, God knows, nobody could blame you for that—you're not mine."

Now it was Optic's turn to laugh, a warm velvety sound.

"It's so weird," she said.

"What's that?"

"I was just sitting here thinking—I know all of these details about your sexuality, your history, your politics. And I don't even know your real name."

He nodded. "Yeah, I got used to using my code name entirely. One of the things that Seraphim did was make sure none of us knew one another's actual names."

"Seraphim—that's the military group that gave you your powers, right?"

"Yeah. Project: Seraphim. I can't really say a whole lot about them, though."

Deosil waved it away. "No, no. No big. I'm only interested in them as it pertains to you." She extended her hand to him, and he took it in a large, warm grip. "I'm Sarah."

He smiled and shook her hand gravely. "Wendell."

Deosil winced. "Eek. I see why you go by Optic." That laugh of his was infectious, and Deosil let herself go with it. It was nice to just sit around with others like her, people who dealt with weird fame, and code names, and DTPA regulations, and all the rest of the shit that came with the Change.

Optic glanced toward the big windows that framed the house's interior. "Think they got lost?"

"Nah," Deosil said. "Mitch just has crazy super-hearing, so they are probably in there chatting so we can talk in private." She turned toward the house. "It's safe to come out now, Mitch."

And as if by magic, about a minute later, a laughing Rusty and a shame-faced Mitch emerged. Optic lost his composure in deep belly-laughter.

"I wasn't," said Mitch. "I mean, I didn't mean to eavesdrop, I just…"

Deosil laughed and bounced up to hug him. "Shut up. You're an Original.

You can hear shit going on for blocks around us. It's part of the package deal. We'll live."

As the night wore on and they retired inside, everyone became more comfortable in each other's presence. From the joking between Rusty and Optic, it even seemed like they'd come to some kind of unspoken okay-place between them, though Deosil wasn't sure how much of that was the alcohol and how much was just genuine camaraderie. Though Deosil was pretty sure that either way, the fact that Mitch genuinely got along with Optic went a long way towards soothing Rusty's hurt feelings. While the three boys chatted, Deosil retreated into her phone for a bit.

"God, that reminds me," Rusty said at one point, glancing over at her. "I need to get a new phone. I kinda fried my last one."

"*Quelle surprise,*" Deosil snorted, face still in her phone. Her tone was sharp.

Mitch regarded her with intense focus for a moment. "What's got you so aggravated?"

"Oh, this forum blows." She sighed, setting the phone down in her lap and taking up her drink again. "At least for reading on mobiles. I'm hunting for that post I remembered. I don't want to message its poster unless I'm remembering it correctly."

"What's this?" Optic asked, looking from her to Mitch, who was a little uncomfortable.

"Deosil saw a post on the volunteer's forums for the Golden Cross," Rusty said. "She thinks she remembered someone describing something that sounded like Claviger's power there. The teleporter that was part of the group that attacked us in Odessa."

Optic's eyebrows rose. "So, you guys are still poking into all of that? Even after the big warning from Uncle Sam?"

"The DTPA isn't Uncle Sam," Mitch growled. "And besides, we're just following up on information. Information that we can turn over to the authorities if something pans out."

Deosil glanced up from her phone with a stern *That had better be all* glare. She glanced back down and then lit up. "Here it is!"

The article was from a post where volunteers recorded the powers of unknown Changed and other weird phenomena they encountered while in the field. The post was from Llorona, dated a week ago or so.

Llorona (05/09/2013 • 14:42)

Has anyone heard of anyone who uses a portal-creating or teleportational power that opens a gateway to what appears to be a field of stars? In addition to transport, the light also causes viewers to experience weird emotional effects, like awe, terror, or religious ecstasy.

The post was one among many and had no replies whatsoever. Deosil sent her a private message via the system, including her phone number, and asked her to get in contact. No one expected Deosil's phone to ring not even a full hour later.

"Hello?" Deosil asked cautiously. "Oh, shit. Llorona! Hey, this is Deosil. Yeah, I'm here with some people who are curious about your answers—mind if I put you on speaker?"

She agreed, and in short order, Deosil was making introductions between those in the room and the tinny-voiced presence of Llorona. "Where are you calling from? It's got to be late where you are," Deosil said.

"Not that late. Just shy of midnight here," Llorona said. She spoke with a calm confidence, and just the slightest hint of a Mexican Spanish accent. "I'm in El Paso right now. Getting your message was a godsend; I'm actually here following up on some information I got about that power."

"Go on," Mitch said, sitting forward in his chair.

"A few weeks ago, I was working a rescue in Mexico. A couple of Echoes tore up one of the larger *ciudades* in Mexico—a very poor neighborhood with a lot of gang activity. Afterwards, though, two of the people my partner and I saved were missing. Just *gone*. As though they'd never been there. I didn't think too much of it, until I was talking to some of the other volunteers, who mentioned that both of them were last seen in the company of my partner."

"Who was your partner?" Optic asked.

"A priest of the Catholic church named Claviger," she said, and Mitch and Rusty shared a shocked look.

"Wait, he was a real priest?" Rusty asked incredulously.

"Well, he used to be," Llorona replied. "I started doing some digging. He claimed that he was part of the Antonine Order—that's an order the Vatican established for the service of both clergy and cloistered who are Echoes."

"But he wasn't," Deosil guessed.

"Oh, he used to be," Llorona said. "But he was defrocked. The Church wouldn't tell me any more than that, but from what I know, you have to do some seriously bad things for the Vatican to choose to turn away one of the Antonines."

"So, you've done some other investigating, I take it?" Mitch asked. "I remember reading some of your reports around the time of the Fated Manifesto."

She chuckled. "You're very kind to remember after all this time, Sentinel. Yes, I did. Part of what I do for the Golden Cross is investigate reports of weird happenings and things, to help discover where the organization is needed most. Some of my digging revealed some interesting facts."

"Such as?" Optic asked.

"Such as increased reports in some places around the world of ecstatic religious experiences. Not necessarily strange by itself, though the Golden Cross does keep track of things like that, because sometimes weird phenomena presage an Echo Event, or are evidence of one of the Changed using their abilities. But these were all the same—no manifestation of powers or miracles other than the weird overwhelming experiences. And from multiple people, as well."

"Other people had gone missing from those places, hadn't they?" Rusty asked, furrowing his brow at the phone.

"Correct. I had a hunch, and though it was hard to find details, there was often evidence of people from fringe communities going missing. In a lot of places that meant even those who were on the outskirts of poor communities, who tend to watch out for their own. So, sex workers, criminals, orphans, counterculture, and queer communities. And they're all young."

"How many are we talking about?" Mitch asked. Both Rusty and Optic leaned forward, but Deosil sat back in her seat, pulling her feet up under her.

"At this point, I've only been able to verify eight instances of religious ecstasy paired with disappearances. I've found three other situations where the ecstatic phenomenon was experienced, but couldn't find anyone who'd disappeared, though if Claviger is taking people who are from unwanted or outsider populations, no one might have even noticed or cared that they disappeared."

"Have you reported this to the police?" Deosil said meekly. "Or the DTPA?"

"*Mija*, they're all outside of the United States. I've talked to the authorities in some of the places, but if they are all being kidnapped, they're choosing their locations well."

"So, no one's searching for these kids but you," Mitch said grimly. He was glowering at the phone, and the others in the room with him couldn't help but exchange glances. That was the voice of a man who was about to *do something*.

"I'm afraid so. I'm in El Paso right now because there are some trans kids who've gone missing from Ciudad Juarez, across the border." Deosil raised a hand to her mouth and looked like she might cry. "Women disappear all the time in Juarez, and the police consider it par for the course. Of course, since the two kids who disappeared were young trans boys, the Juarez police consider them just another pair of girls who've gone missing, and at best I got a promise that they'll check it out. But I know where that promise goes as soon as I walked out of the station."

"How can we help?" Mitch asked.

Deosil's spine straightened. She fixed him with a look of betrayal, and then at Rusty, who couldn't quite meet her gaze. *Goddamn it.*

"Frankly, I could use some help. My investigation is starting to take me into some dangerous places, and while I can handle myself decently, I'm not stupid enough to try to investigate some of this on my own."

"I can be there by morning, easily. Can you text me an address?" Mitch said.

"Oh, thank God. I don't know what I did to secure God's favor enough to get Sentinel's help in this, but I hope someone tells me so I can keep on doing that." Mitch chuckled, promised to see her tomorrow, and Llorona hung up.

It was Optic who finally broke the silence. "Are we sure we're not putting together a team here? This sounds an awful lot like a mission for a team."

"Are you out of your fucking minds?!" Deosil leapt to her feet and fled the room, slamming the glass door to the deck outside behind her. Rusty started to rise, but Mitch stopped him.

"No. She's right. You guys can't get involved in this."

"The fuck she is," Optic said. "I mean, if she doesn't want in, I can respect that. But you're nuts if you think you're going haring off to do this kind of thing alone."

Rusty threw the tall actor a grateful look. "What he said. We're going."

Mitch was standing. "If this isn't just Claviger kidnapping these people—if it's his whole team? They're dangerous."

Rusty's jaw dropped. "No shit they're dangerous! Jesus, do you think I've forgotten the beating I took at their hands?"

"Then why are you so anxious to get back in their company? Is this a payback thing?"

"Christ, no." Rusty shook his head. "Seriously. I don't want to meet those dudes ever again if I can prevent it, Mitch. But Kosma and Oleksander? How much worse must it have been for them? I could at least defend myself, hold out, get away. They didn't stand a fucking chance. And now we know that they're popping all over the globe, snatching up people—queer and otherwise—that nobody gives a damn about?" He paused, staring at Mitch incredulously. "How on Earth could you think I'd just stay here?"

"And no offense to the kid," Optic broke in. "But I'm not a civilian. I've got combat training—superpowered combat training, even. I was the first responder to plenty of sovereign air defensive action. Hell, I held my own against Plasma the last time he tried to come over into U.S. airspace." He paused, and squared his shoulders. "And please don't take this the wrong way? But I'm not asking for permission."

Mitch and Optic stared one another down for a few heartbeats, and frankly Rusty had never been so conflicted in his entire damned life. After a moment, Mitch nodded and then turned to Rusty. "It's important," Rusty said simply.

"Alright." Mitch conceded after another few seconds. He glanced outside at where Deosil stood at the railing, gripping it tightly, in a high wind. He narrowed his eyes and cocked his head to listen. "I'll be right back," he said, and stepped out onto the deck.

The weather was a tumult out on the deck, and Mitch was pretty sure Deosil was the cause. He could sense weird shifting in the pressure systems around them, so much so that a lazy swirling wind was centered on the back part of the house, and if it got much worse, it might generate something truly dangerous.

Deosil's breathing was measured and precise, and Mitch could hear her counting the inhalations and exhalations just under her breath. He paused, and then crossed to stand next to her.

"Give me a second," she said through her labored, iron-controlled breaths. A minute passed, and then two, and Mitch could sense the strange system around them level off and die away. A light rain began to fall, more mist than precipitation. He rested his hand over hers on the railing, and she grabbed his hand tightly. "Sorry."

"No need to apologize. That's some power you've got there."

"It's just so dangerous," she said quietly. "So unpredictable."

Mitch hesitated. "I hope it's not an awful thing to say, but I'm surprised they haven't taught you better control."

"The DTPA?" Her laugh had a bitter tinge to it. "They made me aware of just how scary it could be. Plenty of scientists to explain just how awful a slip-up could be for everyone around me. And to be fair, they've mostly taught me how to tamp it down, you know? How to bring it back under control?"

"Sounds like they've mostly taught you to not use it, rather than how to use it."

She chuckled. "I guess that's a pretty fair statement. That's what they teach most of us."

Though he couldn't tell where the rain ended and her tears began, there was no doubt just how painful this conversation was for her. The fear practically radiated off her.

"So, let me teach you," he said. She hesitated, until he wasn't sure she'd actually heard him. Before he could repeat his offer, however, she turned to regard him with incredible caution—and more than a little of that fear—in her eyes.

"You can do that?"

"After the Original Event, it was just us, you know? No DTPA, no doctors, no scientists. Just us." He leaned against the railing. "Radiant's power was so out of control. Nothing he did seemed to rein it in. We thought his powers were light-based at first, which was why he took that name, but eventually we figured out it wasn't light. It was *radiation*. He and Alchemy knew the proper scientific terms for it, but he could basically generate it on a really wide scale: light, electromagnetism, radio waves, all of that.

"The problem was that he couldn't seem to control it worth a damn. While the rest of us began to master and then hone the uses of our power, he did well to retain basic control of his. Finally, I was the only one who'd approach him in a bad state, because I was the only one protected from his power. It's how our friendship started. The problem wasn't that he didn't have the will-power to do it. It was that he was afraid—not of failure, but of success. All he could think about were the implications of mastery of his power and it kinda freaked him out."

He paused for a moment, staring out at the diffuse light filtering through the misty rain over Portland. She glanced at him. He couldn't miss the tears in her eyes. She was really doing her best to keep under control. He turned to her after a moment. "It's scary, Deosil. I mean, my power is strong, but it's pretty limited. It only does so much. But people like you, and like Radiant? There's almost no limit to what your power will be able to do, one day, and that's terrifying."

She sobbed and covered her face with her hands. Mitch wrapped his arms around her protectively, and kissed the top of her head. "Hey. I get that. But you don't have to be afraid of your power. We'll figure out a way to push you past just the 'not a danger' point and get you into some true mastery, whatever that means for you. You're right to respect your power, but not to fear it. Don't get me wrong—our powers will always cause fear, especially in those who don't have them. But those same people really want you to be afraid of your power as well. Don't give them that."

She looked up at him. "Did you mean that? You're willing to help me figure out how best to control it?"

"Without hesitation."

She nodded. "Okay. Okay, yeah, I'm in."

"Why don't we get started once I get back from El Paso?"

"I don't know if I can go," she said.

"That's totally your call, Deosil. I'd never ask that."

She ran a hand through her wet hair. "You know, it's so weird. It's like, when I was growing up and started trying to live as a girl, there were so many times when things got awful. I was homeschooled for all of my high school grades except my freshman year, which is when I started transitioning. They were so *awful*, Mitch."

"I'm not going to lie, kiddo. I don't know anything about what it's like to be brave enough to be who you are in high school, gay or trans. I can't imagine it."

"I think I knew, somehow, you know? Like, when Rusty first told me about Kosma, and then I read that post Llorona made on the forums? I felt *connected* to something bigger then. But it wasn't until Llorona mentioned tonight that some of those kids who have been taken were trans. It wasn't until then that I knew I had to do something to help."

Her lower lip quivered, and her teeth chattered not from the cold, but from trying to keep from crying. "How many times did I wish I'd had somebody to come and save me? I mean, I was just putting up with bullies and awful transphobic shitheads, and I desperately wanted someone to rescue me. How much more awful must it be to not only wish someone would come save you, but to actually need it? And to know that no one is probably searching for you? It's so fucking *horrible*, Mitch."

"You came out here because you knew you were coming with us, huh? And that scared you."

She nodded, and sniffled. "Yeah. It scares the shit out of me."

He hugged her once more and draped his arm around her shoulder. "Let's go back inside and let those two madmen know."

To their credit, both Rusty and Optic were glad she was coming with them, and Deosil made all the requisite jokes about protecting and watching over Rusty that her relationship with him required. The next few hours were planning and logistics, a now-familiar mode of thought for Rusty and Mitch, and one that Optic threw himself into enthusiastically. In the end, they decided that Mitch and Rusty would fly to Texas the way they had flown to Ukraine. Though Optic's photoassumptive power allowed himself to turn his body into an animate field of photon particles with varying degrees of solidity, allowing him to be there in literally minutes should he choose, Deosil's power didn't lend itself to long-distance or particularly fast flight.

In the end, Optic went for a more solid form that would let him both fly and carry Deosil, who would engineer a good headwind to speed all of their flight to the panhandle of Texas. It was a few hours before dawn when they departed, rising into the sky above the rainclouds and heading for the Rockies.

"Here we go again," Mitch whispered in Rusty's ear as they rose above the wet clouds, and Rusty could only answer with a grin.

CHAPTER EIGHTEEN

El Paso, Texas
May 19, 2013

The address Llorona texted Deosil turned out to be a small taqueria in the Chihuahuita neighborhood of El Paso, just across the river from Ciudad Juarez. She and another woman were waiting for them in the small parking lot behind the taco place, which wasn't large enough to have space to eat indoors. They were standing between a large panel van and a smaller two-door hatchback, and Llorona smiled to see them touch down.

"Look at you four," she said. "It's almost like seeing real *súpers* again." She introduced the woman next to her—a Hispanic woman in her forties, with a generous figure and round face beneath a head of short spiky brown hair—as Donna, who ran the local support group aimed at helping at-risk trans youth.

Donna whistled. "I hope you don't plan on trying to cross the border in those costumes."

"Uniforms," Sentinel said, and shrugged a backpack off his shoulder. "And no. We've got civilian clothes here. They're just awful to fly in, as they get all torn up if you really have to pour on the speed."

Deosil took a moment to pull the headscarf she was wearing off and shake out her hair. "This is literally the first time I've ever regretted not taking one of those suits home," she said, glancing down at her roughed-up sweats. "Thanks for thinking of bringing extra clothes, though, Mitch."

She took the backpack from him, and Llorona opened her van's sliding door to allow the young woman to change in relative privacy. Rusty, Mitch, and Optic donned their civvies over their uniforms. "I went ahead and bought us a bunch of breakfast tacos," Llorona said while they did so. "Early start, I figure?"

Rusty finished buttoning up his shirt, and gleefully took two of the foil-wrapped bundles from the bag she held. The sound he made taking his first bite was practically obscene. "Man, I've missed this," he said, taking a second bite.

"How long has it been since you've been home to Texas?" Llorona asked.

"A long time," he said, with a hint of sadness. "Though I think it's mostly the food I miss. It sure isn't the heat."

Deosil slid the door open, and everyone sat back to eat breakfast, leaning against Donna's hatchback or sitting just inside the van's open door. As they ate and chatted—Rusty pointing out some of the beautiful murals painted on building walls to Deosil, Optic asking Donna questions about her work with the support group—Llorona passed around bottles of water. "Thank you for coming out," she said to Mitch. "I know we've met briefly before, but it was always in a professional capacity. Do you mind if I say something personal?"

He seemed uncomfortable for a moment, but gestured her to continue anyway.

"I just want to say that what the media and the rest of the world did to you—to you and your love—was a great injustice. You inspired so many of us to push against the way the world wants to define us, to insist that we be the ones who get to say who and what we are."

He glanced away, for a moment, and then met her eyes again with a smile. "Thanks," he said. "That means a lot to me."

"And this, what you're doing now? No one could have blamed you if you'd let what they did to you harden your heart, and make you seek shelter from the world."

"If I'm being honest, I kind of did." He took a drink of water and glanced at Rusty. "I wouldn't even be here if he hadn't come looking for help finding someone."

"Oh? Was this the thing in Ukraine? I heard some talk about it, but no details."

"If it turns out that we're right, Claviger is part of a group," he explained. Everyone focused on him, breaking off their breakfast conversations. "If he is responsible for this, then it'll be at least two areas where he has been responsible for missing people: once in Ukraine, with two young gay men, and now here, with another two."

"Joey and Armando," Donna said. "They were both trans. Do you think they're targeting queer kids specifically?"

"If my digging is correct, I don't think it's LGBT victims specifically, no," Llorona said. "I think Claviger may be responsible for other disappearances as well, among disaster victims, sex workers, illegal immigrants."

"So, all people who could go missing without anyone bothering to really search for them," Optic said.

Llorona nodded. "Exactly. These two boys are from Ciudad Juarez. They crossed the border once a week or so to attend Donna's meetings, and they disappeared on their way back from such a meeting. Border crossing records show that they crossed the bridge at the Stanton Street crossing, but then they disappeared right after. The Juarez police are treating them as just another two girls who've gone missing."

"Is that really that common here?" Mitch asked, sounding a little confused.

"It is, yes," Donna said. "All border towns are bad—they're often where the desperate come when they have no other options. And there are *maquiladoras*—large factories—where a lot of the poor come to try and find jobs. Unfortunately, this results in a high transient population, with no one with any interest in looking out for them. Women disappear all the time.

"The official line is the assumption that a lot of those women have either turned to sex work, immigrated illegally across the river, or just returned home to the rural areas they came from. Which is sometimes true, certainly, but many of those women don't do any of those things. They find bodies—sometimes multiples—in the desert occasionally, and they usually go unidentified."

"But you don't think that's what happened here?" Optic said.

"No, we don't." Llorona flipped to some photos of attractive young Hispanic men on her phone. "See these? Joey and Armando don't *present* as women. If someone is preying on women, why would they target these young men?"

Mitch nodded. "So, these kids weren't in any of the situations any of the women who disappear are normally in."

"Exactly. But there's more," Donna said. "I was on the phone with Armando when he disappeared. He'd crossed the bridge and gotten a text saying that his uncle was at his family home. His uncle is an asshole—very bigoted, and has hurt Armando before for wearing men's clothes around the family. Armando was trying to decide what to do, to just change into girls' clothes, or to go over to Joey's to stay instead when I heard Armando cry out."

"Like in pain?" Deosil asked.

Donna shook her head. "No. I would say…in wonder. Like he'd seen something that filled him with awe. He sounded like he was crying, but the kind of crying that you think of people doing who've seen miracles. He muttered something about 'the lights of God' and then I heard him praying and the phone dropped to the asphalt. I tried getting him on the phone, over and over, all the rest of that night, and I finally went hunting the next morning. He and Joey—who'd been walking with him at the time—were both gone, and Armando's phone was on the side of the road, just abandoned there."

"That's exactly what it was like, seeing Claviger's power in effect," Rusty affirmed.

Llorona nodded. "For me, too. But you said he's working with other *adelantes*?"

"Three other Changed, yeah, as far as we know," Mitch said. "One of them is Finnish, from the accent and name, a man who calls himself Kaamos. There are also two women: Velocity, an American who Echoed at the Central Park Event in '81, and another woman. The others called her Mercy, and she didn't show any real superpowers except for what we're guessing is enhanced fighting skills of some kind."

Rusty winced. "Yeah, I went up against Kaamos who has shadow manipulation powers, and Velocity, who's a speedster, but it was Mercy who nearly killed me."

"Just how badly?" Optic asked. His face was set in a frown.

"She kinda broke my everything. Bones, one of my ribs, which she drove into my lung. The doctors said the angle of the hit that did that was different from the one that broke them in the first place, so they figure she probably did it deliberately, as a killing blow." Rusty kept his attention focused on Optic and Llorona as he did so, really not wanting to see Deosil's reaction.

She shook her head at him, glowering. "Your ass should still be in a bed, Rusty. I'm serious."

"It's fine," he said, crossing to her and letting her (ironically) crush him in a hug. "Seriously. See? No pain. One of Vigilance's Echoes has healing power, and he insisted that he use it when they arrived at the hospital. I was in surgery at the time, and he apparently scrubbed up and came right in to help them patch up really difficult injuries. Stuff that might have stuck with me otherwise."

Deosil gave him a *this is so not over* look, and he hugged her again.

Mitch nodded. "Osłoda is a good man. He's one of the few in Vigilance we never had problems with, and he promised me at the hospital that he'd make sure his team investigated their activities in the region."

Llorona smiled. "Then we're all fortunate he was there and willing to help."

"So, if we know they work on a worldwide basis, what are we doing here? I mean, is there much we can get from here?" Optic asked. "Not much chance they left any more clues about where they're operating out of, is there?"

"Probably not," Llorona conceded. "But there's someone who might be able to tell us something. There's a cartel called the Calaveras based out of a ranch just outside of Juarez. They're led by a woman who calls herself Calavera—she Echoed at the same Event I did, the Houston Event. She and I have something of a bad past between us. She was doing some work for the Fated Manifesto back when a bunch of us Echoes were recruited by the Champions to help find them and bring them down. She apparently had a sweet deal and has never forgiven me for messing that up for her."

"You think these people will have worked with her in some way?" Mitch asked.

"Maybe, maybe not. But from your story in Ukraine, it sounds like they do work with some of the criminal element sometimes. I've had similar indications from some of the other disappearance sites. And even if they don't, the Calaveras are very good at keeping track of Changed in their territory. I'd be very surprised if they operated here for any length of time without Calavera and her crew not at least knowing about it. Maybe they can shed some light on the topic."

"So how are we going to get across the border? Fly again? We can't just go through the border crossing—Mitch and Rusty's identifications have got to be flagged by the DTPA after Ukraine."

"They are, yeah," Rusty said regretfully. "They told me as much when I was still at the Cascades facility."

"That's why I wanted to meet here," Llorona said, pointing at her van. "We load you up in your civilian clothes. If they ask you for ID, we have to give it, of course, but most of the border patrol know me and my van from different Golden Cross missions and just wave me through these days. They don't even pay much attention to who's riding with me."

"So if it comes down to it, we're just U.S. citizens crossing the border for a day in Mexico, as happens all the time," Mitch said, nodding. "Otherwise, they'll probably assume we're Golden Cross, and not bother with us at all."

"That's the plan," Llorona said, shaking her keys. "You all ready?"

Donna stepped up to hug her. "Thank you again, Llorona. And all the rest of you. Please phone me if you hear anything, and please be careful. *Vaya con Dios*."

With that, they loaded up into the van, and set off. It was only a few blocks to the bridge, with a short wait to cross. When they pulled up to one of the small stands and halted, the border patrol guard smiled at Llorona behind the wheel. He glanced in and noticed Rusty in the passenger seat, and a few other bodies in the back, but didn't pay them much attention. "Good morning, *señora*," he said. "Who you off to save today?"

Llorona chuckled and shook her head. "Mostly just showing some people around, and introducing them to the area. Nobody in the Cross knows this part of Mexico like I do."

"True." He nodded, writing something down in his booth. He hit a button and raised the small striped bar that blocked their way. "Oh, I saw you on the news the other day, from when you were in Neza, with all those collapsed buildings. You were like a movie star."

Llorona laughed, her hand unconsciously smoothing her hair. "Maybe from a disaster movie! Three days later I was still combing plaster and concrete dust out of my hair. I didn't even dare watch those reports. I know how awful I looked!"

Rusty grinned at the playful banter between them, admiring Llorona's ease. It was clear that she not only knew to what purpose she wanted to put her power, but was doing it, and was respected as a hero for it. He smiled at her as they drove through the checkpoint. Llorona noticed and glanced at him. "What's that grin for?"

"I just think it's cool that they know you, you know? They know who you are and what you do."

"I wish we got the same response everywhere," Llorona said. "Mexico has a strict hands-off policy when it comes to the Golden Cross. The government here doesn't have that many *adelantes*, as the cartels can not only pay better, but also usually keep an eye on the families of those they recruit to discourage them leaving and doing something else."

"Sorry," Deosil said. "*Adelantes*? I heard you use that term earlier."

"It means 'advanced.'" Llorona glanced in the mirror at her. "It's the term I like best. It's used by most of the Spanish-speaking world in the Americas, especially the government and media."

"So it sounds like these cartels hold a lot of power," Optic said, pulling the conversation back on topic.

Llorona nodded as she worked the steering wheel. "It wasn't always like that. It's just that the whole War on Drugs thing has funneled a lot of money into their coffers, and after the Champions were pulled apart, a lot of *adelantes*—both Mexican and otherwise—turned their attention to the cartels. They'd kill off whoever was in charge and take over themselves. These days, most of the big cartels either are run by one of the Changed, or they have a few in their employ, and the really big ones have both."

"Yeah, there's a lot of places like that around the world," Optic says. "In fact, probably a third of the supers we intercepted entering American airspace were trying to get to the United States to avoid being forced into those kinds of situations. The ones interested in using their powers to fight or whatever often stay in their home countries, but Echoes who just end up with powers and no real interest in using them to commit or fight crime—or wars—don't have many options. They're too rare. *Someone* will eventually try to strongarm them into joining one side or the other."

The trip through Ciudad Juarez showed a city struggling under the weight of its own circumstances. Pockets of distinct prosperity had sprung up here and there, like mushroom circles after a rain. But these were oases, in many ways, rising up in the middle of a desert of poverty. Nonetheless, the small *tiendas* and markets were busy with shoppers and workers, prosperous for all the faded and peeling paint. The roads were badly in need of repair, yet were filled with people even at this early hour, bicyclists and drivers dodging roadside pedestrians.

"It's hard to believe there's this level of poverty just across the border," Mitch said, peering out the window.

Llorona smiled. "Most of the world lives like this, though. The majority of the world lives subsistence-level lives, with basic shelter and necessities. What we consider 'normal'? It's uncommon. We've just lived it our whole lives and think it's the baseline. It's not, though. This is."

"There are still places in the U.S. that live like this too, though," Deosil mumbled. Her feet were on the seat, her arms resting on her knees, her head turned to stare out the van's side window as they bounced along the rough road. "I mean, I grew up in California, just outside San Jose, in a shitty little town that was mostly made up of big farms that employed migrant workers, and people who were too poor to escape the town."

Rusty glanced thoughtfully at Deosil, but said nothing.

In a short time, they left the city proper, entering the dry and dusty country-side punctuated by stands of thorny chaparral foliage. Old signs of habitation both past and present were everywhere: here an old rusted out car abandoned on the side of the road, stripped of anything that might conceivably be sold, or old half-falling single-room shacks, some abandoned and some with families sitting in the shade while children played nearby.

About an hour after they crossed, even those signs disappeared, and Lloro-na turned off the major road onto an old road made up of red-orange caliche. She slowed the van to a slow crawl. "Okay. Let's talk about what to do before we get there."

CHAPTER NINETEEN

Just outside of Ciudad Juarez, Mexico
May 19, 2013

Llorona frowned as she drove, like she had a bad taste in her mouth. "The Calaveras are a border cartel, one of the drug running operations that specializes in getting narcotics and similar goods across the border into the United States. They get their goods from other cartels or from production centers they run further south in Mexico or Central America."

"If you know this, there's no way the United States government and law enforcement doesn't know this as well. Why haven't they done anything?" Sentinel asked.

"Jurisdiction, probably," Optic opined, and Llorona nodded.

"That's a big part of it. They've made it very clear to the Calaveras that if they're a big source of trouble for the DEA or other agencies, they'll come for them across the border—they've promised that they can get the authority to do so from the Mexican government." She frowned. "Whether they actually could or not is another question entirely. The cartels have plenty of money in politics here. There are some very good people in the Mexican government, trying to make things better, but there is a lot of money working against them."

"Kinda like corporations in our government, then," Deosil said, leaning forward into the conversation.

Llorona nodded. "I've seen some very distinct similarities, yes. The thing is, none of the cartels really want to test that willingness. The U.S. hasn't tried to get that permission, so none of them want to be the ones responsible for causing them to do so. So, like a lot of the cartels, the Calaveras actually keep a lid on a lot of the trouble that might ordinarily come across the border. Everyone knows that if you mess it up for the Calaveras, the Calaveras come for you, and nobody wants a drug cartel whose leadership are all Echoes gunning for them."

"How common is that kind of thing?" Rusty asked. "I mean, big criminal organizations run by supers."

"Depends on where it's at," Llorona said. "Places that have governments with the resources to offer the Changed a position with some attendant safety and prosperity almost always have a team or two. Even those countries that don't usually will band together with their neighbors and establish one."

"Like Vigilance, in Eastern Europe," Mitch said, and Llorona nodded.

"Exactly. But in a lot of places, the local government can't match the resources of mob organizations, and that's where these situations come from. I mean, I've heard of Changed working with diamond smugglers out of South Africa or human traffickers between the eastern coast of Russia and the United States, for example. But even in those situations, it's usually one or two, working for obscene amounts of money. A lot of those people aren't even necessarily inclined to criminal activity themselves—they're just poor, or working out of fear of what the mob might do to their families, or whatever. Groups of criminally-minded Changed, though? Much rarer, but also much, much more dangerous."

"So who are we dealing with?" Optic asked. Rusty couldn't help but notice the razor-sharp attention he was paying to Llorona's words—probably something left over from his military days. This was a debriefing to him, in anticipation of actual conflict, and Rusty couldn't help but shiver at the thought.

"The group is named after their leader, Calavera. I…know her, to a degree."

Sentinel was thoughtful. "To what degree? What can you tell us about her?"

"Not a lot," Llorona said, glancing at them in the mirror. "You can't miss her—she pretty routinely paints her face in the style of the *calaveras* you see during the *Dia de los Muertos* celebrations."

"The sugar skulls?" Deosil asked,

"Yes, like those. I'm not entirely sure what her power is. She was involved with the Fated Manifesto."

Sentinel whistled. "I know you were involved in helping to take them out. Is that where you first encountered her?"

Llorona's bark of laughter was bitter. "God, I wish. No, she and I both Echoed at the same Event, in Houston. 1986."

Rusty glanced at her from the passenger seat. "I wasn't even born yet."

Llorona fixed him with a sideways glare. "Don't make me turn this van around." He chuckled along with her, and it seemed to alleviate some of the stress Llorona was radiating. "Her right-hand man was part of the Houston Event also. He goes by Matón, which means something like thug, or bully. He lives up to it, too. He broke my jaw when I helped bring Calavera in that time."

"Anyone else?"

"At least one other, from what I've heard. Over the years, her gang's number has fluctuated, so there's no telling. She adds Echoes, and then they piss her off, try to make a power grab, or get out for whatever reason. Only she and Matón are constants."

"So, you got sound control powers, and this Matón got what, super-strength?" Deosil asked after a moment.

"And enhanced durability, yes." Llorona glanced back at the young woman busy on her phone.

"It looks like the Houston Event was a weird one," said Deosil. "Not a lot of the standard energy discharges or large-scale destruction, but there was a lot of lost life."

"It happened on the Day of the Dead," Llorona said quietly. "It was centered on a big civic *Dia de los Muertos* event, across the street from the community church. It was frightening. It was like this white mist descended over everything, and people just went crazy, you know? Screams from all around. You could hear violence everywhere, and people came running out of the fog, appearing suddenly, all covered in blood."

Deosil's eyes were still on the screen in front of her. "The experts later classified it as one of the foremost psychotraumatic Events—most of the damage was psychic in nature, with more people ending up institutionalized than hospitalized. It sounds awful."

"It was," Llorona said quietly.

Deosil clicked her phone off/ "Sorry," she said. "I didn't mean to—"

"No, *mija*," Llorona replied. "It was a long time ago. I'm just distracted, is all."

"So what kind of reception can we expect?" Optic asked.

"Probably not the best one," Llorona replied apologetically. "I've been trying to get in touch with her, but she's so far refused to talk to me."

"Does that mean we're pretty much invading their compound?" Deosil asked. She clearly did not like the idea of that, and frankly neither did any of the rest of them.

"It means we're showing up uninvited, yes," Llorona conceded. "I'm not suggesting we try and fight our way in first thing or anything. But Calavera knows something—it's how she keeps in power. It's impossible to believe that some group of supers would undertake operations in this area and her not know about it."

The road to the ranch turned off the main road and wound its way into the hills, rising and falling through dry scrubland. Cresting a hill, Llorona stopped the van at a welded steel gate. The land was rough on both sides of the road, and the gate's anchoring posts made of steel and concrete sank deep into the ground.

"Dang. That thing looks like you could ram a car into it, and not move it." Deosil whistled as she leaned forward to study it through the dusty windshield.

"I can get it," Rusty said, but Llorona caught his hand.

"No, wait," she said. "Let's get out. I'd rather we didn't approach using our powers if we can help it."

"Sign of respect? Or do you just not want to tip our hand?" Optic asked, sliding the panel door of the van open. Llorona swiveled in her seat to wink at him, and they all got out. It was a quick step around the concrete block anchors to get to the other side of the gate.

They weren't walking for long at all before Mitch pointed up the road, where three plumes of dust marked the approach of men in jeeps. "Company," he said.

"Nobody make the first move, please," Llorona said. "Let's give them the chance to be hospitable first."

"And if they're not?" Optic asked. There was dangerous steel in his voice.

"We're seeing Calavera. That's not negotiable." The soldier grinned at the older woman, and she stepped forward with a bright smile as the three jeeps pulled to a stop some thirty yards in front of them. Men leapt out, men in rough t-shirts and raggedy jeans, men with well-oiled weapons in their hands. Weapons that they pointed at the five of them on the road. Llorona raised her hands as though it were second nature—she was the only one. Mitch stepped in front of Deosil, who seemed glad for the intervention.

Llorona spoke to the men, and it was clear she was explaining why she was here. It was equally clear what the spokesman—a gruff, wild-bearded man with a faded Dallas Cowboys cap and arms full of tattoos—had to say about that. He and Llorona exchanged some rapid-fire conversation, her tone conciliatory, his increasingly agitated as they talked.

In retrospect, it happened way faster than Rusty or Deosil could have anticipated. Maybe it was from a life of movies where the camera makes a point of focusing on the guy about to fire the gun. There was no moment where the weapon clicked into place ominously, where he raised the weapon into a dramatic stance, shouted one final threat.

No, all of a sudden, there was gunfire.

It didn't make innocuous pops like it did on television: it was *loud*. Fortunately, they didn't have to have real-world reflexes when it came to shit like that. Mitch spun on his heel and wrapped his arms around Deosil just before it happened, a movement that was almost comically fast. Deosil shrieked when she realized that the weird sparks flashing in front of her face were bullets pinging off Mitch's impervious field of force he'd wrapped both of them in.

Rusty, however, discovered something about himself. Or rather, about his power—he'd never consciously realized until that moment that some part of his brain was always registering the magnetic field around him. The sudden ripples through it as the metal-jacketed bullets tore through the field were unmistakable, and he reacted faster than he would have ever thought he could, warping that field and sending the bullets careening wide of himself, shoving them into the ground at his feet, or into the air above him.

For Optic and Llorona—the two with the most experience in situations like these—it was a little less blindsiding. By the time the first bravo raised his gun, both of them had already twigged him as the first likely shooter, by virtue of the way the others kept glancing at him, and by how broadly he telegraphed the readying of his weapon. Even before he'd leveled the barrel of his weapon, Llorona stopped speaking and internalized a hum that everyone around her felt in their guts, the sound rendering her immaterial. Simultaneously, Optic exploded into light, shifting the matter of his body into coherent energy, leaving behind a flare in the gunmen's eyesight like glancing up at the sun on a bright day.

Bullets passed through both of them harmlessly, and with that, Gauss acted.

He took a step forward, twisting the magnetic field around him, and then threw his hands skyward, like he was pushing something up. The men howled in shock and pain as guns were ripped out of their grasps by the surging magnetic field that also snatched away jewelry (right out of one guy's eyebrow piercing, in fact), wallet-chains, extra clips, and in at least two cases, grenades. The sudden snatch upward of the metal tipped the men off-balance, and even dragged one entirely off his feet as the shiny steel tips of his cowboy boots were shunted into the air twenty feet above their heads to float in a field of magnetic debris.

The men stared upward for several heartbeats.

"Why did they fire? Why'd they *shoot* at us?" Deosil had a tinge of panic to her voice, like she was on the verge of a breakdown. She pushed herself out of Mitch's arms.

"They asked us to leave," Llorona said, not taking her eyes off the confused men. "I refused. I think we'r–"

"We've got incoming!" Optic said, resolidifying sufficiently to make sound, his luminous arm pointing toward the ranch compound. It took a moment to focus on the silhouette of the figure that leapt skyward from within the compound, in an arc that would send the person crashing down in their midst in that single jump.

"Mine!" shouted Sentinel, launching himself into the air, blowing up dust around them with the force of his propulsion. He didn't need a curving arc to reach the incoming figure—he flew straight there, slamming into the man. The arc of the jump had significant strength behind it, though, and they landed near the cluster at the top of the hill, albeit a dozen or so yards short of where the leaping figure intended on arriving.

Deosil almost felt sorry for the thugs that realized just how badly outclassed they were, who turned and fled to both sides of the road, through thorny chaparral scrub brush and mesquite trees.

"Wait!" The man struggling to rise from the road cried out. He knelt up and threw his hands in front of him, not rising any further. Sentinel rose to his feet, everything in his powerful form suggesting he was seconds from treating the man to the thrashing of his lifetime.

"That's Matón," Llorona said, stepping past their line and crossing to where Sentinel was relaxing into a guarded but ready stance. "He's her second."

Matón chuckled and turned his head to the side, spitting a gobbet of blood onto the packed-clay roadway. His hair was shorn close to his skull, and his jaw was very square. There was something off about his face, like his head was too wide and his neck too thick for comfortable human proportions. He wore a simple diamond stud in each ear, and tattoos climbed up his tree-trunk of a neck, out from under the collar of the expensive tailored white button-up he wore, now torn, dusty, and a little bloodied. He stood and cracked his neck. The man was obscenely massive, standing a least half a foot taller than Sentinel, and his shoulders were half-again as wide as Mitch's.

"Jesus Christ," Rusty said, at Optic's elbow. "That dude's a fucking tank." The two of them crossed along with Llorona, while Sentinel glanced back at them.

"You got this?" he asked them, and Llorona nodded. Sentinel let them step up past him.

"Yeah, Matón just wants to talk, right?" She stepped up to the massive hillock of a man, and he grinned and threw open his arms like he expected a hug. He did not receive one.

"Llorona! How are you, *tia*?" He laughed like a dozen men unloading firearms at them was just a friendly tussle between friends, and she shook her head. Rusty glanced behind him. Sentinel had gone to Deosil and had an arm around her shoulder. He was whispering something to her, and she was shaking like a leaf. Around her, tiny dust devils sprung up in the dusty road and spun away from them, as Deosil worked to get her power back under control. Mitch just stood there, talking to her in a low voice, while she did so.

"You cool?" Optic elbowed Rusty gently, getting his attention without taking his eyes away from Llorona and Matón.

Rusty realized there were tears in his eyes, and he was shaking, too. His stomach roiled, and for a half-second he was pretty sure he was going to be sick. "Uh, yeah," he said cavalierly, and wiped his hand across his face. He fished a bottle of sports drink out of his bag, screwed the cap off, and downed half of it. "Yeah, I'm good. Just surprised me."

Optic clapped him on the shoulder. "You were fucking *awesome*, Rusty. Your reaction is pretty normal for the first time you get fired on. Hell, it's pretty normal for the first hundred times, as far as I can tell. That was some quick thinking, snatching their guns away."

"Not really thinking, just doing. But thanks."

By that time, Deosil and Mitch were crossing to the rest of the group. Deosil broke off to grab Rusty and hug him, making sure he was alright with a cursory glance. Optic and Sentinel let them be, returning to Llorona's side.

"I'm fine, Jesh," he said. "Seriously. Not touched at all."

"Thank God," she said, and hugged him again. "I just froze. Totally useless."

"So did I, Jesh. Seriously." He glanced up at where the guns and other objects orbited one another in the air above them. "I didn't do that. My power did it—I didn't even know what was going on until it had already happened."

"Thank God," she said again, and shook her head. "This is a mistake. We have no business being out here."

"We're okay." He tried to reassure her, taking her hand. She looked at him hard, like she was doing everything she could to keep from crying. Not out of personal fear, though. She was obviously as worried about him as he was about her. "Hey. We've got good people around us, right? We don't have a lot of experience with this stuff, but they do. We can trust them."

She nodded after a moment. "You're right. I'd have been dead if Mitch hadn't–"

"But he did," he said. "He did. Now, c'mon. They're waving us over."

She chuckled, shaking her head. "So what are you going to do about those?" She pointed up at the debris field.

"Eh. Fuck 'em," he said with a grin. "Let them figure out what to do about it."

Mitch walked up to them, concern written across his face. "You two okay? If you'd rather wait at the van…"

"Hell, no." Deosil weakly grinned at him, wiping away tears. "After that? I'm meeting this Calavera bitch to tell her what I think of her hospitality."

Mitch and Rusty exchanged a grin. "I'm good to go, too." Rusty laid a hand on Mitch's arm. "Thanks for protecting Jesh. That was quick thinking."

"We protect each other, right?" Mitch said. He glanced at where Optic, Matón, and Llorona were loading into a jeep. "Let's go. Calavera sent her bully-boy out to invite us in. Apparently, some sort of electrical disturbance fried their radios, and they couldn't hear her tell them that."

Deosil narrowed her eyes at Rusty, who dodged her glance. "Oops."

* * *

A dusty jeep ride later found them at the wrought-iron gate of the expansive ranch compound. From a distance, they could tell it was made up of a huge central house—palatial was not too extreme of a word to use for it—and a half-dozen smaller side buildings. One of them seemed to be a stable, and the immense industrial-looking one that fronted onto large pastureland was probably a barn. Sheltered between the front gate and the front of the house itself was a large roundabout driveway, once well-paved, though starting to show some wear, complete with a mosaic-tile inlaid fountain. At the top of the fountain was a statue of what seemed like the Virgin Mary, but as they parked, Deosil did a double-take and got out of the jeep, walking over toward it.

Tall devotional candles, the kind in glass jars sold in *tiendas* and *botanicas* lined the edge of the fountain beneath the statue's face. The statue was made of concrete, probably poured into a mold. Despite its mass-produced appearance, it was unnerving. Above the long flowing robes, where the serenely benevolent face of the Virgin of Guadalupe might normally be gazing, was instead a human skull, stark in its sharp lines, garish in white and black paint. Hollow eyes gazed down at the level of the fountain's edge so that the figure seemed to be resting its gaze on whoever stood on that side of it. Whereas the rest of the fountain's surfaces were mosaiced in green, blue, and black tiles, the tiles beneath the statue's forward gaze were brilliant crimson, descending from the bottom edge of the robe into the fountain's basin proper, so that the water there shimmered like blood.

Deosil started slightly as Llorona stepped up beside her. "Is that who I think that is?" Deosil said, not quite whispering.

Llorona nodded. *"La Santissima Muerte.* Do you know her?"

"Isn't she a folkloric remnant of one of the old Aztec goddesses?" Deosil gazed back up at the skull-face of the figure. There was a sort of sinister serenity in that haloed visage.

"I don't know about that," Llorona said. "It wouldn't surprise me, though. She's a folk saint—not anyone canonized by the Church, but still prayed to for intercession."

"For what? I'm not all that familiar with her."

"For lost causes, mostly. Things that seem impossible." Llorona paused, chewing over her words. "She's like—you go to her when you have no other hope. When all your other avenues are exhausted, when no one else will answer your prayers. Death is eternal, and is always waiting, so if no one else will listen, maybe Death will, you know?"

"She's the saint of outcasts."

Llorona and Deosil turned to the speaker. She wasn't terribly tall, although the long lines of her jeans made her seem so, as did the heavy leather boots she wore. She wore a vest sewn of brocade in the front panels but leather in the back; it was fastened tightly across her bosom with tiny gleaming silver buttons. Her arms were bare, and tattooed with murals from a bunch of different cultures—some of the artwork was African, some of it Japanese, some of it Egyptian. Deosil knew enough about historical world religions (you pick up weird shit as a pagan these days, she couldn't help but muse) to know that they were all Underworld and funereal images.

Her face was done up in the style of the calavera skulls from the *Dia de los Muertos* celebrations, a pale background against which lines of black and splotches of green and blue and red were painted. Or was it tattooed? Deosil couldn't tell.

"She is," Llorona agreed. "All kinds of outcasts. Criminals and queers, divorcees and drug addicts, prostitutes and cripples."

"Everyone society wants nothing to do with." The woman who could only be Calavera agreed, with an eerie smile. "I've always said that you and I are very alike, Llorona."

"If we are, then it only serves to truly highlight just how different our aims are, then, Calavera."

"Why don't we go in? I was enjoying a relaxing day, and having some guests to join me would be perfect, I think." She turned with no hint of irony, the criminal kingpin acting the part of the perfect hostess, and led them up the massive stone steps to the front door of the ranch house.

They passed through a large galleried entryway, complete with a balcony that overlooked it, a gaudy chandelier hanging above it all, and a large set of stairs to either side of an open archway. Art hung on the walls, some of it which Deosil recognized, a few of which she was sure ought to be hanging on walls in museums. Through the archway, past a set of halls that led further into the house, and they were outside once more, this time beside an immense kidney-shaped pool, with deck chairs and a couple of bravos lounging on the stools beside the cabana-bar, beer bottles in hand and faces wrapped in sunglasses against the bright Mexican sun.

A light wind picked up as they walked down into the pool's vicinity, and strange currents bubbled up in the pool. Deosil prayed no one would notice, but someone did—Sentinel slipped his hand into hers and squeezed it supportively. "You okay, kiddo?" he whispered. She smiled and breathed, and the wind and the water returned to normal. *Just keep breathing,* she reminded herself.

The group awkwardly took up seats beneath a wide pavilion of light linen, not quite dense enough to create full shade, but a relief against the hot sun. The chairs were low to the ground, and it was a little awkward to sit in them, while Calavera took her seat in a chair that was up off the ground, her own little poolside throne, and smirked down at them.

Deosil and Rusty shared a seat, him leaning against the back, and she perched on the side of it, arm resting on his bent leg. Llorona sat cross-legged on another chair, and Optic stretched out like he was there to get some sun. Mitch simply stood, thanking her for the offer of a seat, and examining the hedge that cut the pool area off from the rest of the ranch grounds.

Matón emerged from the big house as well, followed by two more of the cartel's bravos, but the three of them crossed to the other side of the pool enclosure, next to the cabana's massive fridge full of beer and booze. One of the men seemed like he was mixing some drinks while his fellows chatted casually, all acting as though they were not watching Calavera's guests like hawks from behind their sunglasses.

"So," Calavera said, looking out over the pool. "What brings you to my home, Llorona?"

"I'm sorry to come uninvited," Llorona said, glancing upward at the painted criminal with a smile. "I did try and get in touch with you, but I never heard anything back. You can be a little difficult to get a message to, it seems."

"Oh, I got them," Calavera said. Her voice was a low purr, like some dangerous hunting cat, and she turned to regard Llorona with such intensity that Optic and Mitch both tensed, ready for an attack. But she smiled, and even winked at Mitch. "I got them. I was just busy. Didn't have much time for visitors. Fortunately, you caught me on an off-day, as it were."

"Lucky for us," Llorona said.

"Indeed it is. Would anyone like to go for a swim?" Calavera asked, once again the hostess. She smiled as one of her men approached with a large tray, burdened down with mixed drinks in wide, salt-rimmed glasses, and brown and green bottles of beer. "Or a drink?"

Llorona all but snorted at the display of hospitality but took a drink. Optic was the only other who accepted something from the tray. Calavera seemed profoundly disappointed. "Well, if you're not here to drink, and you're not here to swim—I hope you don't take this the wrong way, but you're pretty much an impediment to my plans for the day." Calavera stood, and started popping the buttons open on her vest. Her belly was tightly muscled and smooth, each button opened revealing more and more lines tattooed in her flesh. "Why are you here?"

"Oh, thank God," Rusty whispered. Deosil glanced back at him and smiled.

Llorona stood, taking another sip from her mixed drink, and set it beside her seat. "We're looking for some people," she said. "Echoes, we're pretty sure. Superpowered, at least. They seem to be responsible for kidnappings in a couple of places around the world, and we're interested in them."

"Interesting," Calavera said, and shrugged off her vest. Beneath it, she wore a bustier of some sort—not quite a bikini top, but something that could certainly serve for someone intending on taking a dip. "And you think we're those people?"

"God, no," Llorona said. She said it with a smile that could be taken as reassurance, Deosil noted, but came off as a little mocking. "We know that at least two boys were taken from Juarez, and the MO fits the way they work: teleportation, accompanied by strange lights that create a sense of reverential awe in those who witness them."

"Very strange," Calavera said. She reached down and shrugged her vest back on, though she didn't bother to button it. "So why come to me?"

"You know everyone." Llorona said it like it was a known fact, and Calavera could only smile in response. "And you're careful about safeguarding your territory. They've demonstrated a willingness to work with the local crime elements in the places they operate in the past, and around here? That's you."

Calavera burst out laughing, a merry, throaty sound. "I'm not sure whether to take that as a compliment or an insult, *prima*," she said.

Llorona returned her grin. "It's neither. It's just the truth, wouldn't you say?"

Calavera sighed, and seemed to consider something. She absentmindedly buttoned up her vest again. Deosil watched her, fascinated by the woman's casual charisma. She was so intent that she only half-noticed Rusty when he poked her to get her attention. They both glanced up at Mitch, who'd moved more toward the center of the pavilion, and he nodded their attention toward the cabana.

The men there were watching them closely, all attempt at casualness gone. At least two had hands under the bar. They were all clearly waiting for a signal.

Finally, Calavera shook her head. "No."

Llorona arched an eyebrow. "No?"

"No," the other woman repeated. "No, I haven't heard of these people. I'm inclined to not even believe that they were operating in our territory, but I know you and your little investigative skills well enough to at least say that if they were, they weren't doing so with our permission."

Llorona sighed, a sound of frustration. "So you won't help us."

The glare Calavera gave her was one of purest contempt. "I'm not sure why you ever thought I would, given our background. We Echoed at the same Event, *prima*. That's the only real bond we've shared. Ever. Everything else has been you getting in my fucking way."

There was steel in Calavera's voice, and Deosil's heartbeat spiked. The pool's water began to lazily swirl, as though something large swam beneath its surface.

"Alright, then," Llorona said. "I believe you. I think it costs you a great deal of face to admit that a pack of Echoes outside of your control may have been operating in your territory, so I can't really see you lying about that."

Calavera smiled ruefully. "You know me so well."

"I'd like to talk to Medium, though."

Calavera's carefully constructed smile, the playful facade where she played nice while throwing little barbed jabs here and there—it all fell away to reveal a narrow-eyed hatred. Deosil stood in alarm, and Rusty maneuvered himself to his feet. Only Optic seemed unconcerned, reclining in the deck chair, one leg propped up at the knee.

"That's why you came. That's what you were here for the entire time."

Rusty and Deosil looked to Llorona. This was the first they'd heard about it, although Llorona's face suggested Calavera was right. She was almost *smug* about it. "If you have nothing for me, then surely it's something you want to know as well, no?"

"And what makes you think she is here at all?"

"It's not a matter of thinking, Calavera. I don't make guesses. You know me well enough to know that. Don't play games—at this point, they're just embarrassing."

Calavera's narrowed eyes gave way to a smile, and she laughed, another velvety chuckle. "True enough," she conceded, shaking her head. "How did you know?"

"She was at the Houston Event as well," Llorona said. "And I know that you think something otherworldly happened there. We Echoes from that Event are your only proof of that, though. You've constantly tried to recruit me, and I know you've tried to recruit others, as well. You got Matón. You've tried Pulse, and even Mikael, for God's sake."

Calavera chuckled. "You know, he actually came after me when I approached him? Like, fiery sword and everything. I had to try, of course, but I honestly never expected that response."

"And I know that Medium went missing about five years ago. There wasn't any indication that she'd been kidnapped, however."

"She came willingly. She has family in Matamoros, you know. People who could really benefit from having someone in a powerful cartel to watch out for them."

Llorona clenched her fists. "Oh, I don't doubt that. And I'm sure you've held them over her head ever since."

There was an intensity in the air between them, and it was rippling outward. Deosil was aware that her elemental powers were feeding off it, taking her own anxiety and bleeding into the world around her. The winds picked up in the sky above them, clouds racing past. Though she kept the surface of the pool relatively placid, its depths positively churned like her stomach was, twisting in on itself with fear. She glanced at Sentinel, and he nodded to her—he was aware, his face said, but she might also need that power at any moment.

Finally, Calavera sighed, a deeply irritated sound. She glanced over her shoulder and waved off her men, several of whom had stepped away from the cabana, trying to hide guns at their sides. "It's fine," she said loudly, mostly for their benefit. The men seemed to relax. "It's fine, I'll take you to see her. It's clear to me—and to your friends, I'd say—that seeing Medium was your goal the entire time, no? As surprised as I am, though, it looks like they're more surprised." She smirked, and Llorona glanced over her shoulder at the others, apologetically.

"Nah," said Optic, sitting up from his recline in the chair. "Llorona's got this. We trust her. She knows what she's doing, and knows her shit. Anyone that underestimates her is a damned fool, to be honest."

Llorona shot him an inscrutable glance, and he grinned at her.

"Point taken," Calavera said. "Well then. You know about her, yes. How sensitive she is?"

"I do, yes. I don't know her very well, personally, but we spent some time together after the Event. I know how the littlest thing can set off her power, so she's got to carefully control her environment."

"Well, it's been what, almost thirty years?"

"Twenty-seven."

"Exactly. She's learned a bit more control in that time, and has sharpened her abilities quite a lot in the last five years."

"While she's working for you, you mean," Llorona said, and there it was. Disgust. She shook her head, like the thought of it sickened her, and Calavera could only smile.

"Yes. While she's working for me. I've demanded things of her she never thought she could accomplish, but she's delivered. It's been a very beneficial arrangement we have going on. Do you understand?"

"I do," Llorona nodded.

"But yes. She is still quite sensitive, and it wouldn't be good to subject her to a whole posse of new people all at once," Calavera said, glancing at the rest of the group. "So why don't you and I go in, and we'll see her, and your friends can..."

"No way." Deosil stepped up, shaking her head, fists clenched at her side. "She's not going in there by herself." Llorona shot her a raised eyebrow, but Deosil raised her chin stubbornly.

Calavera chuckled, and regarded Deosil, almost like she was doing so for the first time. "And who are you, *mija*?"

"Deosil," she said tersely. "And I don't mean to be rude, but safety first. We don't know you."

"*Jesh-ull*," Calavera said, rolling the name around her tongue. "An unusual name for an unusual girl, no? Why don't you come with us? One new person isn't too much of a burden. Or would you rather have one of the big strong boys come with?"

"I'll go," Deosil agreed, and Llorona shot her a worried look. Deosil glanced back at Sentinel, expecting to see his concern and unvoiced objection. Instead, he was smiling. *You got this*, his wink said, and Deosil knew he was right.

For some reason, it seemed a little easier to believe in yourself when one of the world's foremost heroes did, too. She smiled at Calavera and Llorona. "Let's do this. This humidity is thrashing my hair."

Calavera chuckled again. "Oh, I like you." She glanced at the others. "I trust you boys will relax here and wait for our return. Please play nice with my boys."

"We'll be fine," Mitch said, and Calavera paused for a moment, staring at him intently, like she was trying to place his face or his voice, but couldn't quite do so.

"Shall we?" She turned, and led Llorona and Deosil away.

"Great," Rusty said. "Now what do *we* do?"

"Get some sun?" Optic chuckled, and pulled his chair out of the shade. He pulled his shirt off, and lay back down in the deck-chair.

"I will turn purple and blister if I do that," the redhead said mock-grumpily. He glanced at Mitch, who pulled up a chair to sit next to him.

"We wait," Mitch said, and reached out to squeeze Rusty's hand.

CHAPTER TWENTY

Just outside Ciudad Juarez, Mexico
May 19, 2013

The interior of the ranch house was gorgeous, Deosil had to admit. It was clearly old, but someone had paid a lot of money to renovate sections of it. Elegant tile lay underfoot. Some of the walls were white plaster, others were paneled in a pale wood, and still others were constructed with mortared fieldstone. Rugs and framed artwork hung on all of the walls, and the ceilings in most of the rooms were very high.

"Nice place," Deosil said as they stepped through yet another anteroom and into a kitchen you could have parked Deosil's car in and still had room.

"Thanks," Calavera said. "It's nice enough to tolerate living way out here. I'm not much of a *campesina* myself, but in my line of work it pays to live away from nosy neighbors. Someplace where you can see visitors coming."

"Someplace with lots of space to bury the bodies?" Llorona joined in the conversation in a sweetly accusatory tone, and Calavera stopped smiling. She arched an eyebrow.

"Always room for one more." Calavera gestured at a doorway off of the kitchen. "This way."

The house was immense, furnished with gorgeous antiques. Deosil couldn't help but be impressed by the ostentation of it all. Calavera was someone who enjoyed the fine life, and she'd figured out how to get it.

"Nice, isn't it?" Calavera smirked, noticing Deosil's wandering gaze. "You know, I can always use good talent." Calavera ran her hand along a beautiful-ly finished side table as they walked through a hallway. Art hung on one wall, and the other was a bank of French doors that opened out onto a gorgeous garden in full bloom. "I've offered your friend here a place plenty of times, you know. You wouldn't even have to get up to anything distasteful. There's always work for those with tender sensibilities in my organization."

"Oh, you've offered," Llorona agreed, and then glanced at Deosil warningly. "You've offered that to others as well. Long enough to keep them on hand, to figure out who they are and who they hold most precious, no? And then what?"

Calavera actually laughed. "I see some of my old employees have been gos-siping."

She turned into an archway and began to lead them down a flight of stairs. Llorona stopped at the top of the stairs, her arm outstretched to keep Deosil with her. "You keep her in the basement?" Llorona clearly had an opinion about that, and it was pretty far from favorable.

Calavera stopped on the landing and turned to look up at them. "No, I don't *keep* her in the fucking basement," she said sharply. "She *has* rooms down in the basement, where she prefers it. It's cooler, no one comes down here to bother her, and the regular noises of the house don't disturb her. My *machos* can get a little rowdy sometimes, and she's delicate. *Entiendes?*"

Llorona threw her hands up placatingly. "Message loud and clear, Calave-ra. You're a humanitarian."

"Fucking right I am," the other woman snarled as she turned away, con-tinuing down the staircase.

Deosil tugged on Llorona's sleeve and the older woman slowed, while they let Calavera get a little ahead. "I don't like this," Deosil whispered.

"Me either, *mija*," Llorona replied, not taking her eyes off of the gangster for even a second. "We just have to let this play out, you know? If we're lucky, she's being legit because she wants us gone as soon as possible."

"And if we're not lucky?"

Llorona glanced at her, a quick flashed apology with her eyes alone. "Then we'd better be ready." The two women picked up the pace, and found Cala-vera waiting for them at the bottom of the staircase.

Deosil snapped her head around, glancing back up the stairs. She could have sworn she'd heard...it sounded like someone else descending the stairs, though no one was there. The stairs were old and wooden, and they creaked loudly as the three women passed. Maybe she'd heard one of them settling back into place? She couldn't be sure. She turned to catch up, stepping through the doorway, into the large wine cellar beyond.

Llorona's hand covered her mouth in horror, the first tears coursing down her cheeks. She sagged against the wall, like she was leaning into it for support, and as Deosil got to her, her knees buckled.

The room was dusty—wait, no. It was *misty*. A faintly luminous fog filled the room, and Calavera stood at its center, her arms crossed. She was smiling at Llorona's distress contemptuously. It wasn't until then that Deosil could make out the other images in the fog. A young woman lay on the ground, her ears bleeding and head shape subtly distorted where the skull beneath it had cracked without any trauma to the flesh. She twitched without making a sound, and the sharp edges of her shattered skull shifted grotesquely beneath her skin as she did.

A boy of maybe fourteen screamed silently, half in and half out of the sidewalk. He looked like he'd fallen and simply *not stopped* when he hit the sidewalk, instead passing through part of it. The edge of a bicycle rack passed through his chest, and he was trying to scream—trying to *breathe*—around it.

And sitting by itself, alone and untended, a tandem stroller. There was no movement from within it, no sign of any life, although the blanket and shade mercifully hid what might or might not be within it.

"Do you remember this, Llorona?" Calavera's voice echoed. Not in the room, but in her *head*. "Do you remember that day in Houston? The day when *Dia de los Muertes* became not about remembering the dead, but making dead of your own? Your screams were the last thing so many people heard, Llorona. Are you still screaming for them now?"

Llorona slumped to the ground, sobbing uncontrollably. Panic flooded Deosil's body, and with it, her power made her aware of a sudden presence behind her. Footsteps slid over dusty floors as arms disturbed the air, all creating tiny eddies in the atmosphere around them. There was someone there, someone unseen but not undetected by the world around them.

Without bothering to try to verify the presence with her eyes, Deosil reached out, seizing chunks of fieldstone mortared into the wall. With a grunt and a push that knocked the wind out of her, she seized the stone with her powers and projected them out of the wall at the invisible figure. The wall behind them exploded outward, sending shards of fist-sized rocks into the seemingly empty space.

They connected, and a thin man was suddenly visible as he slammed into the empty wine rack next to him. He was dressed in a singlet-style t-shirt and cuffed, baggy slacks. His feet were bare, and he bore a knife in each hand. Dark lines were tattooed, eye-liner style, under his eyes, and one of them bled down into a single black teardrop under his eye. He cursed in Spanish as the stones slammed into him, and he fell, knives clattering.

Deosil reached for the storm that raged within her, and cast it out into the world around her. The house shook as a torrent of air gusted through the cellars, catching up dust and small objects, bursting through the doorway behind Deosil and sending a cloud of blinding debris into the room. Deosil dived for Llorona, and tried to pull her to her feet, but she was dead weight, caught in the fit of grief that held her. It was utterly unnatural.

Deosil glanced up just in time to see Calavera close to her. The gangster punched her in the side of the head. Deosil recoiled, but could not dodge in time. The strength of the blow slammed her head and shoulder into the wall beside her. She slumped down the wall, regaining her balance just in time for Calavera's follow-up kick to the ribs.

Deosil sobbed, trying to breathe.

* * *

Eventually, Matón himself came over with another couple of bottles of beer. His men remained behind, across the pool's length at the cabana bar, though they watched their boss carefully.

"You look like you could use another refreshment here," he said in thick-accented English. Rusty accepted one, but Optic hefted the bottle he already had in-hand and sloshed it around to show that it was still half full. Mitch shook his head tersely, and Matón shrugged. "So, are you all a team or something? Or Golden Cross like Llorona?"

"Just friends," Rusty said with a smile. He tugged at the string that hung from the neck of his hoodie. It was hot as hell, but he'd elected to keep his uniform on underneath his civvies, and it was the only thing that would cover the long sleeves of the DTPA-issued garb. "Friends helping one another out, right?" Matón snorted. "If you say so. Me, I get paid for my help."

Rusty could only grin like an idiot, and throw a grimace Optic's way, begging for help. Optic chuckled. "So, that was a hell of a leap, Matón. Out in the driveway," the military man said, sitting up in his chair.

Matón grinned. "When you gotta get someplace fast, you know?" He regarded the three of them and gestured with the neck of his beer bottle at Rusty and then at Optic. "So, I know *el canelo* here is a big magnet, and I seen your movie, with the light and the flying and shit. What do you do?"

Mitch met his question with a clenched jaw, and turned away, like he was distracted.

"Hey," Matón said sharply, trying to get his attention. "I'm talking to you. You look fucking familiar, man. Where do I know you from?"

"We've never met," Mitch said, not bothering to turn his face toward the man. His head was cocked slightly, and Rusty realized he was listening to something. Suddenly Mitch stepped forward, putting himself between Matón and his teammates. "They're under attack. Get there fast," he barked. Rusty stood quickly and started toward the house. Optic, on the other hand, dissolved into a vaguely-humanoid body of light and flashed away into the house. The bottle he was holding fell to the pebbled concrete beneath his chair and shattered.

"Wha–?" Matón managed before Mitch shoved him back and sent him sprawling to the concrete at the edge of the pool.

"I suggest you stay down," Mitch said, jaw clenched. He glanced across the pool where Matón's men were only just reacting to the sudden explosion of action from their guests. "And tell your boys to stand down. No need for them to get hurt."

Matón gathered his feet under him with a growl. "Big mistake, *pendejo*."

The big man shot up at Mitch, lightning quick, with the power of a tank behind him. His big meaty, tattooed fist slammed into Mitch's solar plexus, and then his elbow followed with an upward blow that caught him on the chin, snapping his head back and driving him back a step. Matón's men started forming a half-circle around the pool, half of them chasing Rusty, and the other half moving in to get a clear shot at the big man brawling with their boss.

Rusty paused at the top of the stairs and turned as two of the *machos* trained their guns on him. But they weren't fast enough—the weapons sailed out of their hands, and snapped into the now-also-stolen guns of the other two men. The guns met in the air above the pool with a clacking sound, magnetically stuck to one another fast. Rusty gestured, and the weapons dropped into the deep end of the pool.

Behind him, Optic's light form flashed down the hall. "Downstairs!" Optic shouted as he went past and then was gone.

Rusty nodded. "Go on! I'll be right there!" With a glance behind him at Mitchk, Rusty followed as best he could.

* * *

By the pool, Matón continued to slam his fists into Mitch, over and over, driving him back a little with each blow. The man was insanely strong—probably stronger than any Echo Mitch had ever encountered. Though the blows were greatly dulled by his power, Mitch still wiped blood from his nose.

"Figured it out yet?" Mitch said finally, dropping into what was clearly a fighting stance. Matón looked at him questioningly. Mitch smiled a lock-jawed smile and unbuttoned the top button of his dress shirt. "Know who I am?"

"I don't give a fuck who you are, I'm going to—" The man blanched when Mitch pulled open the top half of his shirt, just enough to reveal his iconic blue-and-white uniform. "Oh *shit*, you're—"

Mitch didn't let him finish that thought, stepping up and slamming into the man's body with a tremendous blow. He put everything he had into the strike—something he almost never did, for fear of hurting someone too badly, but Matón had proven he could take it. Hell, he'd proved that there was a pretty good chance that anything less just wouldn't get anywhere.

Matón's men stared, slack-jawed, as their boss sailed over their heads, landing some twenty yards away, banging into the side of an aluminum-sided storage building, and collapsing it entirely. Mitch pulled his shirt all the way off, tossing it to one side and laying bare one of the most iconic costumes in history, and then cracked his knuckles.

"*¿Quién es el siguiente?*" he asked.

The men fled.

* * *

Even with her arms curled around her head and face protectively—hoping for just a second without new and searing pain in which she could focus her power—Deosil saw the kick coming. She held her breath and braced for it.

But it never landed.

Brilliance lit the basement room like a flash of lightning, and Optic was there, suddenly solid, but still moving very, very fast. His hurtling body slammed into Calavera, and Deosil was sure she heard things in the woman's body *crack* in the meaty impact. Both of them flew across the room, Calavera landing on her back, gasping for breath, and Optic kneeling six or so feet from her, shaking his head dizzily and trying to straighten himself.

The weird misty images dissipated into coils of ghostly fog as Calavera's concentration faltered. Deosil glanced around and found no sign of the invisible dude by the shattered wine racks. Not surprising, really—he was probably using his power again and moving up on her. She was too hurt to help herself or Llorona, damn it. At least like this. She closed her eyes, continuing to lie there, and shifted her sense of self, layering it into the world around her.

The land around them for miles was arid and hot. No real natural bodies of water, other than a creek that was just a muddy smear this time of year. But beneath the dirt and sand, beneath the scraggly, thorny plant life—good, solid stone. Massive plates of flint, remnants of the time when northern Mexico was just another lava field in the early days of the world. Deosil reached with her mind, found the very essence of that stone and then inhaled sharply, invoking those old plates of rock into herself.

Her skin heaved and cracked, solidifying into grey-black flint. Her features sharpened and hair fell away, and when she straightened herself to her knees, her body scraping against the tile floor, a sound of stone on clay. Just in time, too. From out of nothingness came three sharp strikes, and each one connected with her. They failed to draw blood; instead, sparks flew from the steel on flint. She smiled with difficulty, cracking the features of her face as she did so.

"Not good enough," she said, and lashed out with one stony fist. She wasn't a fighter—not by a long shot. But the wide arc of her attack combined with the fact that the invisible man stood staring at her in shock was enough. She connected, with a satisfyingly meaty sound, and the man appeared again, knocked once again to the floor.

Across the room, Optic met Calavera's gaze. "This was a big fucking mistake, Calavera," he said, getting to his feet. The woman glared up at him and the creeping mists began to coalesce around him. "Oh, shit–" He bit off his curse with a gasp as a big man appeared in front of him. He was dark, with tight, curly hair and a big belly. He was clearly a strong man, though, with thickly corded forearms and legs like tree stumps. He was dressed in a stained jumpsuit, with the logo of some department of sanitation.

"Is this who you've become, son?" The big man's voice boomed, and everyone in the room heard it, though no one was sure whether it was in ears or head. "This is how you take care of your brother and your baby sister? All the way across the world, trying to be a superhero, trying to be a movie star, trying to be some *faggot*? Is this how family works in that sick head of yours?" Optic gaped and took a step away from the big man, tears in his eyes.

To his side, Calavera rose to her feet gingerly, careful to not let her pain disrupt the flow of her power. Her power might not have been supernatural, but the ghosts she called on were quite real in their own way.

* * *

In the doorway, Gauss appeared, his hoodie hanging open to reveal his uniform. He stepped up to the stone form of his best friend. "Shit, Jesh," he said. "What are you doing? You hate using this."

"No choice," she said, her voice a stony, rasping echo. "Had to choose: stone invocation or get stabbed a whole bunch of times." Gauss glanced at the unconscious form of the thin knife-man on the ground, and with a flick of his fingers, magnetically adhered his knives to a nearby pipe. They found Optic across the long room; he was slowly backing into a corner, and Calavera was using a wall to lever herself upright.

Gauss spared a glance for Llorona. "You're both hurt. Can you get Llorona out of here?" Gauss was already extending his magnetic senses into the room. Damn it, there wasn't anything strong enough that wouldn't also bring the house down on them if he ripped it out of the wall or ceiling.

"Yeah, I can. You'll be okay?" Deosil asked. He threw her a grin. She exhaled sharply, a small dusty cloud, and restored herself to her normal body. The transformation was weird to watch, up to and including the rapid regrowth of her hair.

"I will, yeah." Gauss held his arms out to his side. Without any weapons on hand, he'd provide his own. The latches on his metal bracers popped open, and a small swarm of gleaming ball bearings emerged like angry wasps from a hive to orbit him.

"Kick her ass," Deosil said. "It seems like she can only use her power on one person at a time."

Rusty nodded and pointed across the room imperiously. The swarming ball bearings all halted, hanging in the air, vibrating for a moment and then took off with a shot. Calavera glanced up just in time and she dropped. The ball bearings slammed into the wall, forming a perfect circle around her. Plaster and wood splinters flew as they tore up the wall. She glanced around frantically, hands running over herself.

"That was a warning shot," Gauss said. He noted that the sudden fear for her life dissipated the mist. Optic was still reeling, though, sagging against a table trying to clear his head. "I can fire these ball bearings with the force of a gunshot, Calavera. Don't test me. Give it up." She nodded once, raising her hands and straightening.

Then, she was in motion, racing across the room, trying to get to Gauss before he could react. Gauss clutched his outstretched hand into a fist and pulled it back. The ball bearings buried in the wall behind Calavera burst outward, destroying that part of the wall, and he slammed the cluster into her.

Despite his warning, there was no way he would use his full power on a living person. But he didn't have to. The ball bearings struck her over and over, turning her run into a sliding sprawl across the floor. With a quick gesture like a maestro conducting an orchestra, Gauss wrapped ball bearings around her wrists, forming a chain of spheres magnetically adhered to one another, and then slamming the two "bracelets" together, forming makeshift manacles. He did the same to her feet. She was bound solidly before she even finished sliding to a halt from when he struck her down.

"If I even get a hint that you're starting to use that power on me, I'll crush your wrists and ankles. For starters. Get it?"

She sighed and rested her head against her crossed arms. "Got it," she mumbled.

"Optic, you cool?" Gauss crossed to the man, who straightened and shook his head. He glanced around and found both Calavera and her buddy on the ground, well in hand.

"Yeah. Thanks." He chewed on his lip and then caught Gauss's eye. "So how much of that did you see?"

"All of it," Gauss said, clasping Optic's shoulder for a moment. "Heard it as I was coming down the stairs. I'm sorry for not getting here in time. You know that's bullshit, though, right? She was just in your head."

Optic glared down at Calavera's supine form like he *hoped* she was trying to get away at that moment or something. "Yeah, she was. And that'll be the last damned time that's the case, I guarantee you."

"C'mon, let's head upstairs. You grab the Vanishing *Cholo* over there. I'll get Calavera."

* * *

The scene pool-side was very calm. Matón and the invisible guy (Soplón was his handle, Calavera said) were still out cold, and Mitch was content to leave them that way. Calavera sat at a table, her magnetic manacles adhered solidly to the chair beneath her.

"Medium isn't here," Calavera said, leaning back in her chair with the air of someone in complete control of her situation. "And there's no way I'm letting you anywhere near her."

Optic grinned at Rusty. "Hey, Llorona. Is Medium an older lady?"

Calavera narrowed her eyes.

Llorona beamed at him. "She is, yes. Have you seen her?"

"I did," Optic drawled, grinning his sparkling grin. "Or at least, someone that might be her. Upstairs, in the attic. I saw her when I flashed through the house earlier, hunting for you and clearing the rooms to make sure we didn't have any additional backup to deal with."

Llorona grimaced, looking a little embarrassed on Calavera's behalf. "I guess you have to try everything you can," she said to Calavera, who refused to meet her gaze. "But that was pretty sad as far as last-ditch efforts go."

Calavera refused to say another word, which seemed to delight Llorona. Rusty glanced over at Deosil with a grin. She wasn't watching the interplay with amusement the way he'd assumed she would be. Instead, she sat at a table in the corner of the pool area, away from everyone, her arms on the table and her head buried in them. Mitch caught his eye, an unspoken question in his face.

Rusty held up a reassuring hand. He got up from his seat and crossed to Deosil, crouching beside her chair. "Hey, gorgeous," he said. "Earth hangover?" He put a hand on her arm, and she turned in her chair and grabbed his neck, hugging him.

"This is the fucking worst," she whispered. "I hate this, Rusty. I'm so embarrassed, and I feel like such a damned loser right now." There was a listlessness and a tinge of despair in her voice.

"Hey, it's not your fault, okay? This isn't you—this is your power. That's all. You did a lot of shit with earth and stone, and you know that fucks you up."

She groaned. "I know. *I know.* Like, logically, I know that it makes me depressed and all energy-drained and *emo.* I know it, but it doesn't help. It doesn't make it better."

When Mitch came over, Rusty glanced up at him. "Just the feedback from her power. Different elements do different things to her. Same as my whole electrolytes stuff with my power."

Mitch nodded. "I think we're heading upstairs to see Medium."

"Why don't we just wait here? Keep an eye on the creeps?"

"You sure?" Mitch glanced a little worriedly at the disarmed gangsters milling about in the cabana, and the chairs where Calavera and her two Echo lieutenants were tied.

"I am." Rusty nodded. "I can keep an eye on everyone, and I'll just shout if something happens. Just keep an ear out." Mitch agreed and glanced at Deosil. He smiled and reached down to rest a hand on her shoulder for a moment.

"Hope you feel better, kiddo," he said, before turning to walk away.

Deosil glanced up and glared at his retreating back. She met Rusty's eyes; the redhead seemed altogether too amused. "Ugh. He's the worst. No one should be that nice, Rusty. No one. It's not natural."

* * *

The door was already half open, from Optic's house-search earlier. Llorona pushed on it slightly, knocking a little as she opened it the rest of the way. "Medium? It's Llorona," she said gently. "We're not here to hurt you."

The older woman stood beside the attic window, in a long white gown and a dressing coat. Her skin was more weathered than wrinkled, and her eyes were gold-hazel. She smiled a thin-lipped smile at Llorona and waved her in. "I know, Blanca. I wouldn't be much of a psychic if I couldn't tell who had bad intentions for me, no? Come in, you and your friends."

Llorona, Optic, and Sentinel entered the spacious attic room. It was comfortable, certainly, but none of them missed the lock on the outside of the door. The woman Llorona called Medium sat down on a small upholstered bench beneath the large attic window that overlooked the pool below. "Well done, by the way," she said with a nod toward Sentinel. "You handled Matón very handily. Though, that's not terribly surprising, given who you are."

Mitch smiled. "You saw that, huh?"

"I did. Better entertainment than any I've had in a long time. Mostly because Matón so richly deserved that beating, I'll admit. He's a nasty piece of work."

"How'd you like to get out of this room, ma'am?" Optic asked, and she smiled, standing.

"I think I'd like that quite a lot."

By the time they got back down to the pool area, Deosil seemed in a better place, standing to introduce herself when Rusty did. It was easy to forget the grandmotherly woman was another Echo when she smiled and pinched cheeks, complimenting each of them on their efforts as though she'd been there to witness it herself.

"You saw all of that?" Rusty sounded skeptical.

"Well, 'saw' isn't exactly the right term for it, but yes. I was aware of what was going on." She stopped and glanced over at the glaring face of Calavera. "In fact, I've known this was coming for hours," she said, smirking impishly. Calavera just closed her eyes and ground her teeth.

"Well, you're coming with us, if you'd like to, ma'am," Mitch said, glancing at the others and finding no objections. Deosil seemed delighted, and Llorona grateful. His gaze stopped on her, though. "But Llorona, why did we come all this way? Was it just as a rescue?"

"Half and half," Llorona admitted. "I think Medium's power can help us." Mitch gave her a severe grimace, brow furrowed, but he said nothing.

"I'm in your debt for the rescue, Llorona. And the rest of you. Anything I can do, I will," Medium said.

"Even if you couldn't help, we'd get you back to the U.S.," Deosil said, squatting next to the older woman's chair, holding her hand. "I'm sure the DTPA will help protect you if that bitch tries anything again." She glanced over to Calavera, still bound to the chair under her.

"Fortunately, Llorona knows my abilities," the older woman said. "So if she thinks I can help, I'm sure I can, and will be glad to." She turned to regard Rusty steadily, and he stopped, suddenly aware that he'd been fidgeting, shifting from foot to foot. She smiled warmly and glanced at the phone in his hand. "You have something for me?"

"Uh…" He bit his lower lip. "I'm not sure…I mean, I don't…"

"She needs a picture, *mijo*," Llorona said. "Of your friend."

"Oh!" He clicked his phone on and flipped through its images. "Yeah, sorry. Here you go." He handed her the phone, its screen filled with the picture Kosma used for his social media. She took it and squinted a bit at it. She smiled at Rusty.

"He has very kind eyes," she said, and then closed her own. She cradled the phone in her clasped hands and breathed deeply. Rusty bit his lip and glanced at Deosil and Mitch, then back at her. Mitch stepped up behind him and rested his hands on the younger man's shoulders, squeezing to show his support.

Medium's lower lip trembled, and she shook her head, the reaction of someone watching a tragedy they could do nothing about. "Ah, no, this poor boy. He was…taken. In Europe, somewhere. Taken by…by terrible people. Echoes, I think…yes, Echoes. They have powers."

She fell into mumbling to herself for a moment. "But it's not just this boy, is it? Others. In Japan? Or China, perhaps. So many other places. Oh! They also took two…boys. Two boys from…from here! Oh, God bless them. Oh, Llorona, these people are *terrible*. The shadow-maker is so cruel. Bloodthirsty. And so is the masked woman. She is *covered* in blood."

Her voice trembled, as though she might break down sobbing. Instead, she took a deep breath, the phone in her hand forgotten, and steeled herself. "They take them. Through…I don't understand. They go into the light, Llorona, and they are elsewhere. Oh, it's like God's glory, but it's not, is it? Not really?"

"No, it's not," Llorona whispered. "Just another Echo's power."

"Terrible, that man. Greedy and deceitful." She paused for a moment and tilted her head this way and that, as though she were scenting the air. "Where did you go, false priest? Where do you...Ah! *There* you are." There was an intensity to her exclamation, like a woman on the verge of victory. "Oh, Llorona. There are so many of them! It's like a refugee hospital. Cots. Bad food and barely enough water. But they take them...they take them to a laboratory of some kind. It's old. Like a hospital built in the seventies, maybe? I can't tell where, I'm sorry."

Llorona knelt beside the older woman. "Please, Medium—what else do you see? Are there any clues? Signs written in languages?"

"It's...it's very blurry, Llorona. Like when I see an Event. So blurry—too much power there. There is a name, though. Not written. I can sense it? Maybe one of them saying it, I'm not sure. Prometheans."

"Prometheans. We at least have a name for them, then, if nothing else." Llorona sighed, frustrated. Rusty stepped forward to take his phone again, and she clutched him, her long thin nails like razor blades against the meaty part of his hand.

"Oh! I see him! I see the boy with the kind eyes!" Her voice trembled again, and she sounded strained. "They are taking...they have taken him into another room. Wheeled him in, slowly, slowly, down dirty halls. There is a tank there, and other children are...there are IVs that run from the tank into their arms. They are all unconscious. Sleeping, or sedated? Not dead, though, no, not dead, thank God."

"Kosma?" Rusty held her hand tightly, ignoring the pain from her grip. "Did they do that to him?"

"Yes." She hissed through gritted teeth. Her grip tightened, as though she might keep hold of the vision by digging into Rusty's hand. "They plug his IV into it, too! There is something awful that drips down into it. Oh, what is that? What is it? It is...blurry, so blurry. It is powerful—is it glowing? Damn it, I'm sorry, I can't tell, I can't see it well."

She released Rusty, and he pulled his hand back, little bloody crescents pressed into his skin. He shook the sting out of his hand, and was about to reassure her when she gasped. Her spine went rigid, and her eyes flew open while she gasped for air.

"A man!" she shouted. "There is a man in the tank—no, not a man. A *corpse!*"

She collapsed back into her chair and then turned in the seat, throwing herself half off the seat and vomiting onto the concrete deck. Llorona skipped around the chair to hold her steady.

Deosil came to Rusty as he backed away, shaking. He stared at her with wide-eyes, and she nodded. "That was fucking intense," she whispered. "She is *totally* the real deal."

After a few moments and a glass of water Mitch fetched for her, Medium sat up in her seat again. "Forgive me," she said wearily. "Using my abilities isn't usually so dramatic."

"Situations where there are lots of Echoes or other superpowered phenomena—like Events—can blur her vision and make it difficult to pick out details," Llorona explained, and Medium nodded.

"There is something strange going on there, Llorona," the older woman said. "I've never seen such a concentration of power as I did there, save during an Event. And there were no superpowered people there that I could tell. Other than who was in the tank."

"Can you describe what you saw in the tank?" Mitch said quietly.

"It was a man. He's Latino, and I could tell he was dead, though he seems for all the world to only be sleeping. His hair is dark, and short, cut close to his head. I could see a tattoo on his arm, a tattoo of a shield inside of a starburst."

Beside him, Rusty noted that Mitch went very still.

She continued. "The machine, the tank he was in, was hooked up to him in many places and it was siphoning out some kind of fluid. Not blood, or anything natural. Even through the blurring, I could tell it glowed."

"What is it?" Rusty asked Mitch, and the older man reached for Rusty's phone. Everyone noticed, and watched him type in something and then flip through results, searching for something, his lips pale and hands trembling. Finally, he stepped up to Medium's chair, handing her the phone. "This. Was this him?"

"Yes," she said. "That was him. How did…"

Without a word of warning, Mitch was suddenly airborne, a straight shot into the air, blowing everyone back a step or two with the force of his ascent.

Rusty snatched the phone from Medium. "Shit," he said. He turned to Optic half in a panic. "Go! Go get him!"

"Why?" Optic asked. "Who is that?"

Rusty held up his phone, showing an old photo of a news conference decades ago. Its picture was zoomed in on two men's faces—Mitch's and that of another, handsome smiling man next to him. Optic's eyes widened, and he nodded, even as his body was dissolving into coherent brilliance that lasered into the sky above.

"Rusty?" Deosil asked, shaking her head. He showed her the picture.

"It's Craig Velasquez, Jesh," he said, his lower lip trembling. Deosil's eyebrows shot upward and she covered her mouth in horror. "The man in the tank is *Radiant*."

CHAPTER TWENTY-ONE

Just outside Ciudad Juarez, Mexico
May 19, 2013

In the air above northern Mexico, Optic searched for Sentinel. This was old hat for him. Part of his responsibilities as a member of Project: Seraphim was doing just this—flying out to meet incoming threats, plucking out their exact location from the vastness of the wide horizon, and intercepting them. Of all the Seraphim soldiers—Updraft, Jetstream, Freefall, Turbine—he was the best at what they called Imperative Engagement Protocol. A fancy name for "intercept right fucking now."

He'd never had cause to be so thankful for that training as now. His training included dossiers on the power sets of the majority of the known flying transformed persons, and Sentinel was pretty much at the top of that list. The day was bright but cloudy, giving Optic almost ideal conditions for tracking Sentinel's flight. Sentinel was telekinetic, and when he poured on the juice, waves of unseen power rippled off of him. He normally kept it controlled, but the closer he got to Mach One, the wider a distortion field he caused.

A distortion field that would leave a visible wake through cloudy or foggy areas. A wide trail of vapor streamed away from one bank of clouds, and also from another behind it, like someone had smeared a line with their thumb through a chalk drawing.

"Gotcha," Optic whispered. For a distortion trail of that width, Sentinel had to be revving high, pouring on the speed—possibly even sacrificing his personal safety field to do so. Fortunately, if there was one thing Optic was good at, it was speed. He concentrated for a moment, setting aside the concern that sat at the forefront of his brain. Sentinel's reaction had been desperate. Crazed, almost, and he had no idea what to expect when he did manage to intercept him.

His body partially dissolved into a field of brilliant golden-white ambient light, and he flashed after the smeared cloud pattern. In this form, he was more hologram than solid man, but that meant that things like wind resistance and gravity didn't affect him. In seconds, he spotted the rapidly retreating figure of Mitch ahead of him—he was heading east by northeast. In a flash, Optic caught up to him, and partially solidified ahead of him.

If there was one thing to be said for Sentinel's flight, it was that psychic movement was precise. When he generated and maintained all momentum with the simple expedience of thought, Sentinel could turn or stop on a dime. He did so, just a few yards from Optic. The two men floated in midair, and Optic solidified enough to form words, though the air was decidedly thin up here. "What's going on, Mitch? Talk to me, man. Talk to *us*."

"This...this is private, Optic. I'm sorry." The bigger man's expression was a maelstrom of shame and grief and rage, barely contained in clenched jaws. Optic could feel telekinetic power rippling off him, like waves hitting the shore just ahead of a big storm.

"Hey," Optic said, and pulled back his mask. "C'mon. We're in this together, man. Come back. Rusty is really fucking worried about you, and the others are pretty freaked out, too. Don't abandon them there."

"They can take care of themselves. They're perfectly capable."

"It's not about whether or not they're capable, dude!" Optic shifted closer and put his hand on Mitch's shoulder. To his credit, Mitch dissolved his protective shielding to let him do so. A good sign, at least. "It's that people who care about you—as friends, or as more in one case—are worried about you. I saw the picture. Let your people *help* you, man. Let us do this with you."

Mitch exhaled, a shaky, trembling breath, and his eyes spilled over in tears for a moment before he angrily wiped them away. He took Optic's arm and squeezed it. "If they've got his body, Optic, I swear to God..."

"They'll fucking pay, Mitch," Optic said, and hugged the man. "We'll all make sure of that, I promise you."

They broke the hug and Mitch resolidified his shielding. "Okay. Let's go back."

As Optic pulled his mask back into place, Mitch caught his eye. "Thanks for coming to get me."

The two men rocketed back toward Juarez. Optic was thankful radar systems were unlikely to spot either of them, crossing and recrossing the American-Mexican border so casually, and smiled as he watched Sentinel ahead of him. He kept his speed to match the older hero's, keeping a partially solid body sheltered behind the telekinetic cone Sentinel generated as he flew.

In short order, they flew in over the Calaveras ranch, and paused mid-air. "They're all still in the pool area. They look worried." Sentinel's voice was steady, but betrayed a little embarrassment.

Optic clapped him on the shoulder. "Just because they care, man. Let's go." He increased his solidity and descended. Everyone in the pool area was watching them: their friends with worried expressions, the assembled goons with frowns and scowls, Medium's face strangely beatific. She stood and met Optic as he landed, taking his hands into hers.

"You're like an angel come to earth," she whispered to him. He smiled and impulsively kissed her on the cheek.

Everyone made space for Rusty where Mitch landed, though he didn't immediately take the spot, hesitating until Mitch met his eyes and nodded. He crossed to him then, and the two men hugged. "You okay?" said Rusty.

"I'm really not." Mitch kissed the redhead on the forehead. He spoke more loudly. "But why don't we get out of here? I'm sure the Calaveras are sick of offering us their hospitality, and I'd rather get out before one of them decides enough is enough and tries to do something stupid."

"That...would be appreciated," Calavera mumbled from her chair, seeming to pay attention to them for the first time since she was bound to it. "The sooner the better."

Mitch stared down at her, considering. "We don't have any jurisdiction, here or in the United States. I'm sure you know that," he said. She simply nodded. "That means we can't arrest you for anything."

"Your point?" Her tone was carefully neutral.

"My point is that while we're not actually law enforcement, we're also not under anyone else's authority. If I hear about you pressganging anyone into your little criminal empire again—Echo or not, superpowers or no—I'm going to come back. And it's not going to be pretty." He made sure the others in her gang could hear as well. "I'll make you famous if I have to. The famous cartel that gets attacked by Sentinel, who comes out of retirement every few months to tear everything they've built apart. Every building. Every weapon. Every goon. Over and over. I'll make sure that being one of your soldiers becomes one of the best-known ways to get hurt in the Mexican underworld, Calavera, and that your enemies know when to look forward to your moments of weakness while you clean up after another of my visits."

She narrowed her eyes. "Are you threatening me?"

"You'd better goddamned believe it," Mitch snarled. "I've been out of this game for a long time. And I know you're feeling cozy, with the Americans putting leashes on their Changed, and all the *adelantes* south of the Rio Grande pretty much in your pocket. But if I'm wearing this uniform again, it's for real. Don't come to my attention again. If you do, I'll definitely make sure I have *your* attention. Got it?"

She squirmed in her seat, jaw locked in rage she couldn't do anything with. Finally, she nodded.

"Good." He turned to the others. "Let's go."

* * *

They were largely silent until almost everyone was back in Llorona's van and on the road. They were thirty or so miles from the ranch when Optic finally rejoined them, flashing through the back windows of the van as a field of light, and then resolving into his normal form. "No one's following us," he said.

Llorona nodded to him from behind the driver's wheel, catching his gaze and smiling. She fixed her eyes on the road ahead, but then glanced at the passenger's seat next to her. Mitch's chin rested on his fist, his elbow leaning against the arm rest of his door. "Mitch?"

He glanced over at her. It was usually very difficult to tell that he was actually older than she was. But not now. The grief in his eyes was palpable.

Llorona couldn't help but wonder—is this what makes people old, then? Not age, or decrepitude, but grief? Do we just accumulate a lifetime of grief, until it builds up and becomes something we call "old"? What did that mean for those whose bodies didn't follow the same rules as everyone else's? She reached out and took his hand, squeezing it.

Mitch turned sideways in his seat, putting his back to the door so he could see everyone in the rear of the van. He reached up and wiped away a tear—like he wasn't even aware he was doing it—and sighed. "Okay. Let's talk about this."

Deosil leapt in. "We don't have to yet, you know. It's obviously very painful, Mitch."

"Thanks, kiddo," he said with a smile. "The fact is, I'm doing something as soon as we get back across the border. Optic seemed pretty sure that you'd want to help in some way, so if we're going to do this, it's sooner rather than later."

"We're in," Rusty said quickly, and Deosil nodded. "What I don't understand, Medium, is how did you recognize him?"

"What do you mean?" she asked.

"Radiant passed away in 1992," Rusty said. "I don't really know how to ask without being too awful, but…"

"How could she recognize him? I've got the answer for that," Mitch said. "It's pretty easy. He looks the same now as when he died."

Rusty and Deosil glanced at one another in confusion, and then at Optic. The soldier was regarding Mitch with a weird expression—incredulity and confirmation chased one another around on his face. "So, that's true, then?" Optic asked Mitch, who nodded. "Originals don't decompose after death."

Llorona's eyes flashed to the rearview mirror. "Wait, what?"

Mitch sighed. "We agreed a long time ago to keep that fact to ourselves, something the DTPA wanted as well. But I guess it's relevant here. So far as we know, only three of the Originals have died: Craig, a Japanese Original named Tsunami, and a woman named Gloria Campbell, who never had a supers identity. All three of them are in the same state as when they died: pale, cold, and obviously dead, but not decomposing in any way."

He rubbed his hands over his face wearily. "The Japanese government have Tsunami's remains, but the DTPA has established a facility we've nicknamed the Crypt to study this phenomenon. I don't entirely understand the science behind it, but their bodies are just not changing. At all. The only signs that they're not just recently dead is the smell. Nothing awful—it's a strange, dusty, sweet smell."

Llorona glanced sideways at Mitch, her demeanor contemplative. "Is it the smell of roses?"

Mitch regarded her with some degree of surprise, his brow furrowed. "I... yeah, I guess it does remind me of roses. The really old-fashioned kind. How did you know that?"

"I didn't," she said, shaking her head. "But there's folklore in the Church. It's said to have been one of the signs of sainthood once—that the body didn't decompose, but instead was strangely preserved and smelt of roses after death."

"Whoa," Deosil said, leaning against the back of her seat and gazing out the window. "What if the miracles and stuff that saints in the past did—what if they were Originals, too?"

"I don't know about any of that," Mitch said uncomfortably. "I just know that if whoever these people are have Craig's body..."

"Then it's not at the Crypt anymore," Optic said. "And they're either complicit, or they've fucked up."

"So, the next step is—wait, that's where you were headed, when you flew off? The Crypt?" Rusty asked.

Mitch nodded. "I've got some questions for them, and intend on getting answers." He paused, hesitantly. "Listen, I'm not supposed to take anyone who isn't cleared for it there. Big DTPA secrets and all."

Deosil smirked. "But you don't give a damn for the DTPA."

"I don't, no. And frankly, if we're dealing with the possibility of these people working with the DTPA—or hell, even *being* the DTPA? I'm not going there alone. It would be stupid." He regarded Optic gratefully. "So, whoever is interested can come along. Just know that there's the possibility of trouble, either violence if they do have some connection, or just bureaucratic otherwise."

"I already know about the Crypt and where it's at," Optic said. "So no one's going to be too upset to see me there."

"I'm in," Rusty said, kneading the muscles of his thighs. "Though I really could use a stop at a store as soon as we can. I'm starting to cramp up like crazy. Got a little over-the-top with the power use back there." He raised a hand at both Mitch and Deosil's immediate concern. "Nothing compared to Odessa, though. Chill."

"Alright," Deosil grumbled, not happy. She glanced back, where Medium appeared to be napping, comfortable in her little nest of blankets. Deosil turned to Mitch. "This is why you do it, though, isn't it?" She nodded toward Medium. "Why you risk your life, do all the crazy things you do. Or used to do."

Mitch let his gaze wander back to the contentedly-resting old lady, and then he met Deosil's questioning face. He simply nodded.

"And you," she said to Llorona, who glanced back in the mirror at her. "You pretty much intended on using us to get Medium out of there."

"About that," Mitch said, fixing Llorona with his steeliest gaze. "In no way am I okay with my or anyone else being lied to and used. This entire goddamned world seems set up sometimes to get things out of us without our permission, to take from us whether or not we want to give. My allies—my friends—don't do that to me. This is the last time you withhold information from us. If you want something, you ask."

Llorona considered him and the rest of the group for a moment. "I won't apologize for it," she said, even though a hint of regret bled into her words. "Though you have my word I won't do anything like that again. I decided a long time ago that I was going to help people in any way I could. I've tried for years to find someone who would go up against the Calaveras to help me get her out, and I saw my chance. I don't really know any of you, and I couldn't risk your refusal. I understand if you're upset, but…"

"Hey, no," Deosil interrupted. "I'd have preferred if you'd been upfront, sure. But you did what was right. The two of you, who've been doing this stuff since before the DTPA was created. You have this need to help people, somehow. This drive. I'm kind of envious. I just feel afraid when I think of doing that too, you know? Like, there's a separation between us. You're *heroes*. I'm just a woman with powers, and I don't know how to bridge that separation."

"It's the DTPA," Optic said. "Part of my training involves counter-programming—the idea that we might need to stand up against interrogation and brainwashing at some point as part of our duties. I can recognize when those techniques are being used, and though they're not overt, the DTPA uses them.

At their big camps, and at every interaction they have with you. They empha-size our vulnerability, and attempt to coerce us into identifying ourselves as law-abiding, while defining what that means constantly. We've grown up on their narrative. It's why I only attended one of those weekends since being kicked out of Project: Seraphim."

"We're not far from the border now," Llorona said. "Let's get Medium across it to my people in El Paso, who can help her get home and likely get her family to safety, too. We can pick this back up after."

* * *

It was late afternoon by the time they met Llorona's contacts in a parking lot at the edge of El Paso, across the street from an old junkyard. Armed with a couple of sugary sports drinks, Rusty had checked out the junkyard and gotten some ideas while they waited. By the time night fell, Medium was on her way home in the cab of an interstate big rig, and the others were back in civvies at a roadside Bar-B-Q joint west of El Paso. The cicadas were loud in the mesquite outside, but the evening was cooling nicely enough to justify them taking up spots at a picnic table outside, letting them eat and talk in relative freedom.

"So, yeah," said Rusty. "We should find the closest train tracks, pull the van onto it, and let me do the rest of the driving."

Llorona balked. "Wait, you want to what—turn my van into a train with your magnetism?"

"Sorta. No physical changes. It's got a big steel chassis, easily enough for me to cushion with my powers, float it a few inches above the tracks, and then drive it like a big blocky maglev."

"Won't that use an incredible degree of power from you?" Optic asked. "Just how many of those sports drinks do you got tucked away?"

"Well, I picked up some salt supplements from the pharmacy aisle. They'll work a bit better than my favorite blue drink for the long haul. But also, it's not like I'm exerting constant force—not like a telekinetic would, for instance. All I have to do is give it enough juice to alter the respective magnetic poten-tial and polarities of the objects in question. In this case, the chassis. I'll have to make changes to it occasionally, but it's not anything constant."

"And what happens when we come into the path of an actual train?" Llorona asked.

Rusty grinned—she was clearly warming to the idea. "I can get us off the tracks. Trains are great big metal objects. I can sense them coming a long, long time before I can see them."

"Or I can get us above the level of the train long enough to pass it by," Sentinel said.

Optic's eyebrows shot upward. "Jesus, I guess you could, couldn't you? I mean, couldn't you just fly the entire van there, with us in it?"

Mitch took a sip of his sweet tea. "I could, probably. I'd be exhausted by the time I got there, though. If something did go bad..."

"Gotcha," Optic nodded, and glanced back at Rusty. "It's a good synergy of your powers, though. Very effective." He glanced around the table. "You know, now that I think of it, there's a lot of really impressive possible synergies at this table."

Optic set his sandwich down and wiped BBQ sauce from his hands. "So, I'm just going to say it. This is sounding like team-talk." Mitch groaned, and Optic shot him a glare. "Just hear me out. We know we can work well together. We outnumbered and outpowered Calavera's people, but that could have still been really bad for us. They're experienced and violent. But we worked together really quickly and naturally. I've been in training with people that took weeks to get us to work as well together as we all did today. That's not nothing."

Deosil stared at him intently. "So, what? Super team? Like in the old days? No offense." She winked at Mitch, who frowned at her.

"I could come up with a bunch of other ideas about how we could work together. Pitch them any way I wanted, but at the end of the day? Yeah. Exactly like that. Like the Champions, or the Order, or any one of the other groups that formed a couple of decades ago—not working for anyone, just good people trying to use their powers to help people and stop threats like Calavera and whoever these others are from using their powers in lethal and greedy ways. What do you say. Rusty?"

The redhead laughed. "Oh, I'm in. I'm so, so in. The day after I woke up from the Gulf Event, I didn't even *know* what my power was yet, and I wanted to be an old-fashioned superhero. No question." He hesitated for a moment, and then glanced at first Deosil, then Mitch. "And honestly, guys? It's something I'm going to do, one way or another. Team or not."

"Right on," Optic enthused. "Jesh?"

"Oh, God," she said. "You guys, we can get in so much trouble."

"But Jesh, there are so many people who are already in so much trouble. Trouble that has nothing to do with government suits showing up and arresting you, and everything to do with all of this stuff. They need help. Like Medium did."

Deosil sighed. "I know. I know all of that. Just, when they send us away to Super-Guantanamo, please assume that I'm 'I told you so'-ing the entire way. I'm sure I won't actually get the chance because of the black bags over our heads." She turned to Optic and shook her head. "I'm in, damn you. Though most of the reason is because I'm sure half of my rescues are going to be of dumbass over there," she said, gesturing at Rusty with her thumb.

The redhead whooped and leaned across the table to hug her, almost knocking over her drink in the process.

"Llorona?" Optic asked, rescuing his plate from Rusty's cross-table onslaught.

She laughed. "I've been doing this kind of thing since the Fated Manifesto. I don't have the most potent power set, and it's always just been me—maybe one or two others, occasionally—so I've gotten used to slow and subtle to get things accomplished. I'm not going to lie, today felt good. To know we could walk out of that ranch having done some good? That felt very, very good. But I'm not young, Optic. I'm not a fighter."

"Maybe not in terms of punching people in the face or whatever," Deosil said. "But I saw you with Calavera. You're a fighter in the most important way, Llorona. You want to do what is right, and you won't stop until it's done. You've got experience dealing with really dangerous situations and people."

Llorona nodded. "I can promise to try. I never got a real chance with the Champions auxiliaries, back in my time. As long as you understand that I'm agreeing to this provisionally—if I'm holding you back or proving to be a liability in what we're doing, I'm out."

"That just leaves you, big guy," said Optic. "Come and lead us, like you did the Champions?"

Mitch knew every eye was on him. He glanced up from his meal, into each face, studying them carefully. Finally, he wiped his mouth on his napkin and set it on his plate.

"No," he said quietly. Their reactions were telling. Deosil's was fear, and possibly regret, like she might reconsider her answer at that very moment. Rusty seemed wounded by the single word and he stammered, trying to come up with an argument, a conversation that would change Mitch's mind. Optic slumped in his seat and looked away, hiding deep disappointment behind an angry locked jaw. Only Llorona met his eyes calmly, waiting for him.

"No, I won't lead the team. I've done enough of that for a lifetime, I'm sorry. I'd still like to be part of the team, but no, I can't play leader. If this team succeeds, it will do so on its merits, not because this costume is calling the shots. Our own two feet, or not at all, okay?"

"Oh thank God." Rusty slumped in his seat and leaned against Mitch for a moment.

"I think you should do it," Deosil said, pointing at Optic with a pickle spear.

"Do what?"

"Lead the team." She challenged him with a smile.

"Whoa, I don't…"

"I agree," Mitch said. "You've got combat experience, military training, and know the value of quick decisions in the middle of a tense situation, using chain of command." Optic turned to stare at the man incredulously.

"Optic for leader!" Rusty crowed, raising his (now empty) glass. Llorona snatched hers up as well.

"Hear, hear," she said. "What do you think, *mijo*? We know you can do it. You ready for a promotion?"

"Shit, you guys." He shook his head again, and laughed. "I don't really know if I can actually lead a team with Sentinel in it, man."

Rusty laughed. "Oh, don't worry. It'll actually be Deosil who's the most impossible to tell to do anything." He darted out of his seat, just ahead of Deosil's lunge, and took off. She gave chase.

"You can do this, Optic. You're far better prepared for this than I ever was," Mitch said. "And you've got me in your corner, okay? Any help, any advice, whatever you need from me."

"I'd be pretty stupid to turn down an offer like that, huh?" Optic asked Llorona. "I mean, the most experienced super-team leader in history is offering to teach me how it's done."

"You would be," Llorona said. "And you don't strike me as a stupid boy." With a grin, Optic clasped Mitch's hand in his own, and shook on it.

"One thing, though," Llorona said, waving over the cackling duo of Rusty and Deosil. "Before I even seriously think of doing this, we all have to be ready. When they can't break us up, they're going to try and change us. They'll come at us from the side and from behind. If we won't stop, they'll offer us legitimacy."

"Is that bad?" Deosil asked, resuming her seat to catch her breath.

"The more 'legitimate' an organization in their efforts to help people, the more they have to bargain and make compromises." She shook her head sadly. "The Golden Cross used to be an organization that did so much good. Now, so much of the money they take in goes towards lawyers and lobbyists, instead of to the poor and disaster-struck. Over and over I've seen it."

She fixed each of them with a very serious face. "So, I'm in, with a promise. We don't ever go legitimate. We wear no symbol but our own, no identity but what we make for ourselves. We don't become military for anyone, or law enforcement, or anything like that. We take no funding from anyone—they will offer us the best toys, if we'll sign on the dotted line. If we can't make it or buy it for ourselves, we don't get it. We may make allies, but we answer to no one else but one another. Agreed?"

"That's really wise," Mitch said. "I kinda wish we'd had someone to tell the Champions that, back in our day."

"Then it's settled," Llorona said. "We're a team."

"Not quite settled," Deosil said, shaking her head. "We need a name. While chasing rust-head here, I was thinking. What do you guys know about the Sacred Band?"

Llorona and Mitch shook their heads, while Rusty just grinned.

"Old Hellenic army. Made up of three hundred soldiers—a hundred and fifty pairs of lovers, renowned and feared for their military acumen, strength of arms, and for their bravery. Each man was said to be dedicated to refusing to dishonor himself on the field of battle in the eyes of his beloved, and so fought twice as hard and twice as strong as a result. When I was young, I remember reading about them, and thinking to myself that the stories of queers in our culture was incomplete. We were weak, we were afraid, we were victims—that's the only story I'd heard about us," Deosil said. "I remember realizing that we'd had warriors, fighters, heroes, soldiers, and that the story they were trying to feed us about ourselves was incomplete. Because it was their version, not ours."

"The Sacred Band," Mitch whispered to himself. "Interesting." No one missed the look he shot Rusty, or the one Rusty gave him in return.

"Okay. Sacred Band, then. It sounds beautiful," Llorona said. "So many team names seem to try and instill fear or suggest military strength. I could be proud to be part of something called this."

"Alright. Sacred Band it is," Optic said, standing and rubbing his hands together. "We'll keep that in mind for the day when we have to tell people who we are. But that's not today. Today, I think we've got a train...or van...a rail-van to catch into the Rocky Mountains, right?"

CHAPTER TWENTY-TWO

The Rocky Mountains, United States
May 20, 2013

The trip to the facility tucked into the Rocky Mountains was strange. If the situation had been different—if they weren't heading for a facility to see what had happened to the remains of Mitch's first love, with Mitch himself doing his best not to give in to the sort of helpless grief that threatened to overwhelm him—it might have been fun. Speeding along the rail, occasionally telekinetically pulled into the sky above a passing train? It was exciting and exhilarating, and Rusty would be lying if he'd said he weren't enjoying himself, on some level.

But still. Weird.

After a while, Mitch slipped out of his civvies, and everyone else did as well (besides Deosil, who once again grumbled about not bringing her Health Weekend uniform). Mitch glanced at them as they secured belts and flexed fingers in gloves. "I need to scout out the entrance. It's not really a road-access sort of place. It's built assuming that only DTPA personnel will be coming in, and that's usually by helicopter."

Llorona's brow knit. "Are you saying we're going to have to fly my van into the mountains?"

Mitch chuckled. "No. We should tuck the van away in case we need it later.

Between all of us, I'm pretty sure we can fly in under our own power." The others agreed, and Llorona shook her head.

"Well, I guess we are showing up as a team," she said, pulling her shawl closer around her shoulders. "Should make an entrance of some kind, no?"

"Yes," Optic said with a grin. "Let's do this."

* * *

It was the middle of the afternoon when the Sacred Band landed on the doorstep to the DTPA facility known as the Crypt. Sentinel carried Llorona, while the other three came in under their own power. To say that their sudden appearance garnered a reaction was an understatement. Optic and Mitch had both warned them that there would be a lot of guns making sudden and very pointed appearances in their near future, but even so, Rusty couldn't help but feel nervous. He wasn't sure he could stop every bullet that might come his way. Those weapons they were pointing at them could unleash an awful lot of rounds all at once, and there were easily a dozen of them, with more on the way.

Sentinel stepped forward, and when he glanced over his shoulder, Optic did too. "Afternoon, gentlemen," Optic said, with a nod. "Is there someone in charge we can talk to, please? My name is Optic, I'm sure you know Sentinel here. We're the Sacred Band, and we've got some very serious questions to ask."

The reactions on the soldiers' faces were something Rusty was pretty sure he was going to remember for a long time. Some of them just seemed confused, like they were sure there was no way they were seeing and hearing this. A few glanced at their fellows, very real concern there; unsurprising, considering how hard the DTPA lobbied to keep super-groups from forming, and teaching people that groups of supers were basically reckless endangerment and property damage waiting to happen.

But it was the reaction from three of the soldiers that clinched it for Rusty. Two of them glanced at one another, as though each wanted to be sure that the other had heard it. Then both of them grinned widely, a shared moment of wonder between two friends.

Oh, they knew who he was, alright.

The third soldier actually straightened up, and lowered his rifle. It was an unconscious action, a shift from wary guardedness to something a little like comfortable relief. It lasted just long enough for him to realize that others around him were not doing the same, and his training kicked in. He returned to a guarded demeanor, though he couldn't help but keep sneaking glances at everyone on the team.

Finally, someone in charge showed up. He had a cragged face and thin lips, with a little grey at the temples and precisely cut military-style hair. Everything about this guy was hard, precise lines and ultra self-control, Rusty thought. He introduced himself as Sergeant First Class Brand, and Optic shook his hand. Their interaction was professional, even a little clipped, but Rusty couldn't help but notice an affinity between the two men. Each knew the other was a military man, and there was some kind of understanding in their interactions that Rusty couldn't begin to follow.

"Sergeant Brand, we apologize for alarming anyone," Optic said, gesturing to the rest of the team behind him. "I'm Optic, formerly of the Seraphim. Can I speak to Liaison Walmer Alcott?"

Brand narrowed his eyes, allowing himself a quick glance at the rest of the interlopers. "What is this about?"

"I'm going to be candid, Sarge," Optic said. "I'm not entirely sure what your clearance is, and I'd rather not get us both in potential trouble laying it all out. Can you radio him? We're happy to wait out here, or we can cool our heels wherever you need to put us while you talk to him."

"It's important, though," Sentinel said from behind Optic. "We don't have a lot of time."

Brand took a couple of steps back into the doorway of the facility and began to speak earnestly into his radio handset. Optic and Sentinel stepped back to the others while the sentries watched them nervously.

"Sorry, I should have mentioned that we'd probably be startling them," Optic said. "Honestly, I was so focused on getting here that…"

Deosil squeezed his forearm. "No biggie. I think we all had some idea about what we were getting into. What now?"

"They're contacting someone I know from my days in Project: Seraphim. He won't have the authority to get us into where we need to be, but he'll know who we can talk to, hopefully with a minimum of bullshit."

"So what do we do if they decide to turn us away?" Llorona asked very quietly. Sentinel glanced back at the doorway, almost as though he were sizing it up.

"It's not going to come to that," he said. "They'll let me in."

"But we don't have any guarantee?" Rusty said, concerned. Sentinel and Optic glanced at one another, and both men nodded. "Are we okay with that?"

"We might have to be," Deosil said with a sigh. "I mean, I don't think we're going to insist, and we're sure as hell not going to force it." Her tone quailed a little as she said it, like she was giving voice to something she was terrified of.

Optic smiled at her, and put an arm around her shoulder, squeezing quickly. "No, we're not going to force it. We're not here to fight anybody. If they insist, we'll wait outside." He turned to Sentinel. "I still don't like the idea of you going in alone, though. Insist that at least one of us come with you."

"We're all going in, or none of us are," Sentinel said. "You guys didn't come all this way to stand around on the doorstep with guns pointed at you. They're not going to treat my teammates that way, and I intend to tell them that, if it comes down to it."

Rusty didn't like the set of Mitch's jaw. He was stressed—not surprisingly, he supposed. A combination of discovering what was going on with Radiant, plus the possibility of walking into a government facility that might be run by people who were involved in all this crap? Plus, Mitch hated dealing with the DTPA to begin with. Rusty reached out and grabbed Mitch's hand, and for a second, Mitch nearly pulled away.

A flush of shame came over his face, and he looked away for a second. With a glance back at Rusty and a smile, he squeezed his hand, and let their grip linger.

"Here we go," Optic said. He turned toward the entry of the facility, spreading his arms. "Alcott! It's been a while!"

The man wore glasses, and his hair was a little long at the collar. He was his late thirties, and though he wore a collared shirt and jacket it all was a little mussed, as though he'd hurried into the coat and buttoned up his shirt while being rushed down to meet them. The man was clearly a bureaucrat, and sort of flustered at the sudden change in his daily routine. The fact that there was a small cluster of important-looking military sorts in a glowering knot behind him—a knot that had clearly hustled him down here—probably didn't help his stress levels either. "Uh, Optic, I, uh, what are you *doing* here?" His question was equal parts bewilderment and blame. "How do you even know where this is?"

Sentinel stepped up. "I showed him. I have some questions that I need answered."

The pale bureaucrat paled a little more. "Uh. Oh, Sentinel. I…"

A woman with an Asian cast to her features stepped up behind Alcott, smoothly disengaging herself from the knot of officers behind her. She laid a companionable hand on Alcott's shoulder, and the poor man jumped. "Alcott, can I bother you to make some introductions?" She smiled at each of them in turn. She wore a crisp skirt suit and no jewelry.

He regarded her and took a deep breath. "I can, yeah. This is Optic—I know him from his days with Project: Seraphim. I worked as the liaison between the Project and the DTPA." He ran out of steam, and then glanced around somewhat at a loss. "I don't really know the others."

"You need no introduction," she said to Sentinel, almost not even letting Alcott finish speaking. She extended her hand to him. "My name is Janice Kimori. I'm the head of Legal for this facility."

"Ms. Kimori," Sentinel said, shaking her hand. "Are you the person we ought to be speaking with?"

"That depends," she said, glancing at Alcott. "Why are you here? And please, call me Janice."

Optic cleared his throat, catching the attention of the faces gathered around them, watching and listening. "It's a matter of some delicacy. Can we go someplace private?"

"Everyone here has the clearance necessary to hear whatever you might have to say," she said.

Sentinel stared at her for a moment, and then leaned forward. "That may be so, but there are some aspects of my private life that I don't care to lay out in front of a literal army of strangers."

She took an involuntary step back, as though retreating slightly, although her calm-and-in-control demeanor never broke. "Can I know what this is in regards to?"

Deosil glanced at Rusty. "And here comes the legal stonewalling," she whispered, and Rusty shook his head sourly.

"I have some questions about the remains of Craig Velasquez." Sentinel's response was icy.

"I am truly sorry, Mr. McCann, but I can't give you any information about that," she said. Optic sighed, and Llorona shook her head.

"You thundering bitch," Deosil said quietly, though from the slight glance the lawyer threw her, she'd clearly heard. Optic threw Alcott a stern look, and the bureaucrat glanced helplessly at the exchange going on. Nodding, he took a couple of steps back, and pulled out his phone and rapidly began texting.

"I understand that you were informed about the nature of this facility early in its creation," Kimori said to Sentinel. "But we're very serious about keeping the confidentiality of those interred here as discreet and private as possible."

"Don't pretend this is for them," Sentinel all but snarled. "I want. To see. His damned body. I have that right."

She shook her head. "I'm sorry, Mr. McCann. You *don't*. There wasn't anything legally binding between yourself and Mr. Velasquez. We've received no paperwork from his family—"

"I was the closest thing he had to family. Me and the other Champions."

"And while I understand that was very true in a personal and meaningful fashion, there's no legal framework for that relationship." To her credit, she at least made the statement *sound* like she regretted saying it.

"When he was brought here, right after he died, I was told—"

"I'm sorry, but you have to understand that we can't be held accountable for what you may or may not have been told in an unofficial capacity by the people who operated the facility at the time. You do understand that, right?"

Rusty was shaking. When Sentinel half-turned away from her, so that she couldn't see the tears forming in his eyes, Rusty didn't know whether to cry or to rage. There must be *something* they could do.

Janice Kimori didn't take her eyes off Sentinel once. "We all have laws we have to follow, Mr. McCann. None of us are above the regulations in place to protect us all." She lowered her voice. "Not here, and not in Ukraine, either."

"Wait, what?" Rusty barked. "Is that why you're not letting him in?"

"Mr. McCann was very clear about how he felt cooperating with the DTPA in any capacity, Mr. Adamson." She addressed Sentinel once again. "We were quite content to maintain a workable, friendly interaction for years, Mr. Mc-

Cann. But you can't have it both ways. We are either in a cooperative relationship with one another, or we are not."

"This is bullshit," Optic said. His voice was low and very agitated. The lawyer glanced at him, and then away, dismissing him.

"Actually, it's the law," she said. She then raked her gaze over the others gathered there. "I'll also make a point of reminding all of you—because I don't know if your friends Optic and Sentinel have seen fit to do so yet—that under no circumstances are you to reveal the existence or purpose of this facility. It is a national security secret, and you can be arrested and tried for treason for doing so. Just as Optic and Sentinel can be right now for even showing it to you."

"Ms. Kimori," said a woman behind them, her appearance through the knot of officials at the doorway something of a surprise to everyone. Rusty couldn't help but notice that her arrival sent several of those officials back into the facility's depths, and the soldiers at the gate redoubled their on-guard positions. This was clearly someone important.

The woman was in her fifties or so. Time had greyed her hair where it was gathered into a neat bun atop her head, and thickened her waist somewhat. Regardless, she cut an imposing figure. Her uniform said Army brass, and as she crossed to the group, she glanced sideways nodding to the now-almost-forgotten Alcott, who returned a grateful nod.

"Why are you interacting with guests to my facility, Ms. Kimori?"

She was taken aback. "Director. You needn't have—I was just explaining to them the legal regulations at play around their visit, and the request they have made."

"And while I'm grateful for the initiative, Ms. Kimori, that isn't your job. Which is frankly a good thing, because if you spoke to the guests of my facility the way I just overheard you talking to these people here, you would lose that job."

Kimori's chin rose indignantly, though she made a show of appearing thoughtful. Finally, she nodded. "My apologies, ma'am. I didn't intend to overstep. It's important that they are aware of the legal ramifications of their visit here, though, and I felt I would have been derelict in my duty to not inform them as expediently as possible."

The Director stared at the younger woman, crossing her arms. "And have you done so?"

Ms. Kimori took the hint and promptly fled, gathering up as much of her dignity as she could while she did so. The Director watched her go, shaking her head, then turned back to the Sacred Band. "I apologize for your having to endure that," she said. "I'm Lieutenant Colonel Eva Rios, and I'm the head of security for this facility. Alcott will show you to my office, and we can talk there, if that will be alright?"

Sentinel nodded, and Optic spoke up. "That will be perfect, Colonel. Thank you for your intervention."

She smiled and gestured to Alcott. "It's him you can thank."

* * *

Which they did, profusely, on the way to Colonel Rios's office.

"Seriously. You saved our asses out there," Optic said, walking beside him.

"I'm just sorry Kimori intercepted you at all." Alcott glanced around, seeing who was nearby. "She's kind of her own thing around here, you know? As far as I can tell, she's got some high-up friends in the DTPA."

"Probably Marque," Sentinel muttered sourly. "She's exactly the kind of bulldog he likes to recruit for his immediate circle of people. I have every faith he's being told about what happened right now."

"That wouldn't surprise me," Alcott said, weakly. They walked into a large office, and Alcott nodded to the young man at the desk, who was on the phone. He nodded as though he were expecting them and waved them through to the door at the back of the room. Alcott opened the door and ushered them in. Before he entered the room, Sentinel stopped and clasped the bureaucrat's hand.

"Thank you," he said simply. "I know that helping us could result in some trouble for you. But we're grateful. I'm grateful. This could have been a much worse visit, but your intervention prevented that. I won't ever forget that."

The man flushed and stammered, nodding all the while. They all walked in, and he closed the door behind him.

"Man. You sure can turn that shit on, can't you?" Optic grinned at Rusty, and both regarded Mitch.

"Turn...what are you talking about?" Mitch wore a perplexed expression.

"He doesn't even know when he's doing it," Rusty said fondly.

"That's why it's so effective," Llorona said, lowering herself into her seat.

"I'm right here, guys," Mitch said, and found a seat himself. Optic and Rusty chuckled, while Deosil stood off to one side, noting the framed pictures and plaques on the wall.

The office was spacious. Like most of the complex, it had no windows, but its lighting was good. No fluorescents, and it was all indirect. The office was painted a rich blue, and all the furnishings were a pale wood polished to a distinct shine. The carpeting was cream-colored, and a massive desk sat in the center of the room, with a small selection of cream-cushioned chairs arrayed in a semi-circle in front of it.

They didn't have long to admire the interior decorating, though, before Lieutenant Colonel Rios was opening the door. "I'm going to be in a meeting, Patrick," she said. "Unless something starts happening out here that involves more dangerous people than the ones in here, or people with more on their collar than me, I don't want to be disturbed." She shut the door, not waiting for his murmured acknowledgement.

She turned to regard them with a smile. She reached down and unbuttoned one of the front buttons holding her coat closed, and shrugged it off. She walked to hang it up, unconsciously smoothing some of the wrinkling out of it as she did so. "So," she said, crossing to the wet bar up against one wall. "Can I get any of you anything to drink? I understand you got here under your own power. That must be a little exhausting."

"Just a water for me, please," Sentinel said. "And we didn't fly the whole way."

She fetched water bottles from the cooler in the base of the bar, and poured a drink out for Optic and Llorona. As she did so, she watched them. She watched them as she bustled around the bar, eyeing them in the mirror along the wall, and she studied each of them carefully when she handed them their drinks.

"We should probably start by introducing ourselves," Optic said finally, as she poured herself a drink once everyone else had something. "I'm Optic, originally from Project: Seraphim."

"That's where Alcott knows you from, I assume?" she asked, flicking her eyes up at him in the mirror.

"It is, yeah," he nodded, and gestured to the others. "You of course know Sentinel. And these are Llorona, Deosil, and Gauss." She nodded to each of them as Optic named them, making her way across the room to the straight-backed office seat behind her desk. She leaned back in it, swiveling slightly as she took them in.

"And you're the Sacred Band?" Her voice held something in it. Humor, maybe, like she found the idea of their team funny? But also wariness. Like a warning.

Optic hesitated. "Uh, yeah."

Rios smiled. "You mentioned the name to one of the guards at the gate."

Optic glanced at the others. "I did?" Sentinel and Deosil regarded him blankly, but Gauss and Llorona nodded.

"Yeah, I was kinda surprised, too," Gauss said with a grin.

"For the moment, I'm going to leave that little revelation elsewhere. It'll be for someone else to tend to, quite frankly. Not my circus, not my monkeys." She raised her glass to them, and took a sip. "Sentinel."

"Please, call me Mitch," he said. She paused, and then nodded.

"Mitch, then. You're here to see the remains of Craig Velasquez?" Her stare was intense, and impossible to pull away from. He couldn't help but admire her presence in the room. It was easy to see how she'd ended up in a position of leadership.

"I would like to, please."

"I'm happy to facilitate that, of course." She typed something into her computer, clicking through a few screens. She turned to him again. "Can I make a suggestion to you, Mitch?"

"Sure," he said, warily.

"You need to sue the DTPA."

Deosil barked a surprised laugh, and immediately covered her mouth with her hands. Everyone else was just as stunned.

"What?" Mitch's voice cracked a little.

"Sue. Not for a financial settlement, but to get court-appointed permission to be able to see him whenever you want. The fact that he has no family on file, and that you and he had a proven relationship? If you can find a sympathetic judge, you can get at least that."

Mitch's eyes dropped, and then he glanced over to find Rusty's gaze. "I will," he said, as though he were just as surprised as anyone to find he was saying it. "I think I know some folks who could help me with that. Thanks."

"Of course," she said with a smile. "It's wonderful that we've been able to make this work on good will, but there won't always be people like me around, Mitch. And there will always be people like Ms. Kimori, who will have to be forced by legal rulings to be decent people."

"Understood. I'll take care of it."

She nodded, and then regarded everyone else with a focused intention before leaning forward on her elbows, her hands clasped in front of her. "Now, do you want to explain to me why you needed an assault team of Changed to pay this visit?"

After a confirming glance at Optic, he told her. Everything, from the story about Rusty's friend in Ukraine, to their trip across the border to see the Calaveras, to Medium's visions.

"And this clairvoyant is reliable?" This she directed to Llorona.

"Very reliable," Llorona affirmed. "Her visions are limited in scope, but not prone to the fuzziness that some clairsentients manifest."

"Useful trick. We still have only her word, though. That's not proof." She regarded Optic. "So, as team leader, you thought it was best for everyone to come because…"

"In case the Crypt was working with the people in question and had handed over Radiant's body willingly," Optic said. There was steel in his voice, a challenge to her to prove it wasn't the case, and she smiled.

"I can't blame you at all. Probably very wise, although bringing civilians into all of this is questionable."

"There's no way they could stop us," Gauss said.

"I just hope you're all prepared for the incredible shit-storm you're about to be at the eye of." She typed something into her computer. "But again, not my circus. Okay, I've got the visitor log. We haven't had anyone in here in over five years to see Mr. Velasquez's remains. Only our own staff, doing the normal tests."

She stood suddenly. "But now I'm curious, too. Shall we go and see for ourselves?"

The route to the heart of the Crypt was long and circuitous. Deosil couldn't help but wonder exactly was behind all of those doors. An elevator ride down, a passage through two guarded security doors, and they finally had a long hallway to walk, a hallway that ended in a massive set of steel doors that currently hung open.

"Not long now," Rios said to them, and continued the conversation she was having with Optic.

As they walked, Deosil couldn't help but notice Rusty's demeanor. He hung back from the group a bit—from Sentinel, specifically, she noticed—and kept glancing up at the bigger man with a worried look on his face. "Hey," she said, wrapping an arm around his neck. "What's up with you?"

He sighed. "It's stupid." He held up a hand, forestalling her *your emotions are valid, stop saying stuff like that* thing she did sometimes. "I know, I know. But it's just...I think what I feel for Mitch is hopeless. Like I said, stupid, you know?"

He gestured ahead of them, as they neared the massive doors that were functionally the portals to a modern-day tomb for Originals. "Like, how the hell do I compete with a dead lover, you know? He feels so strongly for Craig, it's like the thing that caused him to retreat from the world *entirely* for how long? I'm just me. How can I create something as strong as that with him?"

"No, Rusty..." Deosil stopped. What did you say to something like that? How do you answer it?

"Please forgive me for eavesdropping," Llorona said quite suddenly, from just slightly behind them. "I'm going to be very nosy right now, but will shut up once I'm done."

Rusty chuckled, and pulled away from Deosil, shifting to let Llorona between them. "No way. I'm the one whining in the middle of all this, right? Open season."

"Good," she said with a smile, and took his hand as they walked, glancing at him every so often. "I know a thing or two about grief, *mijo*. I think it's lovely how strongly you feel for him, and it's pretty clear he has feelings for you, too. But you're not in competition with Radiant, Rusty. He's not your rival—he's *part* of Sentinel."

She paused for a moment, pulling him to a stop, and regarding him seriously. "I hope you understand that I'm not being hurtful when I say this, but this isn't about you. This is about the grief that is threatening to overwhelm Mitch right now, and has been for years. He's been trapped by it since Radiant died, and the whole world turned against him. We all look to him to save us, but he is the one who needs saving right now. And you can save him—or at least, make him strong enough to save himself—by figuring out how to love

Radiant, too. What is important to Mitch must become important to you, too. That's how love works. That's how relationships form."

Behind her, Deosil just gawked.

Llorona leaned forward to kiss Rusty on the cheek, and then patted that cheek. "Come on, they're getting ahead of us."

It was a few heartbeats before Rusty and Deosil started moving again, both watching her go. "Wow," he said finally.

"I know," Deosil said. "She's good at that whole, whatever that was. Straight-up wisdom bomb, man. In your face, redhead." Rusty chuckled, and pulled her along with him, moving at a quick pace to catch up.

"I kinda envy her kids, you know?" he said as they walked. "I kinda wish my mom was this...I dunno. Understanding? Wise, or whatever? Ow!"

He pulled away from where she'd pinched and shushed him at the same time.

"What was that for?" he asked in an angry whisper, rubbing his arm.

"Rusty, her kids *died* at her Event."

His gaze whipped down the hall ahead of them. Llorona continued to walk, giving no indication that she'd heard any of it.

"Wait, what? Seriously?"

Deosil nodded, and Rusty was chagrined. They quickened their pace, catching up to Llorona as she got to the massive open doors. The security at the door—one man on each side of the huge portal—nodded at them. One turned to the panel in the wall beside him and pressed some command or another. As Gauss and Deosil walked past, the doors began to slowly close, with only a faint mechanical whine. Rusty couldn't help but be impressed by the operation of the machinery at work inside the walls that his powers made him very aware of.

"I thought we'd have some privacy," Rios said. "I'm not interested in being interrupted by Ms. Kimori or anyone else right now. Plus, we'll be able to discuss your concerns without being overheard."

The interior of this chamber was massive—about the size of a basketball court, with high, towering walls, and a ceiling some thirty or so feet up, criss-crossed with steel girders from which lights and other mechanisms hung. The walls of the chamber were stone; the stone of the mountain it was built into, apparently. The floors and the first ten feet or so of the walls were highly polished, but above that, the walls showed rough shearing where whatever method they'd use to carve it out of the mountain's heart left its traces.

In the walls directly opposite the entry were massive bronze panels, roughly ten feet square, embedded in the stone of the wall. Rios led them across the open floor while she swiped through some sort of UI on her tablet. When they got close enough, she shifted the screen, hit a button, and a small green light lit up on the upper right-hand corner of one of the bronze panels that bore an inscription of some kind.

Craig Velasquez.

1965—1992

Champions.

A hero who died that others might live.

Sentinel stepped up to the panel, and reached out to touch the name. Rusty stepped up beside him, hesitantly. Mitch glanced at him, a little bewildered. A little lost. "Is it stupid that I wish I'd thought to bring him some flowers?" Mitch whispered. Rusty shook his head and grabbed his hand. "I mean, I don't even know where I'd *put* them in here." Mitch closed his eyes, and then stepped away from the panel, pulling Rusty with him. He glanced at the Director, and then nodded.

She hit a command on her tablet, and the light turned red on the tomb. With a mechanical hiss, the panel began to pull away from the wall. With it came a white ceramic and glass rectangular case. It was lined with some kind of polymer covering along the bottom, and one of the central panes of glass displayed data of some kind.

The tomb was empty.

Well, not entirely empty. Sitting in the middle of the bier—where a clear indentation in the material showed where Radiant's body had once lay—was a mechanical cylinder of some kind. It was about the size of a roll of paper towels, and had a variety of wires coming out of it, connecting to the glass of the tomb. No, not the glass—the nearly-invisible sensors that lined the inside of the case.

"Mother of God," Rios said, stepping forward. "This is impossible."

She glanced toward the door, and then back at her tablet. "The casket is still receiving all of the data it normally does. That thing in there must be sending false signals to the sensor array."

"I don't understand," Llorona said. "How is this possible? Didn't you say that you have staff in here sometimes? To check on the remains?"

"Not directly," Rios said, tersely. "We try and avoid bothering the bodies any more than we have to. We don't know what will cause them to begin decomposing, if they ever do, so we're dedicated to keeping them in as stable a condition as possible. Technicians come to check and make sure the cases themselves are functioning properly, and our lab assistants come down to take readings, but all of those are derived from the sensor array."

"Without bothering the remains," Deosil said, and the Director nodded.

She considered for a moment, and then glanced at the door again. With grim resolve, she turned to Rusty. "Do you still use the email address attached to your Department file?"

"Uh, yeah?"

"Good." She punched a few commands on her tablet while she spoke. "I'm sending you the visitor logs we've had in the last decade. It's as far back as I have immediate access to. I'm also sending you the personnel roster of technicians who've had access down here."

Her brows were furrowed, jaw set. "All of this is going to be locked down soon. I have to report this, which means that I'm about to have all kinds of investigators and internal affairs people and intelligence agencies in every letter of the alphabet crawling all over me and mine. I'm sending you this information confidentially. The transmission of it is encrypted, but it'll decrypt itself in your inbox."

"Thank you," Sentinel said. "You've risked so much to help us. I wish I could repay that."

She regarded him for a moment, and then took a deep breath. "I have a younger brother," she said. "I'm a decade older than he is. When he was in school, he was taunted and bullied. Mercilessly. It was awful, and I did what I could to protect him, but I was so much older, and we didn't go to the same schools...by the time he was a junior in high school, he'd already tried to kill himself. Because he was gay. It set him back a year in school, and ate at him the entire time, as I'm sure you can imagine. Our parents were, well, they loved him, but they had no idea what to do with all of that. So it was just he and I. We'd talk all the time when I was away—I was already in the service then. He was a wreck a lot of the time, though he ended up in university."

She gave Sentinel a hard look, as though she were willing him to take what she was saying seriously. "All of that changed, Sentinel. All of it, when you came out on public television. It was a moment of epiphany for my poor, struggling younger brother. If the foremost superhero of the Western world was gay—gay, and still very much a hero—then he could find something in himself too to make living worth it. You have to understand. You saved his life. You didn't rescue him from a burning building, or keep some criminal from hurting him. Your coming out saved his life. I know it nearly destroyed you, but it *saved* him."

She paused for a moment to go over something on her tablet. While she did so, Rusty grabbed Sentinel's hand, and met his eyes. Rios glanced back up. "I'm sure that there are so many other people, Sentinel—hundreds, thousands, likely—for whom that single act of heroism was more important than a hundred burning buildings saved or criminals apprehended. This damned world tried to destroy you for it, but at that moment, you also saved the lives of thousands of people, young and old, who looked up to you as the ultimate ideal in heroism."

Without a word, Sentinel wrapped his arms around her, and she let him, though she seemed shocked for a moment before leaning into it. When she closed her eyes, tears spilled. "Thank you," he said.

Rusty watched the exchange uneasily. There was something about Mitch that just made people–

"Guys," he said urgently, snapping his gaze at the open bier. "That device? It just transmitted a pulse of something. Information, I'm pretty sure. A signal of some kind."

"What was it?" Optic asked, stepping forward. "Can you tell?"

"No. Theoretically I should be able to figure out how to unscramble cellular and wireless signals, to read what's in them, but I don't know how just yet." Rusty took a deep breath. "Everybody stand back."

He gestured. The hairs on the back of everyone's neck rose subtly as something happened in the electromagnetic spectrum.

"Talk to us, Gauss," Optic urged.

"Sorry," the redhead said, concentrating. "I'm laying down a field of static. I'm pretty sure that whatever that device is, we don't want it sending or receiving any messages of any kind."

"Good thinking," Optic said. "Llorona, can you–"

His next thought was cut off by a scream. All eyes turned to Deosil, fallen to one knee. "The world...something is *tearing*...something is..." she gasped, and then the glory of Heaven opened up above their heads.

Claviger's portal brought with it shimmering magnificence, a celestial display of strange, dizzying lights that seemed like an invitation to rapture from Heaven itself. Everyone was looking up at it—some in awe, some in agony—when the three objects fell through it just before the light show ended.

"Grenades!" Optic shouted, and his form dissolved into light. In a flash, he raced toward the point in the ceiling where the portal just was, but he was too late, it was gone. Even before Deosil stopped shrieking, Llorona began. She leapt for the Lieutenant Colonel, pitching her voice just so. Both of their forms shivered as the sonic vibration set their physical bodies at odds with the world around them, phasing them out of solidity.

"Get down!" Sentinel flashed between the grenades' path and where Gauss stood over a kneeling Deosil, bracing his arms over them.

As one, Deosil and Gauss reached for the trio of grenades with their powers. Though Gauss seized them up by their metal mechanisms, he wasn't fast enough to prevent their detonation. Deosil evoked the powers of fire with everything she had. She couldn't stop the explosion, either, but did manage to smother the fire that came with it.

With a muted *whump*, the grenades exploded with raw concussive force, the only part of the attack that neither Deosil or Gauss could do anything about. The wave was sudden and loud, but failed to find most of them. Optic, Llorona, and the Lieutenant Colonel were untouched by the wave of force. Gauss and Deosil weren't so lucky. Though Sentinel bore the brunt of the attack's leading wave, both Deosil and Gauss were slammed to the ground.

By the time hearing returned to the Band, alarms were blaring throughout the complex, and the Crypt doors began to open. "Thank you!" Rios stammered as Llorona returned them to solidity. "My God."

The guards outside entered the room, weapons at the ready, and Rios waved them off. "We were just attacked by outside forces. Secure the room and go to threatcon Delta, base-wide. And get me a technician team down here. *Now*. I need to confirm neither of the biers are damaged."

When the guards had scurried out to follow their orders, she turned to Sentinel. "It'll be some time while we investigate this. I'll get people down here to figure out what that damned thing in Radiant's bier is. In the meantime, before you lot get stuck here answering a week's worth of questions, I suggest you get out of here."

"Wait," Optic said as the others turned to go. "If you let us go, that's a guaranteed Relief of Duty for you, isn't it?"

The Lieutenant Colonel hesitated. "Generally speaking, yes, but there are mitigating circumstances. Military protocol has space in it for some of these... edge cases, let's call them." She paused a moment. "The simple fact is that our procedures acknowledge that if one of the Originals—particularly someone like Sentinel—wanted to leave this situation, there's nothing I could bring immediately to bear that would stop him. It would be a literal throwaway of my men's lives."

Mitch was aghast. "Lieutenant Colonel, I would never—"

She held up a hand. "Not saying you would, now or in front of my commanding officers. What I will say is that you and your team decided to leave, and I chose to exercise the discretion my command gives me to not try and stop you."

Optic smiled. "Well, then. Thanks again for everything."

They turned to go as technicians come scurrying into the room, and the Lieutenant Colonel stopped Sentinel. "Sentinel. Go find those motherfuckers, and teach them why you're still the standard by which our world measures power."

Sentinel nodded once, and they departed the facility.

CHAPTER
TWENTY-THREE

Portland, Oregon, United States
May 23, 2013

As much as they would have liked to do as the Lieutenant Colonel encouraged, they weren't sure exactly whose asses to kick, or where to find them for the purposes of said kicking. For a few days, the team camped out at Optic's, who got some frantic calls from his agent. The military wanted to have a few words with him, but Optic asked her to put them off as best she could. They all agreed: they needed some time to investigate some of the names Rios sent them, though after several days, they were all running into the limits of their investigative capabilities.

Deosil paused in the doorway to Optic's room. She hesitated for a moment, then knocked. Optic popped his head out of a hell of a large walk-in closet and waved her in. His phone was cradled between shoulder and ear, and he was listening to someone talk on the other end. Deosil entered the room, but paused just inside the doorway, wondering whether to come back later. She was already here, though. She glanced over at his bureau and smiled. It was extremely neat and orderly, with everything in its specific place. The layout of its contents—a small box for his wallet, pocket change and keys, a modest jewelry box where a couple of rings, a few pairs of stud earrings and some cufflinks sat pressed into some velvet cushioning, a small cluster of deodorant and colognes—made it clear that not only did everything have a place, but Optic wanted it kept there.

Only one thing seemed out of place: a small chain on which a pair of dog tags hung, draped across the top of the mirror's top left corner. It seemed haphazard, but Deosil knew otherwise. She read the name on it.

BEAUCHAMP
WENDELL A.

"You snooping for my secret identity?" he asked, and Deosil jumped with a little *meep* sound. She hadn't heard him come up next to her, apparently having already said his goodbyes and hung up with whoever he was talking to.

Probably his agent. *Again.*

"Oh, God, I'm so sorry, I didn't even–" she stopped when he chuckled.

"Relax, no, I'm just messing with you," he said with a big grin. "Didn't mean to startle you. And it's not a secret—not legitimately. I go by Optic publicly because my agent thinks it helps me to stand out in Hollywood and everything."

Deosil chuckled. "Former names are a sore point for me, you know? So, I try to be really respectful of that for other people."

"I appreciate that." He was thoughtful for a moment. "Do people really ask about your old name, I guess? Not your super name, but your..."

"Dead-name, we call it sometimes. Yeah, they do. A lot."

"I mean, I guess I can see people who've known you a long time, maybe, but even new people?"

Deosil shook her head. "My mom's about the only one who's known me that long, and she'd eat lead before she dead-named me. No, it's only new people. I guess it's a form of forced intimacy, or something? Like, people want in on your secrets, or they want to know something special about you, once they find out you used to have another name? I used to tell people, but way too many new people try to call you by that old name." She shrugged.

"That sounds shitty," Optic said, reaching over to pull down his old dog tags. "They kinda made us change ours. Do the codename thing. Mostly so we could be umbrellaed under the DTPA's identity protection laws, but also I think because they wanted to differentiate who we used to be from what we were now."

"What were you now?"

Optic paused for a moment, regarding the tags, before looking into Deosil's eyes. "Weapons. We were *their* weapons, and I'm pretty sure half the reason they wanted us to use codenames was so we didn't have regular people names."

"So is Optic a name you *want* to use, then?" Deosil shoved the backpack at the foot of the bed over to make room, and sat on the edge of it. "I mean, not out in public. But here. With just us. It sounds kinda like they tried to use your code name to, I dunno. Dehumanize you, maybe?"

"Yeah," he said with that dimpled smile of his, and crossed back to the closet, reaching in and folding the shirt he pulled off the hanger there. "That was their intention. For us, though—that was a brotherhood thing. We were a new family, if that makes sense, and those were our family names."

Deosil nodded. "Yeah, I get that. Pagans take new names sometimes, the same way. It's the name you use with your tribe, you know? We're seeing a lot more of that kind of identity choosing at the DTPA Retreats, too."

Optic fiddled with the shirt a moment before shoving it with several others into the backpack.

"You going somewhere?" she asked with an arched eyebrow. She leaned backwards, her arms splayed out behind her, a kid sprawling on a too-big bed.

"Yeah. When you guys ran into some of the informational walls with those names, I did some digging around, and I think some of the people I know in DC might be able to tell me something. They're not going to do it long-distance, though. Those sorts don't like trails. So I'm going to fly over and see if I can get a sit-down with one or two of them. Probably be gone overnight."

Deosil nodded, chuckling. "Yeah, sounds like Mitch had a similar idea. He's leaving for Seattle right after lunch." She drew her bare feet up on the bed, wrapping her arms around her legs and laying her head against the tops of her knees. "I wish we'd been able to find more, you know?"

"We shouldn't be too surprised, honestly," Optic said absently as he scanned over the rack of ties that hung on one of the walk-in closet doors. "If these people we're after are involved in that sort of clandestine stuff, they're not likely to remain in the public eye—or search engine, as the case may be."

"True," she said, watching him choose two ties and tuck them away into the bag as well. He zipped it up, dropping the bag next to the bed, and sat down next to her. He turned to sit facing her, drawing one leg under him, and allowing the other to trail on the floor, and she twisted in her seat to match his posture, so she was facing him in return. He seemed pensive.

"So, I have something to ask, but before I do, I'm always cool with a hearty *It's none of your business* for an answer, okay?"

"Oh, boy," she said with a suspicious look. "Some of my favorite conversations in life have started off with that kind of statement." She waved him on.

"So, when we were at the Crypt, right? When the Director of Security was telling Mitch the story about her brother? Like, I thought it was a really cool story, even if those kinds of heart-to-hearts do make Mitch act like he's going to have a coronary. But I noticed that you kinda had this look? I've been wracking my brain to figure out what might be behind that, but I can't for the life of me figure anything out, you know? What might have caused it? Assuming I wasn't imagining things."

Deosil nodded. "No, you weren't imagining things." She glanced over toward the head of the bed, where the curtains in the window were drawn aside and a sunny sky shone through. She took a deep breath.

"So, bear with me, because I'm not even entirely sure I know how to express this. It—the Director's story, I mean—it definitely made me think. I've been thinking about it since then, and I kinda realized that I'm a little envious of her brother, you know? I mean, Mitch didn't have it easy, and even today, coming out is still awful for a lot of people, I know. But I never had anybody like Mitch. Someone I could admire—someone who was willing to stand up and admit that they were trans. Someone who was…I don't know. Public enough, celebrity enough, to be a person like that.

"When I was figuring it all out, Optic, I thought I was *crazy*. Like, I never even knew anything about being trans at all, you know? I didn't know it was a thing. I had to stumble through it—not just accepting it about myself, but figuring out what the hell it *was*. I can't help but wonder what my life would have been like if I'd had someone who could do for me and other trans kids what Mitch did for Rusty, and other gay kids, right?"

Optic smiled and leaned forward, arms out, and with just a second of hesitation, Deosil uncoiled and hugged him.

"I'd say that you'd have been as lucky to have them as Rusty and I were to have Mitch," said Optic. "And you're probably not the only trans kid who wishes they had someone like that to look up to, either. I think there are lots of kids who deserve exactly that."

Deosil leaned back, wariness on her face. Optic just watched her, and she sighed.

"Gods, you're not *challenging* me to be that, are you?" She hated that slightly panicky tone that came with the rush of words. "Because I don't...I mean, I think that—"

"Hey, hey, no," Optic said, and reached out his hand. Deosil took a breath, and laid her hand in his. "I'm not. I promise. I can't tell you if you ought to have a public face like that or not. Only you can decide to do that. I'm just saying that I'm willing to bet you're not the first trans kid looking for a role model like that, and probably won't be the last."

He hesitated a moment, and then forged ahead. "But also, you should know, that if we do this thing—this Sacred Band thing—you might not be able to help it. You might not get the chance to decide whether or not you want to be someone's hero. Celebrity will do a lot of cool stuff, but one of the things it will definitely do is get away from you. You won't have a say in how people perceive you, in the stories they tell about you. Are you ready for that?"

She sighed, and then flopped down on his bed. "You're the actual worst."

He laughed, grabbing up his bag as he stood. She grimaced up at him. "I know. I can only barely live with myself, to be honest. See you when I get back." He bent at the waist, kissed her on the forehead, and walked out.

* * *

It was close to four in the afternoon by the time she woke from her unexpected nap. She stumbled out of Optic's room to a house full of lengthening shadows. She rubbed her eyes blearily, walking past Llorona on the phone in the living room. The older woman waved at her and continued to talk in Spanish. She slid the door to the balcony open, closed it behind her and crossed to Rusty, who was on an obviously new phone at the railing overlooking downtown Portland.

"Hey there," he said, glancing up, then back at his phone, and then giving her a double-take. "Whoa, hey, nice bed-head."

She scowled at him, flipping him off with one hand while trying to press her hair down, willing it to lie flat. He chuckled and clicked his phone off.

"You hungry? We saved you some lunch." He gestured inside. "Llorona is on the phone with some of her Golden Cross contacts."

"Maybe in a little bit," she said, biting back a yawn. "Mitch and Optic leave already?"

"Yup," Rusty said, turning away to lean on his forearms over the railing, gazing out over the city. "Optic late this morning. Mitch right after lunch."

Smiling, Deosil bumped his shoulder with her own. "I bet you could have gone with him, if you'd asked."

The natural curse of being a redhead, of course, is the total inability to hide a blush. "Ugh, I know," he said. "At least, he would have probably let me. But he's off to meet important people, it sounds like, and I just..."

"Not sure where you fit in?"

His sigh was deeply flustered. "Not even sure if I have any right to expect to fit in at all, is more like it."

She draped an arm around his neck, and he leaned into her gratefully. "You know he obviously super digs you, right?" she said after a moment.

"Sometimes I think so, yeah. But other times, I'm not so sure." He grimaced again, and honestly Deosil was too good of a best friend to point out how whiny he sounded right now. They both knew, though. "I need to just chill. Let other things get sorted out, with this stuff with Radiant, and the Prometheus Consortium, and..."

Deosil pulled away from him, snapping her spine straight. "Wait, Prometheus Consortium? Do we know something more?"

"Oh, yeah!" Rusty straightened and turned to face her, excited. "Sorry, happened while you were napping. Optic got to DC and started asking some questions. He said that some of the names from the list the Director at the Crypt gave us led to some connections. He said there's something called the Prometheus Consortium with ties to all of those people, and more besides. Some people he knows in military intelligence have been watching some of them for a while. Not sure where he picked up the name or what, but..."

"Wait, wait, wait," Deosil said. "Back up."

"Okay. So, they know that some of the Changed we encountered—Kaamos, and Velocity, that speedster—they're sort of notorious mercenaries. As best Optic can figure, he thinks they're working for this actual conspiracy of people the intelligence community is interested in."

"Uh, wow," Deosil shook her head. "This is some straight-up superspy James Bond bullshit. If these guys are mercenaries, for this consortium or whatever, does that mean they've been snatching up these kids for them? And are they the ones who have Radiant's body?"

"I know, me too. I feel like I need a big board with a bunch of pictures connected to each other by string and shit."

She laughed, and shook her head. "God. Honestly, I'm surprised you haven't done something like that yet, you huge nerd." They both laughed, and he threw an arm around her shoulders. She leaned into him fondly.

They were quiet a few moments, staring out over the afternoon Portland skyline. "So are you really down for this?" he asked, voice sedate.

It was funny how she knew exactly what he was talking about. "Being part of a literal outlaw band of superheroes?" She paused, thoughtfully. She stopped to control her breathing, counting the breaths, like she did when she was stressed. Rusty noticed, but didn't interrupt.

"I am, yeah," she said. "With good reason, though. I mean, the DTPA has drilled it into our heads just how illegal and whatnot doing that is."

"It's not, though," Rusty said, smiling. "I talked with Llorona. They always gave us the impression that forming a team of supers was illegal, but it's not. There are laws in place that upgrade any illegal activities—especially vigilantism—to federal crimes if we do them as a team, but the formation of a team is not actually itself illegal."

Deosil pursed lips at him dubiously. "Really?" She was thoughtful, her brow creased. "I mean, that's what I always thought. But now that I really think about it, I can't remember them saying outright that forming a team was illegal."

"No, but they imply it pretty heavily at the Retreats, and everywhere else we interact with them," Rusty said. "Optic says it's part of how they manage us. Again, all that spy-ops stuff."

Deosil took another deep, calming breath, and then turned back to Rusty, smiling. "You know, they always emphasized to us that we're just normal people. Our powers don't make us heroes or give us the right to engage in vigilante justice."

"Well, I think they're right," Rusty said. "It's not our powers that make us heroes. I think it's bravery and the willingness to do something about things that no one else wants to make right that makes someone a hero. I think ordinary people are heroes every day because of that. It's just that the skill set we bring to it happens to include superpowers."

She stared at him for a couple of heartbeats, with an intensity that made him turn away, blushing. "I know it sounds stupid—"

"No," she said, laying a hand on his, clasping it tightly. "Fuck no. Not stupid. It sounds to me like you've been spending some of that quality time you've gotten with Sentinel lately actually listening to him, and it's a good look on you."

Rusty laughed, and rubbed his face with the palm of one hand. "That's probably better than what I'd like to be doing." Deosil joined him in laughter.

Laughter that was suddenly cut off as she fell to one knee in pain.

"Jesh!" Rusty knelt beside her, anxiously studying her face, trying to figure out what was wrong. "Are you, what's going—"

"They're here," she whispered. The rest of what she said was lost in the boom of a cracking foundation, and the sudden tilting sideways of the whole damned world as it was filled with flying debris.

*   *   *

Rusty couldn't make out exactly what happened. When he returned to his senses, he was surrounded by the debris that used to be Optic's fucking house, torn away from its moorings clinging to the side of the West Hills. From what he could gather, it had slid halfway down the incline, but caught on a mostly level portion of the hillside, just above someone else's house. Though plenty of massive chunks of masonry and steel girder had already rained down on the house below, most of the huge chunks of debris had caught on weird outcroppings of the basalt that made up the heart of the West Hills.

He looked up, coughing from the dust, and found Deosil standing beside him. Her skin was the precise color of those basalt outcroppings, and he noticed that other smaller chunks of stone provided both of them a perfectly round shelter from the fallen debris.

She'd saved them both. *And* the house below them.

"Jesh," he coughed, trying to stand.

She turned to regard him with those creepy cold eyes made of darkest stone. "Get back up there," she said, pointing at the hill above them. He followed her gesture and saw that half of Optic's house—cracked in half like some ill-fated gingerbread construction at Christmas—still clung to the side of the West Hills. "Llorona was in there."

Behind her, inky black tentacles started throwing debris around, cutting a path toward them through the rubble. Kaamos was coming for them, and probably bringing the other Prometheans with him. She followed his gaze, and turned back to him.

"Go!" she barked. "Let me hold these guys off. Your powers will be way more useful if she's trapped inside the rubble."

She turned away from him and exhaled deeply. The basalt coloration drained from her skin, and underneath she was shock-pale and sweating profusely. She breathed a normal cycle of breath as a normal human girl, to steady herself, and then turned her face skyward. She reached her arms upward, as though she might embrace the heavens themselves, and then inhaled.

The piercing blue of the sky above bled into her skin, and the winds came to her call, and she rose unsteadily into the air.

"Go!" she shouted at him again, and then rose higher, speeding toward Kaamos.

Rusty turned toward the remains of the house above, his magnetic senses picking out the largest concentration of ferrous metal still remaining in its structure. The support struts, built into the house's foundation, were still largely intact, sticking out of the hillside like spears thrust into a body. He reached for those with his power, the buzzing intensifying in his head as he made contact, and then he *pulled*.

He catapulted up the hillside in a low direct arc, clearing the trees that hadn't been leveled by the destruction of the house above, and slammed into the girding. He didn't quite manage to slow himself down enough—reflexes were still a little shaken up—but he tumbled as he hit, and righted himself quickly enough, facing outward.

He scanned the direction where Deosil had flown just in time to see her rising from the tangle of Kaamos' shadow tentacles, slicing neatly through them with precisely directed microcurrents of air, thin as blades. She kicked him in the face as she rose and pushed off his skull, gaining height fast. Behind their melee, the trees quaked as Velocity sped toward them up the face of the hills.

She was going to need backup, and soon. But he had a job to do first, and he spun toward the interior of the house. "Llorona!" he shouted. "Hold on! I'm coming!"

CHAPTER TWENTY-FOUR

Washington DC, United States • Seattle, Washington, United States
May 23, 2013

Angel's hadn't changed a bit.

Optic wasn't sure it ever would, really — no reason to, he supposed. When you got a good thing going, why mess with it? The owner of the place was a retired Air Force pilot, and got what he wanted out of the joint: a cool, dark place in the middle of the nation's capital where his old Air Force buddies— and new ones Angel hadn't met yet—could find a place to sip shitty beer away from ground pounders. Those who were most comfortable piloting screaming steel bullets in the blue were a different breed.

Early evening light that cast a glare across the whole bar faded as the door squealed closed behind him. "Still haven't gotten that fucking door oiled, Angel?" Optic called out to the thin balding man behind the bar. Angel Govinda was short but muscled, often wearing short-sleeved button-ups that showed off the muscle and tattoos on his arms. He turned toward Optic with a squint and a grimace, and paused, glaring for a moment before a grin split his face.

"Well, holy shit," he said finally. "You get lost, son? Pretty sure Hollywood's over on the other goddamn coast."

Optic grinned back at him and found a seat on one of the barstools. "Not lost. I'm actually in this shit-hole on purpose. I know, I'm having a hard time believing that, too."

Angel laughed and pulled Optic a beer. Optic took a long drink, and set the glass down in front of him. The old pilot regarded him closely, and shook his head. "Shit," he said, a little more quietly. "You just fuckin' flew over, didn't you? Goddamn Emps."

Optic shifted a little uncomfortably in his seat, though he didn't let the smile leave his face. He glanced up at the mirror behind the bar and scanned the room reflected in it. No one seemed to have heard—or at least, no one was reacting to having heard. Not surprising—there weren't many people in here at this time of day, though that was due to change in another hour or so.

As far as slang terms for him, Optic had heard worse in his day. "Emps" was military slang for the Empowered, a term intended to set them apart from others. The term "Emps and Echoes" was shorthand to refer to the Changed in general, and was often used with one or more colorful invectives on either side of the phrase.

"Speaking of," Optic said, after another sip. "My boys still come in here? Or did they finally wise up?"

"The other Seraphs?" Angel's volume dropped to match Optic's. "Yeah, sometimes. Not Turbine, though. Kid got hurt a few months ago."

Optic winced. "Real bad? I mean, will he recover?" He tried not to show his concern, but Angel flashed him a look—understanding there, Optic thought—and nodded.

"Yeah. Ended up in a brawl over the Atlantic to hear the other boys tell it. Some goddamn fool who spun up a big storm that he was trying to bring to ground on New York or something."

"I heard about that. News talked about the weird unseasonable storm back half a year ago or so."

"That was it." Angel. "I try not to eavesdrop on them, but it sounded like that poor kid got struck by lightning. Pretty bad. Burns all over, heart stopped, fell into the ocean, shit like that. Updraft fished him out and got him to a medical team in time, but he's doing some recuperating."

Optic shook his head.

"No worries, though. Your boys stalled him long enough for the Pile-On Boys to get there," Angel said with a snort. "I imagine Mister Storm of the

Century is rotting away in super-Guantanamo or whatever right now."

The "Pile-On Boys" was their nickname among military types, who seemed to have a physical allergy to referring to things by their actual names. Properly, they were the Extraordinary Intervention Task Force, a project between the DTPA and the Department of Defense. They were Echoes who wanted to put their powers to use defending the United States, so the EITF gave them the place to do just that. Highly trained and pushed to the very threshold of their potential—both physically and in terms of their powers—they were a deadly force of about a dozen supers. They almost never all worked together, usually dispatched in teams of three to five, based on the needs of the mission and who wasn't already working somewhere else.

When the Seraphs intercepted someone entering American air space with the kind of power that prevented them from handling it immediately, they spun up the EITF. In fact, that was why they were called the Pile-On Boys; if the original team dispatched to handle the situation wasn't able to contain the threat in a short time, additional teams arrived in short order, piling on in the fight. It was brutal, but effective.

Optic stood, scooping up his drink. He dropped a twenty on the bar. "Pull one for whichever of my boys shows up, yeah?"

Angel simply nodded. Optic didn't have to watch the old TV screen in the corner for long, which was just as well—he hated news programs in general. After maybe ten minutes, the door opened, and in walked a man in track pants and jacket. The jacket hung open, revealing a uniform identical to Optic's, except with green markings where Optic's were white. He was just shy of six feet in height, with a close-shorn military-style crewcut to his light brown hair, and hazel eyes that twinkled with mischief. He scanned the bar and found Optic's table. Angel pulled the man a drink and handed it to him as he passed.

Jetstream crossed the bar, beer in hand, and finally came to stand at Optic's table, shaking his head. "You know I can't drink this. I'm on duty."

Optic snorted. "You know as well as I do that both our metabolisms burn this shit off way before we even come close to intoxicated."

Jetstream grinned and sat down, making a point to take a drink of his beer.

"Thirsty flight?" Optic asked around a shit-eating grin.

"I could ask you the same, asshole," the handsome Seraph answered. He sat his beer down on the table. "I know for a fact that you can shift your power so that our satellites can't see you at all. So when we got the report about you coming into DC in full visibility mode for us, it was pretty obvious you wanted to see us."

"Well, if you'd give me a goddamned phone number like regular people…" Optic didn't bother to finish that thought. He knew what membership in the Seraphim meant. Full block-out of standard communication was part of it.

"So, what do you want?" Jetstream asked.

Optic shifted in his seat. "I have some questions I think you could maybe help me with."

Jetstream smirked at him and leaned back in his seat. "Maybe."

"Nothing that's actually restricted info, I don't think," Optic said, mimicking his posture. He took up his beer and took another sip. "But first, how's Turbine doing?"

Jetstream's gaze darted to Angel behind the bar, and he shook his head. "I swear to God, that old man." His gaze dropped to the table, and he fidgeted, wiping liquid off the outside of his pint glass before answering. "He's hurt pretty bad, man. We're not supposed to say how bad, but you're one of us. You know him. He's in rough condition. He's started physical therapy. Marque—you know, the Original that runs the DTPA—he arranged to get some Korean lady in who helped with the skin grafts. Fixed him up almost to a hundred percent, which is a shit-load better than the doctors were saying. You can hardly tell that he had about seventy percent of his body fucking flash-fried by that son of a bitch over the Atlantic."

"Who was it?" Optic asked, though he suspected he knew the answer.

"Sorry, man. Classified," Jetstream apologized, and Optic nodded, waving away the question.

"Is he going to make a recovery? Still going to be a Seraph?"

When you've been teammates with someone as long as Optic and Jetstream had been, you learn their tells. Their little signs of stress, of deceit, of whatever it is they've got going on in your head that they're sure won't impact the mission, but almost always does. "What is it? Talk to me, man." Optic said.

Jetstream flashed him a guilty look, and sighed, shaking his head. "I'm not sure, man. They're telling us that he's in bad condition, that he might not even make it back to service. But something's wrong. There's something they're not telling us, and I don't like it."

"Sorry, man," Optic said, and Jetstream shrugged. *What're you going to do?* his body language said, and for a minute Optic's stomach flip-flopped with the pain of missing the people he knew so well that he could read like this.

"Do me a favor, yeah? If he does have to leave?" Jetstream turned his face toward him, and Optic caught the winced grief that flashed there. "Tell him to come look for me. I've got a place he can stay for a while, low key, while he figures out what he wants to do." Optic reached out and tapped the table between them, his demeanor serious. "And I've got access to some damned good lawyers, who'll make sure he gets everything he has coming to him for his service, too. You know they'll try to fuck him out of everything they can, Jet."

Jet's chuckle was weary, but he nodded. "Count on it, man. I think he's got an aunt or some shit he's halfway talked about going to stay with if they do let him go, but, well. He'll be grateful for the offer. You'll be the dumbass who has to put up with his leaving shit everywhere and his snoring, though."

The men laughed then, letting the memories of the foibles of shared living space among the Seraphs wipe away the possibility of tragedy, and it was a little bit like old times again. After a few moments, Jetstream sighed, and put down his now-empty glass. "Okay. You've still got that touch."

"That touch?" Optic arched an eyebrow.

"Yeah. We always said you could have been in intelligence. You can work a contact." He glanced up and held up two fingers, getting Angel's attention. The older man behind the bar nodded an acknowledgement and pulled two more beers. "So, what are you here to find out?"

Optic smiled and leaned back in his seat. "Prometheans. Ever heard of them?"

Jetstream grimaced as Angel brought them their beers. The old pilot waved away the bill in Jetstream's hand. "Yer money ain't any good here, son."

From the smile on Jetstream's face, it was clearly an old exchange between them. Optic wondered when it had started. Jetstream took a long drink, set the beer down between them, and leveled Optic with a serious gaze. "Goddamn it, leave it to you to ask the hard shit." He took a deep breath, and leaned in. "Okay. I don't know anything official—which is good for you, really, because if I did, I wouldn't say shit to you. Just to be clear."

"I wouldn't expect you to, Jet."

"I've heard a little here and there. You know, the way you do sometimes when you're in our line of work, right? Mixing with black ops, intelligence assets, that sort of thing. Me and the boys have heard that name before. Far as I can tell, it's a group. I've gotten the impression that they are a mix—corporate and government, though they're international. Lots of money, and they back a lot of research firms and shit."

"What kind of research?" Optic asked. His drink sat forgotten in front of him.

"Well, that's why I've encountered them, mostly. Heard some of the Choir's people talking about them. Hush-hush, you know, but I think they forget that we've got boosted senses."

"We, hell. You do. Most of the rest of us need equipment."

"So, they're not called Prometheans. They're called the Prometheus Consortium. And they seem to be attaching themselves like remoras to every publicly acknowledged Empowered program, and quite a few that are still under deep cover."

Optic frowned. "So, they're making supers." He didn't like that possibility. At all.

"They're trying like hell, yeah. And in order to do it, I'm pretty sure they're funding all kinds of different Empowered programs all over the world. You know how these programs work, man. Uncle Sam isn't going to talk to Cryptotech, and the Mafia isn't going to talk to either of them. But these guys? They've got money and they've got experience they're willing to share."

"And they'll probably help out anyone's program, as long as they can share in the information." Optic shook his head, and glanced up at the television.

"So, do you think–" Jetstream started, but stopped when Optic stood suddenly, his eyes fixed on the news program.

"Sorry, dude. I have to get back out west." Optic dropped a couple of bills on the table and was out the door. Jetstream didn't have a chance to say goodbye.

There's been no official comment on the Changed involved in the conflict, the blonde onsite announcer said, with a banner across her lower body emblazoned with the words SUPERS BATTLE IN DOWNTOWN PORTLAND. In the background, strange coruscating lights illuminated the Portland skyline, and tiny figures moved in ways humans simply shouldn't have been able. *The local police have established a cordon and are coordinating evacuation efforts from the area, however.*

* * *

The elevator opened after a few minutes' climb. The building was one of the tallest in Seattle's skyline, and the elevator totally private for the use of its occupant and a few others with permission to use it. Despite that, it still took longer than Alchemy liked to reach his offices in the penthouse of the building. He was the CEO of one of the most successful corporations in the world, though, so he had plenty to keep himself busy with his tablet on the ride, scanning through emails his assistant Christopher had tagged for his personal attention.

The door to the elevator opened, and Christopher stood there, coffee cup in hand. He was relatively new and still a little starstruck. Like all the Originals, Alchemy effortlessly maintained an Olympian-quality physique. His dark brown hair was cut conservatively and his jaw and chin completely clean-shaven. His glasses were designer and totally for show, and his suit was too. He was every inch the young corporate tycoon, gunning for old conservative money with cutting edge technology and socially forward ideas about the world and its people.

Alchemy smiled, and gratefully accepted the coffee cup from the young man. "You're here late, Christopher." Alchemy handed him his tablet. "I appreciate the diligence, but I don't expect that kind of work-is-your-life thing."

"It's no problem, Alchemy," Christopher said. "It's one of my workout days, so I'm here late anyway. I saw your schedule and figured I'd stay thirty minutes later to see if you needed anything before I headed home."

Alchemy smiled as the two crossed the small lobby that was the heart of Magnum Opus United, the major industrial international corporation that was the leading employer of the Changed in the United States and several other countries. "That's very thoughtful. I'm going to be burning the midnight oil here, as they say, though. Please go home and enjoy your evening."

"Will do, Alchemy. Thanks."

Alchemy unlocked his office door and paused, turning back to Christopher, who was bustling at his desk, collecting his gym bag and briefcase. "Are we… am I still getting calls from Marque?"

Christopher shot him a wary glance across the small abandoned lobby.

"Uh, you are, yeah. I've been doing what you said. I haven't mentioned it lately, mostly—"

"No, no. No apologies. You haven't mentioned it because I asked you not to. He's being damned persistent, and I don't like that."

"Should I change tactics, sir? Tell him something else?" Christopher flipped open the case on his smartphone, ready to take down any notes. The young man was always active on the thing, his thumbs flying across its surface. Alchemy was pretty sure half of his company operated on those damned thumbs here lately.

"No," he chuckled. "Do let me know when he *stops* trying to get in touch, won't you?"

"I sure will," Christopher said, nodding goodnight. Alchemy remained standing at his doorway, the door unlocked but closed, until the young man was in the elevator. Then, Alchemy waited until he could hear the elevator reach the ground floor, his Originals hearing tuned to the finely-wrought mechanics in the elevator shaft whirring to a stop, and going silent again.

Then, finally, he opened the door wide, and stepped just into the room.

"I recognize that heartbeat," he said into the seemingly empty space. "I just can't place it."

"Evening, Alchemy," Mitch said, stepping out of the en suite bathroom attached to the office. "Apologies for the unorthodox entry."

Alchemy's face split into a wide grin, and he crossed the office to clasp Mitch's hand tightly. "Jesus Christ, you're a sight for sore eyes," he said effusively, pulling the man into a single-arm hug, but quickly letting him go. "No worries, no worries. Like I said, I recognized your heartbeat, even if I couldn't place it."

Mitch gestured at the large window the farthest from Alchemy's massive desk. "I can't believe you've got all this security, but you left one window with a simple latch? What gives? Are you flying these days?"

Alchemy chuckled and waved him over to the small cluster of comfortable seating against the wall opposite the windows. "No. I left that in there for you, man. Well, for you, and a few choice other folks I know who get around the way you do."

"Bit of a risk, isn't it?" Mitch accepted the seat while Alchemy bustled at his wet bar.

"Not really, no," Alchemy said with a grin. "Anyone who is going to attack me is perfectly capable of busting through these windows, despite their composition. I'd frankly rather they didn't make the mess and just entered the damned window there, if they even notice it." He crossed the room, handing Mitch a tall glass of amber liquid. Mitch started to demur, but Alchemy snorted. "It's ginger ale, boy scout. I remembered." Mitch's eyebrows shot upward and he grinned, accepting the glass. "Besides, this entire room is lined with morphic alloy. If I get any choice in the battleground, it's going to be here. Home field advantage."

Mitch chuckled and looked around. The room didn't show any signs of being made of the weird composite metallic-ceramic that was one of Alchemy's earliest inventions, but that wasn't surprising. He could make the stuff appear to be any substance on the planet. He usually had to touch a substance to transmute it, but that was part of the point of morphic alloy. If it was in his line of sight, he could alter its makeup. Steel, glass, plaster—he could even make it mimic compounds not normally solid enough to be used as building materials. Mitch had seen him turn the stuff into some kind of phosphorous metal which immediately ignited itself on contact with air. Frankly, it was a little frightening to think of someone trying to invade Alchemy's office.

Mitch shook his head. "Still a genius, I see."

Alchemy rolled his eyes and sighed, the reaction of someone sick to death of being called that. Understandable, considering how often the words "genius Original" were appended to his name in the media. "What brings you here, Mitch? Please tell me it doesn't have anything to do with the very public trouble I've heard you were involved in over in Eastern Europe."

Mitch drained his drink. "Wish I could, Alc. I really do. But it's tied in with that, but also something bigger."

Alchemy shot him a positively gleeful expression. "I've got some contacts who're attaching your name to the possibility of an actual new team, laws be damned. How true is that?"

Mitch hesitated guiltily.

"You sneaky bastard." Alchemy laughed. "I knew it was only a matter of time. Nearly every one of the other Champions had something else we could be doing, but you and Radiant were only ever superheroes." He sat down at his desk and leaned forward eagerly. "Please tell me you're here to offer me a spot on the team. I mean, I can't accept, but I at least want to be offered, damn you. And I might have some ways to be part of it anyway, even if I'm not putting on a uniform."

Mitch paused, gazing into the ice at the bottom of his glass like he hoped to find the best way to say this. How could he communicate the facts of a situation like this without it dragging the raw emotions along with it, like a riptide pulling something out to sea?

Concerned, Alchemy stood and crossed to him. "Hey," he said, sitting down next to Mitch. For the first time, the man in the room with him wasn't Alchemy the Slick Corporate Original. He wasn't even Alchemy the Champion. He was just Alchemy, the man he had gotten to know over several years of living together in between missions to save people and beat up criminals. Alchemy hesitated for a moment, and then reached out his hand, gripping Mitch's shoulder. "Whatever it is, brother. You can tell me."

Mitch sighed and smiled ruefully. Even now he was starting to tear up. "They took him," he said, and his face crumpled. He covered his face with one hand and leaned back in his seat. The lighting globes in the ceiling burned brightly with what was undoubtedly a hyper environmentally conscious technology. He willed the light to burn away the tears, blinking.

"Who?" Alchemy asked quietly. The intimacy of the other man's concern was unnerving, and Mitch leaned forward, wiping his eyes.

"Radiant," he said, finally looking at Alchemy. "They got into the Crypt, and they took his remains."

Alchemy stood suddenly and walked back to the wet bar. He did so in something of a daze, like the destination was an excuse to just get up. To move, to get away from what Mitch had just told him. He rested the palms of his hands on the surface of the bar, then spun to lean against it. "Who?"

This must be the corporate Alchemy again, Mitch thought. He was calm and composed, perfectly suitable for the public eye. But there was a tightness in his jaw, and Mitch could hear him grind his teeth. His eyes were dark with rage.

"Who was it?" he asked again, biting his words. "Was it Marque?"

Mitch shook his head. "No, no. No one we know—at least, no one I know. They call themselves the Prometheans."

"The Consortium? The Prometheus Consortium?"

"I think so? I don't know. We've run into what I guess are a pack of mercenaries of theirs. They're kidnapping kids, Alchemy. Gay kids and trans kids and runaways and refugees. Sex workers and homeless kids. People that no one bothers to look for, because they're not wanted around anyway."

"The Consortium has its fingers in all kinds of tech and research. It's not a public thing, but I know they're trying to develop a dependable Empowerment process."

"I bet that needs test subjects," Mitch said grimly.

"I don't know a lot about them, Mitch," Alchemy said. "They've approached pretty much every company on the same level as Magnum Opus, but they've never approached me. I guess this is why—my stance on Empowerment projects is a matter of pretty vicious public record."

Mitch stood and crossed to the window. Night had begun to fall, and Seattle twinkled with the coming darkness.

"Listen, Mitch, I don't know what's going on, but they're connected. I'll see what I can find out about them, but you have to be careful. You can't just... the Champions are gone, Mitch. We're not those men anymore. This isn't the same world anymore. You can't just–"

"No." Mitch turned to regard him, and there was something in his expression. Something Alchemy hadn't seen in a long time. "I don't care, Alchemy. About any of that. *No one* is trying to stop them. The people who should be are, by all indications, firmly in their pockets. I'm not going to let them hide behind sinister governmental warnings and threats of legal action. We were once ready to face that when we started the Champions, and for the same reason: because someone should be doing something, and since no one else was willing or able to, we did."

"Shit, Mitch, you're talking about–" His phone beeped at him, a shrill message. His brow furrowed, and he fished it out of his jacket pocket. "Sorry, I have to take this. My informations team don't use this messaging system unless there's..." His words faded as he read the message. He turned to the wall behind the bar and *gestured.*

Mitch had felt it a hundred times before. The world seemed to resist Alchemy's power, insisting that things in one condition were meant to stay that way. Alchemy's power overcame that resistance, however, and the world changed according to his whim. Fortunately, the morphic alloy in the wall resisted the least of any substance, by design. The painting on the wall faded to white, like it had been leached of color, and the effect rippled outward to the wall behind it, draining it of the strong corporate color scheme it seemed painted with. In short order, the entire surface was one plain off-white color, and then its surface rippled. The frame and flat surface of the painting melted into the wall behind it, collapsing into it with a liquid sound, until the wall was completely flat.

Then, it shifted again, small ripples coruscating across its surface until it had turned into a wide plane of black glass. Alchemy gestured again, and a picture flared to life in it, emanating sound and light.

He'd turned the *entire wall* into a television set.

Mitch gaped. Alchemy had always postulated that he'd be able to do this kind of thing one day — to reshape substances in such a way that he could effectively build circuitry and moving parts within the depth of that substance. Creating technology that people could only dream, courtesy of his ability to generate mechanisms too small to normally create, and substances with impossible physical properties.

And he'd done it.

"Holy God," Mitch swore. "Did you just–" He stopped, seeing and hearing the news broadcast.

The camera caught a quick flash of Deosil, landing atop a building and shifting her body into a watery pattern. Her skin shimmered like she was wet and flowing, and the speedster Velocity bolted up the side of the building toward her. Police forced the camera crew away, and the image dropped, returning to a commentator reporter in the newsroom, updating watchers on the ongoing conflict between supers occurring live in Portland, Oregon.

Alchemy turned to say something to Mitch, but the big man was gone. The window on the far side of the office hung open, clacking against its frame in the wind this high above Seattle, and Alchemy crossed to close it. As he reached the window and clasped the latch, he heard the unmistakable boom of Sentinel shattering the sound barrier, and his windows rattled. "Go get 'em, Mitch," he said to the contrail that cut a sharp V-shape through the clouds above Seattle, and turned back to the television wall.

He slid an icon on his phone and held it up to his head as he watched.

"Christopher," he said curtly. "Apologies for disturbing your night. I've got a project that is top priority, and I'm going to need your help. Can you come back in?"

CHAPTER TWENTY-FIVE

Portland, Oregon, United States
May 23, 2013

"Thank God!"

The EMT took an alarmed step backward, jaw dropped, as the young red-head dropped down in front of her, seeming to have hopped off the power line above them. Gauss looked above them both and raised his hands, gently harnessing his power to guide the blanket-wrapped body of an older Latina woman, cradled in pieces of rebar, down from the crux of the power lines above them.

He concentrated carefully, settling her on the ground by the sidewalk next to the man the EMT—a thickly built woman with short blonde hair whose name tag said FLANDERS—was already treating for an arm injury from falling debris. With a gesture, the pieces of rebar unwrapped themselves from the unconscious woman, and she made a pained sound.

"I'm sorry to interrupt, but I need help, please," Gauss said. "She was in the house when it exploded. I got her out, but I don't know how bad her injuries are."

"I'll take a look," the EMT said. "Can you tell me if–"

"I'm sorry, I can't," Gauss said, already rising slowly from the ground. He pointed at the swaying cable-car gondola a few blocks away. "They're going to kill Deosil if I don't do something about it." Without another word, he rose above the street level, pulling himself magnetically first toward the heights of the power pole next to him, and from there to the top of a nearby building.

"Fucking Echoes," Flanders said, shaking her head. She glanced down at the woman at her feet, pulling the blankets aside. "Ma'am? Can you hear me? I need to check your vitals." She glanced upward after Gauss one last time, but he was already gone.

* * *

Portland's downtown wasn't very tall. Its skyline hugged the ground, with a dearth of actual skyscrapers. Instead, the West Hills loomed high above it, home to some of the most expensive property in the city, as well as one of its biggest medical centers. At one point, the city installed an aerial tram, extending a cable mechanism from the medical center to a station on the ground. This station connected with the rest of the city's ample public transportation network, granting ease of access to the medical center that was not only a place of healing, but also where up-and-coming medical professionals learned their trade.

The view from the gondola was spectacular, when it wasn't cloaked in an amorphous cloud of semi-solid darkness.

Kaamos stood atop the gondola, his jaw locked, gritting his teeth. Though the gondola was egg-shaped and rounded, with nearly no flat surfaces, he clung to the massive girder-sized bar connecting the gondola to the mechanisms that actually rode the cabling above with his power, a few of his shadowy tentacles wrapped tightly around the construction. The gondola swayed in midair, its operators having stalled it when the battle between Kaamos and Deosil found its way there.

"I'll snap this fucking cable, you little bitch!" he shouted in his Finnish-accented English, and set the car to swaying even more, far more than it normally might. The screams of the passengers within the car punctuated his threat. "Come out where I can see you!"

From the bright sky above, Deosil dropped like a stone. Literally—her flesh had taken on the tone of the basalt that made up the West Hills once more, with the attendant increase in density and weight. Like a catapult shot, she plummeted out of the sky, feet first, and crashed down onto Kaamos. Hard.

Even though his field of shadows—semisolid, like the touch of ghosts that were physical one minute, before returning to ephemera—blunted the impact of her attack, she still struck him hard enough to hear the meaty *thump*, both of them slamming into the roof of the gondola hard enough to dent it.

Once more the people inside screamed.

Kaamos cursed as he slithered away from Deosil, favoring his left side, hauled toward the side of the gondola by his tentacles, far faster than his own bodily control would have allowed him. Deosil's fists dented the spot where he'd just been lying. He watched her turn her head towards his exact location, despite the suffocating darkness he'd cloaked the entire gondola in.

"I don't need my eyes to see you," she said through clenched teeth. "You're displacing air by your simple existence, Tentacles. That's all I need." She stood and started to walk carefully toward him along the rounded surface of the gondola.

"Maybe, but you've also done more damage to this thing than I could have," he said with a smile she could hear. "For which I'm appreciative."

With that, he pulled himself up above the cable-car, suspending himself by his tentacles on the cables above, and began to rock the car with his other night-black arms. The ambient darkness faded away as he solidified more of them, each gripping and straining against the construction of the damaged gondola.

Rivets began to pop free along its seams, and the sound of metal shrieking against stressed metal filled the air. Deosil nearly panicked. Her earth-form was strong and resilient, but still vulnerable to being unbalanced and toppling off the damned cable car, and she wasn't sure if she could survive a fall of that height even in that form. She could use her air-invocation to get off the gondola, but it was of minimal utility against Kaamos. She couldn't invoke the metal in the gondola—it was too processed—and everything else in the environment was too far away for her power to touch.

She was starting to suspect they knew exactly how her powers worked, and this damned cable-car was an excellent defense against them.

Kaamos sent spear-like tentacles against her, slamming into her over and over as she clung to the central arm of the gondola. The damage they did was minimal, sending small puffs of basalt shards and dust up, leaving small craters where they struck. But they also threatened to knock her off-balance if she let go of the cable-car, and that would send her falling to the ground.

The sudden buzzing in the local energetic ecology was a balm to her senses, because it meant she had new options.

She smiled up at Kaamos. "Time to change what this game looks like," she said. He frowned at her in confusion, and Gauss rose up behind him, a gauntlet of thumb-sized ball bearings orbiting him.

Kaamos noticed too late to stop the sudden stutter-burst of projectiles from slamming into him. They made a sound like a wave of bullets against a side of beef, and Kaamos gave a strangled yelp and fell off the side of the gondola. With a metallic *clink*, Gauss adhered his boots and bracers to the side of the gondola, and watched the man's form dissolve into a bloom of shadow beneath them. It disappeared once it neared street level, the shadows sinuously sliding away behind a building, carrying Kaamos with them.

Gauss glanced over to the window to see the fearful gazes of the people aboard the gondola: a couple of students his age, two others in scrubs, and a mom and her two kids. He waved at them and shouted, "We're going to get you into the station. Hold on!"

With that, he slid up the side of the gondola to where Deosil was resting atop it. She was in her normal human form once more, leaning against the cable-arm of the gondola.

"You alright, Jesh?"

She nodded to him. "Just resting. We need to get these people off this gondola. Can you carry them to the ground?"

"I can," he said, glancing at the ground, and at the distance between the gondola and the station that was its original destination. "But I think it'd be faster to get the gondola to the station. Keep a lookout for me?"

Deosil nodded, standing. She inhaled sharply, and took a deep breath of the clean, cool air of the Willamette river valley's sky, invoking it into herself. Her flesh paled and blued, her hair whipping around in the wind that came off her, and she rose into the air above the gondola, casting her gaze about.

"Do it!" she shouted down at Gauss. The redhead nodded and turned his gaze toward the mechanisms that ran the cables. They'd been braked earlier, and their operators fled shortly after. Gauss adhered his boots to the gondola roof, and then reached out toward the station with hands and power. He clenched his fist and the mechanisms sprang to life.

The cables began to move again, but the car itself gave a great squealing, shuddering protest as more rivets popped free. It was too damaged to make it to the station on its own. Gauss took a deep breath and extended his power down and around him.

From the grim look on his face, Deosil knew this was going to hurt.

Exerting magnetic force, he gritted his teeth, reconnecting the cable-arm to the gondola roof magnetically, sealing them with the force of a high-tesla industrial magnetic generator. The entire car shook and hummed with the sudden influx of power, and small metal possessions of the passengers inside the car took a sudden leap upward, adhering to the ceiling above them. Several of its passengers gave a cry of alarm.

The cable mechanism continued, slowly pulling the car toward the station's dock, and Gauss had to keep pouring on the power to keep the magnetic seal intact. The car was heavy — too heavy to support by passive magnetic attraction, but Gauss could hold it in place by continuing to constantly dump teslas of power into the place where they connected.

"Hurry up, hurry up, hurry up," he chanted, sweat pouring down his brow. He was already starting to feel the ache in his muscles and the buzz of an impending migraine that signaled the onset of his power's effects on his body.

"Claviger!" Deosil shouted above him, gritting her teeth in pain as the priest's power ripped open the world near them with enough violence that she couldn't help but notice. The blackness yawned open ahead of them, and Gauss shut his eyes against the attendant light show that came with it. Even having just glanced at it, Deosil could feel the slight effects of the photosedative effects. Her adrenaline dialed back, and a slight serotonin buzz took its place.

She strengthened her concentration, focusing on the ache in her muscles to push past it, and hoped like hell Rusty could do the same. He wouldn't be able to react to who or whatever was coming through that portal, she knew, so she would have to take care of it.

The gondola began to rock on its mooring as the winds rose around it. The passengers inside screamed and clung to the interior of the car. Deosil was pretty sure that the cable-car could take much stronger winds than this normally, but she understood their terror. That, and it upped the stress on the broken arm-connector, and Gauss had to push to keep the mechanisms magnetically sealed as the momentum from the rocking tried to force them apart again.

Above him, Deosil's skin was the color of the May sky over Portland, all bright blue, the color of heavenly figures in Hindu mythology. The winds around her ebbed and flowed in time to her heartbeat, her very breath. She reached up and out as she flew above the sleek metal car, and the winds came to her call.

She'd never exerted this kind of power and this kind of control simultaneously before, but the air element was kindest to her. She knew it best, and immersion in its warm, wet essence took the least out of her psyche. Though they were invisible to human sight, the torrents of wind gathered around her as she closed her hands into a fist in front of her, pulling the rapidly moving air into a tight sphere orbiting her body with a roar.

Deosil's eyes were closed, but she could sense her environs. The flows of air just stopped in midair, where they ceased to exist in a flat plane facing her and the cable-car. She knew by the strange echoing in her mind (it…it wasn't really groans of actual *pain*, was it?) that was where Claviger's portal was tearing itself into being. She waiting until it stopped growing, and then felt movement. By its sinuous, half-solid feeling through the air, it was Kaamos reaching through, searching for something solid he could use to pull himself through the passage.

There was no way she was giving him that chance.

With a deep, deep inhalation, Deosil held the lungful of air within her until her chest began to ache. Then, with an explosive exhalation that made a sound lost to the roaring winds around her, she shot her arms outward, pointing the winds in the direction of the yawning portal. Winds of a speed not usually seen outside of hurricanes, woven into a single, tight funnel of force, lanced out and into the glowing edges of the portal. Though her winds passed through the passage, they carried some degree of her consciousness with them.

Deosil was vaguely aware of the sudden windstorm that punched through the portal down below, slamming into Kaamos, who stood at its groundward threshold. He yelped, and the force of it slammed him dozens of yards away, into the side of a building. Her consciousness snapped back to her immediate vicinity as Claviger—not even in its direct path, but too near the opening when the barrage of winds roared through his portal—was blown backwards, knocked off his feet.

The portal winked out.

Deosil dropped down to hover near Gauss on the roof of the cable-car.

"Seems Claviger loses his portals if he gets knocked around too much." She glanced at the station, which grew closer as the cable-car descended on its cabling. She looked up the street and swore. "Damn it," she said. "Company's coming. I'll see if I can get in her way."

Before Gauss could ask what she meant, Deosil dropped down to ground level, her skin losing its sky hues in favor of the young woman's own bronze complexion. Without missing a beat, she set her first foot onto the ground, did a weird sliding-step while inhaling, and then exhaled again. This time, the water in the nearby water hydrant sprang to life, bursting out of the small metal fixture with such force that it not only burst its cap, but cut across the road with such strength that when Velocity ran into it, it spun her off-balance and out of control.

The woman didn't even have a chance to make a noise before she went spinning into a parked van. Deosil stepped behind the fire hydrant and continued to extend her arms outward, forcing the water into a tight, spiraling stream with such force that as it continued to strike Velocity, the speedster was forced up against the side of the now-dented van, and nearly lifted off her feet.

"Hurry it up, Rusty!" Deosil yelled up at him. He leapt down from the gondola into the station as it clanked home, and with a flick of his powers popped the its door open. The people within cowered as he paused in the open doorway.

"You have to get out of here!" he shouted at them. "There's a police cordon five blocks north of here. We'll try to pull them away so you have a clear path to run!"

They just stared at him, paralyzed with fear. Biting off a snarl, Gauss left them, hoping like hell that they'd get moving once he wasn't in their line of sight. He just couldn't wait to see, because wherever Velocity was, the other Prometheans wouldn't be far behind.

Gauss crossed the space between the station's open platform and the side of the road where Deosil stood, directing the flow of the water to hold Velocity in place. Just as he got to her side, she gasped, and sagged to her knees. The torrent of water stopped, arcing off and dwindling. Gauss gestured quickly. Velocity slid down the side of the panel van once the water stopped slamming her into it. She pulled herself to one knee, but didn't make it to her feet fully before the dented panel of the van's side popped rivets and tore itself free, wrapping her in the sheet metal with a shriek of twisting metal siding.

"No!" she shrieked as she saw what was happening, but it was too late to react. It wrapped itself around her, its long edges magnetically sealed to one another. Gauss folded the top of it over, crimping the end of it, then knocked it on its side, and repeating the action with the bottom.

Deosil laughed, an exhausted, ragged sound. "Did you just…did you just use your burrito-making skills offensively?"

He grinned at her proudly. "Hey, I'm a goddamned superhero. We really need to–"

And before he could even finish that thought, Mercy was *there*, all white mask and razor-sharp blades. She was a blur of motion — not speed like Velocity but just economy of motion. Perfection of control. Once, twice, three times, she stabbed Deosil, stepping between the two of them and yet somehow ending on the other side of Deosil in her movement, this half-acrobatic, half-murderous barrage of stabs and shifts. Deosil coughed blood, and would have fallen if it weren't for Mercy holding her up by a fistful of both hair and the back of her costume.

"Jesh!" Gauss shouted in shock. The ball bearings he kept secreted away in his bracers and various pouches punched their way out of their enclosures with a hundred small popping sounds. Just in time, too, as Mercy dropped Deosil and leapt for Gauss.

Fortunately, she slammed feet-first into the whirling sphere of steel projectiles, which redirected her forward momentum and made a nasty, bone-breaking sound as they slammed over and over and over into her feet, lower legs, knees, and thighs. Momentum from the impact should have sent the projectiles spinning wildly away, but Gauss had encountered that in his previous fights, and adjusted for it now. He dropped to one knee and amped up the spinning field of magnetism, generating more magnetic force that pulled them back into spinning with power greater than the inertial force generated by the impact.

The result not only kept them from spinning out of control, but it also served to sling Mercy nearly a block and a half away, slamming her into the side of a municipal building. She dropped into the decorative foliage at the base of the building and didn't move.

Rising quickly to his feet, Gauss dashed to where Deosil lay, pulling up one side of the whirling barrier to get it around her, before dropping it back safely over them again. "Hey, hey. Jesh, come on, wake up," he said, and scrubbed angrily at the tears his traitor face kept splashing down his cheeks. He wasn't fucking *crying* because there was *nothing* to fucking cry *about*.

She coughed once, a nasty wet sound that bubbled blood at her lips, and stirred. "Rusty," she rasped at him. "Get away."

"Thank God," he said, sighing in relief, glancing up to see where Mercy was. He couldn't be sure, but he thought she was still lying in the flower bed. "I was super worried that—"

Her hand on his wrist, sudden and like a super-heated vice, shut him up. Her eyes were open and staring into him: eyes of deep, roiling red-orange-black, with a dull glow of their own.

"Oh, shit Jesh," he said.

"Fucking…run," she gasped, and she *reached* again.

Gauss' barrier stopped spinning as he leapt back. His explosive movement was just in time as Deosil was swallowed whole by an immense gout of deep red fire. His leap cleared him from being burned, but it didn't keep his feet under him with the earth began to shake and tremble. It wasn't very strong, and his awareness of the magnetic field told him that it didn't radiate very far away, but there was no doubt what had just happened.

Deep beneath the earth of the Pacific Northwest bubbled a great cauldron of molten rock, and Deosil had just reached down and invoked it into herself.

He looked up. Though she was no longer on fire, Deosil stood and gestured, a single calming wave of her hand, and the tremor subsided. A block and a half away, Mercy rose unsteadily from where she'd fallen, and her gaze snapped to Deosil's immolated form.

I don't know if you just killed me, you bitch, Deosil said in a voice of roaring fire and cracking earth, a terrible voice that clenched a fist in Gauss' gut. *But I'm taking you with me, either way.*

Deosil launched herself down the street, her flames taking her leap high into the air. Though the arc wasn't quite enough to reach the masked knife-fighter, where she landed she melted the asphalt and rode the slick torrent of tarry goo the rest of the distance to her.

In a stunning display of tactical genius, Mercy fled for her fucking life.

Roaring in burning fury, Deosil gave chase. Aftershocks began to pulse across the city's tectonic geoscape, in ever widening ripples, obvious even to Gauss' magnetic senses.

"Shit, Jesh," Gauss swore. He pulled himself magnetically up the side of the sky-tram's ground station, gaining height to see where they were going. He glanced back at the steel burrito that was Velocity's temporary prison, sighed, and then tore off across the city scape beside the river, leaping from magnetic point to magnetic point. To his relief, his vantage let him see that the tram passengers had fled the station, heading in a wide arc around their battlefield toward the police cordon. He did his best to ignore the ache that had become a shriek in his muscles, and the sunburst of pain that was trying to blossom behind his eyes.

At this juncture, he wasn't sure which was more likely: Deosil killing Mercy, or Deosil causing a volcanic fucking eruption in the middle of Portland. Either way, he pursued, hoping to prevent both.

* * *

It was the shaking of the ground that woke her where she lay in the back of an ambulance. Small, sterile-packaged medical equipment — masks and tubing, weird rubber shapes and vacuum-sealed syringes — slid out of overhead compartments left partially open and rained down on her.

Llorona sat up with a gasp, reached up, and pulled away the oxygen mask covering her mouth. The doors of the ambulance stood open, and outside she could see the side of a Portland street, with a handful of people clustered around the ambulance. They were in various states of injury. An EMT — a strong-looking woman with short blonde hair and a small smear of soot-and-blood across her forehead that she probably didn't know she had — glanced up from where she was caring for an older man in his fifties. His suit coat was cut away, and his good white collared shirt underneath was soaked through with blood.

Immediately, Llorona dropped the oxygen mask and began to unbuckle where she was safety-strapped to the gurney.

"Ma'am!" The EMT half-stood, though she couldn't make it all the way to her feet without releasing pressure on the man's abdominal injury. The man groaned at the jostling, like he might pass out. "Please, I need you to stay back—"

"I'm a trained emergency responder with the Golden Cross," Llorona said, shifting out of the gurney and moving to the entry to the ambulance. "I'm fine, and you look like you could use some help."

Sighing in frustration, the EMT nodded and reached up with one hand, and Llorona leapt out of the back of the vehicle, steadying herself with the EMT's assisting hand. Landing, she turned around and assessed her surroundings. She knelt next to the ambulance worker.

"Here, let me," she said. "I can apply pressure easily enough. That woman over there—the one by the tree—she's having breathing problems." Hesitating for only a moment, the EMT nodded her thanks and retrieved her kit and a mask-and-tubing, and crossed to the woman quickly, speaking in confident, soothing words to the woman who would be in a full panic if she had the oxygen to do so.

"It's alright, sir," Llorona said to the half-conscious businessman. "You're in good hands." He nodded weakly at her, and leaned his head, with a slight thunk that made Llorona wince, against the heavy chromed bumper of the ambulance. Continuing to apply pressure and occasionally checking his pulse, Llorona looked around.

People were clustered here, just behind a police cordon. They were still pouring in from the zone where she could only assume was where the fight was going on. Goddamn the Prometheans. They'd clearly been investigating the Sacred Band at the same time she and her friends had been investigating them. It was unlike anyone these days to make these kinds of attacks in broad daylight in the continental United States. She didn't need a particularly high degree of cunning to figure out what was going on here. She muttered the whole plan quietly to herself, using the words as much to soothe the businessman (by tone, at least) as to pick apart the plan.

The Prometheans sought a fight with the Sacred Band where the DTPA and other law-enforcement agencies can engage them quickly. The EITF shows up in full force — as they always do when there is danger to a major urban area from a superpowered brawl. The Prometheans get out thanks to Claviger's powers, leaving the Sacred Band to shoulder the blame. With the Sacred Band in prison, there would be no one to step up to whatever it was the Prometheans were doing. Even if anyone were willing to believe them about the Prometheans, it would take too long to track them down and do something about them.

End result: The Prometheans get away scot-free. The Sacred Band gets prison time *at least*.

The blonde EMT — Flanders, her name-patch said — came up next to her. "Keep pressure on it for just a few moments more, please," she said, while she checked his breathing and heartbeat with a stethoscope, and double-checked his pulse. "Thanks for your help," Flanders said, with a grim smile. "Not enough hands with all this bullshit going on."

She glanced nervously at Llorona. An ambulance pulled up, and she waved the EMTs over, directing them to take the man with the bleeding laceration, rattling off what was wrong, and what was needed, following them as they did so. She nabbed up some of the extra supplies they carried — "Thanks, used all of these up!" — and returned to her ambulance, where Llorona stood. Both women glanced toward the barricades.

"Looks like it's slowed some," Llorona said.

"Yeah. Overheard the cops say that the fighting had pulled a little further south, deeper into the South Waterfront." She glanced back at Llorona nervously. "You're one of them, aren't you?"

Llorona gave her an appraising smirk. "Golden Cross credentials give it away?"

"That, and it was some flying ginger kid who brought you here."

"Several of us — my friends and I, who are all Echoes, yes — were in a house up there." She pointed up toward the slash of devastation that cut an obvious line down the eastern ridge of the West Hills. "They attacked us. My friends aren't doing this out of fun. They're fighting for their lives right now."

The EMT nodded, and Llorona glanced down the street, past the police barricade. "Where did you say they were?" Llorona turned to her and asked. Flanders shook her head. Llorona grasped her hand. "Please. These are two good kids. Young kids who don't deserve to be *murdered* by these people. You and I both know that police response is to get people out of the way and then wait for the EITF to show up and sort it out. These people — our attackers — are stone cold killers, and I'm *not* going to let them die."

Flanders looked down at Llorona's hand, and then back into her eyes.

"Please," Llorona said. The silence hung heavy between them, Llorona pleading, Flanders resisting. She was probably worried about being an accessory to whatever superhero-powered crime she was imagining Llorona and the others were up to.

"You gotta tell her," a thin black man sitting on the curb a few yards away said. He was holding a small kid in his lap, the little boy's head in bandages. "That redhead kid, he saved me and my brother here from this straight-up shadow monster. He coulda gotten away really easily, and just left us there, but he didn't. He distracted him by letting the creep punch on him for a while. Gave me and Petey time to get away."

The little boy—who couldn't be older than ten or so—nodded solemnly, watching them with big wide brown eyes, one of which was beginning to develop a deep bruise. Flanders tore her gaze away from them and back at Llorona sharply. "I can't believe I'm doing this," she said, with another glance around to make sure no one else was listening. "Last I heard over the radio was that the fight was in that park south of the Ross Island Bridge. Elizabeth Caruthers Park, it's called. They're trying to tighten the cordon, so it's not going to be easy to get there."

Llorona took her hand once again in her own, and raised it to her lips.

"Thank you, so much. Don't worry. I can get there." She paused, and smiled back at the EMT. "I'm Llorona, by the way."

The blonde woman smiled. "Emily. Flanders, Emily Flanders."

With that, Llorona turned and dashed off.

"Go kick their asses!" Pete's big brother shouted after them, and little Petey hollered a "Yeah!" His brother shushed him.

"Yeah," Emily Flanders whispered, and then turned to the brothers. "Hey, Petey. Can I take a look at your head really quickly? How bad does it hurt? Do you feel like throwing up?"

* * *

The rumbling got worse the closer she got to the South Waterfront. So did the heat, burning off Portland's normally humid air — inhaling it was like taking a breath in a clay oven. Llorona prayed that this was something that Deosil was doing intentionally, but she had her doubts.

Finding them wasn't too difficult. She had to admit that the DTPA was right in one regard: fights between the Changed always wrecked the terrain. She couldn't help but feel for the people who'd been injured and terrified by the fight.

This could *never* happen again.

She was terrified herself of the EITF's arrival. She'd seen them in action against superpowered gangsters before once, out in New Mexico. They were brutal and to the point, a superpowered black ops team, and she did not want to end up on the pointy side of that particular weapon. That said, though, it was weird that they weren't *here* yet.

A moment before she saw the blur, she heard the strange buzzing sound of hyper-fast boots on pavement. Fortunately, decades of operating in disaster situations honed Llorona's intuition and made her willing to trust it without second thought. She shrieked, and her body phased out of sync with the world around her, just as Velocity tore around a corner and ran *through* her. Llorona gasped with the sensation, stopping her sonic field, but Velocity was long past her and almost a full block away. She screeched to a halt, and the two women turned to regard one another.

Llorona wasn't sure that she could hit the speedster with one of her screams, but she didn't have to. A noise above them turned out to be Gauss, skating along what Llorona assumed were the steel girders inside the stone facade of one of downtown Portland's older buildings, and with him came his cloud of steel projectiles. Without missing a beat, they shot toward Velocity like a swarm of angry chrome wasps, but she was too fast — the orbs slammed into the concrete sidewalk where she'd just been standing, leaving a spiderweb of cracks in the pavement, and a total lack of Velocity.

She was gone again.

Gauss dropped down next to her. "Don't know how she got out of the burrito, but she clearly isn't interested in doing it again. Let's get above the street," he suggested, and she hesitated, decided not to ask, and nodded. He wrapped his arms around her, and jolted upward, getting her to the top of the building. It showed some signs of combat as well, and even a few spatters of blood. As they reached its height, Llorona stepped away and found blood on her sleeve and side.

"Gauss, are you injured?" she asked, turning him half around. Two deep furrows gashed his uniform down the back, long slices that split the tough material. Blood soaked either side of the injuries.

"Yeah, a little," he mumbled. "Mercy got me just before you got here. I'm barely feeling any pain from them, though, and I'm pretty sure they've stopped bleeding. I'll get them patched up as soon as we get Deosil out of this mess." He gestured to the sidewalks below, and his ball bearings tore themselves loose from the sidewalk with the sound of concrete crumbling and flew back into his orbit.

"What's going on?" Llorona asked. She was not happy about having to leave his injury as it was, but she also had to recognize the situation they were in. He wasn't dying from it, so it would have to wait.

"She's out there," he said ominously, pointing toward the patch of green a block or two away. The ground was cracked and shattered and steam emanated from those cracks. A lambent flame moved among the greenery, and a bed of flowers and small patches of lavender shriveled and blackened. Some of it was still burning. Off to one side was a concrete circular splash pad: a shallow pond, with small domes of concrete sticking up out of it, which occasionally emanated little splashes and jets of water, sending them into the air, intended to cool hot days.

It would have been a pleasant sight were it not for the demon-girl who stood in the middle of it. The water of the splash pad had already turned to steam, and it hung heavy around her. Deosil was no longer actively on fire, but her skin was soot-black, and bore small cracks in that glowed a cherry red, pulsing in time with her breaths.

"What's going on?" Llorona repeated, glancing at Gauss. The young man met her gaze warily, and then shook his head.

"I don't know." His voice was small, and tired, and out of hope. "Jesh...I don't know. Her power is crazy strong — I don't think I ever knew just how strong."

"And neither of you ever would have, if the DTPA had anything to say about it," Llorona sighed. "Is she out of control?"

"Kinda?" he said, all uncertainty and concern. "I think she's hearing voices, Llorona."

"*Dios mio.*" The older woman crossed herself. Llorona leaned over the edge of the building, staring intently. "Is that Mercy down there? Darting from cover to cover, staying just out of her line of sight?"

"Where? Yeah. They've been..." He swallowed. "They've been hunting each other for a few minutes now. Mercy hurt her pretty badly earlier. I think she's running on elemental mojo and pure rage right now, Llorona. I saw the stab wounds; Jesh is really injured."

"Very likely true. So, here's what we're going to do. You're going to get the drop on Mercy while I see about helping Deosil out of her tailspin. What about the others?"

Gauss shook his head in aggravation. "I had Velocity wrapped in steel earlier, but I'm betting Kaamos freed her. Except for when she started hunting you just a minute ago, I haven't seen anyone but Mercy for almost ten minutes now."

"That's bad," she said. "Keep an eye out — they're probably regrouping."

"Gotcha," Gauss said. "Give me a minute to pounce on Mercy, and then you move in. Just don't hurt her, okay?"

"Never." She said it with a vehemence that gave Gauss no choice but to trust in it.

He quickly got both of them back to the ground, and they split up. Llorona approached head on, using cars and other terrain to work her way quietly around the park's edge. It was hard going — she had to make sure that Mercy didn't see her, while also keeping track of the possibility of ambush by Velocity or Kaamos.

She really, really wished either Sentinel or Optic were here in the middle of this with them. The area trembled again, this time more stridently. No time for wishing, though. Time to *do* something, and she was in the area to do it.

For his part, Gauss skated parallel to the park on the light-rail tracks that ran next to it. He was practically a speedster himself with that speed, and Mercy couldn't help but see him coming. At the last moment, he flung his ball bearings across the distance between them, scattering them shotgun-wide. Desperation gave flight and power to the attack.

Mercy ran toward them, knives in hand. She leapt, putting one foot down on the park bench in front of her, and kicked upward. *Damn it*, Gauss swore

— the arc took her over most of the ball bearing spread, which he'd fired wide rather than high. She pulled her feet upward at the last moment, carrying herself entirely over the deadly barrage, and came down on the other side of it. She landed into a smooth forward tumble, and was running toward him again.

She dove for him, knives first. He could already tell that those wickedly sharp things were ceramic or something else distinctly non-metallic. He'd paid the price earlier in their fight for making assumptions about them, and had no intention of adding another couple of slashes to the ones that ran down his back, narrowly missing his spine.

Reacting quickly, he reversed the attraction of his gear to the metal of the light rail track. He did so faster than his body could prepare — she was coming too fast and he had no choice — so he was suddenly fired into the air as out of a cannon, all boneless rag-doll that arced upward. As he did so, however, he also pulled on the train track itself, pulling the area directly under him directly upward.

It tore itself free from its moorings and bent in half.

Mercy couldn't stop in time — where once had stood a boy she was preparing to bury those blades in, there was suddenly a seven-foot-tall arch of rail-steel, and she slammed into it. She grunted with the impact, skidded halfway around it, and slid by, slamming and sliding into the pavement knee-first and tumbling the rest of the way to the ground.

Unfortunately, Gauss couldn't get his power under control in his mid-air tumble, and he took an uncomfortable dance with gravity himself. He pushed a buoying field of magnetic energy beneath him, pushing his gear away from the metallic grillwork that formed the foundation of the sidewalk. There was too much momentum and not enough magnetic power in time to avoid impact entirely, but instead of slamming into the sidewalk, he skidded sideways away from it, sliding face-first into a charred length of flowerbed, raising a massive gout of ash and still-burning cinders.

Halfway across the park, Deosil watched Gauss skid helplessly to a stop. She shrieked in furious rage. The heat in the area spiked a good ten degrees immediately, and waves of heat roiled off of her. Suddenly, there was someone in her path.

"Deosil!" Llorona shouted. She wore her shawl tied to the lower part of her face, hoping to filter out some of the heat and soot. Deosil turned toward her in a rage, but then paused.

The young woman was clearly angry — she lashed out verbally, but all that came out was a strange, snapping glossolalia, nonsense words that gave form to what she was experiencing while in the grip of the elemental powers she communed with.

"Deosil, please, you have to listen!" Llorona said again, raising her voice. "You're tearing Portland apart. You've got to pull back, or you're going to trigger a tectonic event of some kind. Portland is built over an active volcano, and you're going to push it into an eruption. Please!" The shaking of the ground nearly knocked her off her feet, and she stumbled into Deosil. The contact seared her skin, though it wasn't bad enough to raise an actual burn. She gasped with the sudden pain and snatched her hand away, though, pressing it to herself with teeth gritted in pain.

As though someone had thrown a switch, Deosil exhaled a ragged, hot breath, and sank to her knees. The lambent flame beneath her skin faded and died, the cracks disappearing, and the strange earthy-sooty flesh began to flake off, leaving her rich bronze skin smooth and unmarred beneath.

She wrapped her arms around Llorona and burst into tears. The older woman pulled the weeping girl to her, smoothing her hair. "Shh, shh, *mija*. It's okay. You're alright. You're safe."

Llorona pulled away from her for a moment, feeling around the girl's torso. "Let me see, yeah? Rusty said you were injured badly — let me check you?" Deosil sat back on her heels and pulled the top of her DTPA uniform up enough to see three nasty stab wounds. The skin around them was puckered and angry, but the bloody middles were sealed and scabbed over with what had to be burnt blood.

"*Dios*," Llorona swore, poking at one of them carefully. "They look *cauterized*."

"Down!" Deosil tackled Llorona, shoving both of them aside. Three vicious tentacles speared into the ground where they'd just been. One of them slashed across Deosil's leg as she tumbled aside, and she shouted in pain.

Llorona found Kaamos some ten yards away. A field of ambient darkness floated about him, discoloring the already sooty air and blurring his image. The edges of that field were gathered together into a half-dozen writhing tentacles. Without a thought, Llorona shrieked, pitching her voice high and her focus tight, a lance of pure sonic force.

Kaamos' head snapped back with the impact, and blood burst from his ears. He tumbled over backward, and his shadows retreated around him, pulling inward defensively. He disappeared into his own ambient cloud, and Llorona took that moment to pull Deosil to her feet. Before either woman could say anything, the cloud of twisting, roiling shadows lashed out, a pair of viciously barbed, thick coils of condensed darkness. Llorona pushed the still-stunned Deosil aside, and shrieked instinctively, pitching her voice to let her phase.

Unfortunately, the lashing barbs of darkness were not themselves entirely solid. The attack struck her, and so invested was she in her phasing defense that she could not dodge or roll with the blow. Her scream cut off with a strangled gasp, and blood was everywhere.

"Llorona!" Deosil rose to one knee. Instinctively, she leapt, reaching upward as she did so, arms raised high. Kaamos was already turning toward her, his tentacles rearing back to strike. When she came back down, she brought the winds themselves with her.

The air above them darkened ominously and spontaneously. Pressures shifted, and all their ears popped with her efforts as a thin, tight rope of coiled wind spun itself into being, and then arched down, following Deosil's path to the earth.

A tornado, stories tall but only about as big around as a person's torso, shot down out of the sky like a lightning bolt, right on top of Kaamos. The winds snatched first his cry and then his entire body upward into the air. He shot upward, with only a slight arc to his flight, and came down a short distance away, slamming first into a parked car, and then the street with a sickening *thud*.

"And stay down, motherfucker," Deosil said as the winds died around her. She turned to Llorona, who lay unmoving and bleeding. "Oh, no."

Quickly, she cast about. Mercy and Gauss's fight had taken them to the far end of the park, and it looked like it might be moving further south still, into the city streets again. She glanced between the running battle and Llorona lying bleeding in the burnt grass. "Hold on, Rusty," she implored as she picked the slight Latina woman up, fireman style. She spared one last glance in their direction before moving toward the police cordon.

CHAPTER TWENTY-SIX

Portland, Oregon, United States
May 23, 2013

Gauss knew that if he stood still for even a moment, Mercy would kill the hell out of him. So, he did what any reasonable, healthy young person with a murderer in hot pursuit would do — he kept moving. He could get away from her if he wanted to. There were plenty of surfaces with sufficient ferrous metal on or just beneath them that he could rocket himself along easily enough. But he also wanted to keep her attention, so it became a game of cat and mouse.

Dart away, around a corner.

Come sneaking back, just enough to get her attention, and renew the pursuit.

He hurled projectiles at her as he zipped past, slamming into her. Largely ineffectually, he had to admit; she was clearly tough.

That one point where she was hot on his tail and he tore past an alley, and slammed the trash dumpster he saw inside it into her as she passed? That was definitely a story he was going to tell later, if he fucking survived. He was pretty sure he was going to use a line—something about "Sometimes the dumpster comes to the trash instead"—as part of it. He'd seen Deosil carry away a badly injured Llorona. Though he didn't like the idea of being left along with mask-and-knife here — he was pretty sure her superpower was to be an actual monster from a slasher flick — he was glad that both of them were probably on their way to medical attention.

Gauss paused in the mouth of an alley between two buildings. He hadn't seen Mercy in a little too long, and that made him nervous. He landed and spun his ball bearings into a defensive field, pouring all his juice into doing so. He extended his magnetic senses around him. Human bodies distorted the magnetic field just like everything else did, though the warping was too subtle for him to detect anything out beyond a block or so.

Still. Nothing. He didn't like that.

Head awhirl with images of Mercy growing frustrated and going back to knife Deosil instead, Gauss left the alley, and peered down the abandoned city street.

Fuck. Nothing.

He broke for the light-rail line nearby at a dead run. As he moved, he noticed belatedly the big delivery truck parked beside the sidewalk was missing its passenger door. He made the mistake of slowing warily as he noticed it. It was less caution and more confusion that did it, though. Something that Mercy presumably anticipated.

She dropped down from on top of the truck's roof, hr footprint" in the local magnetic field disrupted by the proximity of the much bigger, much more ferrous truck. She carried with her the passenger door, and she'd thrust it in front of her as she fell, angling it so it was between her and the pattern of his spinning ball bearings.

She dropped down right *into* Gauss's field. Ball bearings slammed into the door, denting it and imbedding themselves in it as they impacted.

And then Mercy slammed the bottom of the fucking door into Gauss, using the full force of her leap from the truck top. His magnetic field blunted some of its impact, but Gauss went down as if poleaxed, and his defensive ball bearings flew in every direction. He lay there, stunned but vaguely conscious as she threw the door aside. "Now, little boy," she said viciously. "This bullshit ends." From the small of her back, she drew her knives as she dropped gracefully on top of him, her knees pinning his shoulders.

Desperately Gauss tried to fight past the pain and the spinning in his vision, a combination of his injuries and the toll on his body from protracted use of his power. She shoved the point of one knife under his chin, lifting to press painfully against the sidewalk under him. He tried to reach for his power, but he couldn't focus enough to *breathe*, much less touch the magnetic field around him. His breath came in short, sobbing gasps.

Cold eyes regarded him through the eyeholes in the white mask. "Wish I could say I regretted this, kid," she whispered. "But it's just business."

The point shifted, tracing a burning line down his neck to the hollow of his throat, just above his collarbone.

And then in a sudden flash of blue and white, and with the definitive sound of bones breaking, she was gone. Gauss was dimly aware of the sound of her slamming into a plate glass storefront nearby, and then Sentinel was helping him sit up. "Rusty, are you all right?"

The redhead moaned and wiped blood away from this throat. "Yeah. She didn't…she didn't get a chance to–"

Sentinel spun, on guard, and then froze. "Mata Hari," he said, his voice strangled.

"Oh, *shit*." Gauss tried to get up, but couldn't.

Mercy rose from inside the shop. Her mask was shattered, most of it lying outside of the shop, its pieces scattered in with those of the plate glass window. The woman on the other side of it was lacerated with a dozen or so shallow cuts, though the one that ran from her temple to her cheekbone bled profusely. She was beautiful, with high cheekbones, full lips, and a delicately pert nose beneath dark, mysterious eyes.

Though her hair was shorter, her face somewhat battered, neither man had any problem recognizing her. Mercy was the Original named Mata Hari, a woman with a long history of espionage both corporate and international, who was wanted by nearly every major law enforcement operation on the planet, and was known to have been integrally involved in the Fated Manifesto.

She was the woman who killed Radiant.

Mata Hari paused just long enough to throw Sentinel a mocking half-smile. "Damn, Sentinel. I wish you'd left me a little time with the redhead there. I was hoping to make it two for two in the competition to see how many of your boyfriends I could end."

And then, she disappeared into the back rooms of the shop.

Sentinel roared in fury and took off, launching himself into the shattered storefront.

"Mitch, wait!" Gauss cried, but it was too late — he was in hot pursuit. The interior of the building basically exploded outward as something inside slammed into load-bearing walls and the entire thing started to come down.

Desperation and adrenaline let him ignore his weakness and injuries, and Gauss pulled himself magnetically away from the two-story structure before it could collapse on top of him. He slingshotted across the street and skidded to a halt just above the hood of the car he'd yanked himself towards. He half-slid and half-tumbled across it, ending up on the sidewalk on the other side of it.

For just a moment he let himself breathe as the building finished falling down behind him. Choking dust billowed up and covered the block, and debris rained down on the street on the other side of the car.

This was fucking terrible. Sentinel was going to kill Mata Hari, and though he knew he should stop him, he wasn't sure he could. Or wanted to, really. Fuck her. She *deserved* to die.

Still. This was Sentinel, and the idea of him killing someone was…it was too much. Taking a breath, Gauss closed his eyes, already watering from the grit in them (where the hell had he lost his goggles, anyway?). He listened and felt for the eternal hum in the world around him, and locked onto it, until that hum was just an extension of his own awareness.

Two blocks away, a pair of human-shaped distortions in the magnetic field brawled. He could tell immediately which one was which. Sentinel was strong and fast, his silhouette bigger than Mata Hari's. But she was faster, and dexterous beside. The way Sentinel was swinging, he was going to do some real damage if he hit, but she had no intention of letting him do so.

Gauss snapped his eyes open as someone appeared beside him, manifesting into the magnetic field far too close to him for comfort. He scrambled away, or tried to, until he saw it was Optic. "Hey, whoa, whoa," Optic said, his hands reaching out to steady him. "It's just me, Rusty. Sorry. Just me."

"Shit," Gauss said. "You must have been in light form. I didn't detect your approach *at all*."

"I saw you lying here as I flew over. What's the situation?"

Gauss shook his head and wiped muddy tears off his face. "He's going to kill her, Optic."

Optic looked up, where even now both of them could hear the sounds of the fight. He put a hand on Gauss's shoulder. "No, Rusty, it's Sentinel, he's not—"

"Optic!" Gauss interrupted him, clutching his hand. "Mercy. The woman in the mask. It's Mata Hari. It's always been Mata Hari."

Optic's eyes widened and he stood, searching in the direction of the fight, peering through the cloud of dust. For a moment he gauged the distance, and then glanced down at Gauss.

"Go," Gauss said, pulling himself upright to lean against the car. Optic nodded and then flashed away, more light than body.

* * *

The EMT finished field-bandaging Llorona's wound, her mouth set in a grim line and her brow furrowed angrily the entire time. "I knew I shouldn't have let you go back out there," she muttered to the unconscious woman and turned her attention to Deosil. She found she wasn't the only one watching Deosil carefully. The three cops standing by all had their guns trained on her. For herself, the young woman didn't seem to notice, so intent was she on cradling her injuries. She seemed like she was trying to put pressure on them.

"Do you…" Deosil swallowed like it was hard to do. "Do you know Llorona?"

"We met earlier," Flanders said, dragging her medical kit over as she crab-walked into position next to Deosil. "Can I see your injuries?"

"Don't know. Those guys seem like they might start shooting at any second. Might not be too safe to be near me."

Flanders glanced over at the three cops. Two of them kept looking to the other, unsure of themselves and frankly afraid. The third, a much older officer, had a steely glare that refused to pull away from Deosil—just like the muzzle of his gun.

"Officer," Flanders barked. "Can you kindly point that firearm elsewhere?"

"She tore up the South Waterfront," he said in a tone that suggested she was an idiot for even asking.

"Well, I didn't, and I don't deserve to get shot. I'm about to start giving medical aid here, so can you kindly either drag me away in cuffs or put the gun away? I trust your firing discipline, but your rookies there have had their fingers actually on their triggers for the last two minutes, and they're looking really fucking twitchy."

They couldn't get their fingers off their triggers fast enough to avoid him confirming the EMT's words. "Christ," he bit off, and lowered his weapon. None of them holstered them, but fingers were off triggers and barrels weren't pointing at bodies anymore. Emily shook her head; it'd have to do.

Deosil chuckled. "Not their fault. Echoes are serious business. Their training says so."

Flanders snorted. "Five square blocks of devastated city says so, sweetheart." She pulled up the hem of Deosil's tunic to examine some of the injuries under the soot and blood.

"I know. I didn't think it would last as long as this. I didn't know how else to hold them off. Fucking EITF should have been here by now. I've been... we've all been running on desperation and pain up here."

"Yeah, tell me about it," Emily whispered, glancing over her shoulder. "I heard the cops' radios a while ago, after Llorona left earlier. Sounded like the EITF was delayed or something. They're mobilizing SWAT."

Deosil cringed, but nodded. "They don't have a choice. What else can they do?"

"You seem pretty calm about the idea of being in the sights of police snipers."

"Not really. I just...they teach us what to expect, if the shit hits the fan this way. Honestly, I'm surprised they haven't started shooting yet." She was thoughtful. "No, I take that back. They're probably trying to figure out who we are and what we can do."

"It make that much of a difference?" Flanders asked as she began to clean one of the nasty, newly cauterized injuries on Deosil's torso. The girl hissed in pain, and then chuckled raggedly, a forced sound.

"Yeah, it does. They take a shot at someone they can't take out—like someone too tough to injure with regular bullets, or someone like Gauss who can sense them coming and prevent them from hitting him—then the cops are suddenly a target. Their training is really specific about not letting that happen. So, they wait it out, clear the space, and hope either we kill each other off, or the EITF shows up to bust heads legally."

"I don't mind saying that I hope they get here soon."

"Me, either," Deosil agreed, wincing as the EMT covered the injury in gauze and tape. "I think that—wait, what is that sound...?"

Velocity was on them before anyone had a moment to react.

Her decision-making was sound, tactically. She started by disarming the cops, shattering bones with punches from the brass-knuckle-like ridges built into the gauntlets of her costume. Wrist, forearm, shoulder of gun arm, elbow of opposite arm, and then both knees—in that order. One cop after the other.

The snapping of bone sounded like the popping of someone going to town on bubble wrap, along with sudden screams of agony. The three officers were down.

As awful as it was, Deosil was grateful for the delay. It gave her time to push Emily Flanders towards the back of the ambulance, where the door hung open to reveal Llorona strapped to a gurney, unconscious.

"Get her out of here!" Deosil cried. She reached for the flowing, sluggish waters of the Willamette River nearby, inhaling its essence into her from across the distance.

In a moment, Velocity was on her. She didn't stop to gloat or threaten—this was a woman with experience fighting other superpowered folk, and she knew her best asset was her speed. So when she came for Deosil, she was in full motion and swinging like a brawler.

Fortunately for Deosil, she was ready. The essence of water was motion and fluidity. It flowed around obstacles and threats. Deosil spun and ducked, weaved and stepped past Velocity's attacks. She couldn't avoid them all—the speedster was frankly too fast—but most of the blows were glancing strikes at best, and more than enough of them missed to keep Deosil on her feet.

Her martial arts instructor would be proud of her, Deosil thought distantly. Her footwork was perfection, given the situation. Slide the foot, shift balance as part of a dodge, withdraw her trailing foot. She did this, over and over again, occasionally throwing her arms up to deflect strikes to the center of her mass, absorbing the energy of the blows.

Water also disperses energy quickly, reacting to kinetic strikes with ripples and shudders. To those who were watching—Emily from the back of the ambulance, struggling to get back to her feet and the gurney locked down, the incapacitated cops, writhing on the ground in pain—it looked like she was taking more damage than she was. The entirety of her essence was directed to her defenses, sliding and shifting away with each blow avoided, even "riding" the power of some blows into a backward tumble that brought her back to her feet as Velocity closed the distance. All with one purpose: pulling her away from the ambulance.

"Goddamn it!" Velocity swore, taking a step back. The two of them were across the street from where they'd started, in a parking lot full of cars, but empty of people altogether. Deosil could tell that Velocity's endurance was flagging.

"You don't have to do this," Deosil said, anxious to get her to talk. She knew there was no way that she'd be able to talk her out of violence—they were clearly used to it and committed. But if she could just keep her busy, not only would it give the bystanders a chance to get out, but it would also give Deosil an opportunity to try to catch her breath.

She was hurting. Her nerves fired all up and down her body, bombarding her with painful awareness of contusion and burns, trauma to skin, to muscle, to bone. She was only standing because she had to be, because if she didn't, this bitch in front of her was going to straight-up murder her.

"You shouldn't have interfered," Velocity said. "You should never have—"

"I know you and whoever you work for were counting on that," Deosil said. "But that wasn't ever going to happen. Not once we knew." She exhaled, and then watched Velocity, waiting.

"Then you have nobody to blame for your deaths but yourselves." As soon as she started moving—hell, before she was done talking, Deosil inhaled sharply, reaching for the occult essence of the vast body of stone beneath her feet. Velocity's blow was committed and landed before she was even aware of the change in Deosil's skin.

She *howled* as she slammed her fist into the solid stone of Deosil's earth invocation, and both of them heard bones crack. She tried to step back, but Deosil was already moving, stepping forward to snatch the woman up by the front of her costume. Stone hand seized a fistful of the material, bunching it up and yanking her up off the ground, and then Deosil punched her over and over with her other hand.

She punched until bone broke. And she kept punching. At some point, her fear and adrenaline and anger dissolved her earth invocation, and she dropped the woman. Deosil fell with her, and kept punching until Emily Flanders pulled her off her.

"Hey, hey, hey!" The blonde EMT barked in her ear, and bodily hauled Deosil off of Velocity's prone and bloody form. "Stop! She's down! She's not moving, kid."

Deosil took one ragged breath, took in Velocity's bloodied, broken face, and burst into tears, sinking to her knees in horror. Emily spared her a saddened glance as she began rendering the unconscious woman first aid.

* * *

The fight between Mata Hari and Sentinel was bad. It was worse than bad—it was historical, Optic knew. That kind of fight would go into the history books as one more reason to fear supers. The two of them raged up and down Portland's waterside district, tearing up the scene.

To be fair, Sentinel was the one doing the damage—Mata Hari's strikes were surgical and perfectly executed. She came into the fight knowing that Sentinel's force field was weakest when he was using his other powers, so she kept him flying or timed her strikes for when he was lifting heavy things. Those were the moments she struck, and Sentinel was bleeding profusely from what seemed like a dozen superficial wounds, and another handful of deep, ugly punctures.

Optic fought too, diving out of the sky to strike her from behind. He learned after a time or two that she was seemingly impossible to actually surprise—whether or not she was fast enough to react (and she usually was), she seemed to be always aware of attacks. He mitigated this to some extent, keeping his distance and attacking her from surprising angles, directions that gave Sentinel room to move or to set up his own attacks. She definitely felt it when he managed to strike her with one or two of his photonic punches, but he didn't manage it too often.

Finally, though, the end was inevitable. She'd been fighting defensively, moving closer and closer to the river with each exchange. Optic noticed it, and apparently Sentinel noticed it as well. He'd been moving slower and slower, keeping out of the air, boosting his defensive shielding. She slashed through the air at him, landing another couple of glancing blows, and he seemed to reel.

But he was ready. He was more than ready, from where Optic watched. He was *baiting* her, and she took the bait, turning to flee as fast as she could toward the river. The moment she spun on her heel, Sentinel *lunged* and snatched her up in both his arms. Optic could hear the terrible snapping sound from there, and Mata Hari went limp in his arms.

And Sentinel continued to squeeze, shouting in fury the entire time.

"Fuck," Optic said, and dropped out of the sky. "Mitch, you can't kill her!" Optic solidified and grabbed Sentinel's meaty arm. "Please, don't do this, man. I know what she did—she deserves to die, but you're not the one who does that. It's not how the Champions operated, Mitch, and it can't be how Sacred Band does, either!"

Sentinel's grip on her slackened, slightly. Optic could tell that he wasn't applying killing pressure any more, but he continued to clasp her tightly. "Why shouldn't I?" he asked hoarsely. His voice cracked from grief and exhaustion, and Optic could see tears running down his face. "She killed him! He's gone because of her, Optic. How can you ask me not to end her miserable life?"

"Because that's not what we got together for, Mitch." Optic leaned in close, starting to pull on Mata Hari to take her out of his hands, though Mitch resisted. "Our justice system is fucked, yes, but she killed him on national television, Mitch. Once she's in custody, they're going to *fry* her. She's one of the biggest wanted terrorists in the world, and the United States government *can't wait* to execute her. Don't do this. Don't dirty your hands. Don't ruin our name—Sacred Band's name—before we've even started. We're going to have to be better than any other team in your day had to be, because they're going to be hunting for an excuse to arrest and incarcerate us."

Mitch hesitated, and looked down at the woman he was holding. She was breathing shallowly. His grip shifted, and he released her into Optic's hands a little more.

"I know the world has asked so much from you, Mitch. And it's taken even more. But as your teammate, I need to ask for one more thing. You have every right to kill her, every personal reason valid a hundred times. But I'm going to ask you as your teammate—as your team leader, Mitch, like *you* wanted me to be—I'm going to ask you to let her go and help me get her to medical help. Because if you don't, they're going to brand our whole team as murderers, and while you and I are sons of bitches who've probably done our part to earn that, Llorona and Deosil and *Rusty* don't deserve that."

Mitch closed his eyes, strain carving deep lines in his face. "You're right," he whispered, and handed her over to Optic.

"Rusty is a couple of blocks that way. Last I saw him he was in bad shape," Optic said, indicating a direction with a nod of his head. "Right now, we need to make sure everyone on our team is okay. Priority one, yeah?"

Mitch wiped his eyes, and nodded. "Roger. I'll find Rusty."

"I'll get her to secure medical treatment and be right back." Optic rose into the air, his flight slow enough to remain solid so he could carry his burden. Mitch nodded to him, and the man flew away.

Mitch found Rusty half-conscious against the side panel of the debris-dented and dust-covered car. He stood for a moment, just looking down at him, exhaustion and grief like a millstone around his neck. He knelt next to the redhead, who opened his eyes.

"Hey," he whispered.

"Hey yourself," Mitch replied. He ran hands over Rusty's body, checking for injuries.

"You..." the young man winced. "You taking advantage, mister?"

Mitch chuckled, despite himself. "You can't be in too bad a condition if you're flirting with me."

"You're the one getting all handsy up in here," Rusty said, and winced in pain as he sat up. He took a deep breath, and looked around.

"Where is—"

"We're okay for the moment," Mitch said, and shifted to sit next to Rusty, his back against the car. He hesitated for a second, and then placed his hand down on Rusty's. The redhead smiled at him as he took the bigger man's hand, clasping it tightly.

"Did...did you..." Worry creased Rusty's brow, and he faltered.

"She's alive," Mitch said quietly. "Optic stopped me. I don't know how, not really, but..."

Rusty made a strangled sound and leaned into Mitch, wrapping one of his arms around the man's own, and clung there for a minute. "Thank God," he said and pulled away slightly. Tears had scored muddy tracks down his dusty face, and he just managed to smear it.

"He's a good leader," Mitch said simply.

In a few moments, Optic returned and he wasn't alone. A banged up Deosil was with him, and he carried with him another, half-conscious form: Claviger.

"Ah!" Rusty hefted himself to his feet and everyone ignored the quick loss of balance as he did so that had him nearly falling down again. Deosil crossed to him and then they were hugging, apologizing and scolding in shifts.

"We have to finish this," Optic said as Mitch stood to examine their prisoner. "If the Pile-On Boys get here, this entire affair becomes DTPA and DoD jurisdiction, and they aren't going to go after the people these dickheads work for."

"So, what are you thinking?" Mitch asked.

"This one is going to use his power to get us to the Promethean headquarters, wherever that is. And we finish this, and get anyone who is still alive out of there once and for all. We're here to rescue these people—this fight was not us finishing this mission."

Hesitantly, Mitch nodded. "Agreed. Have you seen or heard from Llorona?"

Optic nodded. "She's in pretty bad shape. In an ambulance headed for the hospital last I saw. I found them trying to convince Deosil to do the same."

Rusty and Deosil joined them.

"I refused. We're seeing this through to its end, whatever that means," Deosil said. She was frightened, but more than that? She looked *resolved*. This was not the same fearful young woman who'd driven them back to Portland after Rusty's stay in the DTPA's Cascades hospital.

"Agreed," Mitch said with a smile. "Now help me get Claviger conscious again, would you?"

Rusty pulled Optic aside.

"Hey, I just wanted to..." Rusty paused. "I just wanted to thank you."

"For what?" Optic's brow furrowed.

"For not letting Mitch kill Mata Hari." He looked embarrassed. "I guess I just assumed that, you know, you were military, and..."

Optic laid a hand on the younger man's shoulder and squeezed. "I get it. This might shock you, but military tactics are about preserving life as best we can, even in awful situations."

He glanced back at Mitch, who was watching bemusedly as Deosil made a small stream of water from a nearby hydrant dance around her weaving fingers, dropping a cupful or so onto Claviger's sputtering face.

"Besides. Killing changes you. Nobody knows that better than I do, Rusty. And it would have definitely changed him. And I couldn't stand to see that happen." He glanced back at Rusty, a shy smile creeping across his face. "You weren't the only one that idolized Sentinel as a kid, you know. Hell, he's the reason I signed up for the Air Force and then Project: Seraphim in the first place."

Rusty just stared at Optic for a moment, and a smile broke across his face. "Yeah?"

"Yeah. Dreams of flying, man. All my life."

"Hey, you two," Deosil said. She crossed to them as Mitch continued to hold onto Claviger. "We know where we're going now."

"I wonder if we shouldn't find some place to hold up? Patch some wounds, get a breather?" Optic said.

Mitch shook his head. "They'll know their team failed to kill us. They'll know we know where they are. They're probably wiping evidence and shutting everything down right now."

"So that means the people they took–" Deosil said.

"Are evidence, too," Optic said grimly. "Alright. You're right. We go now. Guess we've all got to just rub some dirt in it and keep going."

Mitch turned to the battered old priest. "Open the portal now. You and I are going through first—I can get back to here from anywhere in the world you take us, so this had better be the right place."

The old man nodded wearily. "Believe me, I have every investment in you and yours taking out the Prometheus Consortium. They tend to have nasty imaginations when it comes to failure, so the more trouble you can cause them, the less they'll have to come after me with."

"Do it, then," Optic said, and the priest raised his hands and opened the gates of Heaven.

CHAPTER TWENTY-SEVEN

Central Forest Reserve, Dominica, the Caribbean
May 23, 2013

It was gut-wrenching and dizzying, like the world's most insane roller-coaster. But the effects on the body were nothing compared to what it did to... the emotions? The spirit? Maybe even the soul? Exaltation was a term that came to mind, the sense of being in the presence of some great Mystery, an unknowable, ineffable thing that transcended the human experience. It was like coming home, in some way, and might have inspired the formation of entire religions, if it weren't over so fast.

They stepped through Claviger's gate into the swelter of an island jungle, the light of the day bleeding away quickly in the west. Sentinel was the first through, pushing Claviger—hands bound behind him—ahead of him. They were followed by Optic, who was almost immediately airborne, circling low overhead.

"Where's the base? This is the middle of the jungle," Sentinel all but growled.

Claviger sighed. "This is the only spot I know. They never actually allowed us into the base—we've never seen it. Our job was to deliver the...packages here. That's all."

"You mean kidnap victims." Sentinel set the thin priest at the rootball of a wiry broadleaf tree, and the older man slid down to crouch at its base, watching them warily. "Don't give me any trouble," Sentinel warned, and Claviger nodded. Sentinel turned and reached out to Gauss as he stumbled through, keeping him from falling. The pupils of his blue eyes were blown wide, and he shuddered as he steadied himself against the bigger man's arm.

"Whoa," Gauss said. It was almost night here, though the heat of the day hadn't dispersed yet. Deosil emerged last, and Gauss caught her hand to steady her. "You okay, Jesh? You really took a beating back there."

"You both did," Sentinel said. "If I had my way, you two would be getting medical attention right now."

"Llorona's going to be getting enough of that for all of us," Gauss said.

"She's also going to be taking the heat for all of us with law enforcement," Deosil reminded him, clearly unhappy at the thought.

"No, she's not," Optic said, landing beside her. "We're finishing this, and we'll be going to see the authorities. She's not taking this blame for us."

"We're not outlaws. We'll take responsibility for our actions, once doing so doesn't put even more people in danger." Sentinel glanced at Optic. "You see anything?"

"Nothing for a good distance, as far as I can tell. Thick jungle canopy, though. Could be hiding anything."

"No, there's something," Gauss said, looking around. "Big concrete and metal complex, about...mile and a half away or so? I think that—ah, crap!" He snapped his head around and gestured, yanking a metallic object to him from the concealment of the underbrush with the sound of rending metal and a quick flashing arc of electricity from its base. He held it up for the others to see—a camera.

Optic turned to regard Claviger furiously. The priest held his hands up. "I don't have the camera locations memorized! I didn't even know they had one at our normal landing point. Besides, the security team has tons of cameras, but they only have so many eyes at one time," he said placatingly. The sweat that rolled down his forehead was only partially because of the lingering heat. "They only saw us if they had that camera view active. Besides, *we're* the ones they usually sent to investigate things like this."

"Speaking of the rest of you, where did Kaamos end up?" Deosil asked the older man. Gauss realized it was the first time he'd seen the man face directly since his capture.

The priest shuddered a little. "He bribed me to get him out of Portland," Claviger said. "He asked me to open a gate for him to Reykjavik, where he knows some people. He's gone to ground."

"What do we do with him?" Gauss said to the others, gesturing at the priest. "We can't just let him go."

"We're not," Optic said. He turned to Claviger. "Here's what you're going to do. You're going to open up a gateway to that room in the Crypt. I know you can—you've done it before. We're going to leave Gauss's shackles on you, and we're going to drop you in that room. You're going to go through, and be arrested, and you're going to admit your full role in all of this. If you're very lucky, you'll be the first conscious member of your team to be able to rat out what you and the other Prometheans have been doing, and so you'll be the one who gets to cut a deal."

Claviger didn't say anything, but he did furrow his brow. Optic held up a hand.

"You'll probably have time to escape before they can scramble a response, in all likelihood. And that's fine—you'll fucking wait for them anyway. Because if you run, we are going to tear this little globe apart until we find you, and your power is anything but subtle." Optic paused and smiled. "Do the right thing, though, and we'll put in a good word on your behalf."

The priest smirked. "I don't get the impression that your reputation is going to be any better than mine, once all is said and done. American laws consider us pretty much the same thing right now, don't they?"

Sentinel raised his chin and glared at the smaller man. "Maybe in the short term. But you're smart—do you really want to gamble on it staying that way?"

Claviger sighed, and held his hands out to Gauss. "No, not with Sentinel on the team. There'll be people positively salivating to back your re-appearance as a superhero, or whatever. Your offer is probably the best thing I've got going for me. Ready when you are."

The former priest closed his eyes and concentrated, and space rent itself once more with a cascade of shimmering celestial light. Deosil winced as he did it.

"You cool?" Gauss asked, worried.

She nodded. "It just kinda hurts the world when he does that. Really messes it up."

Sentinel stepped between Claviger and the coruscating portal. "Wait. I'm going through first." Claviger sighed and nodded. Sentinel stepped through, and the gathered group waited.

After a couple of minutes, Gauss looked to Optic. "What do you think is taking so–"

At that moment, Sentinel stepped back through with a smile on his face. "Sorry. I took a second to rouse the MPs. They're waiting for him on the other side." Claviger groaned and shuffled through the display of numinous illumination.

After a moment, it closed itself without a sound, though it left a strange psychic echo, like a ringing in the mind rather than the ears.

"Okay," Optic said. "Let's do this."

* * *

"I'm not sure how I missed that," Optic said unhappily. The compound was half driven into the base of a small range of mountains in the middle of the wildlife preserve.

Sentinel hovered in midair next to him. He pointed to the expanse of jungle-hued netting and overhangs. "Sight baffles and camouflaging. Probably intended to prevent drones and satellites from spotting them mainly, but it works pretty well against fast fly-overs."

"Good thing that's not all we have to rely on, then," Optic said with a grin over at Gauss, using his power to keep himself and Deosil aloft beside them, just above the tree cover.

"That much steel and concrete fucks with the local magnetic field. Messy," Gauss said.

Deosil frowned and glanced at Gauss. "I can sense it, too."

"Really? How?" Optic asked.

She tsked. "I'm not sure. It's weird. It's like the jungle is really wild, and the compound sticks out because of the contrast. I don't normally notice the difference, because most wild areas transition pretty gently into settlements and everything, but this sticks out like a sore thumb."

"I bet that's something you could cultivate with some practice," Optic said with a smile. "It's a useful ability."

"What's the plan?" Sentinel asked.

Both Optic and Deosil turned their attention back to the compound ahead. "Two directions," Optic said, after a moment of studying the compound tucked into the shadow of the higher terrain. "Me and Sentinel come in high, and start tearing shit up. Terrorize those armed guards."

"Who are they, do you think? Local military?" Gauss asked, concern on his face.

"Definitely not." Optic shook his head. "Mercenaries, guaranteed. An outfit like this might operate with the blessing of the locals, but they're not going to trust them with any part of their security. These are professionals."

"What...what are we doing?" Deosil asked the question almost like she dreaded the answer.

Optic smiled at her. "While we make a big noise, you and Rusty get to that front gate and rip it up. We need an easy get away for anyone we free. We don't know how long we'll have or what sort of rescue situation we can reasonably set up, so the more we can facilitate escape at every stage of the operation, the better. An operation like this also has employees that are...well, if not innocent, many of them are either ignorant of what's going on, or they're desperate enough to collect the paycheck anyway. Any sign of trouble, and they'll get off the scene themselves, which is what we want."

"Cool. We can do that." Gauss reached out to squeeze Deosil's hand, and she smiled at him gratefully. "Should I static radio in the area, too?"

"Definitely," Optic said. "We don't want them radioing for help—the fewer targets we have to deal with, the quicker and neater we get this wrapped up."

"Can we tell anything about the rest of the compound?" Sentinel asked. "The parts we can't see?"

"Just that it exists," Gauss said. "We get in a little closer, I'll be able to tell lots more, but the vehicles and structure outside of it is blurring things in the magnetic field too much for me to get any detail."

"Alright, then," Optic said. He looked at Sentinel. "Let's make some noise."

Deosil and Gauss watched the two of them speed off: Optic straight up into the night like a flare, definitely attention-grabbing in his arc toward the compound. Sentinel shot off in a low arc, circling around the compound so he could come up behind it, approaching behind the cover provided by the mountain itself.

"They're so badass," Deosil said with a grin. She looked at Gauss, and found him peering off in the direction Sentinel had taken. She snorted, and elbowed him. "Wipe up the drool, coppertop. We got a job to do."

He bumped her shoulder with his own, and the two sank low beneath the jungle canopy and floated closer.

* * *

At the peak of his arc, Optic resolidified. He floated in midair for a few breaths, and then began to fall. He angled his body downward, headfirst, arms tucked tight against his body. The wind beat against his face mercilessly, and he closed his eyes against the fury of his own fall. He'd done this before: a leap into the air, all brilliance and light, and then a shift to his non-photonic body. Those watching him simply saw a light rise above them and then wink out entirely. Watchers couldn't help but keep searching the sky for a threat, and in the dark, there was almost no way to see him plummet toward the earth.

A couple of stories above the ground, Optic opened his eyes, squinting against the wind, and decided he was close enough. In a burst of light, he shifted and exploded like a flashbang above the ground. Soldiers searching the dark sky above them were blinded and dazzled, and he swooped in, coming just above the ground and solidifying enough to tear his way through the camo netting that shrouded the open center of the compound.

He ducked even lower as the netting shredded to flap in the night breeze, and paramilitary types scattered like bowling pins. He didn't even have to touch most of them: simple tactical logic said that when a man who looks like a living laser comes at you, you get the hell out of the way. He heard more than one of them shouting into radios that only piped back crackling static, and he silently thanked Gauss.

Mercenaries panicked and fired weaponry at him, bullets whizzing through his light-body, once again phased completely insubstantial. Optic almost wanted to laugh, because they were treating him like the big threat. He couldn't blame them of course—all the light and fury of his approach, and the suddenness of the attack was intended to make them think exactly that.

It is because of this that they were entirely unprepared for the massive boulder that landed in the middle of the compound's motor pool. As a cohesive unit, they stopped and craned their heads upward to see the most recognizable super in human history floating above them, illuminated in the night sky by Optic's brilliant light. In one hand, held straight up above his head, Sentinel hefted a second boulder, easily as big as the first. With his other, he saluted them.

And then he dropped the second boulder.

Nearly a dozen armed and armored mercs fled for cover, just as the second boulder impacted the first from about fifty feet in the air. The stones cracked against one another, and stone shrapnel and pulverized earth exploded everywhere.

If their plan was to make lots of noise, they succeeded. Civilians streamed out of the offices in the main compound, and out of the two motor pool garages, all of them aiming to get as far from the compound as they could. Chunks of stone and bits of fencing animated themselves to leap into the paths of those who sought to diverge from Deosil and Gauss's planned escape routes, and those fleeing quickly righted themselves to take the paths already planned for them.

In less than five minutes, the compound was largely abandoned, save by the few actual defenders who remained. And they were fair game as Gauss and Deosil caught up.

Sentinel caught Optic's attention. "Hold up." He pointed to something on the horizon, and Optic stopped sniping light blasts at mercenaries behind cover long enough to get a look at it. "What is that?"

Optic stared at it for a moment, and his face fell. "Shit."

"Is it a missile? Are they firing ballistics at us? At their own base?"

Optic shook his head. "Nope. Not a missile. I'll be back." Without another word, he shifted into a sudden torrent of white-gold light and flew to intercept the low-flying projectile, with its streaming tail of fire and smoke.

"Okay?" Deosil said. "What the hell was that?"

"Trust your teammate," Sentinel said. "He knows what he's doing. We've got this well in hand."

Deosil nodded. "Alright, good point. I've got a cluster of mercs behind those overturned jeeps over there. Rusty?"

"Got 'em," the redhead said, and metal shrieked nearby.

* * *

Turbine pulled up short as Optic materialized in front of him, and hovered there for a moment, occasionally sputtering jets of flame and force beneath him to keep him aloft. "Holy shit," the jetfire generator said, and set down on the forest floor. With a glance behind, Optic followed him.

"It *is* you," Turbine said with a laugh, and stepped up. For a moment, Optic thought it might be a feint of some sort, but Turbine wrapped him into a hug.

Turbine was skinny, verging on scrawny. Hell, even in his Air Force days, he'd struggled to keep his mass up to required standards. The last time Optic had seen him, he was wearing a regulation military cut, but now the man's hair was wild and windblown, hanging down over his goggle-covered eyes. He was also grinning like a fool.

Optic eyed what he wore warily, though. It wasn't his black and red Seraph uniform. Instead, he wore a more form-fitting version of the black and grey pattern the mercs at the Prometheans compound were kitted out in. "You're not here as a Seraphim, are you?" Optic said.

"No, man. Took a job with the Knighthawks crew." He paused for a moment, glancing over Optic's shoulder, and then shook his head. "Let me guess. You're the disturbance?"

"Me and some friends, Turbine. Good people, just trying to do the right thing." He looked pained. "I don't want to fight you, brother, but…"

Turbine held up his hands, forestalling him. "Nope. No fighting. They just hired me and assured me my contract wasn't for fighting supers. They're not paying me enough to do that—I'm a glorified scout, that's all."

Optic studied him for a moment and shook his head. "What the fuck, Turbine? Why are they paying you *at all*? Do the Seraphim know you're out here doing this?"

Turbine pushed his goggles up onto his head, shamefaced. "No. No, they don't. The brass has to know I'm gone by now, but I doubt the team does."

"I talked to Jetstream. They think you're still sick, man. They're *really* worried about you." Optic couldn't help his accusatory tone.

The guilt cut deep lines on Turbine's face. "I just can't *do* that shit anymore, Optic." Turbine pulled his goggles off entirely, and the pain in his eyes was real. "It wasn't getting electrocuted that did it. That was just the final straw. I couldn't fight those kinds of battles any more. I wake up with nightmares, man. I can't stop shaking sometimes. I nearly blew out the wall of my apartment because when I woke up to a thunderstorm. I thought I was *fighting* over the Atlantic again. I just…I can't."

"So, what? You bailed?" Optic did his best to keep judgement out of his voice, but Turbine's wince told him he hadn't quite managed it.

"It was too much. We don't get medical discharges, man. It's in those contracts we signed at the beginning of the Seraphim trials. They were going to either force me to keep serving or to lock me up. They don't ever intend on letting any more of the Seraphim go, man. You don't know this, but they did you a favor when they drummed you out."

After a moment, Optic reached out and pulled his old buddy close, embracing him. "Good for you, man."

Turbine pulled back warily. "Yeah?"

"They don't have a right to treat us that way, brother. We're not fucking *property*. We sacrificed everything to serve our country in this way, but that doesn't mean we give up our rights as human beings." He glanced back over his shoulder. "Look. When you get the chance? Ring me. Same number as when I left. I've got lawyers that I think can help you—they did great things for me."

Turbine shook his head. "You still trying to look after me?"

"Somebody needs to," Optic said with a grin, shoving the man away. "You were always pretty shit at looking after yourself."

The two men regarded one another affectionately, until a loud noise behind them pulled them both back into what was going on tonight.

"Well, what are you going to do now?" Optic asked. "When you report what you saw here, what are the Knighthawks going to do?"

"Man, screw the Knighthawks. Not paying me enough for all of this," Turbine said, and stepped back to clear space for his blasting power. "I'll get back to base and give them a doomsday report, basically. They'll pull their men off the field to try and salvage as much of their force as possible. The bigwigs in that facility aren't paying the company enough to get all their men wiped out. Take care of yourself, Optic. I'll be in touch." He pulled his goggles back down over his eyes.

"You better be, asshole," Optic said fondly, and turned his face away as Turbine rocketed out of the clearing.

* * *

When he returned to the compound, it was a ghost town. Admittedly, a ghost town that seemed to have suffered a catastrophic avalanche from the scattering of boulders and other rocks dropped from a height. He landed next to Gauss and Deosil. The young woman sat cross-legged on the ground.

"Uh, is she alright?" Optic asked Gauss. "She looks green. Like, literally green."

The redhead chuckled. "Yeah. She's invoking the plant life of the area. She can do that to heal injuries and whatnot if she's out in the wilderness."

Optic was impressed. "Huh. Neat trick. Here comes Mitch."

Sentinel landed among them. Deosil opened her eyes and smiled up at him, and the green drained out of her face. She stood and stretched languidly, rotating joints and extending limbs, checking for lingering pain and injuries. From her grin, she seemed happy with the results.

"Showoff," Gauss muttered, rubbing at a sore spot on his side, and she blew him a kiss.

"So, what's the situation?" Sentinel asked, checking back in the direction Optic came from.

"That was one of the Seraphim. Former Seraphim, now, it turns out. Not going to be a problem for us—he's withdrawn."

"Good," Sentinel said, glancing at the cavernous interior of the compound's front face, which was torn away, revealing an interior of cinderblock and corrugated steel construction. "The defenders have retreated further into the compound. Gauss says they're behind a thick set of steel doors right about where the compound drills into the base of the mountain proper. Shielded by bedrock, mostly."

"That going to be a problem for us to get into?" Optic asked, with a glance at the redhead.

Gauss scoffed. "It's a steel door. No. We were just waiting for you to get back before we punched our way into there. Wanted to make sure you weren't going to need back up."

Optic grinned. "Let's do this, then."

"I'm not going to be able to stop the bullets if I'm hauling on the big security doors, though," Gauss said after a moment studying it. "The minute those open even an inch, they're going to start firing through it."

"Stand behind me," Sentinel told him. "One hand on my back. I can shield us both."

They got into position, Sentinel standing facing them, shoulders wide and stance broad. Gauss stood behind him, and with a moment's hesitation, laid his palm into the middle of the wide, muscled expanse of Sentinel's back. He glanced at Deosil for a half-second, grinning like a loon, and she rolled her eyes at him.

A crackle across his skin caught his attention, and Sentinel spoke. "Ready when you are."

"Here we go," Gauss said. He leaned around Sentinel and reached for the doors with his magnetic power. The anchors used to secure the doors into the bedrock of the mountain's roots were too strong to simply rip them from their moorings. Likewise, the locks they had in place were strong and complicated.

Gauss closed his eyes and winced as he tickled magnetic fingers across the internal workings of the door's locking mechanisms, finding the places where hinges gave and internal pieces pivoted on pins. Poking and prodding with his power, the door clicked and pinged ominously, and Gauss could only imagine what the soldiers on the other side of it were thinking as it made little metallic noises at them.

"Aha!" With a final surge of magnetic power, Gauss overrode the mechanisms that sealed the locking pins in place, shoving them aside and up along their normal paths, and a loud bang came from somewhere inside the door. He clenched his fist and yanked back, and the doors began to open.

That's when the bullets started flying.

Gauss nearly lost his concentration over his power the first time he actually saw a bullet fly toward his head only to crumple and deflect away a few scant inches from his face, repelled by Sentinel's telekinetic shield. With a yelp, he ducked back fully behind Mitch. Over and over again they came and ricocheted away, Gauss wincing as the only noise they made were from pinging off of equipment and vehicles around them.

Finally, though, with a final grunt from Gauss, the doors slammed open.

Before the soldiers within were even done wincing from the sudden loud noise, the small entryway into the complex was filled with dusty, swirling winds that blew grit into eyes and forced everyone to take a few steps back.

"Now, lightning bug!" Deosil shouted to Optic, who flashed among the soldiers, shifting states between physical and photonic over and over, a strobe light display that landed with fists. In a moment, he stood in the midst of groaning soldiers, mostly solid again.

"Don't call me *lightning bug*," he groused, pointing at Deosil mock-sternly. She grinned at him. "Okay, but like, no promises." He glared at her for another moment, before winking.

The four of them advanced carefully into the outer area, a vault used for storage of some kind, and Gauss dealt with the much smaller door ahead of them. The electronic keypad entry system squawked indignantly as he scrambled it, pulling open the door magnetically.

The hallway ahead was tiled, some twenty feet wide or so, with a simple metal door at the end of the long corridor. Stepping into the hallway, Sentinel caught his breath, and the others followed shortly after.

"Shit," Gauss said quietly.

The walls to either side of the hallway were all glass, each of them showing a lab. The labs were themselves separated by walls, and the coloration on the glass suggested that they were one-way mirrors, allowing those in the hall to view what was going on inside each of the labs.

"I kinda assumed everything would be all creepy and sketchy, you know?" Deosil whispered. The labs themselves were top-notch quality, all glass and gleaming metal and sterile white surfaces.

"Yeah, I figured it would be all Frankenstein's horror show," Gauss whispered, though he wasn't sure why.

"I'm betting it's horrific enough for them," Sentinel said, pointing. Each of the labs held several gurney-type beds, with benign-seeming electronic monitoring equipment tracking their vitals. "Rusty, can you get these locks open?"

Gauss shook himself. "Yeah, of course," he said. "They're maglocks." The lock ahead of Sentinel buzz-clicked, and then swung itself open. He closed his eyes, and a moment later, every other lab lock in the facility did the same.

Sentinel stepped into the lab in front of them, and Deosil followed. Gauss glanced at Optic. "Something wrong?"

"I'm not sure," Optic said. He turned and walked a little further up the hallway, staring at the lab interiors as he went, and Gauss followed him. One lab in particular stopped him cold, and before Gauss could ask him, Optic flashed into his light form, moving through the clear pane of glass, rematerializing on the other side of it.

The teenaged girl in the strange bed was Asian. The head of the bed was a readout display of some kind, and halfway down, more machinery curved around her, cradling her from solar plexus to thighs. This curve of white plastic and glass displayed a variety of different bars and numbers, but Optic wasn't focused on those. She was clearly plugged into this machine in some way, and Optic looked stricken.

"Do you know her?" Gauss asked, having come into the room after Optic?

"What?" Almost in a daze, Optic turned toward his teammate. He shook his head. "No, no, I...shit."

"You're kinda freaking me out, Optic," Gauss said, and Optic looked up at him with big eyes.

"This equipment, Rusty. I've seen this before." He looked down at hit, and ran a hand over its pristine lines. He reached down under the curve that covered her and pulled back a thin bit of IV tubing. The line was full of a weirdly luminous, viscous liquid and Gauss's eyebrows rose. "Rusty, this is the equipment that was used to Empower the Seraphim. To Empower me."

"Is...is that the–"

"Isotope extract derived from Radiant's remains?" Sentinel asked from the doorway. He crossed to it and paused. "It looks like it."

Optic dropped the line like it had stung him. "Shit. Shit! "Mitch, do you think—I mean, what if–"

Sentinel laid a comforting hand on his shoulder. "What if they used Craig's remains to give you your powers, too?" Optic's face crumpled, and Sentinel hugged him.

"It's possible," Sentinel said, putting his forehead to Optic's, and then pulling back to look him square in the eyes. "We don't know enough to make assumptions, Optic. It might just be that the Prometheans are replicating technology used in successful Empowerments before theirs. It might be that they flat-out stole or purchased the technology. We don't know enough yet. But no matter where your powers came from? You're using them to do the right thing, and there are people here who'll be alive because you're doing so. There's nothing else Craig would have wanted you to do with them."

Optic sniffled, and nodded, wiping his eyes. "Fuck. Yeah, you're right."

Gauss realized that Deosil was standing next to him, looking pale and haunted. He hadn't even seen her approach.

"You okay, Jesh?"

She shook her head. "No. I mean, I've never seen a...some of those people in the beds are *dead*, Rusty." She covered her mouth with her hand. Gauss pulled her into a hug and she sobbed against his shoulder.

Gauss looked over at a grim-faced Sentinel, his hand still on Optic's shoulder.

"But that means that some of them are still alive," Optic said. "Let's get our shit together sufficiently to get them out of here."

Deosil nodded, wiping her eyes. "Yeah. Fuck yeah." She turned to look at Optic and Gauss. "You two start in one of the other labs. Sentinel and I can start in here." Gauss hesitated a moment, glancing back at Sentinel, and then left the room. At the back of the lab, Sentinel studied the IV lines with the strange compound, following them with his fingers to where they went into the wall. He laid one hand on the flat of the wall and studied its surface while Deosil began unhooking IV lines.

* * *

"Holy shit," Gauss said from out in the hall. "That's Kosma!"

Kosma was in one of the labs with the weird slightly luminous IV lines, one of which was inserted into his arm. Gauss started examining the bed he was in, and found the release catch that opened the swoop of glass and plastic electronic displays that covered the middle part of Kosma's body. With a push, he arced it up over the bed.

Kosma was thin and sick-looking, with sunken cheeks and sallow skin. Darkness marred the hollows of his cheeks and under his eyes, and he was slightly clammy to the touch. He wore a dirty medical gown and a simple wristband with a barcode, as well as a variety of sticky pads that adhered monitoring devices to his body. Gauss laid hands on either side of where the IV entered his arm.

"Hang on, hang on," Optic urged the frantic Gauss as he flashed into the room. "Check his vitals. I'll see what he's hooked up to and make sure we can get him free without hurting him."

Biting his lip, Gauss nodded, checking for a pulse at his neck. It was there, but it was faint. Bending close, he could tell he was breathing. Not deeply, but it was slow and steady. In a few minutes, Optic had the IV needle out of his arm, and the monitoring stickers off of him. As far as both could tell, he was simply sleeping.

"This is the guy, I take it?" Optic said with a twinkle in his eye. "Never took you for the long-distance boyfriend sort, Rusty."

Gauss flushed. "No, it's nothing like that. He's just a nice guy. Met him online. He's studying to be an architect, too."

He watched as Optic fidgeted with him some more, straightening his bed gown and pulling the covers up over him to warm him. "Honestly, I doubt he'd even recognize me. Since he went missing, I've been so driven trying to figure out what happened to him, get him back to safety, that I…" He trailed off.

"Never thought about what it would be like to actually meet him?"

Gauss nodded. "Basically. I mean, I doubt he'd even remember me, you know? He's been such a big deal in my brain for weeks now, but I'm basically a stranger off social media to him." He smiled wanly. "Stupid, huh?"

Optic smiled up at him, clearly holding his tongue. Gauss narrowed his eyes. "Alright, say it. You've clearly got something to say."

"I don't want to stir the shit, but you asked me." He reached out and put a hand on Gauss's shoulder. "You kinda *do* that, Rusty."

Gauss brushed his hand off, bristling. "Do what, exactly?"

"You get *focused*. You create roles and identities for people you like, for people you're interested in, and you kinda let it get away from you. You spool out these entire dynamics between you and the person you've projected onto them, and then it hurts your feelings when the real people don't measure up to what's created in your head."

Gauss' jaw snapped shut, grinding his back teeth, and rage drew his eyebrows together. "So, what, I'm a creepy obsessive?"

Optic just shot him *that* look. "Shut up. You're doing it right now. You're projecting some bullshit onto what I just said." Gauss blinked in confusion, and bit his lower lip, like he'd just been slapped.

Optic stepped closer, and put an arm over his shoulder affectionately. "All I'm saying is this—the only thing wrong is that you're impatient. You want closeness with people, but you're kinda running out ahead of them. Give people time, let the actual relationships develop into what they are, instead of imagining what you want them to be and being hurt when the other person is left scrambling trying to catch up to that, okay?"

Gauss realized he was holding Kosma's cool hand, and side-eyed Optic. "Shit. I totally did that with us, didn't I?"

Optic chuckled, and bumped his forehead into Gauss' playfully. "You sure as hell did, crackerjack. Scared the shit out of me, too. I just..." He paused, caught Gauss' gaze, and then glanced into the next lab over where Sentinel stood over another gurney, his back to them. "I just don't want you to keep making that mistake, okay? You deserve good people in your life, and they deserve the real relationships that develop between you two, and not the ones you're projecting there out of impatience and fear. Alright?"

"God, shut up," Gauss whispered, mortified. "He can probably hear us talking right now."

In the other room, Sentinel smiled.

"Something amusing?" Deosil asked, glancing up at him as they unhooked another kid—this one a young Polynesian boy—from the machines.

"Nothing," Sentinel said, shaking his head.

Deosil craned her neck to see the other lab. "Are you eavesdropping on those chuckleheads?"

Sentinel bit his upper lip and dropped his gaze, abashed.

* * *

It took the better part of an hour before everyone was seen to. Nine of the twenty-eight prisoners were dead, and Sentinel and Gauss flew another three to a nearby hospital in one of the coastal settlements. By the time they returned, some of the prisoners were starting to wake up, and their signs were good: warmth and color returned to them quickly.

Optic and Deosil were exploring the rest of the compound, trying to find the room that Medium had seen, without much luck. "It's beneath us," Gauss said when they mentioned it to him. "At least, I'm pretty sure it is. It's the only part of this construction that I can sense that we haven't found access to. I think a concrete tunnel might connect to it from the interior of that storage room at the end of the hall, maybe?" In the end, it was only because of Gauss' magnetic senses that they could even find the damned stairwell down, so well-hidden was the door to the passage.

Gauss paused at the top of the stairwell. "Kosma is waking up. You guys go ahead, okay? I'm going to stay up here."

Kosma was struggling to sit up in his bed when Gauss returned to the room he was in.

"Hey, hey. Careful. Let me help you," he said. "Are you in any pain?"

Kosma shook his head. "No," he said in thickly accented English. "I feel very weak."

"You've been here for a while. Probably under for a while. What do you remember?"

"I…I remember being here, but only for a short time. Sasha and I were… wait, where is Sasha?" He scanned the room, not recognizing any of the others there. His imploring eyes found Gauss, who looked away helplessly. With a sigh, Kosma sat back in his bed. "He…he is dead. Yes?"

"I'm so sorry, Kosma," Gauss whispered. He hesitated for a moment. "I don't know if you remember me, Kosma, but my name is Gauss."

Kosma squinted at him, bleary-eyed. "I…think so? From the architecture group?"

"Yeah. When you went missing, some of your friends got worried, and I did too. We—my friends and I, I mean—we came looking for you. I'm sorry it too us so long, but…" Gauss trailed off. "They didn't make it easy to find you. I'm just sorry it took us so long."

Kosma looked at him for a moment, like he was struggling to understand. He swallowed thickly. "I…I am tired," the young man said, and lay down again, turning his face away so no one would see him cry. Gauss stepped out of the lab to give him some privacy, stopping in to check on some of the others, but not before he'd wiped the wetness from his eyes.

A few minutes later, his teammates came rushing up from the storage room. Sentinel and Optic didn't pause, but practically dove for the exit, while Deosil paused to get him.

"C'mon," she said frantically. "Sentinel said he heard some engines inbound up above."

Gauss closed his eyes for a half-second, and then nodded. "Yeah, he's right. Two choppers, it feels like. Rotor blades of some kind, spinning fast. They're almost here."

They emerged from the remains of the compound's front facade in time to watch the choppers touch down thirty or so yards away. They landed, blades still spinning, and a single man emerged. In his suit and sunglasses, the thickly-built man was unruffled despite walking through the dust-storm caused by the helicopter's turbulence.

"Fuck," Optic said, and a quick glance at him showed that Sentinel recognized the man, as well.

"Marque," Sentinel said in a neutral tone that somehow contained both contempt and a warning.

The man's craggy face split into a grin. "Mitch, old buddy. Long time."

Gauss and Deosil glanced at one another warily. Marque wasn't just the head of the DTPA. He was its founder, and one of the Originals who founded the Champions decades ago. Though he didn't have Sentinel's raw power, Marque was a kinetic manipulator, able to shift, adjust, reverse, and bleed off momentum and kinetic potential in the world around him. He was a cunning combatant, too, and more than one group of opponents had found themselves essentially fighting one another, so skilled was his ability to redirect and divert attacks, defenses, and even simple movements on the battlefield.

"Marque." Optic greeted the man coldly, and Marque simply nodded to him. Belatedly, Gauss recalled that it was Marque's testimony at Optic's military hearing that convinced the service not to make exceptions for superpowered folk. Not surprising, considering the fact that Marque was the only one of the Champions to publicly speak out against Sentinel and Radiant's relationship, generating all manner of conflict and dissension within the team's.

Radiant's death may have been the catalyst for the end of the Champions, but it was Marque's actions that surely sealed that end.

Marque turned to Deosil and Gauss. "I don't think we've met."

Optic spoke up first. "These are two of my teammates, Deosil and Gauss."

The man hesitated a moment, reaching up to pull his sunglasses off with his thick, scarred hands, and give the two of them his squinting regard, up and down. He turned to regard Optic, who met his gaze with a challenge of his own. And then he dismissed all three of them to turn his full attention onto Sentinel. "You've got to be fucking kidding me, Mitch."

"Not kidding, no." Sentinel's response and spine alike were steel.

"You pack of jackals are in a world of trouble," Marque said casually. "Legal troubles from top to bottom."

"Cut the bullshit, Marque," Sentinel said, refusing to rise to the bait. "We both know that I'm the one who called you. I'm the one who told them at the Crypt to get into contact with you and why."

"And that makes you think that I'm not going to arrest the lot of you for what you did here today?"

"What *we* did here? You mean rescuing the people inside there from being illegally experimented on to try and turn them into Empowered?" Deosil barked, and Marque snapped his regard to her.

"Watch your tone, young lady," he said contemptuously.

"I don't *fucking* think I will, no," she replied. "Where the hell were you and the DTPA when these people needed you?"

"We don't have a mandate to operate outside of the United States, and I don't think that—"

"Then there's no problem here, is there?" Optic replied coolly. "Unless Dominica is going to try and punish us?"

"They just might—"

"Nope," Gauss said, with a smile. He pointed over Marque's shoulder. "At least, that's what whoever was on the other end of the radio said, the one talking to the guy in that helicopter. They said they were fine letting the DTPA claim everything on this site, since they don't have the resources to deal with it."

Marque glared at him. "Some conversations are private, junior."

Gauss rolled his eyes. "They probably shouldn't be held over public airwaves where any old magnetic nerd can listen in on them, then, huh?"

Marque paused for a moment. "I can see why you're hanging with these miscreants, Mitch. Same disregard for law you've got."

"We're *not* criminals," Optic said. "We haven't operated in any capacity other than in self-defense inside the United States. The DTPA has no authority in Dominica, or anywhere else we have operated. And my lawyers assure me that while there is legislation that tries to criminalize the formation of a team like ours, there are plenty of attorneys who are just itching for the opportunity to get that legislation examined under a legal system that isn't anxious to make the scandal of a queer American hero disappear forever."

Marque glanced at Sentinel, and then away quickly.

"Look," Gauss said. "I'm part of the DTPA. So is Jesh. And the whole program works. We know it does. But it's not everywhere, Marque. It can't be everywhere. It's pretty clear that there are lots of people in the world that other governments don't give a shit about, and the DTPA can't do anything about that. Do I wish that something like a worldwide DTPA existed? Maybe, if I thought it could be trusted to treat everyone fairly. But that's not even on the table. Someone needs to help people."

"And that's going to be you?" Marque sneered at him.

Sentinel bristled. "You're *goddamned* right it is. It *should* have been *us*," he said, gesturing between Marque and himself. "And it was, for years, before you threw me to the media's shark tank and bailed on the team, getting out with cushy contacts for yourself while you could, you *fucking* coward."

Marque tightened his fists. "Try something, Mitch. I'll have the EITF here so fast, your head will spin. I've got the entire team standing by, waiting to flag Crossroads to teleport them in here."

"I'm pretty sure even if you do, you're not going to risk letting them operate extranationally without your life being at risk," Optic drawled. "And no one here is attacking you."

Gauss couldn't help himself. "Besides, where the hell were the EITF in Portland earlier today?"

Marque smiled that contemptuous smile, never taking his eyes off Sentinel. "Occupied elsewhere. Besides, if you brats want to play superhero? Maybe it's a good reminder to our country just why it is we have an EITF."

Deosil's jaw dropped. "Are you fucking kidding me? You let us nearly get killed just so you could–"

"Enough," Optic interrupted. "He knows what he did, and now we all know it, too."

Marque was contemplative for a moment. "What about Radiant's remains?"

"You're not getting them again," Sentinel said bluntly.

"You don't have the right or authority to–"

"No," Sentinel said, his deep voice gravelly. "*Fuck* that. It's bad enough that you morons lost his body to begin with, but especially now that we know someone might possibly use his remains to create Empowered? Hell no. I'll make arrangements to see that he's interred someplace safe and private."

Marque stepped forward, and Sentinel raised his chin, daring him to try something.

"Look, this is stupid," Deosil said. "Like Rusty said—we're DTPA. We will always err on the side of getting the proper authorities involved with these situations. But the proper authorities won't always handle it, because they can't, or they won't. And those things are worth handling, even if that means jail time or worse for us. You guys spin a good 'self-preservation' line, but I'm *done*. I'm ready to sacrifice whatever it takes to ensure that I use my abilities to help people who don't have my abilities, and who don't deserve to be crushed under heel because of it."

"The DTPA does good work," Optic said. "We'd rather work with you than against you. But that's up to you. The fact is, we're out to do some good for folks who get overlooked or pushed down in the world. We've got the strength to do some pushing back, if it comes to that."

Marque sighed. "As far as I'm concerned, I'm willing to chalk all of this up to extenuating circumstances. I want you to know that I'm going to find out who this Prometheus Consortium is, what they want, and I'm going to see that they're brought to justice. My agents already have the members we scavenged from Portland—Mata Hari and Velocity—in interrogation."

He paused, and then turned to Sentinel. "And I promise you, Mitch, that bitch is going to fry for Craig's murder. I swear it. But I'm warning you. Don't push this, especially not in the States. I can't protect you if you break the laws."

"We're establishing a team," Sentinel said calmly. "We're called the Sacred Band, and Optic is our leader. There are too many places where people who don't have the power of the local privileged class or ethnicity get stepped on. They deserve justice and protection, too. If those places don't want us to show up and interfere, then they'll make sure they take steps to see that the right thing is done."

Marque contemplated Sentinel's words, and then put his sunglasses back on.

"Does that include the United States?" he asked, dangerously.

"That most especially includes the United States," Sentinel growled in return. "Best make sure the people getting protected are the ones who deserve and need it the most." He turned to the others. "We should go. Too much more of this, and he's going to start pissing on things so we know he owns them."

Marque and his men gave them some breathing space. True to his word, he made sure the victims were seen to first and foremost. The sudden military presence made Kosma uncomfortable, so Gauss made a point to stick close to him. He accompanied them downstairs to the vault where the team unsealed the tank and gently pulled Radiant's body from the chemicals within. Gauss lifted him out of it, suspended on a bed of his ball bearings, and gently placed him into the steel coffin they'd obviously used to transport him there.

Sentinel rested his hand on the lid of the compartment once Gauss sealed it. Gauss stepped away to give him a moment in peace, and found Kosma seated nearby.

"How are you feeling?" he asked, and Kosma nodded up at him.

"Tired. And hungry." The young Ukrainian man hesitated for a moment. "And sad."

"I'm so sorry about Sasha, Kosma," Gauss said, crouching down next to him. "We tried to get here as soon as we could, but–"

"No, my friend," Kosma said, looking at him. "That you came at all is a miracle I had no right to pray for."

Optic and Deosil walked back into the room.

"Ready to go?" she asked.

"May I come with you?" Kosma asked meekly. "I do not wish to stay with these soldiers."

Gauss looked to Optic, who regarded the young man cautiously. Then he nodded. "Absolutely. We'll get you to the States, get you rested and healed up, and then figure out where to go from there. Make sure you're recovered from all of this."

"Going to be a bit of a rough flight with all of us, isn't it?" Sentinel asked, his hand still resting on the steel tube.

"Not so much, no." Deosil grinned at Optic.

"While we were outside, I had my people charter us a plane. The air strip is maybe ten minutes by air from here, and the plane should be here within the hour. It'll get us home in no time." Optic smiled at the relief that came over everyone's faces.

"You okay, coppertop?" Deosil asked, and Gauss shook his head wearily.

"I am. Sort of. It's frustrating. Not figuring out who the Consortium is, or what they want, you know? Feels unfinished."

Sentinel and Optic traded a glance, and Sentinel gestured for Optic to go ahead and turned to Gauss. "Thing is, Rusty, it's never that simple. I know in an ideal world, we'd have bust in here and found all the answers to our questions. But the forces on the ground usually only ever see a part of what's going on, you know? But that's no reason for us to stop looking into it, either."

In short order, they emerged from the facility, Gauss carefully controlling the movement of the steel coffin, levitating it at the center of their group. He remained casual, but it was clear that he and the others anticipated an attempt from Marque's people to seize it. Fortunately, that didn't happen.

As the team and Kosma headed for the edge of the compound, Marque spoke one last time. "Mitch. Don't take this too far. This isn't the world we got our powers in. Don't drag these kids into trouble you can't protect them from."

Optic turned to him. "We know exactly what we're getting into, Marque. Thanks for the warning. And I've got one for you." He watched as his allies got airborne.

"We'll be watching."

And with that, they were gone.

CHAPTER TWENTY-EIGHT

Portland, Oregon
May 24—June 1, 2013

The chartered jet eventually got them where they wanted to go, but not without some additional scrutiny. The Department of Transformed Persons Affairs was waiting for them on the ground when they arrived in Portland, with no less than Director Belinda Veracruz herself at the head of a small knot of agents. Beside her, looking a little rough, stood Llorona, beaming a smile up at them.

Local police were a short distance away, in riot gear, looking nervous. Standing among them were two members of the Extraordinary Intervention Task Force, the "Bully Boys," as some liked to call the Department's team of superpowered agents: Bulwark, who could create force fields to contain or defend targets, and Melee, a superpowered hand-to-hand specialist, his signature shock batons in their hip holsters at his side.

"They are clearly expecting trouble," Deosil said as she glanced through the open door in the side of the plane. "Why is Blanca here? She should be in a damned hospital!"

Optic peered over her shoulder at the tableau below. "Hmm. Everyone stay cool. Kosma, you stay on the plane for now."

The young Ukrainian man looked very concerned. "You can't fight. I'll go with them."

Optic looked back apologetically. "Real talk here. If they want you, you will have to go with them, yeah. We can't fight them over it—there's no winning that sort of thing. But if they do take you, I'll have my lawyers on it immediately, alright?"

The young man swallowed nervously, and nodded. Deosil and Optic descended first, followed by Gauss. Sentinel stepped out of the plane but remained standing at the top of the stairs, arms folded forbiddingly and a stubborn glower on his face.

"Director Veracruz." Llorona gestured to Optic, shifting as she did so to stand with her team. "Have you met Optic before? He's our team leader."

Belinda Veracruz flashed a shiny politician's smile at him and shook hands. "Oh, I'm very aware of who Optic is and what role he plays here, courtesy of an emergency memo sent to the Board of Directors at an ungodly hour last night. Marque used quite a lot of capital letters to communicate just how imperative it was that we knew who all of you are."

"Sounds like Marque," Llorona said with a smile, one which Veracruz mirrored.

She glanced at the others. "Deosil, Gauss. Good to see you both again."

She took a moment to acknowledge Sentinel at the top of the stairway. He wasn't even looking at them—his attention was fixed behind them. She craned around to follow his gaze to where Melee and Bulwark met his glare with scowls of their own. The two of them seemed a little less sanguine about the possibility of a tussle with the famous arch-hero. She smirked at Llorona. "I see Mr. McCann is making friends, as usual."

Optic smiled his best Hollywood smile. "He's just feeling protective of the young man aboard the plane, Director Veracruz. Kosma has been through an incredibly traumatic experience by faceless figures. Sentinel feels—as do we all—that the young man could do with some rest and recovery before he has to face down the bureaucratic might of the DTPA."

"Please, call me Belinda," the Director of the Pacific Northwest said, nodding her head. "As it so happens, the Board of Directors agrees with you."

Deosil and Gauss looked at one another in surprise. "Wait, you aren't going to take him into custody?" Deosil blurted.

Belinda smiled. "No. In fact, we would appreciate it if your...well, your team would be willing to take him in for a while."

Optic narrowed his eyes. "What's the catch?"

"The catch is that we'd need you to publicly lay claim to doing so. And to have your lawyers apply for asylum on his behalf."

"What?" Gauss stared at her a little open-mouthed, like he couldn't understand what he was hearing.

"We have it on good authority that he's probably in danger from his home government, if he develops powers," she said with a slightly conspiratorial touch to her smile. "We understand that he's a young gay man, is he not?"

"He is," Optic said hesitantly.

"Which means that as a young man with new superpowers, if he returns home, he is going to find himself under the auspices of a government program that will—to put it lightly—take a dim view of his orientation, will they not?"

Optic, Gauss, and Deosil exchanged horrified looks.

"He would," said Llorona. She gave every indication that not only was this not news to her, but that it was something she'd been thinking about. "As a superpowered Ukrainian citizen, he would be automatically considered a government resource, assigned to Vigilance."

"Not Vigilance itself," Belinda said. "But to the governing body that runs Vigilance, yes. The member states who are part of Vigilance's mission all consign their Changed citizenry to that organization. Even if they have no ability or inclination to fight, they are still considered a resource to be lent out to member state governments or industry, depending on what their abilities are."

"He's queer, though," Gauss said. "He can't go back there."

"Exactly our point," Belinda said, with a comforting smile. "That's why we want him to apply for asylum in the United States. The Department is prepared to back his application. Behind the scenes, of course."

Llorona *tsk*ed. "Oh." She hesitated. "Assuming he develops powers."

Director Veracruz smiled at her. "So far, three of the other survivors have. We're willing to risk it, even if he doesn't develop any."

"I take it in return, the Department would like the opportunity to do some testing on Kosma?" Llorona continued. "Since literally every one of the other new Promethean Empowered are citizens of countries other than the United States?"

"Son of a bitch." Optic scowled. "I should have seen that one. All of them have manifested powers? There were nearly two dozen survivors."

"We won't know for a few more days." Director Veracruz held both of her hands up. "I won't dance around it. Llorona has the right of it. You know we have strict ethics for testing and observation, though, and those are just as in place for him as they are for any of you. Plus, he'll have you as advocates."

"Damn right he will," Deosil growled. Director Veracruz smiled at her.

"We could try to get asylum for him on our own," Optic ventured.

"You could, yes. But unless that's a legal battle you are willing to wage over the next couple of years in international courts? I suggest you accept our help. The nations of the world have something of a hands-off policy when it comes to one another's Changed citizens. Even if an American citizen gains powers inside Vigilance's territory, for example, they remain an American citizen. Nations who try and seize those assets risk all-out war, just as though they'd tried to lay hands on another country's nuclear weapons."

"Jesus, are we just weapons to you people?" Deosil looked sick.

Director Veracruz fixed her with a no-nonsense stare. "You are weapons to altogether too many governments of the world. We don't treat you like objects, but there are too many places that would, in a heartbeat. We have to protect our own, and part of that means ceding national sovereignty to citizens. Usually."

"She's right, *mija*," Llorona said, laying a hand on Deosil's arm. "It's *bad* in some places."

"So, if we accept, what are the terms?" Optic said.

The Director held up one finger. "You provide him a living space and keep track of his whereabouts. This isn't a license to disappear somewhere in the U.S. He's got freedom of movement as long as someone on your team is aware of his whereabouts, and ideally is accompanying him, especially if you leave Portland."

Llorona nodded. "Go on."

"He will accept regular examination and testing of his abilities, and give us a full debrief of his experiences. He holds nothing back that he can remember." She raised a second finger. "We do testing for one week every three months. He'll be seen in the DTPA headquarters in Seattle."

A third finger. "Finally, he avoids speaking to the media unless we approve the interview. If we come to him with a media opportunity, he agrees to do it. This will absolutely mean him coming out publicly."

"That's a hell of a demand!" Gauss raised his voice, and the security forces nearby straightened and shifted a little closer. Optic laid a calming hand on Gauss's shoulder.

"We understand that," Director Veracruz said. "But a request for asylum must include an impetus, and that has to be part of the public record. We're not going to march him in front of the cameras—at least not right away—but his orientation is going to have to be known for this. There's no way around it."

"We can't agree to that on his behalf," Optic said. "We can't agree to any of it for him."

"I understand."

"So, what does he get in return?" Deosil asked.

"Besides political asylum?" Director Veracruz arched an eyebrow. She looked thoughtful. "The Department is willing to provide a modest stipend, payable each time he completes a round of testing. We will also work to ensure that he *gets* the asylum he's applying for."

"Work," Llorona said. "Or schooling, whichever he wants to do. He's studying architecture, and he deserves to finish his education, or get a job, if he wants. He deserves some normalcy. That means visas."

Veracruz sighed. She glanced at one of the aides beside her and nodded. The young woman brought her phone up, dialing, and then pressed it to her ear. She stepped away so she could speak in privacy. "I'll work to get that, too. Though it might take a little time." She looked at the four of them. "Thoughts?"

"I'll do it," Kosma called down from the top of the stairs. Sentinel stood beside him, a supporting hand on his shoulder. "I accept."

"Mitch has been telling him what we're talking about," Optic said quietly.

"Good." Director Veracruz smiled, clearly unsurprised. "Saves us the time of going over it again."

They all turned as Kosma descended, Sentinel close on his heels. "Thank you, Director," Kosma said, extending his hand to her shyly. "I know I have no right to ask these things, and that you're putting your Department in a difficult position on my behalf."

Now Director Veracruz looked slightly surprised. "I...well, you're welcome, Kosma." She looked at him thoughtfully. "Despite all the cold bureaucratic nonsense, please know: we *hate* what was done to you. It's cruel and horrible, and no one should have to endure that. While we would like to know more about your experience, I'm genuinely glad to be able to provide a little sanctuary from all of that, in whatever way I can."

Kosma smiled and shook her hand. "I'm grateful for your help, Director, and for your department's."

One of her aides produced some documents for him to sign, and after that, the Department staff were gone, with a promise to be in touch later.

"Let's get you some rest," Optic said to Llorona fondly, giving her his arm.

"Thank you, *mijo*." She sounded exhausted. "I couldn't let them meet you without being here. Dealing with the Department takes a deft hand sometimes, and I've dealt with them longer than most."

Deosil hugged her carefully. "You're honestly just the best. Let's get you to a bed, though."

Optic turned to regard Kosma. "Welcome to the U.S., Kosma. Let's see about getting you some rest, too, and then we'll figure out what we need next, yeah?"

"Thank you so much, all of you," Kosma said, at the edge of tears. "This is a far, far better outcome than I had any right to hope for. I think I would just like to sleep for a few days."

* * *

Optic's house was wrecked, of course, thanks to the Prometheans. His insurance and the city were already going round and round with the Department of Transformed Persons Affairs. It was almost fifty years since the first superpowered people had appeared, and the powers that be still hadn't figured out who was liable in cases of damage caused by their powers. It was one of the reasons why the Denisov Measure tended to stress the Changed finding affiliation for the use of their powers: if they were law enforcement, military, or corporate, it meant there was someone clearly responsible for the damage they might do.

Fortunately, Optic had the means to ensconce the team in a hotel downtown. They claimed a pair of two-bedroom suites that faced one another in the penthouse, with a door connecting them. Gauss set up Kosma in one of the bedrooms. He complained of a headache, and Gauss got him some painkillers and water. The young man was asleep before Gauss closed the door and padded out of that suite and into the adjoining one.

Though she'd been set up with one of the bedrooms in that suite, Llorona wasn't in bed yet. Gauss arrived to find her stretched out on one of the sofas, her head pillowed on Deosil's lap, facing the other sofa across the room where Sentinel and Optic sat. Optic was telling her about meeting up with Turbine as they caught her up on what she'd missed.

"Is he all settled in?" Llorona asked Gauss as soon as he walked into the suite's common room.

Gauss nodded. "Yeah. Already snoring by the time I shut the door."

"Good," she said. She waved her phone at him. "He's got an appointment with a doctor tomorrow to make sure there aren't any immediate medical concerns."

"Good idea," Gauss said, sliding into the spot between Sentinel and Optic. He brushed up against Sentinel as he did so, and the smile he got for it was dizzying. "This is swanky, man," he said to Optic, who grinned at him.

"It's not bad. Not quite the ridiculous degree of some places I've stayed when doing press tours and shit, but it'll do for a while. I've got to hunt for a place to rent until my place gets back to order."

"I'm so sorry about your beautiful home, Optic," Llorona said mournfully. "Those horrible people."

"Honestly, I'd been putting off getting some small changes done here and there, so I guess I can take the hint." Optic looked at Gauss. "Rusty, you willing to help me figure out the best way to put some of those things into play? We'd talked a little about some ideas you had for the place."

"Me?" Gauss's eyebrows shot upward.

"Yeah, you." Optic snorted. "You're the architecture student around here, and you were the one with the ideas about the big glass walls in the bathrooms and bedrooms, right?"

"Yeah! I mean, thank you, yeah. I'd love that."

"Cool. When the time comes for me to meet with the folks doing the rebuilding, I'm gonna rope you in to talk with the architect about some of that."

"Totally," Gauss said, smiling. And after a moment: "Thanks."

"For what? I'm the one getting free advice by taking shameless advantage of my teammate," Optic teased, standing. He glanced across the room and found Llorona dozing lightly on the other sofa, Deosil's hands soothingly gentle on her head. "We ought to get Blanca to a real bed."

Llorona inhaled and forced her bleary eyes open. "I really should. I'm sorry—these pain meds they have me on are no joke."

"Hey." Deosil tweaked her nose playfully, staring down at her from above. "You got the hell beat out of you and still made it out of the hospital to come play negotiator for us with the DTPA. You've earned your fucking rest."

Llorona chuckled her deep, throaty laugh and reached up to boop Deosil on the nose fondly. "I wasn't about to let them make things worse. They were obviously feeling skittish, and you all were coming down off at least one fight already. I know what that can do to threat assessment psychology."

"And we definitely appreciate it," Optic said, crossing to stand over her. "But you need your rest. Those are orders."

"Oh, well if they're *orders*," Llorona teased, and struggled to sit up, wincing and hissing in pain as she did so, even with Deosil's help.

Optic glanced over at Sentinel, who was already rising from the sofa. "You wanna carry her to her room, big guy?"

Llorona laughed. "Don't you dare," she said. "I'm not so injured I can't walk, and I am not about to be princess-carried to my bed."

"Aww, but I was looking forward to it," Sentinel teased her, and she laughed, holding a hand to her injuries.

"There are a lot of people who would kill to be princess-carried by Sentinel, you know," Deosil said. She glanced across the room to Gauss. "Some of them even in this room."

The sheer murder Gauss shot her with his eyes alone was practically a new superpower, and she laughed. Sentinel blushed furiously, a quick flush of red up his neck and across cheeks and even the bottoms of his earlobes. He leaned down and helped Llorona stand. "Here, at least let me do this," he said, giving her an arm to lean on. She sighed as she let him pull her up and gently bolster her movement with his telekinetics.

"Thank you, Mitch," she said fondly. She gave a half-hearted wave to the room. "I'll see you all in a few hours."

"Get some rest," Optic said. "We'll have something to eat for you when you're up and about again." He glanced down at his phone and stepped out onto the balcony to make a call.

Gauss all but flew across the room to the sofa, settling in next to Deosil. "You suck," he hissed at her with a shove, and she giggled, shoving him back.

"I'm sorry, I could *not* resist. Gods, your face,"

"I'm trying not to make him uncomfortable, Jesh," Gauss said, concern knitting his brow.

"Then, maybe you should remember that he can hear all of this," she said, pointing at the closed door to Llorona's room.

"Fuck!" Now it was his turn to blush furiously.

"Look, just chill," she said, leaning into him. "You are allowed to be a grownup about being attracted to someone. You can be honest about it without that somehow implying an obligation from them to respond in some way, you know?"

He sighed, leaning his head back against the sofa and pressing the heels of his palms against his eyes. "I know," he said after a moment, dropping his hands in his lap. "I do, I know that."

"Okay, good," she said, and leaned in to kiss him on the cheek. "You're a fucking *catch*, coppertop, and he is no dummy. Just let shit happen in its own course without worrying *about* it happening, yeah?"

He smiled. "Thanks, mom."

"*Pssh.* You should be so lucky to have a mom as damned cool as me," she said, ruffling his hair and standing. She was immediately on her phone. "I wonder if we can get some food delivered."

Gauss groaned. "That sounds amazing. I'm fucking starving."

"You used your powers a lot lately, for some pretty hefty shit," Deosil said, scrolling around on her phone. "I'm surprised you're not all wiped out."

"I had a lot of recharging to do on the plane," he said. "And Optic got them to stock the plane he chartered with some stuff for me. Bananas and some of that pediatric drink they give to kids and stuff. It's apparently better for replenishing electrolytes than the sports drinks I usually go for."

She glanced fondly at the glass doors to the balcony, where Optic was still on his phone, leaning against the railing. "He's a good team leader."

"He is," Gauss said with a smile. "So, what are *you* going to be doing now?"

Deosil sighed, and clicked her phone dark, curling up on the sofa again with her legs under her. She rested one arm on the back of the sofa and cradled her head in it, looking at him. "I don't know, honestly."

She chewed at her thumb nail for a moment. "I have a few obligations right now—mainly festivals and Pagan Pride stuff I've committed to. But that's only over the next four or five months or so. I've already gotten like ten thousand messages from my mom, so I might go and see her for a few weeks. Prove I'm not actually dead from supervillains or whatever."

"God, I know. I called my mom once we got into PDX but ended up having to cut the conversation short. I made sure she knew I was okay but I *did not* have the answers she wanted." He hesitated. "I think I really scared her."

"Yes," Deosil said. "I honestly am super dreading talking to my mom because I know that me saying 'I'm fine' over and over isn't going to do shit to make her feel better."

"You really should go do that, you know," he said after a moment.

She groaned and shoved him. "I know, it's jut so exhausting to deal with other peoples' fear and worry. Especially when you're as wiped out as we are right now, you know?"

They both looked up at the sound of the door to Llorona's room closing gently. Sentinel stepped back into the common room. "Sorry to interrupt," he said.

"You're not interrupting," Deosil said. "You used to do this superheroing thing. How do you manage the...well, the fear of the people who love you, you know? Like, how do you deal with being the one who is injured and worn out, but also having to be the one who makes everyone feel better at the same time?"

Sentinel shook his head, sliding into the sofa across from them. "You just do it. Just like you're saying. You make the phone call, you listen to them being afraid and anxious and freaked out, and you assure them you're okay."

"What if you're not okay, though?" Deosil asked quietly, and Gauss turned concerned eyes to her. He grabbed her hand and squeezed it tight.

Sentinel looked away, sadness in his face. "I don't know that my answer for that is a good one. A healthy one, I mean. I always just told them I was okay anyway. Even if I was doing it from an infirmary bed." He hesitated for a moment. "The fact is, they can't really understand why we do it. The drive. Maybe I don't either, honestly. But for me, it felt like being that invincible hero you have to pretend to be in the field had to extend to my family and loved ones, too. Because if I showed them the hurt. The scars? I know they would want me to stop, because they love me and care for me. And there's only so many times you can have that conversation with the people you love before it starts to weigh you down. To weigh *me* down."

"That sounds lonely," Gauss said sadly.

Sentinel closed his eyes. "It's why the Champions became my family. They understood. I could be vulnerable—genuinely vulnerable, about this, at least—around them, because they knew what I was experiencing. They were experiencing it with me, most often. And I'm not honestly the best with sharing my…feelings, or whatever, but…" He trailed off, searching for the words. "But if I was hurting or torn up because of how things on a mission played out? If people were injured or killed because of my not being there, or if we were dealing with governments being horrible, or just whatever it was. My teammates were people I could talk to about that, and they could handle me being sad or angry or hurt without automatically questioning why I was doing it at all. Does that make sense?"

"Kinda," Deosil said with a sad nod. "It's a lot like being out and queer when you move away from your family. You realize that after a while, it's exhausting to constantly tell your family about the daily shit of being queer, right? Like, oh, some dude clocked me today at the store, and he followed me around and called me a slur. Or, a friend of mine was bashed, and we're all getting together to make sure they get home from the hospital alright and have meals for a couple of days. Our families don't know what this shit's like, and it's exhausting to tell it to them and reassure them that you're alright, when you're just *not*."

"But you can't tell them that," Gauss said. "Because then comes the 'I'm just worried about you living this lifestyle' and all the rest of that."

"You're hurting, but then you are suddenly responsible for making them feel better about living your life, too. Like you don't have enough emotional healing to do so recently after coming out, but then you're also responsible for their emotional wellbeing when it comes to fearing for you out on your own?" Deosil looked from Gauss to Sentinel.

Sentinel blinked. "I'd never thought of that. I mean…" He sighed, and looked away, shamefaced. When he spoke again, he was quiet. "I was outed, but I've never been out. If that makes sense. My family knew I was super-heroing with the Champions, of course, and I kept them at arm's length, emotionally. Because of this. But I've never talked to anyone in my family or friends about being…being gay. I just…" He shook his head. "I don't know what I'm trying to say. Just that I guess I didn't realize how similar the two things were. You guys are probably better prepared for this than I ever was."

They lapsed into a companionable but exhausted silence, until Optic stepped back inside to find Gauss and Deosil on their phones, and Sentinel leaning back against the sofa with his eyes closed. He opened them at the sound of the balcony door sliding shut. "Everything alright?" Sentinel asked, and Optic nodded.

"Yeah. Just some stuff that needed tending to."

"We were thinking about food," Deosil said, flashing her screen at him. "There's a gyro place not too far from the hotel. Rusty and I could go and grab some food."

"Would you? I'm starving," Optic said gratefully. "We can call the order in, and I can get it on my card."

She stood, smiling. "Team leader doesn't mean you have to pay for *everything*, you know."

He chuckled and threw his hands up, surrendering. "Alright. Honestly, I don't really know how any of this works—we didn't have to pay for anything ourselves in the Seraphim. It was all just *there*, you know?"

"My treat," she said. She looked back over at the sofa, where Gauss's attention was still on the phone. "C'mon, coppertop. Stop reading about yourself and let's go get some food already."

He blushed and clicked his phone off, standing. "Hey, they're actually saying some really nice things. About us, I mean. I'm actually kinda surprised."

Optic nodded. "Yeah, my lawyer was saying something about the city of Portland wanting to get in touch with us to talk about what happened. I think they want to know if we're sticking around here, or what."

Gauss stopped, scrunching his face up. "Oh. I guess I just assumed that we'd be based out of Portland. I hadn't thought about *not* being here."

"Well, don't worry. I told them that we're here for now. You're here, and I've got a house here. I'm selling my place in L.A. to help cover some other stuff that's bound to come up."

"Wait a minute," Desoil said. "You're selling your home in L.A.? What does this mean for your career?"

Optic winced. "I'm not cashing in my chips in acting. I just feel like this is what I need to do right now, more than anything else."

"What Deosil said about food earlier also applies to everything else, Optic," Sentinel said seriously. "You don't have to pay for everything just because you're the team leader. I've got some savings. I'm no Alchemy, but I've got some money socked away."

Optic smiled. "No worries. We can figure all that out. For now, since the lawyers and publicists are mine, it's honestly just easier to do things this way. But we'll add that to the list of things we need to figure out."

Gauss looked thoughtful. "Hey, when you talk to your people, or whatever, again? Would you ask them to let the city know that I'm happy to help with the rebuilding? My powers are really useful for big scale construction and repair."

Optic stared at him for a moment, considering. "Hmm. You know, that would look really good for us, you out there using your power to help the city."

"Especially since, uh, we kinda caused some of that damage," Deosil said quietly.

"Exactly," Optic said. "I'm going to bypass my lawyers and get in touch with the city to make that offer directly. Good thinking, Rusty."

"Alright! If we don't go and get some food now I cannot be held responsible for what happens next," Deosil said, with an impatient little stompy dance by the door.

"Go and get our witch some food already." Optic laughed, waving them out the door. She and Rusty left, chatting amiably.

"It's good to see them bounce back from what we just saw. Just did," Sentinel said after a moment.

Optic turned and studied him. "They're both strong and dedicated. They'll be alright. We all will."

Sentinel looked at the closed door as if his gaze could follow the duo's departure through it. "God, I hope so."

* * *

By the time they got back with a big paper bag full of foil-wrapped gyros, Llorona was up, comfortably stretched out on the sofa once more. Her feet rested in Sentinel's lap, and Optic was on the phone again out on the balcony.

"Hey, gorgeous." Deosil smiled at her. "Want a gyro?"

Llorona groaned. "Honestly, no. But I need to eat anyway. These medications they gave me are making me a little nauseous."

"Sorry, Blanca," Gauss said. "Want me to pop downstairs and grab you something else?"

"No, *mijo*." She smiled at him. "It's the meds, not the food."

"We passed a corner store on the way. Can I at least go see if they have something for the nausea? Maybe get you something fizzy and clear to drink? Grab some pink goop?"

Llorona hesitated, torn between not wanting him to bother and that sounding good. He didn't give her a chance to tell him no. "I'll be right back!" He was out the door in a wink, Llorona watching him go fondly.

"He's so good," she said after him, and then glanced at Sentinel, whose eyes were fixed on the door. After a moment, he realized she was talking to him, and met her eyes. She was smiling, and though he smiled in return, his gaze darted away, a flush on his cheeks. After a moment, she said, "You could do much worse, you know."

He flushed again, and his eyes crept up to where Deosil was unpacking the bag of food. When he didn't say anything, Deosil winked at the two of them. "I think I'm going to go and see if Kosma is hungry. Back in a few."

He sighed as the door clicked shut behind her. "I know. It's occurred to me." He chewed on his lip. "He's just...he's so *young*, Blanca."

She laughed. "Maybe. But you're going to need to make your peace with the fact that you've waited a while. Which is fine, we all have to do what we have to do, but you're in your sixties, Mitch. In a handful of years, everyone is going to be much younger than you."

He snorted but didn't deny it.

"But also? You were outed, but you never came out." He threw her an unsure look, but didn't say anything, waiting for her to continue. She smiled gently at him. "You got to the part of coming out where everyone knows. But you never got to the part where you starting living your life as an out gay man. Making decisions about where you want to live so that you have community and dating options. Telling your family and navigating the terrain of them becoming comfortable with your queerness, and you becoming comfortable with their acceptance or not. You never settled down to *live* your life, Mitch."

She sat up, crossing her legs under her and taking his hand. "Which isn't bad. We all grieve differently, but it's sort of like Radiant wasn't just your lover. He *was* your identity as a queer man. But when he died, he didn't take your queerness with him."

"It was just…" Sentinel hesitated, searching for the right words. "Easier, with him. I guess. He knew everything about being gay and all that, and he basically held my hand through it."

"What he taught you was the queerness of those days, Mitch. And that was good, for then." She chewed on her lower lip. "Mitch, one of the things that happens with queer people is that our development, for lack of a better word? Our development as queer adults is often shaped by when we come out. Straight people don't have to think about it—they come into their sexuality in line with their physical and emotional maturation.

"But because we are often stuck hiding who we are, you can have queer people who are the same age who are of radically different levels of maturity in their queer identities. If you have two people in their forties, one of them might have been out for twenty or thirty years already, while the other may have only come out last year. They're not at the same place, in terms of that maturity."

Sentinel frowned. "So, you're saying that you think I'm, what? Behind the curve?"

"Mitch, you are *exactly* where you need to be. But you're worried about your age respective to his, when you ought to be considering where the two you are *at*. You're hardly cradle-robbing if he's the one guiding *you* through being a queer adult in the world today."

He looked at her, startled. For a moment, it seemed as though he might say something—to deny or refute her point, but after opening and shutting his mouth a few times, he sighed. "You're probably right."

"It's honestly the worst part of being my friend," she teased him. "I'm right all too often."

They both laughed, and he wrapped her in a hug.

"Seriously, though. You were comfortable with Radiant taking the lead in your relationship. I feel like a good deal of your hesitation is the idea that because you're the older one, you're expected to do that with you and Rusty."

Mitch just nodded, looking away and running a hand through his hair. "Yeah. I think that's pretty accurate."

"So then. Let *him* lead. You've been hiding out in backwater places, hiding not just your queerness but your actual identity for years now. He, on the other hand, has been out since he was in his teens, and is a young queer adult who has been through the wringer already. If you're more comfortable being guided when it comes to things like your romantic dynamic? You could do so much worse than him, Mitch. He adores you, and you don't have to pretend to be anything you aren't around him. He knows your grief and your life, and he cares very deeply for you."

"You don't...you don't think it's just some kind of..." He trailed off. "Hero thing?"

She laughed. "Oh, you had better believe it is. At least originally. But Mitch, there are so, so many unhealthier perspectives to start a relationship off from than one where he respects you for being kind, brave, and selfless." He exhaled sharply, a half-laugh that suggested he hadn't thought of it that way.

"And that was then. Before he knew you personally. That respect is still there, but he also cares for *you*. He's one of those heroes now, too. He's seen you vulnerable, and understands what you've been through. I don't think there are a lot of illusions about who you are and where you've been."

Sentinel leaned back against the sofa, chewing the inside of his cheek. He shot her a narrow-eyed look. "I take it you've already had this conversation with him, huh?"

She grinned. "Nope. My conversation with him was very different." She winked. "But yes, we've talked about how he feels. And how you obviously feel as well."

Sentinel looked up at the door and then at Llorona with a smile. "Alright. Let me chew on this one for a while." She grinned at him.

* * *

Within the week, they'd all given up any ideas about things "going back to normal," whatever that meant. Llorona was recovered enough to answer a call from Grace—the head of the Golden Cross—asking if she felt well enough to coordinate the relief effort for the recent unseasonal storms in the Amazon Basin. Small communities all up and down the countryside, both indigenous and otherwise, had been devastated by the unexpected weather. The Cross needed someone to take point for both media and in organizing the ops on the ground.

"You're not healed yet, Blanca," Optic reminded her sourly when she told them.

"That's both very true and very kind of you to remind me," she replied. "But I can sit a sofa here or I can sit a desk there. I'm going to go and be useful."

Unwilling to let her go off on her own, Deosil asked Blanca to get her old Golden Cross ident re-activated with the organization. Headquarters was frankly thrilled: an elementalist of Deosil's power was invaluable when it came to this sort of operation. In short order the two of them were gone, less than twenty-four hours after Blanca got the call from a harried Grace.

Gauss gave Kosma the grand tour of Portland, introducing him to some of the city's architectural sites and even taking him down to his university to look around. Summer term was in session, and it gave Gauss the chance to double-check his registration for fall. Both of them noticed that more and more people seemed to recognize Gauss, which led to them receiving an out-of-the-blue invitation to a party that weekend, held just off campus. Kosma demurred, clearly not ready to be around that sort of environment, though he insisted that Gauss should go.

Kosma did more than heal during this time, however: he also came into his powers. His headache from the first night in the hotel bloomed into strange sensory input that overwhelmed and panicked the young man. He was fine alone, but anytime others came near him, it happened again: a slow build of emotions he couldn't control, slowly driving him into a frenzied state of mind. The team learned to withdraw and leave him alone. After a day of this, Optic made a call to the DTPA, who sent a physician and two agents over.

After administering a light sedative, the agents helped figure out that he was manifesting receptive empathic power: he could sense the emotions of those around him, without filters and magnified by his nascent abilities. They left him with a tablet computer with a full suite of videos from a Department specialist in getting psychic phenomena under control.

Soon enough, he was joining the others for meals, though his control eroded faster than he liked, forcing him to flee to the solitude of his room when it happened. Kosma slowly began to unfold from the shock of the past weeks, even confiding in Gauss his memories of Sasha. Grief bubbled up during those conversations, of such intensity that Gauss all but panicked when it first happened.

"I don't know what to say, or what to do when that happens," he confided in Optic and Sentinel after it happened again. "I'm not good at this shit. Ugh, I wish Jesh or Llorona were here."

"Hey," Optic said. "Don't sell yourself short. There's a reason he's opening up to you, Rusty."

Sentinel agreed. "Honestly, Rusty—in these cases, most people just want to talk. They don't need you to have all the answers or to counsel them. They're not looking for you to fix anything. They're talking to you because they feel safe and un-judged. You don't have to *do* anything. Just listen."

Optic stayed busy. Reconstruction began on his home in the West Hills, repairing the damage the Prometheans did. As the team leader, he gave an interview or three to various media outlets, turning the full force of his charm to speaking on behalf of the team. His legal team carefully coached him on how to skirt the edges of the Denisov Measure's restrictions, useful when he was asked questions about what he thought about the restrictions the law placed on his team's efforts.

After some initial protective anxiety—he was sure the Consortium was going to find a way to strike back at them—Mitch was distant, giving Rusty and Kosma room to explore both the city and their growing friendship. Mitch took some time in Seattle with Alchemy, who seemed determined to get him operating in the current decade. This included a new phone (which Rusty delighted in teasing him about having no idea how to use), as well as long conversations about figuring out what he wanted from this new life out of the shadows.

Rusty also managed to corner him to have a talk. The roof of the hotel was technically off-limits to guests, but the staff turned a blind eye to them occasionally being up there, given the local excitement over having the team in residence. Mitch frequently found himself there, watching the sun set and the city spin below.

"You lurking up on the roof again?" Rusty smiled as he crested the edge of the roof, rising up to it from their suite balcony below.

"Guilty," Mitch said with a dimpled smirk. "I've never been good with the ground view, I guess. I prefer a wider perspective."

Rusty settled into a sitting position on the lip of the roof next to the bigger man. "Kinda distant, though," he said simply, and Mitch looked at him with a frown. He crossed his arms and nodded.

"Yeah, kinda," he said. After a moment, he realized that could be taken in two ways. "Sorry."

Rusty smiled and bumped Mitch's shoulder with his own, a quick little jostle that was both friendly and sort of intimate. "Nothing to be sorry about."

Mitch took a deep breath, opened his mouth, and then shut it again, biting his lip. He glanced sideways at the redhead next to him, a strained look on his face.

"Dude," Rusty said. "You look like you're in pain."

Mitch chuckled and shook his head ruefully. "God. Sorry, I know. I'm just very bad at this sort of thing."

Rusty swiveled in his seat, pulling one knee up to his chest, and letting his other leg dangle off the roof's edge. He crossed his arms, resting them atop his raised leg, and then settled his chin there. "What sort of thing?"

"How I feel. For starters. About you?"

Rusty took a deep breath. "How *do* you feel?"

"I don't *know*." He sighed, exasperated. "No, that's not true. I *do* know. Sort of? I'm just…" He trailed off again, shaking his head in frustration.

"Hey." Rusty waited until Mitch looked up at him. "Say as much as you want. As much as you feel comfortable with. No matter what you say, we're going to be cool."

"I'm…really attracted to you." He said it like it pained him to say so.

Rusty blinked. "Seriously?"

Mitch's eyebrows shot up in alarm. "What? I mean, yes. *Yes*, seriously. Was it not–" He stopped. "Sorry. Like I said. Really bad at this."

Rusty smiled at him fondly and laid a hand on his shoulder. "No, no. You're not. Bad. You haven't done this a lot, but there's nothing wrong with that." He hesitated. "You just caught me by surprise, a little. I'm kinda used to being the one who falls for the other guy, you know? I usually make the first move, right? Not totally used to someone being into me, too."

Mitch smiled. "I won't lie—I'm sort of grateful you expressed it first. It was already there, with me but you kinda gave me permission. If that makes sense." He hesitated. "God, am I messing this up?"

Rusty laughed warmly. "No. Would it make you more comfortable if I went first?"

The look Mitch gave him was a mixture of relief and embarrassment. "Probably?"

"Cool." Rusty regarded Mitch with an intensity that made him fidget. It was everything Mitch could do to not look away. He held the look for what seemed like forever before speaking up again. "I *really* like you. I'm trying to be smart about it, to not just fall for you completely, because that's something I kind of do. Something I could do really easily with you. You deserve someone who takes you seriously—who takes any potential 'us' seriously. I don't have a lot of experience with that, but I really want it with you." Rusty hesitated a moment before speaking again. "I know you've got a lot going on. A lot of scars. And honestly, they scare me a little."

"I know, I'm sorry—"

"Hang on, let me finish," Rusty said. He scooted closer, pressing his leg warmly up against Mitch's side now. "Not because it's a *problem*. They scare me because I don't want to hurt you more. Or to push you in any way you're not ready for, you know? I've always just kinda leapt in. Both feet, into the deep end. I don't know why, except that's just sort of me. Maybe it's because I'm scared that if I take it slow, the other person will discover I'm not worth it? The work of building a relationship, I mean."

Though he wanted to interject, Mitch stayed quiet.

"But the thing is, you're worth the extra time to me. So, if you aren't interested, I'm saying that's okay. But if you are? I'm willing to take this at whatever pace you want to set, because I trust you enough to know that any hesitation isn't about me. It's not because you think I'm a dumb kid or whatever."

"God no!" Mitch turned toward him fully and took his hands. "Rusty, you have to know—*please* know—any slowness or hesitation on my part isn't because I'm not interested in you. It's because of me. Because I just don't know what I'm doing when it comes to all this."

"I do know that," Rusty said reassuringly and squeezed Mitch's hands. "That's what I'm saying. Though I'm not *used* to it, I can take this slow because I trust you, Mitch. Maybe more than anybody else. You tell me it's because you're navigating your way around the bad shit that's happened to you, or your own inexperience, or whatever? And I *believe* you. I believe you enough to trust that you're not just being nice, and trying to find a way to let me down. I *trust* you."

Mitch closed his eyes, taking a few deep breaths. When he opened them again, intensity shone in their green depths. "I do want to pursue this. I don't know what that looks like, and I'll probably need a lot of patience from you. But I do want to try."

The grin that split Rusty's face was almost painful, and he laughed. "Can... can I kiss you?" He drew back. "I mean, if you think that would be–"

And then they were kissing on that rooftop in downtown Portland for quite some time.

* * *

Over the next week, the Band left the safety of Optic's hotel suites. It started with an interview with a local radio program who wanted to hear their side of the terrorist attack. Though the hosts really pushed for the "exciting, fighting" parts of the story, giving each member of the team a chance to tell what happened from their perspective, they did exactly what Optic's publicist wanted them to do: focus on their self-defense and the use of their powers to mitigate the damage the Prometheans were doing.

They also delved into the backstory to the attack, and told—for the first time to American media—what they found in the horrifying medical facility in Dominica. The calls from listeners started coming in hot and fast then, with the expected range of questions and commentary. Overall, though, the interview was a success, and ended up being replayed on stations across the United States, and then the rest of the world.

The next day, Eleanor, Optic's main publicist put in a call to the team bright and early, to update them on what was going on. "Last of all," she said over the speaker phone, "I've arranged a meeting for tomorrow."

"Who with? And when?" Optic asked. "I've got a few appointments that–"

"Not with you. With Gauss."

"Me?" Rusty squeaked.

"Optic mentioned that you wanted to help out. With repairs to the city?" she confirmed. "I've got you an appointment with the city to talk about doing just that. The meeting will be with the city planning commission, a rep for the city's insurance company, the companies they're contracting to do the actual repair work, and a DTPA liaison."

Rusty regarded the phone like it had just turned into a live, coiling rattlesnake.

"Are you still there?" Eleanor asked after a moment, impatience in her voice.

"Uh, yeah. I am. Sorry." Rusty swallowed. "That sounds really intimidating."

"It's cool, Eleanor." Optic broke in smoothly, with a wink to Rusty. "He'll be there."

"They're going to offer you a stipend," she said. "But don't take it."

"No?" Rusty seemed a little disappointed.

"No. The optics—pardon the pun—will be better if you show up to do this pro bono. You're not a professional, so doing the work for free means no one will pitch a fit about you taking a job you're unqualified for and it'll avoid some union issues. And it really cements the team's efforts to build the community up out of goodwill."

"Uh, okay, sure," Rusty said. Deosil reached over and squeezed his hand.

"Don't worry, Eleanor," Llorona reassured the voice over the phone. "He'll be ready."

The meeting went off better than Gauss could have anticipated, thanks in part to the DTPA liaison who met him outside of the city planning offices and gave him some solid pointers for making it through the meeting. In the end, they planned a news conference for the next day—complete with Gauss in uniform. They held the news conference at the base of the skytram station, still shut down after the battle with the Prometheans. Several of the people Deosil and Gauss rescued that day were there, and the media ate up the images of them thanking Gauss for his heroism. Quite the crowd showed up, including a small cluster of protesters calling for the arrest of the Band, though they were outnumbered and shouted down by quite a few new fans, many of whom held signs that lauded the team not just for their heroism, but for their queerness as well.

"It was really amazing," Rusty said afterwards over dinner at a local burger joint with the team. "There was a sign that said 'Sacred Band: The Champions for Queers' and it kinda choked me up a little, you know?"

Deosil got a little misty-eyed. "Really? Gods, I *love* that."

Mitch got quiet and a little distant at that, but Rusty reached under the table and squeezed his hand. A bit later, after the conversation had drifted again, he spoke up. "Hey, so, I wanted to let everyone know. I've spoken to Rusty about this already, but I wanted to make it official. I'm not going to be getting a place in Portland."

Deosil looked up from her plate, stricken, and looked to Rusty, concern on her face. He met her look with a smile and a wink. *It's all good*, his nod to her said.

"So, what's the plan, then?" Optic asked, popping a French fry into his mouth.

"I still own my parents' old place. In Montana. Since I disappeared, I've let it just sort of sit there. I think I'd like to get it put back into decent condition. Make it livable again. Probably to sell it in the future, maybe, or at least pass it on to family."

Llorona perked up. "Oh! Have you been in contact with your sister?"

Sentinel shook his head, looking a little embarrassed. "No. No, not yet. I'm sure I will, soon enough, but I think I just need a little time."

"But it's not like he's abandoning the team or anything," Rusty said quickly. "I mean, he can fly from Montana to Portland in less time than it takes to drive from one side of Portland to the other."

"What is everyone else doing now?" Llorona asked after a moment of introspective quiet around the table.

"I've got school starting back up soon," Rusty said. "I'd really like to finish my degree."

Deosil nodded. "You better." She smiled across the table. "Optic offered me one of the bedrooms at his place once it's all done."

Optic winked. "Totally. It'll be a big help to me, too. Kosma is going to be staying with me as well, but I will probably be out a lot. I've got the last bit of contractual promotionals for Skylight to finish up, and it would suck to leave him there all on his own."

"It'll be fun," Deosil said with a grin. "Especially since you're getting that hot tub built into the back deck."

"I'll be returning to work with the Golden Cross," Llorona said after a moment. "Call on me anytime for team needs, of course, but my work with the GC is important to me."

"And to them," Deosil said. "You're pretty integral to how they function, from what I understand."

"Do they have any issues with your affiliating with us?" Sentinel asked, concerned.

She smiled. "No. The Golden Cross has always disavowed letting affiliation impact how its volunteers work with the organization. Plus, Cobalt may have put in a good word with the rest of the organization."

Sentinel chuckled. "Tell her I miss her, next time you see her?"

Llorona smiled warmly. "I will. I keep trying to get her to do something radical, like get a phone number for herself but…"

"It's not easy for any of the former Champions," Sentinel said, shaking his head. "Even decades after we broke up, the merest hint of easy accessibility means constant requests from media, law enforcement, special interest groups, and all the rest of it."

"Hey, as long as we've got *your* number, that's all I'm worried about," Optic joked, winking.

"Always," Sentinel said, waving his phone around.

"So, it sounds like we're all in on this," Optic said after a moment, looking around the table. "There's no telling what this is going to ultimately end up looking like. Probably going to be a wild ride the entire time."

"To the wild ride, then," Llorona said, lifting her glass, as her teammates did the same. "To the Sacred Band."

SPECIAL THANKS

To my first editor and friend **Steve Berman**, who believed in *Sacred Band* from the first time I mentioned it to him. And to **Chaz Brenchley**, whose keen eye and red pen definitely improved the first edition of the novel. Likewise, thanks to **Madeline Schrader,** whose insightful comments and editing work made this edition as sharp as it is.

To my own personal team of superheroes, my beta readers **Brian**, **Kurt**, **Steve**, **Jeff**, **Jamie**, **Marina**, **James**, **Laurie**, **Joshua**, and **Samuel**. Your superpowers are to literally make me better at this thing, and that's an incredible gift.

To **Mel**, for providing me with my first visualizations of my Sacred Band.

To **Meredith**, for putting together the Sacred Band's Theban shield icon.

To all the Ronins at **Green Ronin Publishing**, the sassiest and most amazing work family a writer could ever want.

To **Jaym, Nicole, Hal**, and **Chris**, for believing in *Sacred Band*, and welcoming it into the Nisaba family.

To the **Gray Havens Writers Retreat** crew, for always supporting my work and me as a writer.

To each and every one of you who bought either edition of *Sacred Band*. These heroes are for you.

To the patrons of my Patreon (http://www.patreon.com/oakthorne), whose avid hunger for more *Sacred Band* has encouraged and uplifted me, giving new height to these weird, queer flights of fancy. Thank you for loving this work and loving this world.

Thank you. I couldn't have done it without all of you.

ABOUT THE AUTHOR

Joseph D. Carriker Jr. has been playing roleplaying games for over thirty years now, and making them professionally for almost twenty. *Sacred Band* is his first novel, and he is glad to see it back on shelves thanks to Nisaba Press. His second novel, *Shadowtide*, is a fantasy novel set in Green Ronin's *Blue Rose* roleplaying game setting. Joseph lives in Portland, Oregon with his poly constellation family, and likes to think he does his part in helping to Keep Portland Weird.

JOSEPH D. CARRIKER JR.'S
SACRED BAND
CHRONICLES CONTINUE!

Since their public debut the year before, the Sacred Band have found themselves standing in a bright spotlight, every move closely watched by suspicious governments and legions of adoring fans alike. As they struggle with the challenges and the benefits of newfound fame, the team is about to face their greatest challenge yet—the shadowy force that has erased other superheroes teams in the past. Can the Sacred Band overcome the mysterious foes who have erased so many before them? Or will this turn out to be...a TERMINAL VENTURE?

COMING IN 2021 FROM

NISABA PRESS

TERMINAL VENTURE

SACRED BAND CHRONICLES · BOOK II

JOSEPH D. CARRIKER JR.

NISABA PRESS draws the rich detail and excitement of collaborative storytelling from the world of roleplaying to create immersive fiction for all readers to enjoy.

We believe everyone should see themselves reflected in our stories. By actively seeking out and amplifying the voices of under-represented writers: women, people of color, and LGBT+, we strive to be inclusive of all readers.

While currently focused on exploring the richly detailed worlds created by Green Ronin Publishing, Nisaba Press's vision extends to a future filled with speculative fiction set in all manner of places, times, and genres.

WWW.NISABAPRESS.COM